I0522549

Season of Defiance

Season of Defiance

Susan Schroeder

Season of Defiance

© Susan Schroeder 2017

This book is a work of fiction. Named locations are used fictitiously, and characters and incidents are the product of the author's imagination. Any resemblance to actual events or places or persons, living or dead, is entirely coincidental.

All rights reserved. Without limiting the rights under copyright reserved above, no part of this publication may be reproduced, stored in a retrieval system, or transmitted, in any form or by any means (electronic, mechanical, photocopying, recording or otherwise), without the prior written permission of the copyright owner of this book.

Published by
Lighthouse Christian Publishing
SAN 257-4330
5531 Dufferin Drive
Savage, Minnesota, 55378
United States of America

www.lighthousechristianpublishing.com

Chapter One

The soft silver light of a full moon shines benevolently on the wigwams of the peaceful Mohican village deep in the forests of Massachusetts. Crickets sing their midnight concert. A soft rumble in the distance, steadily growing louder, silences the crickets, but the women, children and old ones of Rafe's adopted tribe sleep on undisturbed. Moments later a dozen mercenaries ride into the village, dismount, and surge into the wigwams with their pistols drawn. Then they herd the rudely awakened, bewildered women, children, and old ones out of their homes to a clearing in the village center.

The mercenaries don't know it, but chance has favored them, for all the men of the peaceful Mohican tribe are away on a hunting trip. Ten-year-old Rafe would've gone too, except that he'd come down with a high fever the day before the hunt, and so despite his strenuous protestations had been left behind. The lead mercenary, a man chosen by his employer, the Lord Brookstone, because of his naturally cruel nature, has no idea which of the dark-haired, dark-eyed children is the half-breed child they've been hired to retrieve, for the Lord Brookstone had no description, having never seen the child after his birth. "Which of you is the young Lord Rafael Zacharias Brookstone?"

A few villagers stir restlessly, but none are willing to betray Rafe, whose veins run with both the noble white blood of his dead mother and the Delaware Indian blood of his dead father. "Hand over the young Lord Brookstone, or you'll pay the consequences!" the mercenary threatens, but still the villagers refuse to speak. The mercenary addresses his men. "Line up all the children old enough to walk."

The men roughly herd the children into a line facing the group of villagers. Although fear is readily apparent in most of their eyes, they all remain stoically silent. "I shall kill each of these children, one by one, beginning with the youngest, until someone tells me which is the young Lord Brookstone," the lead mercenary says.

"If you kill all the children, you'll only end up killing Rafe too," the oldest, frailest member of the tribe points out defiantly.

Cursing vilely in his rage that the old one has discovered a flaw in his plan, the mercenary snags the revered one by his hair, bends him over backward, draws a whip from his belt, and whips the man mercilessly. Everyone in the village flinches with each blow, yet, unwilling to render the old one's sacrifice useless, they remain silent. But Rafe's gentle nature cannot stand to see anyone suffer for long, and especially not for his sake. He steps forward. "I'm the one you're looking for. I'm Rafael Zacharias Brookstone."

Grinning triumphantly the lead mercenary drops the old one on the ground like a piece of rotten fruit then roughly grabs Rafe's arm. Mistaking Rafe's febrile trembling for terror, he says, "Have no fear boy, we haven't come to harm you. Your life, at least, is safe." He lifts Rafe into the saddle of a sleek, bay gelding from Lord Brookstone's famous stables brought to carry Rafe home in the style the Lord Brookstone's heir deserves, and then addresses his men. "Kill them all! Lord Brookstone wants no one left alive."

Shouting vile curses in Mohican Rafe scrambles from the saddle and grabs the rifle barrel of the mercenary aiming at his adopted aunt. "Stop!" Rafe struggles to disarm the man, but he's weakened by his illness, and so his attack on the muscular, full grown man is as effective as a flea attempting to pierce the hide of a buffalo. With a sweep of his arm the mercenary easily knocks Rafe aside. His back smacks hard against a tree knocking the breath from his lungs. Then he slides to the ground senseless. When he regains consciousness, he's being led away, tied securely to the saddle of the horse, through the village center, which is littered with the bloodied and twisted bodies of everyone he knows and loves.

* * *

John and the other men return the next morning heavily burdened with meat from a successful hunt, but their anticipation of a feast dies at first sight of their slaughtered loved ones. After a grief-stricken search they discover that all are dead except Rafe, who is missing. John instantly realizes what must have happened, for he'd always known someday Rafe's white grandfather would have his revenge against him for saving the infant's life.

* * *

John and the other men of the village attacked the mercenaries as they laughed over their morning campfire over how easily they'd earned their pay. Armed only with knives and bows against the mercenaries' flintlocks, the Mohicans, celebrated warriors, are easily slaughtered, although John kills three mercenaries before he takes a shot in the heart. In all, three mercenaries lose their lives in the brief battle, but every last one of the Mohican hunters die, all of them like uncles to Rafe, who helplessly watches the battle still tied to the saddle of his fine, glossy, thoroughbred stallion.

As a mercenary leads Rafe's horse past the broken and twisted body of his heart father, Rafe tearfully whispers his last farewell. "Nio Ktochwah nen, John." *I love thee, John.*" Then he added in English, "Forgive me."

* * *

After a hard three-day ride, Rafe is brought, struggling defiantly, and screaming curses in Mohican, to the bedside of his dying grandfather. "Such a fuss," the dying man complains irritably. "Rest easy, boy. Look around you. We've done you a favor taking you from a rough wigwam in the woods to live in this fine manor house."

Rafe has already looked around. He's not in the least impressed by the magnificent surroundings, the rich woods of the house and furniture, the plentiful and expensive Moorish rugs and the other luxurious accessories, or the fine paintings by a famous English artist of his grandfather's day. He cares nothing for such trappings, and even had he cared, he's far too angry and heartbroken over the slaughter of everyone he cared for and loved to be comforted by material comforts. "What do you want with me?" he demands, glaring defiantly at the ancient, wasted white man in the huge four-poster bed propped up by four heavily stuffed feather pillows in bright white pillowcases with French lace edging. His wispy gray hair is so thin that it's barely noticeable, his pasty hands covered with age spots shake and tremble even at rest, and his eyes are so cloudy it's impossible to discern their true color. He doesn't answer Rafe's question, for he's lost in his memories of ten years ago.

Rafe's mother, Ophelia, was Lord Brookstone's only living child, as his disgraced and disinherited son and heir had died six years before. Late one night while walking home alone under a new moon after tending to a sick friend, Ophelia was set upon and raped by a drunken Delaware Indian scout well known for his rash, selfish behaviors, for which vile act Rafe's father he was relentlessly tracked down then immediately hanged, making Rafe fatherless before his mother even knew he was conceived. Nine months later Ophelia died in childbirth making Rafe an orphan only minutes after his birth. Some claimed she'd died from shame over bearing the dark-haired, dark-skinned, dark-eyed, half-breed. But the old Lord Brookstone knew otherwise, for with her last breath his daughter had given her half-breed child the family names of Rafael after her beloved dead brother, and Zacharias after himself. No one would grant such honor to a child they were ashamed of. Despite the knowledge that his daughter had cherished the child, however, the old Lord Brookstone wanted no mixed blood namesake reminder of the reason for his daughter's death haunting his life. He wrapped the newborn Rafe in a blanket, mounted his swiftest horse, rode to a secluded spot on the far, east end of his estate, and casually dropped the hungry, cold, wailing infant into a rushing river. Then that Mohican guide, John, had appeared as if by magic and scooped the thrashing and choking infant from the frigid waters. "You've thrown away this child. Now he's mine," he'd proclaimed above the wailings of the angry infant, and then rode away with the rapidly calming babe crooked in his arm without allowing the stunned Lord Brookstone a chance to reply.

"What do you want with me, sir?" Rafe demands again, tearing the old man from his reverie.

"You are my grandson, my daughter's boy, my sole heir," the sick old man rasped. "I've brought you back to serve the noble Brookstone family as lord of this grand estate."

Rafe is stunned temporarily speechless. This is the same man who tried to drown him as an infant, and now he wants him as his heir? Surely the old man's illness has robbed him of his senses!

"Well boy? Have you not even a word of thanks to offer your grandfather for saving you from the cruel fate of growing up a complete savage among the Mohicans?" Lord Brookstone demands breathlessly.

In a voice barely more than a whisper and as cold as the frosty winds of deepest winter, Rafe replies, "The only thing I'll offer you is your death at my hands even as you had your mercenaries kill everyone in my village, *grandfather.*"

The old Lord Brookstone laughs, amused by this grave threat from a mere slip of a trembling boy, then is taken by a coughing fit that spews blood across the front of his nightshirt, cheeks and chin. Lord Brookstone's thin, gray-haired, wrinkled dutiful attendant dunks a clean white cloth in the water of the nightstand bowl and dutifully begins to wipe the old Lord's blood-spattered face clean, but he irritably shoves the attendant away then addresses Rafe. "You're too late to kill me, impudent boy, for I'm already dead. That's why I've brought you here. I'm in desperate need of someone to carry on the family name and run this great estate, and our young Pastor Henline has convinced me that although your father was a drunken Delaware, once you're properly trained, the Brookstone blood you inherited from my dear, departed daughter, and the nobleness of our line, will overwhelm the savage half of your nature and make you worthy of the Brookstone name."

"I care nothing for your name or your great estate, old man! May it go to the dogs! My duty is to my tribe, the Mohicans, not to you!" Rafe replies defiantly.

"Those savage Mohicans were not your tribe, child! The noble family of Brookstone is your tribe!" The sick old man's chest heaves with the effort of speaking, and he's forced to take a moment to catch his breath before he continues his argument; one he hopes will sway his young heir, for if Pastor Henline was correct and the boy was anything like his mother, he won't be able to resist coming to the aid of people in need. "This estate which shall soon be yours takes many to run it. Many depend upon it for their livelihood, men, women, and children. It's your duty as the Brookstone heir to oversee the estate and assure that those who earn their living from it will never fall upon hard times, and that they and their children will never go hungry, or lose their homes here."

"I'll be no one's master," Rafe stubbornly insists.

Color darkens the Lord Brookstone's otherwise pale face as fury takes hold. "Obstinate child! Will you let innocents starve to death? You've already caused the death of your Mohican foster father and everyone in his village, and because you failed to die in the womb, you killed my beloved daughter. How many more innocent deaths will you callously make yourself responsible for?"

Rafe pales and inhales sharply, but he offers no reply. He doesn't need to, though, for Lord Brookstone sees the guilt reflected in the boy's expressive dark brown eyes. His rheumy eyes light up in triumph. So Pastor Henline was correct! Like his mother, the child has a strong conscience, a useful weakness, for he can use it to turn the boy to his will. Suppressing a victorious smile, Lord Brookstone presses the final attack. "Do you truly wish to live out the remainder of your days accompanied by the knowledge that your stubborn pride destroyed the lives of countless innocent workers and their families? Are you not responsible for enough harm already?"

Rafe glares coldly at the wasted old man, trembling from head to toe, not only from fever, but from rage, his fists clenched so tightly at his sides that his knuckles whiten and his fingernails bite into his palms.

"Surrender your stubborn pride and assume your rightful place as my heir," Lord Brookstone concludes weakly, his short speech having exhausted him.

The mere thought of prospering the estate of the man responsible for the mass murders of his adopted family revolts Rafe, but even as the vile man says, enough lives have already been ruined or prematurely ended because of him. His conscience couldn't abide even the thought of adding more lives to the already too long tally. Furthermore, he has nowhere else to go, for everyone he's known and loved is dead. Then he suddenly realizes that denying him the ability to run away is exactly why Lord Brookstone ordered the mercenaries to slaughter everyone in his village. A dark fury seizes control of his heart and he's tempted to kill the vile man on the spot, except that it's plain Pachtamawas, the Mohican word for God that Rafe prefers to use, is already killing the vile man for him. "It seems I have no other choice but to take my place as your rightful heir," he concedes sullenly.

"Ah…" Lord Brookstone smiles triumphantly. "You'll make a suitable heir despite the savage in you, but you must marry pure white blood so that in only one more generation the savage blood in the Brookstrone line will be completely obliterated." He looks to his hovering attendant. "Douglas, summon Leopold."

"Yes, my lord." Douglas hurries out.

"You're trembling, my boy. Sit. Rest." Lord Brookstone nods at a red satin upholstered chair with a high back.

Rafe reluctantly sits in the ostentatious chair, but only because he has no wish to collapse in weakness in front of his enemy. He sits silently, sulking, uncomfortable despite the soft, overstuffed cushions and his worn, comfortable buckskins, until Douglas reappears, accompanied by a tall almost scarecrow-thin man in his early forties with brown hair and gray eyes. Lord Brookstone, who'd seemed to be fading while they waited, perked up. "Ah, Leopold. At last." He gestures weakly at the scarecrow man. "Rafe meet Leopold Aspenwall, our family barrister, and your guardian until you're of legal age. He'll assure you receive the proper training and education for a Brookstone lord."

Rafe has spent many of his winters in the missionary settlement of Stockbridge with John, met many white missionaries, and observed their social habits. He slides out of the chair and bows gracefully. "Pleased to meet you, sir."

"The same, young sir," Leopold replies stiffly. He then addresses the old Lord Brookstone. "It seems it will be far less difficult to train this savage than we thought, sir." He sounds relieved.

"Yes. His dark looks belie his good Brookstone blood. Although, I would've wished he had more of his mother's coloring, for he looks far too much like his father, especially with that long hair flowing down his back. See that it's cut to a properly fashionable length first thing tomorrow morning."

"As you wish, sir," Leopold says.

Rafe wants to object to the cutting of his hair, but he's well aware he has no power here. Yet. Once he is older, though, he'll take complete control of his life, including the length of his hair.

Lord Brookstone coughs up more blood. The dutiful Douglas once more moves in to wipe it away and once more Lord Brookstone irritably shoves him away. "Leopold take the boy to his room. We'll talk more tomorrow after breakfast."

"Yes, sir. Come boy."

"I'm not boy. My friends call me Rafe, but you are not my friend. You may call me Rafael," Rafe says insolently.

Leopold scowls. "Come then *Rafael*." He puts sarcastic emphasis on the name.

Rafe's eyes narrow, but he obediently accompanies Leopold down the long hallway with fabulous paintings decorating the walls created by the same famous English artist as those in the Lord's bedroom. They walked on rich and expensive rugs spread on highly polished oak floors, but all of this extravagance makes no impression on Rafe. It's the everlasting beauty of nature that he appreciates, not houses and their effects that inevitably crumbled to dust.

His room is as sumptuous as the rest of the manor. A blazing fire burns in a fireplace large enough to roast a boar in, warming the vast space that would easily house half the wigwams in his village. Rafe stares in incredulity at the four-poster bed large enough to comfortable sleep four boys of his size, at its six plump, goose-down pillows, and lush coverlet. The thought of sleeping in that monstrous thing is abhorrent, as is everything else in this house. But at least he has the satisfaction of witnessing the old Lord Brookstone's death in a fitful and bloody paroxysm the very next morning.

Chapter Two

Thirteen Years Later

Rafe knelt in the high brown grass and watched the black fox casually canter across the meadow. A gust of wind blew a lock of his glossy, shoulder-length straight black hair across his cheek. He absently tucked the bothersome strands behind his ear as his dark brown eyes followed the fox's progress. It stopped suddenly and looked in his direction, perhaps alerted by the slight movement he'd just made, but Rafe's buckskins blended so perfectly with the brown grasses and he sat so still that although he looked directly into the fox's amber eyes it didn't sense him. Although armed, Rafe wasn't there to kill the fox, but merely to observe; for he felt a kinship with all wild things since like them he too was misunderstood and mistrusted. Despite that he is undeniably handsome, with fine, even features, shiny black hair, lightly tanned skin from both the sun and his native genes, strong, and lithe, a skilled hunter, proficient with bow, knife and pistol as well as in hand-to-hand combat, holding a title and a high place in society, because of his origin and mixed blood, like the wild animals he continually endures the unjust suspicion and prejudice from all but a few of the people in his life.

The baying of dogs startled the fox and dragged Rafe from his contemplations. As the fox raced into the woods at the north end of the meadow, a pack of six hounds bounded in from the south baying loudly, and a group of four riders emerged from the thick trees behind them their red felt coats marking them as a hunting party although it's early spring and not the season for hunting. Rafe scowls at sight of the lead rider. Charles Huntington is the same age as Rafe, nearly as tall as Rafe, and nearly as handsome as Rafe too, being well-built, with light brown hair and blue eyes. He's an affable gentleman unless he's looking at or talking to Rafe. Then his sky blue eyes turn cold and hard and his fine features contort with the intensity of his disdain. Rafe stood up then stepped lightly out of hiding to confront the hunting party, his black, mid-calf high, brown suede boots barely making an imprint in the soft ground.

The group reined to a halt and Charles glared at Rafe with plainly evident disdain. "Rafe," he acknowledged coldly.

"Charles," Rafe returned with equally evident disdain.

"Lord Huntington," Charles corrected imperiously.

"Lord Huntington is a title of honor and you've not yet proven yourself worthy of such," Rafe retorted frostily.

His statement drew the ire of the single female rider, a petite woman barely twenty with large blue eyes and golden blond curls styled in early 1700's high fashion. "Rafe, I'll not tolerate you speaking ill of my husband!" she chastises, her delicate, white leather glove-clad hands tightly gripping her horse's reins in her indignation.

"I only speak the truth Sarah, of which you are well aware," Rafe countered stubbornly.

Charles turned a bright shade of angry red. "It's you who's unworthy, Rafe, for although you may have inherited your grandfather's vast fortune and the title of Lord Brookstone you're still the product of rape, and a half-breed as well, both of which make you an abomination in God's sight! It's a shame your grandfather failed to drown you on the day of your birth and then compounded his error by allowing that Mohican savage to foster you, for its certain the world would be far better off without your despicable presence tainting it!"

Rafe listened to Charles's tirade openly defiant, but inwardly heartsick. He'd trained and learned beside Charles for six years in their boyhood and during that time they'd become as close as natural brothers. But ever since the misunderstanding involving Sarah six years ago that had ended their friendship they never met without some sort of disagreement or unpleasantness ensuing. For five years after the incident Rafe had done his best to repair the relationship, but Charles had steadfastly refused to forgive, and so Rafe had given up on him. Charles finished his rant with, "If there was justice in the world, you'd be a slave instead of the owner of the largest and richest estate in the territory!"

Rafe's dark eyes narrowed. "I'm no more an abomination for the unlucky origin of my birth than you are special for the undeserved luck of yours," he said in the quieter than normal tone he used whenever he was outraged.

"He has you dead to rights there, husband," Sarah interposed.

Rafe gifted her with a winning smile of perfectly white, straight teeth.

Like most women Sarah had always thought he was dashingly handsome, and especially so when he smiled. So when that smile was directed at her, she couldn't help but blush and return it.

Charles noted the exchange and it infuriated him. Even before the incident with Sarah that had ruined their friendship, Charles had been convinced, although erroneously so, that Rafe, fully aware of his physical attractiveness, used it to unduly influence the fairer sex in his favor. He twisted in his saddle to glare at his wife sternly and she lowered her eyes, put in her place although no words had been exchanged. Charles then refocused his ire on Rafe. "I'm of a mind to have you brought up on charges, half-breed."

Rafe raised an eyebrow. "This is my land, and you are here uninvited. If anyone has a right to file charges, it is I against you, for trespassing."

"We are not trespassing!" Charles exclaimed self-righteously. "Your grandfather allowed all to hunt freely on his land. Everyone knows that."

"Aye, but this land is mine now, and I am not my grandfather," Rafe replied.

"Anyone can see that," Charles sneered. "You have absolutely no Brookstone traits, much to your detriment."

Rafe's left hand strayed toward the hilt of his ever-present knife in its colorful beaded sheath. "Leave my land Charles before I'm forced to throw you out! You, particularly, are unwelcome."

Charles drew himself up imperiously. "I shall leave when I'm ready, and should you attempt to harm me or my companions in any way I shall be justified in using force against you!"

"Allow me, Charles," interposed one of the two other male riders, a husky, blond, bearded man riding a glossy bay mare. He then aimed his loaded hunting rifle at Rafe. "I'll make certain the abominable savage never again dares to disrespect his betters."

Rafe drew his knife so quickly and fluidly that it almost seemed to magically appear in his hand. "Try it, Micah, and learn which is more deadly, your bullet or my thrown knife."

"Rafe," said the fourth rider, a sturdily built man closer to thirty than twenty years of age with blond hair, and eyes as green as a mountain lake. "You're barely tolerated as it is. If you kill a white man, no matter how justified," he looked at Micah pointedly, "they'll hang you in a heartbeat despite your noble blood."

"He who started this fight must end it, Duncan. I'll sheath my knife when Micah lowers his rifle," Rafe said stubbornly.

"You heard Rafe, Micah," Duncan commanded sternly, but Micah ignored him.

"Micah!" Sarah chastised her older brother sternly.

Micah slowly lowered his rifle, and only then did Rafe sheath his knife. "Take your dogs, and leave my land," he commanded.

Charles made no move to leave, but continued to glare at Rafe coldly.

"I suggest you honor Rafe's wishes, Charles," Duncan said with the authority of an elder friend.

"Yes, please Charles, let's be off," Sarah pleaded. "I'm cold, and it's time for tea."

Charles hesitated a moment longer then he whistled his dogs in and after a dark glare at Rafe, reined his horse around and galloped off followed closely by Micah, then Sarah, who looked back at Rafe and smiled apologetically as she rode away. Duncan delayed his departure to speak to Rafe privately. "While I agree that this is your land, Rafe, and so you have every right to throw off uninvited guests, you'd be wiser to 'play better' with Charles. You know well that he's a man of influence and highly respected, with the power to sway public opinion against you should he so desire."

"He's already swayed public opinion against me, Duncan. I have nothing to lose. But tell me, why do you spend time with that ruffian anyway? You're far better than he."

Duncan grinned. "That's what Charles says about my spending time with you; but Charles is no more a ruffian than are you. He's a good man and as true a friend to me as you." He pulled on the reins of his horse as it tried to dance in a circle, impatient to follow after the others.

"Everyone is your friend, Duncan. But there are some you'd be better off not associating with," Rafe said.

Duncan chuckled. "I presume you speak of Charles?"

"No. As you pointed out, Charles is a man of good standing and well respected among the upper classes. I was speaking of myself. You'll lose your exalted position in high society if you continue to associate with me."

"Pshaw! High society," Duncan said derisively. "I care little for those snobs who think far more of themselves than they deserve."

Rafe couldn't help but grin, for he felt the same.

Sarah had stopped her horse several dozen yards away. "Duncan!" she called impatiently.

Duncan nodded to her, indicating he was on his way. Then he said to Rafe, "I must catch up with the others. I'll come around later tonight, and then we shall discuss the faults of high society in greater detail, chief among them their continued failure to recognize your merits. Will that suit you?"

Rafe nodded and smiled. "I shall look forward to it."

Duncan smiled, saluted Rafe with a finger to his forehead then finally allowed his horse the freedom to canter after the others.

Chapter Three

It was nearly midnight by the time Duncan arrived at the Brookstone manse, but he knew Rafe would still be up, and he also knew exactly where to find him. He left his sleek, dappled stallion in the hands of Rafe's stocky, surly, grizzled, head groom Cabel then walked to the back of the house and entered the English garden where he knew he'd find Rafe stargazing, for it was one of his favorite activities. He sat sideways on the nine-inch wide, three-foot high circular wall of the garden's center fountain, his left leg bent, one moccasin-shod foot resting on top of the wall the other supporting his weight on the ground. Duncan stopped to admire the fountain's life-size statue of a voluptuous female in Greek dress with a tipped jug balanced on her hip from which poured a constant stream of water. The statue fit perfectly with the flower gardens and decorative stone garden benches, but Rafe looked uncomfortable here and out of place too in his plain buckskins that he almost always insisted on wearing, except upon the extremely rare occasion when he was invited to a social gathering.

Rafe smiled and nodded a friendly welcome at Duncan who then sat down beside him on the fountain wall. Despite the seemingly affable reception, however, Duncan could literally feel the melancholy radiating from Rafe like cold off of ice, and he was tense too, like a spring wound way too tight and ready to break. "Quin'a month'ee?" Duncan asked, Mohican for 'how are you', that Rafe had taught him.

Rafe shrugged disconsolately and continued to stare into the garden seeing things far away and long dead, not the beauty of the moonlight illuminating the flowers all around him.

"I'm guessing you're missing your adopted home in the woods again?"

"I always miss it. I was happy there. I'm not happy here. You know that."

"Yes I do, and that's why I've always wondered why you don't give up this life that you so despise and return to what you love."

"There's nothing to return to, and even if there were, after all these years I'm now half of one world and half of another, but belonging to neither. Furthermore, for better or worse I'm the Brookstone heir. I have responsibilities to this estate and those who run it, and my heart father taught me better than to run from responsibility." With a visible effort Rafe tossed off his melancholy then smiled. "Besides, why would I wish to leave behind such a valued friend as you?"

Duncan chuckled. "Indeed. That would be a grave loss." Then he sobered. "I think there's more to this glum mood of yours than merely missing what once was, though. Are you blaming yourself for the deaths of your adopted Mohican family again?"

Rafe looked away and although he said nothing, Duncan had his answer. "It's been thirteen years. You need to forget about it," he advised.

"How can I forget that everyone in my village is dead because of me! My sense of honor demands I make amends, but the only way to do that is to restore life to the dead. Since that is impossible, I'm left with only my guilt and my nightmares."

"There was nothing you could've done to prevent their deaths."

"I could have killed those mercenaries!" Rafe spat angrily.

"You were ten years old and weakened by fever besides. How could you have prevailed against an entire squad of trained mercenaries?"

"I don't know. Somehow..." Rafe stared gloomily into the pool, watching the coruscating rings formed by the cascading water pouring from the Greek goddesses' pitcher. His dark eyes followed the path of the outermost ring until it broke against the edge of the stone wall. In the light of the full moon as the water settled, Rafe could clearly see his wavering reflection, dark hair, skin, eyes all distinctly marking him as unacceptable as was his ignoble origin. Charles and everyone else, except Duncan, Rafe's friends Lisbeth and Pierre, and Pastor Henline claimed he was a cursed, savage animal, irredeemable, and unworthy of God's love, and although Rafe had accepted Jesus into his heart upon a visit from a missionary when he was yet a child living with the Mohican, sometimes, he wondered if everyone was right. After all, hadn't he killed his mother with his birth, which made him singularly cursed? Hadn't he betrayed his adopted tribe every single day by prospering the estate of the man who'd ordered the slaughter of everyone in his village? But the only way to end that betrayal was to dismiss everyone who depended upon the estate for their livelihood, betraying them instead. It was a bitter trap with no escape.

"How do you say stars in Mohican again?" Duncan asked in an effort to distract Rafe from his obviously bitter reverie.

"Anakusak. Geshoch is sun, aki is earth and soganahn is rain, but you didn't come here for a lesson in Muhekaneok. How went the mood after I kicked you off my property?"

"As you can well imagine, Charles was livid, but he soon calmed down. He's really quite an agreeable person—,"

"When I'm not around," Rafe finished for Duncan, and then grinned crookedly.

Duncan laughed. "I suppose that's true, which I find strange since I was given to understand that you were once as close as brothers?"

Rafe nodded. "The Huntington estate borders ours and Charles and I are the same age, born in the same year, two months apart, so Leopold arranged for me to train alongside Charles. We learned everything together and thus became like brothers."

"What happened to ruin your relationship?"

Rafe was initially surprised by the question, since even as everyone knew the shameful circumstances of his conception, so everyone also knew of the scandal that had permanently ended the friendship of the two richest young lords in the territory. But then again Duncan had only been in the colonies for six months and he didn't associate with those who liked to gossip. Before he could answer, though, Duncan blanched, realizing his error. "Forgive me. I shouldn't pry into matters that are none of my business. You don't have to answer that."

"No, I don't mind. It's common knowledge anyway. I'm surprised you don't already know. Sarah was the cause of the rift between Charles and me, although it wasn't her fault."

Duncan raised an eyebrow. "Did you and Charles duel for her hand?"

Rafe chuckled. "If we had, Charles would not be alive today." Then he sobered. "When Charles was sixteen, his family and Sarah's arranged their engagement. You know how it works, two families of fortune and good bloodlines assuring the continued survival of the line. Charles was ecstatic, for he'd had a crush on Sarah since he was twelve. Sarah, however, was headstrong, and although she liked Charles well enough, she rebelled against having a mate chosen for her, which manifested in flirting with me. I knew she was only using me, but I liked her too and the attention was flattering and annoyed Charles, which amused me. So I encouraged her in the game, for that's all it was; or at least that's how I justified my dishonorable actions.

"We flirted shamelessly in front of Charles for months, but when I realized Charles had graduated from simply annoyed to insanely jealous, I told Sarah we had to stop. She'd never desired to hurt Charles either and so for the next three months we stayed clear of each other. Then late one night during the winter solstice holidays and only a week before their wedding, Sarah rode alone to my estate and threw pebbles on my bedroom window until I awoke and opened it. She sobbed that she needed to talk to me and although I knew better than to entertain an affianced woman alone late at night, I took her into my parlor despite.

"She threw herself into my arms and lamented about her upcoming nuptials and being forced upon a man she respected and liked but didn't think she loved. She said she had some money of her own and she wanted me to accompany her to France where no one would think to look for her. I had enough sense left in me despite her tears and the headiness of her warm body in my arms to refuse to pursue such a dishonorable course and by it also betray Charles, a man I loved. I refused her entreaties gently but firmly then settled her on a settee in my parlor with a cup of hot tea to warm her while I went out to order my carriage readied to take her home before someone discovered her missing.

"Upon my return she said my refusal to run away with her had set her thinking and she realized she'd been foolish and had made a mistake in thinking that she didn't wish to marry Charles. She said it was rebellion and nervousness over the imminent nuptials that had caused her hysterics then thanked me for not taking advantage of her, hugged me, and kissed me on the cheek.

"That's when Leopold, Charles, Charles's father, and Sarah's father burst in on us. All manner of harsh words were exchanged and I was even accused by Charles of using evil native magic to spirit Sarah away and steal her affections. Although Sarah and I vehemently protested our innocence, none would listen to a woman under an enchantment or the half-breed savage who'd cast the spell." Rafe spat out the words *half-breed savage* as if it burned his tongue to say them. "Even Leopold didn't believe me," he added with a trace of resentment. "Sarah was quickly bundled off by her father.

Charles's father paused long enough to inform me that I was lucky Leopold had convinced them not to press charges against me, before he too stormed off. Charles was about to indignantly follow his father out, but I grabbed his sleeve and tried to reason with him, to explain that it was all innocent. He labeled me demon spawn and proclaimed that from now on we were enemies. Since then, Charles has never spoken civilly to me or of me either."

"I'm sorry," Duncan said. "Perhaps I could talk with Charles. As a close friend, I might succeed in making him see the truth of the matter."

"Thank you, but nothing you say will change Charles's opinion of me. It's as much as set in stone. Besides, Sarah's and Charles's relationship has improved significantly since the birth of their son, Laird, last year. I have no wish to do anything that might ruin it such as dredging up incidents that should best remain buried and forgotten." Rafe stood up. "It's late and the road is dark. It's a wonder you didn't injure yourself or your horse on the way here. Will you do me the honor of being my guest for the night?"

"I'd love to. Your guest rooms are the most comfortable in the territory," Duncan said.

Rafe grinned. "Flatterer. Sarah is well known for her efficient hospitality, while Leopold and I are bachelors who run a casual household with no woman's touch to be seen."

"Which in my opinion is far more conducive to a good night's sleep than the regimental order of a tightly kept household," Duncan said, grinning.

Rafe laughed and slapped Duncan lightly on the back. "Then, my friend, you shall indeed sleep soundly tonight."

Chapter Four

Rafe had never required much sleep. Six hours or a little less was more than sufficient; so he was awake well before Duncan. He summoned his butler and instructed him to have the cook prepare a hearty English breakfast of the home-grown food of the estate: fried fish, potatoes, beefsteaks, chops, and beer for Duncan. Rafe despised the taste of alcohol of any sort, perhaps a psychological side effect of having had a drunken father even though he'd never known the man, and didn't even know his name.

Duncan was awakened by the lush aromas of cooking meat and potatoes, and by the time the hearty fare was laid out on a table in the morning room, he'd joined Rafe there. "Good morning, Duncan," Rafe greeted him with a ready smile. "Hungry?"

"Famished." Duncan inhaled appreciatively. "It smells wonderful!" He sat down across the table from Rafe and looked over the laden table with evident satisfaction. "For all that you've never been to England you serve a proper English breakfast. I'd venture to say that even my picky older brother, Henry, would be satisfied by this spread!"

"Well eat hearty. We're out for a ride after breakfast. I have something I wish to show you," Rafe said.

"What is it?" Duncan asked.

Rafe smiled. "If I told you, it would spoil the surprise."

Duncan took seriously Rafe's suggestion to eat hearty, but Rafe ate lightly as always. Then Duncan and Rafe walked out to the stables where two fine, black thoroughbred stallions awaited their pleasure, already saddled, reins held by Cabel sporting his ever-present scowl. Duncan openly admired the horses' sleek, broad lines and chests, their flowing manes and tails. "What fine horses! Finer even than Lord Huntington's stock. Who is their sire?"

"Warlord, of Sir Marmaduke Benning's stock," Rafe said.

"Sir Marmaduke Benning? I don't recognize the name," Duncan said.

"He was renowned in England in my grandfather's time for breeding extraordinarily fine horses," Rafe explained. "He and my grandfather were good friends and they remained in touch after my grandfather moved to the colonies as a young man to marry my grandmother. These horses were a gift from Sir Benning on my sixteenth birthday, in 1710." Rafe patted the neck of the glossy stallion closest to him. "This one is Al-Hadiye, the gift. Yours is El-Marees, the south wind."

Duncan patted El-Marees on the nose. "I have never ridden the south wind. It should be an exhilarating experience," he grinned, pleased by his pun.

Rafe chuckled. "I promise it will be that and more, for El-Marees is my finest horse. Shall we be on our way?"

Duncan nodded eagerly and they mounted up. "You mentioned your sixteenth birthday and then I realized I don't know when your birthday is," Duncan said as they cantered off.

Rafe glanced at Duncan uneasily. "Why does that matter?"

"Oh, well, I only just attended Lady Sarah's birthday ball and I wish to have plenty of time to decide which of the many beautiful women I met there that I should escort to your birthday ball. I presume I will be invited?"

"My birthday is in mid-September, but there'll be no birthday ball," Rafe said tersely.

"Don't you care for balls?" Duncan asked.

"I do not, but that's not the reason I won't have a birthday ball. My birth caused my mother's death. It's not a day to celebrate," Rafe replied.

"Many women die in childbirth. It's the way of nature, not the child's fault," Duncan said.

"It is the child's fault if that child happens to be a half-breed, and conceived in rape besides," Rafe responded bitterly.

Duncan had witnessed the undeserved prejudice levied against Rafe by every level of society from the lowest to the highest. He'd also witnessed Rafe's non-reaction to it, and so had always assumed he weathered it unscathed, but now upon hearing the bitterness in Rafe's tone, he realized Rafe's indifference had been a façade meant to deny his antagonists the satisfaction of knowing they'd hurt him. "Forgive me. I didn't mean to bring up a painful subject," he apologized.

Rafe responded with an easy smile then he said, "It's I who should apologize, for because of my aversion to birthday's you'll lose out on a chance to escort a pretty woman to a dance."

Duncan chuckled. "No harm done. I'm fairly certain I'll have other opportunities for escorting pretty women."

"I have no doubt you will," Rafe agreed.

They rode side by side through green, leafy woods, crossed a meadow dotted with clumps of white and blue wildflowers, waded their horses across a swift-running, but shallow creek, rode up a steep, grassy incline and down the other side then Rafe reined Al-Hadiye to a standstill, Duncan reined up El-Marees, and they dismounted. They tied their horses' reins to low-hanging tree branches and then Rafe motioned for Duncan to come along. Duncan fell in beside Rafe, making a great deal more noise than his friend who as much as ghosted through these dense woods on the east end of his property. After a tenth of a mile of stealthy walking, Rafe motioned for Duncan to kneel behind a thick clump of four-foot tall shrub-oak. Duncan knelt with a questioning look. Rafe smiled and put a finger to his mouth warning Duncan to silence then parted the bushes.

Duncan's green eyes widened with delight. Three cubs cavorted with a vixen, nipping playfully at her legs, racing away then attacking each other, growling and rolling on the ground with their tiny, sharp teeth clamped on tails and noses looking for all the world like interconnected furry, snarling balls. Rafe let the bushes fall silently back into place and then motioned for Duncan to back away. They returned to their horses and as they rode off, Duncan commented, "So it wasn't because you didn't want Charles on your land that you chased us off. You were protecting the vixen and her cubs."

Rafe nodded. "I see no merit in killing foxes or any other animal merely for sport, and especially not at this time of year when cubs are still dependent upon their mothers."

Although Rafe had not spoken with rancor, Duncan winced. "I'm sorry. I know better. I never should've let Charles convince me to hunt out of season, but he can be quite persuasive."

"Well do I know that," Rafe said. "When we were growing up Charles's convincing arguments persuaded me to engage in all sorts of mischief. When we were inevitably caught, Leopold and Charles's father always blamed me and my savage nature for involving Charles in immoral conduct and I was punished harshly, while Charles, as my victim always escaped punishment."

"That's patently unfair," Duncan empathized.

Rafe shrugged. "Charles's father could never believe his precious son could misbehave, and Leopold was thrust suddenly and against his will into fostering me, even as I was thrust unwillingly into his care. He did his best by me and I love and respect him for all the sacrifices he's had to make on my behalf, willingly, or no."

They rode in silence for a while after that each caught up in their own thoughts, and then Rafe spoke. "I know I'm not like the rest of your friends…"

"You're far better," Duncan finished for Rafe and then grinned.

Rafe chuckled. "Most would argue against that; but why did you ever call on me to begin with? Why didn't you ignore me as everyone else does, except Pierre and Lisbeth Calbrith?"

Duncan's grin widened. "I'd heard the stories of the demonic, half-breed, Brookstone heir who wandered the territory at night seeking small children to roast and eat, and I had to find out for myself if it was true."

Rafe snorted. "That ridiculous rumor." It didn't seem to matter that no child was missing or had ever gone missing. People still insisted on believing the outlandish story.

"Ridiculous indeed, for you only roast and eat adults who hunt vixens out of season," Duncan joked.

Rafe laughed. "Indeed."

"In all seriousness, though," Duncan said. "I've never met a man with more honor and integrity than you. I'm proud to call you friend."

"Thank you," Rafe said genuinely touched. "But if you wish to find an even better man than you claim me to be you need only look in the mirror. My life has been much improved by your friendship. I value it greatly."

"Then our mutual friendship is good fortune for both of us," Duncan said. "But now that we're finished complimenting each other until we blush like shy maids, I'd like to see if this horse lives up to its name. I challenge you to a race. First to the stable wins."

Rafe rose to the challenge with relish, for he had a deeply competitive streak in him perhaps as a result of a need to prove that he was as good or better than all those who unjustly despised him. "I accept, but you should be prepared to lose."

"How so? Did you not say I have the superior horse?" Duncan asked.

"Yes, but are you the superior horseman?" Rafe asked, grinning confidently. He urged Al-Hadiye to a gallop and then a full run, and couldn't help laughing out loud, glorying in the smooth gait of his muscular horse and the wind ruffling his hair. Duncan shouted in annoyance at Rafe's head start, and then gave El-Marees his head.

It was a close race, but Rafe's horse won by a nose. They dismounted and handed their lathered horses over to the care of the perpetually scowling Cabel then walked to the house side by side, laughing and clapping each other on the back. Cabel glowered malignantly at Rafe's back before he turned away and sullenly tended to the horses.

Chapter Five

Rafe hated dressing up, but Pierre and Lisbeth had personally invited him to their anniversary ball at the end of August and thus he found it impossible to refuse. He studied his reflection in the polished plate he used as a mirror. His glossy, straight, black hair was pulled back in a ponytail and tied with a black satin ribbon. He wore black breeches, jacket, and a waistcoat, with a fine white silk shirt underneath, the French lace spilling out over his waistcoat at the breast and pouring out the ends of his jacket sleeves. His outfit was finished off with white silk stockings and brass-buckled shoes. Everything was of the finest quality, at Leopold's insistence, which Rafe thought a ridiculous waste of money. He certainly felt ridiculous and he thought he looked ridiculous too. With a resigned sigh, he set the polished plate on top of his dresser then since it was raining and an unusually cool night for August as well Rafe pulled his black felt overcoat out of the wardrobe and donned it. He absolutely refused to wear the matching black felt top hat though despite that it was the height of fashion and Leopold said he looked dashing in it.

Rafe bounded downstairs then strode outside where Cabel, surly as ever, waited impatiently, holding the reins of Al-Hadiye. To avoid being soaked by the rain, Rafe could've taken the luxurious, black, Brookstone carriage with its solid gold Brookstone crest composed of a large letter "B" in the middle of a field of fleur de leis, and its soft, white leather seating and white velvet curtains, but he rarely used the conveyance, for he had absolutely no use for such pretentious splendor even if it did keep him dry. "Thank you, Cabel," he said, taking Al-Hadiye's reins then fluidly mounting without using the stirrups. "I'll be back late so there's no need to wait up. I'll groom Al-Hadiye myself."

"Yes, Lord Brookstone," Cabel said with subtle emphasis that made it sound more like sarcasm than respect.

Rafe frowned. It was bad enough that he must constantly endure the disrespect of everyone else; he had no desire to have to put up with such annoyances from his hirelings too. "Attitude, Cabel," he chastised gently.

Cabel made a courtly bow that he somehow also made seem disrespectful. "Forgive me, sir. I'll try to do better in future, sir," he said snidely.

Rafe's ire rose and he considered firing the man on the spot, but he couldn't find it in his heart to put him out of a job, and too, Cabel did a fine job of supervising the care of his horses. So he ignored Cabel's insubordination as he'd done hundreds of times before and rode off.

He arrived at the ball as one of the later guests. The well advanced in age Calbrith butler met him at the door, smiling welcomingly, genuinely glad to see him, for Rafe was the only one of the Calbrith's countless friends and acquaintances who ever inquired after his welfare or even remembered his name. Rafe knew the names of all the other Calbrith servants as well, even as he knew the names of his own servants and estate workers, and also like his own servants and workers he always treated the Calbrith servants with the utmost respect. Several years ago, while the Calbrith's were away on an extended stay in Europe, Rafe had referred Joseph's dying wife to specialists and then paid all the expenses so that her life had been extended by nearly a year and her passage in the end greatly eased. "Good evening, sir," Joseph said respectfully. "I trust you're well?"

"Quite. How's your arthritis?" Rafe asked.

"Much better since you sent over that ointment, sir and thank you for asking," Joseph said as he helped Rafe out of his wet coat. Then Pierre hurried into the foyer to greet Rafe, one of the few of his guests that he granted that particular honor.

Pierre was in his early forties with streaks of gray at his temples battling for dominance with the light brown in his hair. He was accompanied by his wife, a few years older than Rafe, the beautiful, dark-haired, brown-eyed, Lisbeth. She looked absolutely stunning in a white ball gown imported from France with yards of the finest imported lace gathered in the modesty ruffle and edging the three-quarter length sleeves. The dress's stomacher was decorated with yellow silk ribbons and embroidered yellow roses, and matching ribbons and roses festooned her shiny black curls.

As always, Rafe brightened considerably at the sight of her. Three years ago, recently widowed, Lisbeth had taken pity on Rafe who'd fallen ill with a high fever while Leopold was away on business and everyone else had refused to nurse him, even for a fee. Rafe's lonely, arid heart had responded with love to Lisbeth's tender ministrations. When Leopold had returned and realized Rafe's infatuation for Lisbeth, he'd insisted that Rafe take a holiday at the beach to speed his final recovery; and then while Rafe was away, had introduced his friend and fellow barrister to Lisbeth. Six months later she and Pierre were married. Although Rafe had initially felt betrayed by both Leopold and Pierre in their scheme to take Lisbeth from him, in his heart he knew Pierre was a far better man for Lisbeth than he could ever be if only because Pierre was accepted and even revered by the upper strata's of society, while he could never hope to rise to such grand heights of acceptance. More importantly, though, Rafe saw that Lisbeth was deliriously in love with Pierre. So he'd set aside his jealousy and anger, and now the three were solid friends. Pierre affectionately draped his arm across Rafe's shoulders. "Thank you for coming. We know how you hate attending balls."

"It's not the event I hate as much as the men staring at me hostilely as if I'm some demon newly arisen from the pit while the women shrink from me as if I might rape them or kidnap and devour their children behind their backs," Rafe complained.

Lisbeth lightly rapped Rafe's left arm with her closed fan, which was white, with yellow roses to match her dress and the decorations in her hair. "My dear Rafe, you're too self-conscious," she chided. "It's quite the contrary, with the women at least, who wholeheartedly admire your exotic, dark, good looks, and the men are only jealous of the women fawning over you and ignoring them."

Rafe smiled. "You're sweetly innocent to think so. One of your many singularly adorable traits and the reason I have always loved you."

Lisbeth blushed and smiled prettily. "Of the many charming traits I hold dear about you, Rafe, the one I enjoy the most is that you never fail to flatter me."

Pierre scowled in mock anger. "Enough flirting with my wife, young man. Let us find you a pretty, young, unattached maiden upon whom to focus your attentions."

Rafe grinned and winked at Lisbeth over his shoulder as Pierre steered him into the already full ballroom; then apologetically abandoned him to greet another newly arrived important guest. Rafe looked longingly at the open double doors at the opposite end of the ballroom leading into the gardens, wanting to escape from this room full of virtual strangers he knew despised him, and his desire to escape only heightened when he spotted Charles standing near those doors among a group of other highly respected persons looking easy, confident, accepted, with his arm wrapped possessively around Sarah's slim waist.

As if Charles could feel Rafe's eyes on him, he looked in Rafe's direction and then frowned darkly and excused himself to stride briskly across the room and confront Rafe. "What business do you have in polite society, Rafe?" he demanded belligerently. "Shouldn't you be out dancing half naked under the full moon around a fire with the other heathens, or something equally vile?"

"I was invited by Pierre and Lisbeth in person. You?" Rafe demanded coolly.

Having received a written invitation hand delivered by a servant, Charles was at first at a loss as to how to answer and still remain superior to Rafe, but over the last seven years he'd become quite adept at hurling barbed comments at Rafe. "I'm sure you manipulated that invitation somehow; perhaps by making Lisbeth and Pierre's fell guilty over their love for each other. You simply refuse to accept that Lisbeth picked the better man, you vile demon spawn."

It was the name-calling more than the accusation that made Rafe's dark eyes smolder with restrained rage and his hands form into tight fists at his sides. He took a menacing step toward Charles, but then Duncan was suddenly between them. He was accompanied by a man who looked much like him, only a little older, but who respectfully kept a few paces back. Duncan put his palm on Rafe's chest. "Rafe, restrain your anger," he warned in a low voice. "Don't lose what little respect you've so laboriously earned."

After a second's hesitation Rafe visibly relaxed, which deeply disappointed Charles. Having practically grown up with Rafe he knew that with the proper baiting he could force Rafe to lose control of his temper, which he otherwise kept tightly restrained. Then Rafe's savage nature would've been exposed to all, proving him unworthy of polite society. "Indeed be wary Rafe. You nearly exposed your true nature this time and revealed you are no true gentleman," he said, still attempting to make him lose his temper.

Rafe stiffened. Duncan put a restraining hand on Rafe's forearm and then addressed Charles sternly. "You're my friend, Charles, but so is Rafe, who before God is as good as any man, if not better. Treat him with the respect that is his due not only as another human being, but as the Lord Brookstone."

"On the contrary, Duncan, Rafe's a lying, manipulative, half-breed bastard. I strongly suggest you open your eyes to his true nature before he takes advantage of your naïveté and slices your throat while you sleep as a guest in his house, as you so often unwisely do."

Rafe couldn't let such a foul accusation go unanswered. "I'd never willingly harm anyone, including you, Charles."

"A blatant lie! Your desire to pummel me a moment ago radiated from you like heat from the sun! If Duncan hadn't intervened, you'd have beaten me to a bloody pulp. I dare you to deny it!"

Rafe couldn't, and so he glanced away self-consciously, and inadvertently made eye contact with the stranger who'd accompanied Duncan. The man quickly lowered his head, embarrassed at having witnessed a private argument. Rafe wondered who the man was and why he hadn't discreetly walked away then Charles drew his attention away from the stranger. "Admit it, Rafe," he said. "You may have some people completely fooled by your lies and you're pretense of salvation, but you'll never fool me. I know you too well, *brother."* He then walked away deliberately denying Rafe an opportunity to reply. Rafe glared malevolently at Charles's back, but he broke it off guiltily when he saw Duncan's disapproval.

"What did Charles mean by your pretense of salvation?" Duncan asked.

Rafe glanced uneasily at the man who'd accompanied Duncan, unwilling to discuss such personal matters in front of a stranger. Duncan followed his gaze. "Oh, I'm so sorry." He addressed the stranger. "Henry, my apologies as well. I've been quite rude. Rafe, this is my brother, Henry Letourneau, come to visit from England, arriving only last week. The Calbrith's were gracious enough as to insist that I bring him to the ball, and I was about to introduce you to him, when…hm." He cleared his throat. "Henry, this is my good friend, Lord Rafael Brookstone, whom I've taked so much about."

Rafe smiled, crooked his left arm behind his back, and performed a slight, gracious bow. "I'm pleased to meet you Henry, and my apologies for the unpleasantness you witnessed. I'd like to make it up to you by inviting you and Duncan to tea at my estate tomorrow."

"No need to apologize for the unpleasantness. It was quite plain it wasn't of your doing," Henry said graciously. Then the orchestra finished the final strains of a waltz and started on another. "If you'll excuse me sir, I've promised this dance to a particularly ravishing beauty." He hurried off without either refusing or accepting Rafe's invitation to tea, but Duncan answered for him.

"We'd be glad to come for tea tomorrow; but you never did answer my question. What's this Charles was sputtering about your salvation?"

"It's a long story, but the gist of it is that even though I accepted Jesus as my Savior back at the Stockbridge mission when I was only seven, no one—all of them influenced by Charles, no doubt—believes that a soulless half-breed bastard and child of rape is included in God's plan of salvation. They're far more willing to believe I'm destined for eternal damnation."

"How do you know that? Have they ever said it directly to your face?" Duncan asked.

"They're far too proper to say it to my face," Rafe said. "But I've overheard it whispered often enough that sometimes I even half believe it myself."

"God loves you as much as anyone," Duncan reassured Rafe.

Rafe smiled, but doubt and sadness tinged the edges of it. "Charles used to say the same, but now he openly disparages me for my ignoble origin and claims salvation is impossible for such as me."

Duncan rested his hand on Rafe's shoulder. "My friend, God is the God of all. If you believe, then you're His. Promise me you won't ever let anyone or any untoward circumstance convince you otherwise."

Rafe couldn't make that promise, for he feared he couldn't keep it. A thick fog of doubt already clouded his soul. "I'll keep your words, the words of a friend, in mind," he said instead, and smiled to ease his refusal to make the promise.

Duncan was far from satisfied with that answer, but decided not to press the matter now. He withdrew his hand from Rafe's shoulder. "We'll talk more on this tomorrow. Now I insist you stop looking so glum and enjoy yourself. Shall we visit the sweets table and overindulge?"

Rafe didn't care much for sweets, but to please Duncan he accompanied him to the sweets table. Duncan filled a plate with sweets and they both filled two glasses with punch then stood on the sidelines. Rafe noted Duncan wistfully watching the dancers. "Why don't you join them?"

"And leave you alone in this room full of ogres to fend for yourself? I wouldn't think of it," Duncan said.

Rafe grinned at the vision of a roomful of green-skinned, hairy ogres dressed in all this flaunted finery. "I appreciate your concern for me, but I've somehow managed to survive all by myself before you came along and appointed yourself my protector. I'll be fine. Go. Enjoy yourself. I insist."

Duncan brightened. "Well, since you insist…" He set down his plate and cup then approached a pretty young lady with springy black curls and extraordinary emerald green eyes and was soon enjoying himself as ordered. Rafe stood alone, envying the ease with which Duncan fit in, coveting that sort of acceptance, but knowing he'd never own it. Bored, his eyes roamed casually around the room, and then he thought he saw Cabel rushing past the open double doors leading to the garden. Cabel had no reason to be here, so Rafe wondered what he was up to and started for the garden to find out. However, before he was halfway across the ballroom he was waylaid by a thin, wiry servant he didn't recognize holding a tray of filled glasses. "Would you like some port, sir?"

"No. Thank you." Rafe sidestepped around the man.

The servant quickly stepped in front of him. "You really must try it, sir. It's new, a special blend. Quite sweet. Quite satisfying."

Rafe decided to take a glass if only to make the persistent servant go away. He accepted the glass that the servant carefully selected from among the others on the silver tray before the servant then hurried away. Rafe studied the red liquid, shining, beautiful. Despite his general distaste for alcohol he impulsively decided to try a sip and see if perhaps this new beverage might be different. He took a sip, and made a face. It tasted awful, not sweet at all, but quite bitter, and as bad as any other alcohol he'd ever tasted. He'd heard, however, that sometimes the first sip was a shock and the second sip was better, so he took another—and nearly spit it out it was so vile. He dumped the remains of the port into a nearby planter set the glass on the floor beside the planter, and then feeling a bit lightheaded continued out to the garden.

By the time he stepped outside it had escaped him why he'd wanted to come out here, but it was a pleasant night, so he decided to continue down a path of white crushed stone lined with evenly spaced white marble benches on both sides. He followed the snaking path all the way to a little cul-de-sac with a fanciful fountain depicting a smiling female angel with wings outspread, holding a small, blue-painted bird in the palm of her outstretched right hand. It had always annoyed Rafe that people insisted on portraying angels as female when not a single female angel was mentioned in the Bible; but he was forced to concede that it was an eye appealing statue. He clasped his hands behind his back and studied the graceful lines with an artist's eye, for he was a skilled painter and sculptor himself. He found it hard to concentrate, however, so he gave up on studying the statue, closed his eyes and breathed in the warm night air, scented with the gentle fragrance of the yellow and red roses from the garden. Unfortunately, that exercise only made him feel even more lightheaded. He opened his eyes, and tuning out the distant strains of the orchestra, tilted his head back to look at the stars.

He caught the scent of her distinctive French perfume well before he heard her light, satin-slippered footsteps crunching on the crushed stone pathway. "It's a beautiful night, isn't it?" Sarah breathed, stopping beside him.

Rafe, at six feet, towered over Sarah at four foot ten. The top of her head barely reached his broad, muscled chest. "Yes. It is indeed a beautiful night." He kept his eyes on the stars and his hands clasped behind his back in case anyone was watching, so that there'd be no cause for any misunderstanding. After an uncomfortable silence, Sarah spoke again. "Rafe, I regret the trouble I've caused between you and Charles. The two of you were once so close and I ruined it all. I've tried to explain what really happened that night, but Charles will hear nothing of it and continues to insist that you placed an enchantment of some sort on me."

Rafe looked fondly down upon Sarah. "You were not to blame for the split. Charles was already drawing away from me, realizing there was a social hindrance in maintaining a friendship with the widely despised half-breed lord. You and I being caught alone together, innocent though it was, merely gave him the excuse he'd been looking for to break off our friendship."

"You're not a social hindrance," Sarah objected. "If you need any proof, you need only look at Lisbeth and Pierre. They don't seem to be losing any friends because of their relationship with you." She gestured at the full ballroom.

"Lisbeth and Pierre are French," Rafe pointed out. "People expect certain—eccentricities from the French."

Sarah laughed and then so did Rafe, which made him lose his balance and stumble back a step. Sarah had never once seen the always surefooted Rafe lose his balance. Alarmed, she hastily grabbed his arm at the elbow. "Do you need to sit down?" she asked concernedly.

Rafe massaged his forehead with his left hand, trying to rub away the fog. "No. Sorry. I had some port earlier, but surely it couldn't have had this much of an adverse effect on me."

"Perhaps you're ill? You do have a tendency for high fevers." Sarah placed her palm on Rafe's cheek to check his temperature. Rafe gently grasped her wrist to remove her hand and protest further that he was fine.

"I'll thank you to keep your filthy, half-breed hands off my wife!" Charles shouted.

They both hastily pulled away from each other, looking guilty. "Charles, it's not what it looked like. I—," Rafe began to explain. Charles punched him forcefully on the chin making him stumble backward. Enraged, he surged forward and attacked Charles with a frenzy fueled by anger too long restrained. He was vaguely aware that he was not only acting out of character, but against his ethics, and although he heard Sarah begging him to stop, he couldn't control himself. A strong hand grabbed the back of his suitcoat at the neck. He shoved the one interfering with his desire to pummel Charles with the full force of his uncontrolled rage. There was a loud crack as the person hit his head on the edge of one of the marble benches lining the path when he fell then Sarah screamed. "Duncan!"

The name finally brought Rafe to his senses. He released his grip on the ruffled, French lace decorating the front of the white, silk shirt of the now nearly unconscious Charles, who collapsed moaning in a jumbled heap at Rafe's feet then stared in horror at Duncan's body lying absolutely still at the base of one of the stone benches, open eyes staring at a scene not of this world as a dark pool of blood steadily spread under his head. "No," he breathed in horror. "What have I done?" Sarah wrung her hands indecisively, torn between helping her good friend, Duncan, or her husband, but then Henry rushed up and knelt beside Duncan, freeing her to assist Charles. He gently lifted Duncan's broken head then seeing he was beyond aid glared up at Rafe accusingly. "You've killed him, that's what you've done!" He tenderly set Duncan's bloodied head on the ground then sprang to his feet and shoved Rafe with the strength of grief and outrage. "Murderer!"

Rafe stumbled backward then instinctively thrust out his left hand and grabbed a low-hanging tree branch, preventing a fall. He pulled on the branch, sloppily righting himself as if he was drunk, and then let the branch spring back into place. A few leaves broke off and drifted down, one landing on Rafe's shoulder, another on top of his head. "I—I didn't mean to hurt him. I only wanted—," He broke off his explanation as Henry deliberately turned away then knelt, sobbing, and tenderly gathered Duncan's body into his arms. Rafe glanced uneasily at the gathering, murmuring crowd, sensing their anger towards him, and then at the bereft Henry and back at the crowd again. "I—I—didn't mean to—it was an accident! I swear!"

Charles struggled to his feet assisted by Sarah. "Liar! You killed him on purpose because he was attempting to prevent you from beating me to death for defending the honor of my wife!"

"No!" Rafe denied against the disapproving murmurs of the crowd.

"There are witnesses, Rafe!" Charles swept his arm across the crowd then gloated triumphantly. "You've forgotten yourself and revealed your true nature and everyone has seen it! You'll hang now, you demon spawn!" He swiped at a line of blood on the corner of his mouth with the back of his right hand, but only succeeded in smearing it across his cheek. "Well? Why are you all standing there agape? Seize the murderer and someone summon the constables!"

A man broke from the crowd and ran off to summon the constables. Three more men advanced menacingly on Rafe, who warily backed away, his chest heaving from his recent exertions and fear. Then he saw Pierre and Lisbeth. Pierre had drawn Lisbeth protectively close as she wept into his chest. Arrin locked gazes with Pierre, who stared back at him in shocked horror. Rafe turned away unable to bear having his friend look upon him that way and his eyes fell upon the angel fountain, which was no longer smiling, but scowling—at him! And the outstretched hand that had once held a bird was empty with the index finger pointed accusingly at him!

"No!" Rafe stumbled backward then turned away from the accusing statue and raced away with a drunken gait. He heard someone shout "Stop!" then the pounding footsteps of countless pursuers. He didn't head for the stables and Al-Hadiye, however, but raced swiftly away on foot across the dark fields, his black clothing lending him camouflage in the dark shadows of the moonless, cloudy night. Stumbling like a drunk over the, muddy, uneven ground, Rafe headed for home. Despite his clumsy steps he was making good headway, but then he caught his left foot in a hole and fell hard. Even though he painfully banged his right knee and badly twisted his right ankle, he didn't cry out, though, for he'd been taught by John that a man never acknowledged such inconsequential and passing things as physical pain; and although Rafe had now spent three more years away from John's influence than he'd had with him he still held firmly to all of the Mohican scout's teachings over and above everything the white man had taught him.

He struggled in agonizing pain to his feet while looking frantically over his shoulder, fearing someone would pounce upon him while he was down. Luckily, he'd left his pursuers so far behind that he was in no danger of that happening. He resumed running, ignoring the sharp pain that shot up his leg from his ankle every time his foot hit the ground. He raced for five miles over rough and uneven land, scrambled over low fences, somehow avoiding another spill then burst in through the back door of his manor house, which opened into the kitchen, cold and empty at this late hour, everything neatly put away, counters clean, sourdough starter sitting on a counter in a covered bowl to the left of the pump.

His chest burning from taking in too much cold air as he ran, his ankle throbbing, legs rubbery, Rafe raced up the back servant's stairs. He knew the authorities would come for him soon, and although he was willing to pay the consequences of his actions he knew he wouldn't receive a fair trial. His life as the Lord Brookstone was over. He would have to run away to somewhere far away where no one knew him. He would change his name, take a job as a laborer; but first he needed to change out of his blood-spattered clothing, stuff a few other items into a bag, and he'd need to stop in his study for some cash.

With a shaking hand, Rafe lit the candle on the table beside his bed, and then limped to his wardrobe. When he reached out to open the door, he noted for the first time that his hands were red with Charles's blood and the skin of his knuckles was broken and seeping blood. It was then that the full realization of what he'd done washed over him. He'd brutally assaulted a man and murdered another! His stomach heaved. He hurried across the room to his bed, knelt, pulled out his chamber pot, and violently threw up then threw up again and after that retched and heaved although nothing more came out, as his body attempted to rid itself of the horror of his crimes.

He was still uselessly heaving over the pot feeling as if his guts were being wrenched out, when Leopold burst into his room and the shock of being confronted by his foster father ended the useless heaving. He struggled unsteadily to his feet favoring his throbbing, sprained ankle then wiped his mouth on his sleeve. "Leopold—,"

"So you are here! They said you'd run this way," Leopold spat.

Rafe silently cursed. Leopold knew already! How was it that bad news always traveled so fast; especially when it concerned him?

"There are two Constables downstairs with Charles and some man who claims to be Duncan's brother. They say you drunkenly sexually assaulted Sarah, beat Charles, and when Duncan tried to stop your violent crime spree you killed him. From the sight of Charles and the blood spray on you and the state of your hands I must believe that you assaulted him, but the other things? Are they true? Are you drunk? Did you lay hands on Sarah and kill Duncan?"

"It's not how it sounds, sir. We were in the garden and Sarah was only checking me for a fever when Charles came upon us and misinterpreted the situation. He punched me, and I think there was something in the port I drank that made me lose control and beat him in return. Then Duncan intervened and I shoved him… But I swear by almighty God that I never intended to harm anyone. It's as if I was forced to watch a mad man that is me, but not me while unable to do anything to stop it. I—I don't know what's happening to—," Rafe's knees buckled.

Leopold grabbed Rafe's left elbow and supported him until he could stand on his own, albeit unsteadily. "You'd best wash your face and at least clean Charles's blood off your hands before you go down to the constables." Leopold grabbed the pitcher on the nightstand and poured water into the bowl, snatched up the white washcloth hanging on the dowel underneath the bowl beside a white towel. He wet the washcloth and handed it to Rafe, who took the cloth with a trembling hand, wiped his face clean then draped the cloth absently on the rung and dipped his hands in the water, inhaling in pain as it stung his cut knuckles.

As he watched the water in the bowl turn red with Charles's blood, he became sick to his stomach all over again. He swayed a little and grasped the bars on either side of the bowl to steady himself.

Leopold handed him the towel. "Look at you! You can't even stand straight! How much port did you drink?" he demanded disgustedly.

"I only took two sips," Rafe said, noting that his voice trembled even as his hands still did.

"You must have had more than two sips to be so drunk that you're throwing up and can't stand without support," Leopold said accusingly.

Rafe gripped the towel so tightly that the broken skin over his knuckles started seeping blood again. "I swear I only took two sips of port then I started feeling odd." He ran his left hand across his face. "I didn't mean to use such force… and then that angel statue…" Tears blurred his vision. He hastily blinked them away, for Mohican warriors never cried. "It must be true what they say about me. I am a soulless abomination; a cruel, depraved creature that would kill a friend!" He disconsolately tossed the white towel over the washbowl, covering the bloodied water.

"You drank too much and discovered you're a violent drunk, the hard way. That alone doesn't make you cruel and depraved or even soulless; merely unwise." Leopold was trying his best to be supportive, as was his duty as Rafe's foster father. But it was difficult to do when Rafe was looking and acting so much like his drunken natural father, whom Leopold had despised well before the man had raped Ophelia.

Rafe gripped the washstand with both hands and leaned toward the polished silver oval to look intently into his dark eyes, hoping to see a clear indication that he was not cruel and depraved or soulless, even as Leopold claimed. But he saw no light of God's ownership in his eyes, only a deep darkness mocking him for thinking he was better than the half savage he was. Hopelessness and despair took advantage of the opening Rafe had given them and swooped in, wrapping their tentacles firmly around his heart. He straightened and turned away from the mirror. "I suppose we had better go downstairs before they come up after me," he said resignedly.

Leopold fell in beside Rafe, but didn't offer to help him as he limped downstairs leaning heavily on the banister, favoring his swollen ankle.

Constables Richards and James waited at the bottom of the stairs along with Charles and Henry. All but Constable James had drawn their pistols. He held a set of manacles. Richards gripped

Rafe's right shoulder firmly with his strong, nubby-knuckled hand. "Lord Rafael Zacharias Brookstone you're under arrest for the murder of Duncan Letourneau and the brutal assault on Lord Charles Huntington. Resist and lord or not I won't hesitate to shoot you."

"I have no intention of resisting, sir," Rafe said. "I know I've done wrong. I'll willingly pay the consequences of my actions, whatever that may be."

"You'll most likely be summarily hung," said Constable Richards with a trace of triumph in his tone.

Rafe nodded. "Yes, I know."

"Constable James, the restraints," Constable Richards ordered.

Constable James stepped up to clap the manacles on Rafe, but Leopold hastily stepped in between them. "I really don't think it's necessary to restrain him, sir."

Constable James knew Leopold held a great deal of authority in these parts, but he was unsure if it extended to this particular situation. He looked to Constable Richards for guidance, but Charles spoke first. "With all due respect, sir, it's absolutely necessary. He's murdered Duncan, accosted my wife, and assaulted me. Then he ran, attempting to escape justice. Do you seriously think he can be trusted not to try to escape again, harming anyone who stands in his way?"

Leopold addressed his answer to the constables. "Sirs, although Rafe is apparently a violent drunk even as his father was, he's sober now, and furthermore, he's lord of a most highly respected family; so yes, I do think he may be trusted, and I beg you not to lead him away like some common criminal."

"Drunken, violent behavior is no less acceptable in a lord, sir," Constable Richards replied. "If anything, he should be made an example of so that all will know that no one is above the law. Now leave us to our duty, or we'll be forced to take you in as well."

Leopold drew himself up indignantly. "How dare you, sir! Do you know who I am?"

Rafe knew Leopold was far more worried about what everyone would think of his fathering abilities if they saw him led away in manacles than he was concerned for him. However, he most certainly couldn't let them arrest Leopold for it. "They have the right of it, Leopold. I should be treated no differently than anyone else who has broken the law." He stepped around Leopold and held out his arms so Constable James could snap the manacles onto his wrists.

The cuffs were rough and un-sanded around the edges. Rafe briefly wondered if that was on purpose so that the manacles would tear his skin or, if it was merely poor workmanship.

Then he was led away. Leopold followed them as far as the porch then watched from there as his foster son was ushered down the front stairs to where Cabel waited smugly, holding the reins of Al-Hadiye and two other horses, a caramel-colored stallion, and a white mare belonging to the two constables. Rafe wondered how Cabel had so quickly retrieved Al-Hadiye from Lisbeth's and Pierre's, but he didn't ask, for it was insignificant. He mounted Al-Hadiye, with some difficulty due to his injured ankles and the manacles, as the constables mounted the other two horses then they rode away with Rafe in between them, as Cabel grinned spitefully.

Chapter Six

Rafe wished he could start this day over with the knowledge of the tragedy that would occur if he attended the ball and then simply not attend. Failing that, he wished he was only in the throes of a particularly vivid nightmare and that the echoing hooves of the three horses on the silent deserted cobblestone streets was only his heartbeat or the rain drumming on the roof and translating into his dream. But as they approached the red brick walls of the jail it was plainly evident that they were all too real and no dream. They rode up to the hitching rail in front of the building and then without having to be ordered to do so, Rafe dismounted along with the constables, a little awkwardly because of his manacled wrists and swollen ankle then limped inside followed closely by the constables.

A young constable waited inside the jail, leaning back in his chair with his booted feet resting on the desk in front of him. As everyone entered, he hastily stood. "You caught him! Where was he?"

"He was at his home, no doubt preparing to run," Constable Richards said.

"They always do, but we always catch them." The man smirked at Rafe.

"Indeed." Constable Richards agreed. He pulled a small, black, metal key from his waistcoat pocket then unlocked and removed Rafe's manacles and hung them on a peg on the wall behind the desk as Constable James shoved Rafe into the cell. He stumbled forward onto his wounded ankle and sharp pain shot up his leg to his hip, but he resisted grimacing in pain, unwilling to grant his jailors the satisfaction. Then he limped the few remaining feet to the uncomfortable wooden bed with its lumpy, straw-filled mattress and sat down on it. "What happens now?" he asked.

"Justice," Constable Richards said curtly. He closed the barred door with a loud, depressing clang.

Although Constable James had never spoken with Rafe before tonight, he'd watched Rafe stoically enduring the open disdain of all he met, never complaining, never paying back disdain with disdain, and he'd come to respect the young lord; a respect that had only deepened with Rafe's willingness to pay for his crimes and his cooperative attitude. Thus, he felt Rafe deserved an explanation. "We'll return early tomorrow morning to take you before Judge

McKitrick. In the meantime try to rest. You'll need your wits about you when you face him. He's not known for mercy." He then accompanied Constable Richards out, leaving the young constable on guard.

"Thank you for ruining what would've otherwise been my night off with your drunken lack of self-control, half breed," the young constable said contemptuously before he disgustedly sat back down in his chair.

Rafe ignored him. He lay down on his back on the bed all too aware of his throbbing ankle and the straw poking through the mattress and digging into his back, and stared gloomily up at the white plaster ceiling trying to grasp the awful truth that he'd actually killed his best friend. It was impossible to even imagine that he could commit such a heinous act; almost as impossible as to accept that he'd actually beaten Charles into a bloody, pulpy mess. If only Duncan hadn't interfered; but then if he hadn't, it would've been Charles he'd killed instead. He recalled his last ride with Duncan a few months back and Duncan's childlike delight in the fox cubs at play. Now Duncan was dead because of him. He'd killed his good friend in a sort of drunken rage; but why had a mere two sips of port had such an adverse effect on him?

Rafe closed his gritty eyes and crooked his left arm over them. If he'd cared enough to notice, the fine weave of his black silk jacket felt incredibly smooth against the skin of his eyelids. "Pachtamawas," he prayed silently, using his favored Mohican word for God, reserved for his most intimate requests. But then he abandoned the prayer as he recalled the darkness reflected in his eyes in his washstand mirror, which along with his violent behavior tonight proved he was soulless and totally irredeemable; for no man who possessed a soul could be capable of brutally assaulting a friend and killing another without reason or provocation. He moved his arm from across his eyes to rest across his chest, and stared out the tiny window of his cell and the absolute darkness it framed which exactly mirrored the darkness that had enveloped his heart with the realization that there was no hope for him. An aching lump arose in his throat. He swallowed several times to ease it, but then shameful tears welled up in his eyes. He silently, furiously, commanded himself to cease the shameful flow, to bury the pain, but the tears obstinately refused to stay away, and then even had the audacity to spill out and run down his cheeks!

Chapter Seven

After a sleepless night on Rafe's part—the young guard had a solid rest, snoring loudly—Constables James and Richards returned and the young guard left. Rafe limped to the front of the cell and waited patiently as Constable Richards inserted the black metal key in the door then opened it. The hinges creaked and groaned and then the door clanged loudly against the bars behind it grating on Rafe's already raw nerves. "Time to meet the judge, Lord Brookstone," Constable Richards said, drawing his pistol. "Don't give us any trouble or we'll be forced to—,"

"Shoot me, I know," Rafe interrupted tersely, irritable from guilt and lack of sleep. "It's your favorite threat," he said as he limped from the cell.

Constable Richards scowled and his finger tickled the trigger of his pistol as if he was considering shooting Rafe despite lacking true provocation. Constable James, however, suppressed a grin of amusement. Rafe compliantly allowed Constable James to lock the abrasive manacles on his wrists then he was taken across the street to the church, which also served as the courthouse and school. Despite the sharp pain that shot up his leg from his torn ankle with each step, he made himself walk normally, for he would grant no one the satisfaction of knowing the contemptible half-breed was in pain. He also adopted an air of calm self-assurance, camouflaging the truth that he was trapped in the unyielding grips of trepidation and despair.

It wasn't the fear of hanging that had him in turmoil though, for he would readily embrace death and the end of his misery and guilt; especially now that he was convinced he was soulless and there was no hope for him. What bothered him was the possibility of a sentence of lifelong confinement in a dungeon, never again to feel the wind caressing his skin, or to inhale the fresh scent of the wet earth after a rain, or to gaze upon the stars. Losing all those needful things would be a fate far worse than death.

Rafe and the two constables paused momentarily at the closed, elaborately carved, heavy double wooden doors of the church each nine feet tall, made of six panels of polished mahogany and held together with two wide bands of black-painted metal at top and bottom. Normally, Rafe would've appreciated the beauty of the natural pattern of the wood, but after last night his soul had become dulled to all beauty. Then Constable James grabbed the oversized, curved, black metal door handle on the left door and pulled it open. Rafe's eyes widened briefly in stunned surprise at how many had gathered to see justice applied to the half-breed, demon spawn, undeserving of the largest estate in the territory and the honorable name of Brookstone. Every seat was filled. Those men left to stand lined the back and side walls, packed shoulder to shoulder. The room had already grown stuffy from the combined heat of so many bodies. "Move on," Constable Richards growled impatiently and then shoved Rafe making him stumble forward.

He grimaced involuntarily as fiery pain shot up his leg from his sprained ankle. Then his dark eyes anxiously searched the crowd for Leopold, seeking the comfort of someone on his side, however incompletely. It didn't take long to find him, sitting in the front row. Their eyes met and Leopold nodded at him, a silent command to be brave. Ever obedient to his foster father's commands, Rafe thrust his shoulders back and walked down the aisle with his chin up. He stopped in front of the podium and then since no chair had been placed there for his comfort, he stood, favoring his sprained ankle.

Various people hissed derogatory words at his back as eternally long minutes ticked by. He heard them calling him murderer, demon spawn, bastard, half-breed, drunkard, rapist, and although outwardly he stood strong and confident, he flinched internally at each accusation, convinced now they were all true. Then finally Judge McKitrick walked in looking majestic, although portly, in his black robe and white wig. He took a seat on a high stool behind the podium and looked down his aquiline nose at Rafe, whose spirits sank to their lowest level yet; for it was readily apparent from the derision and prejudice in the judge's demeanor that there was little hope of receiving a just sentence.

"Lord Rafael Zacharias Brookstone," Judge McKitrick boomed in a deep voice that carried extraordinarily well. "You stand before the court today accused of accosting Lady Sarah Huntington, brutally assaulting her husband, Lord Charles Huntington, one of our most respected citizens, and killing Duncan Letourneau when he tried to intervene on their behalf. I've already read the written testimony of the witnesses and it appears—,"

Sarah, seated in the sixth row in between Charles and Micah, jumped to her feet. "Sir, a grave injustice is about to be carried out."

Judge McKitrick was initially incensed that anyone had the audacity to interrupt him, but then he took appreciative notice of

Sarah's uncommon beauty. "Who might you be, young lady?" he asked congenially.

"Lady Sarah Huntington, sir, the woman Lord Brookstone is accused of accosting. Sir, nothing improper occurred between us. He was a complete gentleman. It was all a grave misunderstanding. My husband is known to have a quick temper, especially where Rafe is concerned, and—,"

"Sarah," Charles hissed. "Sit down. You're making yourself a spectacle." He grabbed her hand and tried to pull her into her seat.

Sarah stubbornly tore her hand free from her husband's unwelcome grasp. "I will not sit down! The truth must be told."

Charles indignantly sprang to his feet. "Woman, this is men's business. I command you to sit down!" he said loudly and firmly.

Sarah's eyes widened. Charles had never treated her so rudely, and in front of a crowd of witnesses too, including workers from their estate! Her chin started to quiver and her eyes filled with tears.

Rafe by nature could never allow any injustice to pass unopposed if he was around to do something about it. Forgetting his circumstances for the moment, he instinctively came to her defense. "Sarah is your wife, Charles, not your property! Abstain from commanding her to obey you as if she were one of your slaves!"

A heated fury seized control of Charles. He rushed from his seat toward Rafe, hands fisted, favoring his right leg. His face, which had been in shadow until he stepped into the aisle, was now illuminated by a shaft of sunlight streaming in through an adjacent window. His fine features were so bruised and swollen as to make him unrecognizable to one who didn't know him well.

Rafe winced guiltily. He'd done this! "Charles, I'm—," he started to apologize.

"Do not presume to tell me how to treat my wife, son of Lucifer!" Charles snarled then delivered three strong, fast jabs to Rafe's stomach doubling him over in pain. He had to tap into a monumental amount of self-control to prevent himself from wrapping his manacle chains around Charles's neck and strangling him in front of everyone, which most definitely would've brought a roar of indignation from the crowd rather than the roar of approval Charles's had earned. He slowly, painfully straightened then looked to Leopold expecting him to object to the unjust attack, but Leopold looked directly at him and said nothing! Rafe looked to the two constables standing with their arms crossed on either side of him, but neither of them found it necessary to reprimand Charles either.

"Beat the half-breed bastard to a bloody pulp as he did you!" someone in the crowd shouted, and others cried their agreement.

"Go ahead. Have at him. We won't stop you," Constable Richards said in an undertone to Charles.

Anger surged up in Rafe and burned what remained of his self-control to ashes. He raised his arms, the chains of the manacles chiming musically, intent on following through on his original impulse to strangle Charles if he dared to touch him again, no matter the consequences. Several things happened at once; Sarah cried out in dismay, the two constables tensed, preparing to take Rafe down, and at least a dozen men sprang to their feet to aid them. Leopold also sprang to his feet, but only to chastise Rafe sternly. "Rafe! Mind yourself!"

Rafe reined in his anger and lowered his arms then looked apprehensively at Judge McKitrick, wondering, contritely, how much further he'd influenced the judge against him. His answer came soon enough. "Well, young man. That was a helpful demonstration of your naturally violent nature," Judge McKitrick remarked. "I understand now how you so easily lost control under the influence of drink. It seems you have quite enough trouble controlling yourself while sober."

Rafe said nothing in his defense, for after his recent demonstration of quick temper, what could he say?

Charles hissed triumphantly under his breath, "You've done yourself in now, Rafe."

Judge McKitrick straightened his wig, adjusted his black robe, and then cleared his throat. "If everyone will take their seats…" He waited for Charles and everyone else to sit back down. Rafe, forced to remain standing, although he wanted to collapse from weariness and pain, was reminded of Isaiah 57:20. *But the wicked are like the tossing of the sea, which cannot rest.*

Judge McKitrick cleared his throat again. "I must tell you, young sir, I knew of your foster father, John, although I never met him. I understand he was an honorable man, who would've been sorely dismayed by how thoroughly you've abandoned his teachings."

Rafe hung his head in shame knowing it was true.

"Well?" Judge McKitrick asked impatiently.

Rafe looked up, confused. Had he somehow missed a question? "Sir?"

Judge McKitrick sighed exasperatedly. "This is your opportunity to explain your hot-tempered, drunken actions of last night young man."

"I cannot explain them, sir, but I assure you I wasn't drunk. I'd had only two sips of port. I think now it must have been drugged, for afterward I felt dizzy and not quite right. When Charles punched me, I found myself unable to maintain control, and when Duncan intervened, I reacted without thinking and shoved him. It was never my intent to harm either of them; and especially not Duncan. He was one of the rare few who accepted me unconditionally despite my ignoble origin and mixed blood. I valued his friendship greatly."

Judge McKitrick raised a skeptical eyebrow. "Then please explain recently drawing your knife and making a threat on Duncan's life simply because he was hunting on your grandfather's land. Or is this how you treat those whose friendship you *value greatly*?"

Rafe was temporarily struck dumb by this twisted accusation.

"Well, boy?" demanded Judge McKitrick impatiently.

"Who told you this vile lie, sir?"

Micah stood up. "It's no lie. I was there, and I'm one of those you threatened to kill!"

Rafe turned to confront Micah. "It was you who threatened to kill me that day, not the other way around!"

Charles again rose to his feet. "Sir, Micah was merely defending us against Rafe, who threatened to kill us all, claiming we were trespassing on his land which we all know is open to everyone."

Rather than argue uselessly with Charles, Rafe turned back around to present his case to the judge. "It's my land now, and I've closed it, particularly to those who hunt out of season. But I threatened no one's life. I merely asked Charles and his hunting party, of which Duncan was a silent and non-confrontational member, to leave. I drew my knife only in self-defense when Micah then threatened to shoot me."

"So you say, but it's the word of a half-breed bastard against nobles, isn't it," said the judge, "and you still haven't answered my question."

Rafe rubbed his stinging, gritty eyes with the heels of his hands. "Forgive me, sir, but would you repeat the question?"

Judge McKitrick sighed heavily and then, slowly, deliberately, as if Rafe was half-witted, he said, "I asked if you sincerely expected us to believe, given your naturally savage nature, that you killed Duncan accidentally?"

Rafe's temper flared, and he was tempted to reply that if he was truly naturally savage, he'd fight his way to freedom and escape once and for all the prejudice and unjust judgments continually levied against him by stubborn and obstinate white people. However, he knew such a statement, no matter how true, wouldn't help his case. "It is the truth, sir."

"The truth is it now, sir?" Judge McKitrick mocked.

Rafe swallowed the vile curse words he wanted to spit in response to the judge's insulting tone. "Yes, sir."

"No, sir," Judge McKitrick countered. "The truth is that you killed Duncan in anger for coming to the aid of Lord Huntington, who was merely attempting to prevent your drunken assault of Lady Huntington."

Rafe nearly exploded in frustration. The judge wasn't listening to him! He'd already said several times that he wasn't drunk! "Sir, I detest the taste of all alcoholic drinks. As I already told you, I barely had two sips of port, and that only because the servant insisted!"

"Your defense is weak, sir, for it has already been made quite clear by your violent behavior before me this day, as well as by the testimony of Lord Huntington and his brother-in-law, Micah Anderson given privately after you were taken into custody last night that you were not acting against your nature at the ball, but fully in accordance with it. Furthermore, your assertion that someone drugged your drink is ridiculous, for who would have anything to gain by doing so?"

Rafe had no answer, although he'd puzzled over it as he'd lain awake all night. He'd eventually concluded that someone had wanted him to make a fool of himself at the least, which answered the *why;* but *who* was driving him to distraction, for it could be anyone. They all hated him.

"Sir, may I address the court?" Leopold asked.

Judge McKitrick had been Leopold's roommate at law school, and they were still friendly so he willingly obliged. "Very well, the Court recognizes Leopold Aspenwall."

"Thank you, sir." Leopold came to stand beside Rafe. "You all no doubt may wonder how I may defend a man with Indian blood who has killed a white man and badly beaten another in a drunken fury. I will tell you. As Rafe's foster father these last thirteen years I can attest that Rafe's good deeds far outnumber the bad. He alone donated the funds to build an extension to the hospital, two new schools in the neighboring parish, a church, and the orphanage. Now, because of an unfortunate accident the first time he ever drank too much you forget all the good he's done and have the audacity to put him to trial! It's—it's scandalous, and that's all I have to say about it, sir."

"Come now, Mr. Aspenwall, surely you know an individual may practice good deeds merely to win the accolades of men without that charity actually having any meaning to them. People do so all over the world every day. Who would crave the accolades of men more than a widely despised half-breed?" McKitrick reasoned.

"This may be true for some, sir, but I assure you that Rafe's good deeds are genuine and heartfelt," Leopold asserted firmly. "He gains his satisfaction merely in the doing. He does not seek the accolades of men."

Rafe was both relieved that Leopold was at last coming to his defense and surprised he was saying benevolent things about him, for although Leopold had never treated him unkindly, he hadn't exactly showered him with love. Despite that lack of warmth Rafe had come to love Leopold for the small kindnesses on rare occasions, for kindness from anyone had been in short supply ever since he'd been forced to watch the slaughter of his loving, adopted tribe and then compelled to live in the white man's world.

"Hogwash!" Charles interposed disgustedly. "You never wish to hold Rafe accountable for his misdeeds, sir; which is why he's grown as bold as to assault me and murder Duncan!"

"That is patently untrue, Lord Huntington. I have properly punished Rafe for every mischief he has ever perpetrated!" Leopold countered.

Judge McKitrick banged his gavel on the podium. "Enough! Lord Huntington, please sit down."

Charles reluctantly sat down and the judge turned his attention back on Leo. "As for you, Mr. Aspenwall, I understand your reluctance to believe your foster son would willingly harm another, as I'm sure you did your best to bring him up properly. However, I fail to comprehend how you could forget that his arrogant Indian father was both a drunk and a rapist. It's obvious to everyone but you that despite your foster son's good Brookstone blood, the natural father's bad blood is dominant in him."

"I'm well aware of all that, Joe, but in light of Rafe's previous good deeds, I think he deserves a little—," Leopold began to argue.

"I don't care what you think, Leopold! You're not the judge! I am! Return to your seat!" Judge McKitrick shouted.

"But—,"

"Now, sir, or I shall cite you for contempt," Judge McKitrick warned frostily.

Leopold opened his mouth to argue further, and then apparently thought better of it, snapped his mouth shut, and reluctantly returned to his seat his shoulders sagging in defeat. McKitrick straightened his wig, which had gone askew when he'd shouted, straightened his black robes, his white tie, and then he addressed Rafe. "Now, young man, do you have anything else to say on your behalf?"

Rafe shook his head. If Leopold's protestations were of no use, no argument from the vile son of a drunken rapist who was one half despised Indian besides would sway the judge.

"Then I shall pronounce sentence." Judge McKitrick looked sternly down his nose at Rafe. "The spiteful murder of an innocent man that you called a friend and who was only attempting to prevent you from committing a heinous crime in your drunkenness is ample evidence you cannot control your temper and thus cannot be allowed to remain free. Furthermore, the guard we posted outside your cell has informed me that you've demonstrated absolutely no remorse. Ever since you were recovered from those savage, murderous Indians—,"

Rafe had listened to the scurrilous claims against him in quiet resignation, but now that the honor of his adopted tribe was besmirched he couldn't keep quiet. "My tribe was peaceful, sir! It was my so-called honorable, white grandfather who ordered his mercenaries to slaughter them, men, women, children, and the honored old ones, merely because he wished to deny me a home to return to! It's you white men who are savage and murderous!"

The courtroom exploded in exclamations of angry outrage. Judge McKitrick had to bang his gavel on the podium nine times before order was restored. Then he once again straightened his robes, adjusted his wig, and addressed Rafe. "You've only further proven your rancorous nature with this outburst, young man; but if you're quite finished, I'll continue pronouncing your sentence." He glared at Rafe sternly. "Are you quite finished?"

Rafe nodded sullenly.

"Very well." Judge McKitrick cleared his throat. "Despite the half of your noble Brookstone blood, I've always feared you'd one day submit to the savage half of your nature and irreparably harm one of our citizens as your father did. Now you've proven me correct. There's no doubt that a sentence of death is most certainly what you deserve. You shall be hung as soon as the gallows is built; and since you have no heirs—," Judge McKitrick paused. "You do lack heirs, sir, do you not? Or have you sired a bastard by rape, even as your father sired you?"

"I would never take a woman by force, sir," Rafe said indignantly.

"That's yet to be disproven, but no doubt you've sired heirs through the local prostitute or a tavern wench, or perhaps by a secret marriage you were forced into as a result of impregnating a respectable farmer's daughter?"

"I have no heirs, sir, bastard or otherwise," Rafe said. He deliberately failed to mention that he was still a virgin. That was far too personal for the ears of such a crowd, and he doubted they would believe it anyway.

"Then since you refuse to admit to an heir, your estate will be forfeit to the state," Judge McKitrick declared.

"No!" Sarah cried, springing to her feet. "You're making a terrible mistake!"

Charles sprang to his feet, embarrassed that his wife was once again defending the man who'd brutally assaulted him. "Sarah, sit down. Calm yourself," he said sternly.

Sarah put her small, delicate hands on Charles's left forearm and looked earnestly into his face, her large blue eyes swimming in tears. "Please, Charles. If anyone is in the wrong here, it's I, for if I hadn't followed Rafe into the garden, none of this would've happened. Help him. I beg of you. If you've ever loved me, help him!"

Charles most definitely did not want to help Rafe. He finally had the despicable, bastard, half-breed, rival for Sarah's affections exactly where he wanted him, on the brink of hanging! However, he did love Sarah with all his heart, and furthermore, he could never deny a request from her when he looked into those beautiful, blue eyes; especially when they were filled with tears. Then he realized he could have it both ways. He could ingratiate himself to Sarah, while also assuring that Rafe suffered unendingly under his own hand for the remainder of his days; far better than seeing Rafe hung, the satisfaction of which would only last a few days at most. "Sir," he said, addressing the judge. "May I speak?"

Judge McKitrick nodded obligingly.

"As one of those wronged, I beg the right to grant mercy to the accused. Allow me to transport Rafe to my plantation in the Caribbean, there to work off his debt against me and society as my slave until such time as it's proven he's a changed man or until the end of his days, whichever comes first; which, considering Rafe's naturally violent nature will most likely be the latter."

Judge McKitrick considered this request thoughtfully for some excruciatingly long minutes while Sarah waited anxiously. Then the Judge nodded. "I shall grant your request. However, this changes the disposition of the estate. It shall now be held in trust by Leopold Aspenwall until such time as Lord Brookstone may reclaim it or until Lord Brookstone's death when it shall revert to the state if there are no heirs sired in the meantime.

"Hand over your signet ring, sir," he then said to Rafe.

Rafe grasped the signet ring on his left ring finger of a Phoenix in flight. Leopold had handed the ring over to him on his fourteenth birthday judging he was ready to take over the running of the estate. Rafe had immediately set about making changes. The worker's living conditions had all been upgraded, homes rebuilt or remodeled, regular medical care was provided, along with plenty of nutritious food, and the estate worker's children were all educated by a private teacher hired by Rafe out of his own discretionary funds. Leopold had argued that Rafe's changes would only make the workers lazy and demanding, but instead the estate was producing three times what it had under the oversight of Leopold and before that the old Lord Brookstone. With those same workers in mind Rafe found he was reluctant to hand over the ring and turn the estate back over to Leopold, who would undoubtedly undo all the changes he'd made.

"Constable James," the judge said. "Please take custody of the ring and turn it over to Leopold Aspenwall."

Constable James held out his hand demandingly. Rafe reluctantly pulled the ring from his finger, his manacle chains chiming with his movement, and with a trembling hand dropped it into Constable James's waiting and open palm. The constable carried the ring to Leopold, who then pocketed it, avoiding eye contact with Rafe.

"You may now return the convict to his cell until arrangements may be made to transport him to Boston, from whence passage shall be arranged on a ship to the Caribbean." Judge McKitrick banged his gavel once on the podium. "Court is dismissed."

The constables each grabbed one of Rafe's arms and propelled him through the darkly mumbling, glaring crowd and outside where Rafe unexpectedly came face to face with Henry, whom Rafe now realized hadn't been at the trial. "Henry, I'm so sorry. I never meant—,"

His apology was rudely interrupted by the forceful meeting of Henry's fist with his jaw, a blow so unanticipated and so powerful that both constable's lost their grips on his arms and Rafe stumbled backward and then fell. "You should be dead instead of Duncan, you evil half-breed!" Henry snarled, and then stormed away.

"That was well deserved," Constable Richards remarked.

Rafe rubbed his bruised chin, the manacle chains ringing a doleful accompaniment. "Indeed," he agreed dispiritedly.

His agreement annoyed the constable for it left him without the opportunity to counter with another snide comment. He grabbed Rafe's arm roughly and dragged him to his feet then shoved him in the direction of the jail.

As Rafe was once again locked into his cell, he cursed Charles for his interference. Why couldn't his obstinate, one-time pledged brother have let him be hanged? Then he'd at least have oblivion to look forward to. Now he had nothing ahead of him but years of unending misery as Charles's slave, a fate far worse than death.

Chapter Eight

Constable Richards sat with his feet propped up on the desk, leaning back in his chair, snoozing, with the jail door open to let in a breeze on this hot, September day. Rafe took advantage of a little privacy to kneel in prayer. Ignoring the pain of his still untreated sprained ankle he bowed his head while working up the courage to pray and risk facing God's rejection.

Charles walked in.

Rafe hastily rose to his feet. Constable Richards startled awake and then stood up. "Good morning, Lord Huntington," he said respectfully.

Charles nodded at the constable then addressed Rafe. "You're wasting your time praying. You can't fool God any more than you've fooled any of us."

Constable Richards snickered.

"Why have you come, Charles?" Rafe asked so frostily that it was amazing ice didn't instantaneously form on the white plastered brick walls of the cell.

Charles assumed an air of offense. "I have magnanimously granted you the opportunity to redeem your soul by working off your debt to society on my plantation and this is the reception I receive?" He visibly checked himself. "Wait, I misspoke. You're an abomination that lacks a soul to redeem, so you must be content with merely working off your enormous debt to society. You'll have to live until you're toothless, bent, and gray and I'll make sure you work quite hard for every last one of those years. With any luck you'll die knowing your debt is paid."

The only outward evidence of Rafe's fury was a malevolent gleam in his dark eyes. "If you're entertaining thoughts of abusing me, I suggest you reconsider," he threatened quietly.

Charles knew that tone and that look all too well. He'd seen it often enough in their childhood when their arms master had deliberately pushed Rafe too hard in their training sessions. So he knew Rafe was at his most dangerous now. Ordinarily, he would've made a hasty retreat after another snide comment to cover up that he was afraid, but the cell's bars presented a safety barrier that gave Charles the courage to continue his taunts. "I warned everyone not to expect any good from you, but they were all so easily deceived by your noble bloodline and your silver tongue and your extraordinary good looks. If only they'd remembered that Lucifer is God's most beautiful angel, they would've recognized before you assaulted Sarah, beat me, and killed Duncan that you can't suppress your evil nature any more than the moon can become the sun, and they would've hanged you before you killed an innocent man."

Rafe thrust his body against the cell bars, putting him only a few feet from Charles, but given the bars between them they might as well have been separated by miles. Grasping the bars with both scabbed knuckled hands, he said, "You wouldn't have the courage to make such vile accusations without these bars between us."

"It takes no courage to speak the truth," Charles countered.

Rafe gripped the cell's bars so tightly that the scabs on his knuckles cracked and seeped blood. It provided pleasing evidence of his success in taunting Rafe, but it wasn't enough for Charles. He aspired to even greater heights of offense. "If you owned a shred of decency, you'd end your despicable life now and save me the expense of transporting you to the Caribbean and feeding you until you die of overwork." He then used his usual method of denying Rafe a reply and walked out, grinning triumphantly.

"Lord Huntington told you off properly, didn't he, half-breed scum," Constable Richards remarked smugly.

Rafe knew better than to provoke a constable, so he suppressed the angry reply that sprang to mind. Instead he merely retreated to his lumpy mattress, leaned against the cold, hard wall, and stared glumly out the window at the passing clouds.

An hour later Pastor Henline walked in. He was a muscled man in his mid-fifties with graying brown hair and warm brown eyes. Lisbeth and Pierre came in behind him. Rafe was too depressed to bother walking to the front of the cell to greet them, and besides he'd rather avoid the pain of walking on his sprained ankle.

"My dear Rafe, how are you holding up?" Lisbeth asked as she tucked a loose lock of her glossy, curly black hair behind her ear.

"I'm well," Rafe lied.

"Is there anything we may do for you?" Pierre asked.

"You may release me from this cell. The key ring is hanging on that peg on the far wall," Rafe joked.

"You know we can't release you," Pastor Henline said, glancing at Constable Richards warily, as if he was afraid the constable would arrest them for the mere mention of helping Rafe escape. "Perhaps we could help in some other way, though. If you'd confess to the folly of your drunkenness, we might be able to persuade Judge McKitrick to grant you a few allowances that will make your life more comfortable until you're transported."

Rafe had long ago forgiven Pastor Henline for suggesting to his white grandfather that he steal back his only surviving heir from his adopted tribe, but now he was tempted to withdraw his absolution. "Charles visited me. He claims I'm evil. It seems you agree with him. Sir."

"I believe you're no different than anyone else. We're all sinners," Pastor Henline said.

"And in this tragedy you're only partly to blame," Pierre interposed. "For its no fault of yours that something in your makeup inherited from your natural father makes you vulnerable to violence when you drink."

Rafe stiffened. "I never thought *you'd* partake of such ridiculous notions, Pierre." He looked to Lisbeth. "Do you share your husband's opinion?" His overly dark eyes locked on hers pleading with her not to disappoint him.

Then she did. "But of course, Rafe. That's why we came here today; to beg your pardon for failing to note that after all this time you'd succumbed to your father's blood in you and become a drunkard. Why did you keep it secret from us? If we'd only known, we could've warned the servants to refuse you any alcohol and prevented this tragedy."

Rafe knew Lisbeth had spoken with good intentions, but all that mattered was that like everyone else she thought he was the same as his wicked father. "You all so easily believe ill of me," he lamented.

"What else are we to believe when we all witnessed your crimes?" Pierre asked defensively.

"Believe I'm better than that," Rafe said softly in Mohican.

"I'm sorry?" asked Pastor Henline.

Rafe shook his head. "Thank you for coming, but I'm exhausted and would like to rest now." He lay down on his lumpy bed with his back to them and almost immediately heard them depart. He closed his eyes, but although he hadn't slept for the last three nights, sleep refused to grant him respite from his troubles. After several hours of uselessly pursuing sleep he sat up, rested his back against the wall, and stared forlornly out the barred cell window to his left at the black, starless night sky. "Pachtamawas," he prayed silently as tears welled up in his eyes. "As the Creator, you have the right to reject me, soulless half-breed, seed of an abominable act that I am, but learning I was in error to believe You loved me has come upon me so hard and swift that my heart grows faint. I would that You'd have been more merciful and let me know the truth gradually; or is it that I don't deserve such kindness?" A single tear rolled down Rafe's cheek. He hastily swiped it away with the back of his left then glanced at Constable Richards, who fortunately hadn't noticed his shameful lapse.

Leopold walked in looking bedraggled and rumpled. Rafe's wounded heart was comforted by the visit, but as with Pierre, Lisbeth, and the Pastor, he lacked the desire to rise to meet him. "Leopold, I hope you also haven't come to accuse me of lying."

Leopold bristled. "How dare anyone besmirch the Brookstone name!" he said.

"Yes, how dare they," Rafe remarked bitterly. As usual, Leopold cared more for the family's reputation than for him.

"Who was it? Charles?" Leopold demanded.

"He as well," Rafe said then changed the subject. "What time is it?"

"It's a little after midnight. I've just come from arguing with Joe—er—Judge McKitrick, that as you have never been in trouble before and you're a lord of a noble family of good name, he should declare Duncan's death an unfortunate accident."

"He refused I presume, else Constable Richards wouldn't be sitting calmly at his desk but would instead be retrieving the key to let me out of this confounded tiny cell," Rafe said.

Constable Richards snorted. "If I have anything to say about it, you'll never be free again."

"I'm sorry, Rafe," Leopold said. "It's not fair that you should suffer so abominably for a single drunken lapse in judgment when previously you've been a model citizen; but don't lose hope. I'm quite persuasive. Joe has never resisted my arguments for long."

"Thank you for your efforts on my behalf, sir…" Rafe's voice trailed off despondently.

"However?" Leopold prompted.

"I can't help noticing you're asking for leniency instead of working to prove my innocence, even though I told you I was not drunk. Why is it that you never believe me, even though I've never once lied to you?" Rafe complained.

Leopold was at first prepared to adamantly deny that he never believed Rafe, but then he realized he couldn't, for he had always doubted Rafe. He couldn't help it. He was too aware of Rafe's father's wicked blood in him. "I'll investigate your claim that the port was drugged," he conceded, attempting to make up for his lack of faith.

Rafe's eyebrows shot up in surprise then he looked relieved. "Thank you, sir."

Leopold nodded acknowledgement. "You look haggard. Get some rest. I'll report my findings to you by tomorrow noon." His black wool cloak swirled about his legs as he turned and then briskly walked out.

Rafe lay down on the lumpy straw mattress and tried to summon up hope now that he had at least one person believing in him enough to actually investigate matters. However, hope continued to evade him, for the truth was that even if his port had been drugged, he'd still brutally assaulted Charles and killed Duncan. Those heinous acts couldn't be taken back no matter how they'd been instigated. Worse, now that he knew God had rejected him, there would be no forgiveness, no end to the guilt; and with that dismal realization, came an even deeper despair that wrapped its claws in a stranglehold around his heart and whispered a promise to remain a faithful and constant companion.

Chapter Nine

Rafe paced his small cell in agitation, although it aggravated his sprained ankle. It was well past noon on the second day after Leopold had promised to investigate his claim that the port was drugged, and he'd heard no word from him. When, finally, the jail door opened Rafe looked to it hopefully, but it was only Constable Richards, who carried a tray covered with a blue, flowered cloth. The mouthwatering aromas accompanying it gave a solid clue that it was Rafe's lunch. He sat on his bed as was required whenever a meal was brought then Richards opened the squealing cell door. "You should particularly enjoy your lunch today," Richards remarked, setting the tray down on the floor. "Lady Sarah Huntington prepared it especially for you."

"Then it's entirely possible Charles poisoned it when she wasn't looking," Rafe remarked dourly.

Constable Richards shrugged. "You should have been hung, but as you managed to avoid that just sentence, I would be pleased to see you earn what you deserve in another manner." He slammed the cell door closed with a loud and angry clang.

Rafe tentatively approached the tray, nudged it with his foot then stepped back quickly, as if he thought the food might suddenly burst into flames. He was fairly confident that Charles wouldn't actually try to kill him, but it wasn't outside the realm of possibility that Charles had slipped something into the food to make him so miserable he would wish he was dead. The joke was on Charles, though. He already wished he was dead. Since he was stuck living, however, and had no wish to increase his suffering, he decided to leave the food untouched despite that he was ravenous. Constable Richards didn't care one way or another if Rafe ate, but when Constable James came on duty an hour later he observed the untouched food with dismay. "You didn't eat. Didn't Constable Richards tell you Lady Sarah Huntington made the meal especially for you?"

"I'm not hungry," Rafe said, and then his stomach grumbled and revealed his lie.

Constable James scowled. "Refusing to eat is petty and furthermore hurts only you. But suit yourself." He opened the cell door, picked up the tray, and after firmly closing the cell door, he carried the tray out of the jail. Rafe sat on the floor in the corner of his cell with his back against the wall, stretched out his right leg with the throbbing ankle, bent his other, and rested his left wrist on the knee. Then he stared gloomily out the cell's window while ruminating despairingly on the many years ahead in which he'd be forced to serve under Charles's harsh and unforgiving hand; years sure to seem twice as long for their misery.

In the midst of imagining a discouraging scenario of Charles whipping him for no reason, Leopold finally walked in. Rafe surged to his feet and walked to the front of his cell barely noticing the shooting pain in his ankle in his eagerness for the hopefully good news Leopold brought. "At long last! What have you discovered?"

"That you used guilt to manipulate me into believing your lie that your port was drugged," Leopold replied coolly.

Rafe's spirits sank so low that they scraped a hole in rock bottom and he silently labeled himself a fool. He should've known better. Justice was not for the likes of him. "I spoke the truth," he asserted half-heartedly, without any hope Leopold would believe him.

"Then why is it that although I've interviewed everyone who was at the ball, including the servants, I'm unable to discover any evidence whatsoever that you were anything but drunk that night?"

Rafe suddenly recalled that Cabel had miraculously shown up with Al Hadiye before it was even known that he'd come back without him. "Cabel; did you ask him—,"

"I trusted you as you asked me to, and you made me look a fool! A cruel way of rewarding my faith in you!"

Rafe bristled. "Sir, you cannot seriously believe I'm so dimwitted as to drink too much and then accost the wife of a highly influential man before scores of people who are already constantly watching my every move in the hope I'll prove their prejudice is warranted!"

"I didn't think you were so dull," Leopold said. "However, it's plain from the evidence that you did do exactly that. So I'd like to know why you sent me on this useless chase when you knew all along I'd find nothing. Whatever did you hope to gain by it?"

"Justice," Rafe said despondently.

"Justice!" Leopold spat. "It's more likely you were hoping to avoid justice."

"No, sir—," Rafe began.

But Leopold wouldn't let him talk. "Why the old Lord Brookstone ever thought a half-breed would ever be capable of doing the family name justice is beyond me!"

Tears welled up in Rafe's eyes, which both angered and embarrassed him. He'd withstood injustice and prejudice every day of his life for the last thirteen years without even flinching, but ever since the ball the tears sprang up at the slightest provocation! It was ridiculous! He was a warrior, for heaven's sake! "So then you too are finished with me," he stated forlornly.

"I'd love to never see you again, but unfortunately Constables James and Richards are unable to transport you to Boston as they must assist in the transport of a gang of criminals from Downing parish to prison in Philadelphia. Therefore, Charles has offered to transport you and I've agreed to help him, for since I failed as your foster father to teach you right from wrong, I feel it my duty to make amends by seeing you safely on Charles's merchant ship, the Lady Bountiful, headed for your penance of a life of slavery." Leopold whirled around and stormed out.

Rafe pretended not to notice Constable Richards' victorious sneer. He retreated to his lumpy bed and spent the rest of the night lying on his back staring up at the ceiling and unsuccessfully willing his heart to stop beating.

<h1 style="text-align:center"><u>Chapter Ten</u></h1>

After a week of confinement in the tiny cell, the walls were starting to close in on Rafe. Worse, although he was beyond exhausted, sleep continued to elude him, except for a few hours here and there, denying him more than temporary respite from his circumstances, and he also had a throbbing headache with vision disturbances that had started at his temples then spread to the rest of his head and neck. He'd endured these painful headaches often during the first few years of his forced new life as Lord Brookstone, but they'd subsided when he'd finally resigned himself to his fate. Now he had a much harsher fate to accept and the headaches had returned. He assumed they'd plague him until he resigned himself to this new fate, if he ever could.

Leopold had always treated the headaches with a mixture of opium and vinegar rubbed on the forehead, but Rafe he was convinced Constables James and Richards would take pleasure in disallowing such treatment. So he didn't even ask, thus robbing them of the potential satisfaction. He paced his cell, ignoring the dual pains of his sprained ankle and his throbbing headache, on the edge of demanding to be let out of this suffocating cell. Then Constable James came, accompanied by Leopold dressed in traveling clothes and armed with a loaded pistol. He carried a set of Rafe's buckskins under his right arm, along with a set of clean undergarments, thick cotton socks, and the heavy, black, calf-high boots Rafe always wore when traveling.

Rafe came to a standstill. Apparently it was time to begin his journey to a life of slavery; the precursor to even more misery. But it was at least the end of his smothering confinement in the tiny cell. Constable James let Leopold into the cell then Leopold handed Rafe the socks, underclothes, buckskins and boots. "Your traveling clothes." He spoke with no trace of his customary sociability.

Rafe took the clothing without comment then set it on the bed while he stripped off his four-day-old, rumpled and blood-spotted black suit, undergarments, socks, and uncomfortable dress shoes. He felt self-conscious undressing in front of two people watching him sternly, and thus as each succeeding layer was removed he felt his face growing hotter. He turned his back on them to hide his embarrassment and dressed as quickly as possible. Then Constable

Richards clamped the heavy manacles with the rough edges onto Rafe's wrists, drew his pistol and motioned for him to start walking.

Rafe was nearly blinded by the brightness of the sun after so long in the dim cell. He closed his eyes and lifted his chin to the sky soaking up the sun's warmth, and enjoying the soft caress of the wind on his skin. For the first time since Duncan's death the ever-present tension in the muscles of his neck and shoulders eased. Then he opened his eyes and was surprised to see that the Brookstone coach awaited, its roof loaded with supplies. He'd expected to be transported in a prison wagon. He was not surprised, however to see Henry and Charles both armed with pistols and mounted on two fine bay stallions from Charles's stables. The horses snorted almost in unison creating tiny double clouds of vapor in the cool, early September morning air. "Why are we taking my coach instead of the prison wagon?" Rafe asked Leopold.

"It's no longer your coach, Rafe. It belongs to the estate," Leopold corrected tersely.

Rafe resisted rolling his eyes. "Then why are we taking the Brookstone estate carriage?"

"The prison wagon is in use. Thus, it was suggested we use the Brookstone carriage as the next best way to keep you contained."

"Like the vicious wild animal that you are," Charles couldn't resist adding nastily.

Rafe ignored Charles. "I see no horse for you, sir," He said to Leopold. "Will you be driving the coach?"

"Sometimes. Charles, Henry, and I will trade off," Leopold answered.

"Enough delay," Charles said impatiently. "Step into the carriage, murdering demon-spawn." He rode his horse into Rafe, battering him with the horse's chest and making him stumble sideways onto his bad ankle.

Sharp pain shot up Rafe's leg, and his temper flared. He glared at Charles darkly. "Mind yourself, Charles!" he threatened quietly.

Charles noted the fury reflected in Rafe's abnormally dark eyes, but that telltale sign wasn't necessary to know how Rafe felt. Charles could literally feel the anger and resentment emanating from Rafe. It hung thickly in the air between them like a dense, invisible veil. Well aware that even manacled Rafe was fully capable of unhorsing him and delivering the beginnings of another sound beating before anyone could intervene, he drew his loaded pistol; and then so did Henry. "Are you threatening me?"

Rafe was strongly tempted to respond in the affirmative, but then he glanced from Charles with his drawn pistol to Henry with his drawn pistol, Constable James with his drawn pistol, and lastly Leopold, who so obviously lacked even a trace of sympathy for his plight. Opinion and power being thus stacked against him, Rafe was wise enough to yield to it. "I meant no threat. Forgive me if I made it seem so."

Charles gloated openly that he'd made Rafe apologize to him and in front of others too. "I accept your apology, and I shall even forgo your punishment in the interest of not wasting time. Now step into the coach, Lucifer's child," he commanded imperiously.

Rafe opened the door and stepped inside the coach left leg first, but before he was fully inside Charles leaned over from atop his horse and slammed the door shut. Rafe had to quickly pull his right leg in to prevent the door from smashing on his sprained ankle and he shot a dark glare at Charles before he settled onto the soft cushions of his, or rather the Brookstone estate's luxurious personal conveyance. The carriage leaned slightly to the right as Leopold climbed up into the driver's seat then Rafe heard him slapping the reins on the backs of the two coach horses and the coach lurched forward, headed north. Normally an admirer of all nature, today Rafe failed to appreciate the glorious, dense stands of tall, leafy trees, with smaller trees taking root at their bases and the thick, green bushes they passed as they traveled down the road. At some point, the soft, cushioned seats, the gentle swaying of the coach, and exhaustion lulled him into slumber.

The dream started out benignly. He and Duncan walked companionably through the woods on the east end of his vast estate. Then for no reason Rafe drew his knife, knocked Duncan to the ground, and started determinedly sawing off Duncan's head.

Rafe startled awake, pulse racing, sweat beading his aching brow. He wiped his painfully aching brow with his left hand, dried his hand on his pants then rubbed his eyes and stared out the carriage window to his left at the crisp, high noon shadows of the passing trees marking the road like the black bars of the suffocating cell he'd only recently escaped from. Bright, swirling lights and colors that almost always accompanied his more painful headaches danced around the black shadows, making him feel ill. He closed his eyes and leaned over, resting his elbows on his knees and then cradling his seemingly eternally aching head in both hands.

* * *

Around sunset, Rafe's headache finally waned to a point where it didn't make his eyes water. Leopold parked the carriage in a shady glade beside a swift-running creek, while Charles and Henry dismounted and led their horses down to the water for a long drink. A moment later Leopold opened the carriage door. "You may disembark, Rafe," he said in a business-like tone.

Rafe stepped out onto a thick carpet of dried leaves, which released a pleasant aroma and crackled underfoot as he made his way to a crumbling log. He sat down on the most solid spot and stretched his leg with the sprained ankle out in front of him as he watched Leopold unhitch the coach horses then take them down to the river for a drink. As he passed by Rafe, he said, "Make yourself useful by unloading that." He pointed to the basket lashed to the back of the carriage.

Rafe obediently struggled to his feet and limped to the basket. He loosened the leather lashings, but then discovered that the short connecting chain on his manacles made it impossible to spread his hands wide enough to lift the basket by the leather handles on either end. He slid his hands under the basket instead, lifted it then leaning backward and resting the weight of the heavy basket against his chest awkwardly carried it to where Charles and Henry were now setting up camp, having just finished watering their horses.

Charles snatched the basket from Rafe without a word of thanks, set it down then shoved Rafe roughly away from him, forcing Rafe to have to take a quick back-step to avoid a fall. Shooting pain blazed through Rafe's sprained ankle and up the side of his leg to his hip. Already irritable from suffering a monster of a headache all day as well as being cooped up in the carriage, the additional pain pushed Rafe over the edge. He shoved Charles with the full force of his rage. Charles stumbled backward and his back slammed against a nearby tree trunk with a loud 'thwack'. However, he recovered quickly and advanced on Rafe threateningly, his hands balled into tight fists at his sides. "How dare you put your filthy hands on me, your master, slave!"

"You will never be my master!" Rafe spat. "I'm superior to you in every way! If you need proof, ask Sarah why she pleaded for my life at the trial after I so brutally assaulted you. Ask her why she came to me the week before your wedding begging me to run away with her so she wouldn't have to marry you!"

Charles's nostrils flared and he struck Rafe on the chin, knocking him onto his back on the ground. Charles didn't quite there, though. He whipped out his already loaded pistol, straddled Rafe, and thrust the pistol's barrel into his chest. "I should kill you!"

Rafe seized the opportunity to end the nightmare his life had become. "Do it then. Rid the world of an abomination and a scourge, if you have the courage."

"Oh trust me, Rafe, I have the courage." Charles pulled the trigger.

"No!" Henry roared as he knocked the gun aside, making the shot go into the ground beside Rafe instead of into his chest. "What do you think you're doing!"

Charles looked up at Henry in shocked surprise. "Have you so soon forgotten it was your younger brother he so brutally killed?"

"Of course I haven't forgotten, Charles. I wish as dearly to see Rafe dead as you; but as gentlemen of honor we must abide by the law, else we're no better than this criminal. Holster your pistol."

Charles's hand trembled with uncertainty.

"Don't become a vile murderer like him," Henry said.

Charles hesitated a moment longer before he shoved his pistol into his holster, sprang to his feet, deliberately kicking Rafe in the side, and then stormed off into the trees to sulk in private. Leopold was just then returning to camp with the carriage horses, whistling tunelessly. He stopped in mid-note, however, when Charles brushed angrily past him, and then he noticed Henry scowling and that Rafe had a new bruise on his chin. "You have a new bruise, Rafe," he remarked accusingly.

"A gift from Charles," Rafe said.

"How earned?" Leopold demanded.

Henry interposed, "He shoved Charles into a tree and then would've beaten him bloody, except that Charles defended himself."

"Assaulting Charles is how you came to be in this mess in the first place, Rafe. Why must you continually instigate violence against others? Have you learned nothing from the consequences you now pay for such sins?" Leopold said disgustedly.

"Indeed I have, sir. I've learned two things; there is no justice where I'm concerned, and you will never cease assuming I'm always the instigator," Rafe said resentfully.

"You are always the instigator, exactly like your despicable father," Leopold spat. "I failed to wean that despicable trait out of you, but it seems his wicked blood flows too strongly in your veins. It wouldn't surprise me at all if you've committed rape like your father as well!"

Rafe's eyes widened at the unjust accusation and then he looked hurt. "I am not my father, sir," he denied softly then retreated to a nearby tree with a large, above-ground root. He sat down between two of the four, thick, off shoots with his back against the trunk and then nursed both his wounded heart and his wrists, which were seeping blood from the raw wounds caused by the constant rubbing of the rough spots on the manacles.

Charles returned a short time later and sat down at the campfire beside Henry, who along with Leopold offered him sympathy and compassion. Rafe watched, nursing resentment. He craved sympathy and compassion like a parched man in the desert craves water. It was patently unfair that although he lacked a single friend and was even denied God's love he was denied the slightest comfort, while Charles who neither deserved nor needed the emotional support received more than his fair share!

Eventually, Henry opened the food basket and passed out hunks of fresh sourdough bread with Muenster cheese and lush, red apples, to Charles, Leopold and reserving a hefty portion for himself. He brought Rafe a small portion of only bread and cheese on a tin plate and wordlessly placed on the ground beside Rafe's knee. Rafe left the food untouched, for resentment, the headache, and the accompanying nausea had most thoroughly robbed him of his appetite. Eventually even the smell of the food became too much to bear. He picked up the plate and flipped the contents onto the ground. Several chipmunks raced from nearby bushes and pounced on the bread and cheese then carried it away chattering excitedly over their unexpected feast. Before the tragedy at the ball, Rafe would've smiled at the sight, but now he only watched numbly.

"I saw that, Rafe," Henry said indignantly. "Since you feel inclined to waste your food you'll have no breakfast tomorrow. Perhaps after going hungry you'll be less inclined to throw away what you don't deserve in the first place!"

Weary of the mistreatment, Rafe snapped, "Pettiness is unbecoming in a gentleman."

With a roar of anger Henry charged, knocked him onto his back and wrapped his fingers tightly around his neck. "How dare you lecture me you despicable, murdering half-breed!" he snarled.

Rafe's vision started to darken, but he made no effort to pry Henry's hands loose. Death by strangulation was merely another if more painful way to end his misery.

"If you wish an answer from him, you'll have to let him breathe, Henry," Leopold interposed calmly.

Henry released his stranglehold on Rafe, whose face had started turning blue, but not without first banging Rafe's head painfully on the rocky ground once. Then he stood up and stormed off muttering unkind words about murdering half-breeds under his breath as Rafe turned on his side and greedily sucked in air.

<u>Chapter Eleven</u>

After nearly twenty-four hours, Rafe's pounding headache and nausea finally abated and he'd been able to eat a light lunch and afterward to nap. He awoke at sunset when the carriage halted for the night. Charles opened the carriage door, gripped Rafe's left arm at the elbow, dragged him out, and shoved him onto a short, squat boulder large enough to seat two comfortably. "Sit there and don't cause any trouble this time, Lucifer's child," he snarled.

"Stop calling me that, Charles! With her dying breath, my mother gifted me with the name of her beloved brother. Respect her memory and call me by it!" Rafe demanded.

"Ah, but she was unaware that you'd someday become unworthy of the name," Charles retorted. "Undoubtedly, looking down upon your wickedness from heaven now she'd approve of your being stripped of it." Charles walked away smiling smugly, well pleased with himself. He joined Henry in pulling their rifles from the roof of the coach then they set off to catch a few rabbits for dinner.

As the sky slowly darkened and the stars winked on one by one in a black velvet sky with a full moon, Leopold busied himself setting up camp. He finished as the crack of several gunshots reverberated through the night air then sat down on the boulder beside Rafe. "Sounds as if there will be meat for dinner," he remarked. Rafe looked up at the night sky and refused to answer. He wasn't in the mood for polite conversation with one of those who'd been mistreating him for days, or at least had been in collusion with those who had.

Leopold looked up too. "The stars are beautiful tonight aren't they?"

Rafe nodded once, unable to summon up the disrespect to continue ignoring his foster father.

"I know there's a verse in the Bible about the stars and the moon, but I can't recall it," Leopold said.

"It's 1 Corinthians 15:41. The sun has one kind of splendor, the moon another, and the stars another and star differs from star in splendor," Rafe said.

"Yes. That's it. You've always had a superior ability to recall God's word," Leopold said as Charles and Henry walked into the clearing each carrying a large rabbit by the ears. "It's a mystery to me then how you can justify walking so completely outside of God's will."

"It's easy when you completely lack remorse," Charles interposed.

"I told Judge McKitrick at trial that I regretted killing Duncan," Rafe swiftly countered.

"You've never once expressed regret over killing Duncan," Henry said.

"How would you know? You weren't even at the trial, but waiting outside to waylay me," Rafe accused resentfully.

"I was not waiting to waylay you. I was delayed making the funeral arrangements for my murdered brother. However, Charles has told me every detail of the trial, and that you not only failed to express remorse, but even went so far as to claim you were innocent of any murderous intent!" Henry said.

"Even as I was," Rafe maintained. "It was an accident."

Charles snorted. "Come now Rafe, you can't expect us to believe such a ridiculous claim. We all know you are a murderer from infancy, having killed your mother with your birth."

"As Charles says," Leopold added.

Rafe could bear the jibes from Charles. He'd had six years of practice at it. He could bear the jibes from Henry too, for Henry had a right to be angry with him for killing Duncan. When Leopold took their side against him, though, it broke him. He sprang to his feet ignoring the sharp pain flaming up in his sprained ankle, his hands clenched in tight, white-knuckled fists. "I must thank you good Christian men, for without your unceasing efforts I would've never realized my entirely hopeless state," he said stiffly then limped to a nearby tree and sat down under its benevolent sheltering branches resting his back against the trunk. There was nothing he could do to ease his emotional pain, but he did his best to ease his physical pain by stretching out his sprained ankle in front of him and shoving his manacles up his arm as far as they would go, which was only half an inch. It helped for a short time until the manacles slid back down. Rafe pushed them up. They slid back down. He pushed them up. They slid back down. He gave up. It was as futile as trying to convince Henry, Charles, and Leopold that he suffered guilt and remorse.

Later Henry begrudgingly brought him a plate of rabbit stew. Rafe forced himself to eat while resentfully watching Charles and Henry laugh and converse cheerfully without a twinge of guilt over their mistreatment of him. Leopold, however, glanced guiltily at Rafe from time to time as if he wished to apologize for taking sides against him earlier. Rafe dared to hope that perhaps he still had someone on his side after all, but as the evening wore on and Leopold remained distant and aloof, he silently chastised himself for a fool. Wasn't everything that had happened to him since he'd accidentally killed Duncan proof enough that hope was not for such as him?

* * *

In the morning after a cold breakfast the men set off again. At mid-day, Leopold parked the carriage in a grassy meadow, wordlessly let Rafe out, and handed him a full water skin. Rafe nodded his thanks and then carried the water skin by its strap to a flat spot on the grass ten feet distant from the others. He set the skin down in the thick, soft grass and lay on his back beside it among bright yellow, red, and blue flowers, crossed his arms behind his head, closed his eyes to block out the sun's glare, and let the soft whispering of the wind in the trees and the harmonious chirping of the birds ease his troubled mind and heart, at least as much as was possible for one devoid of hope. A little while later he heard Leopold saying grace. He opened his eyes, for he refused to even seem to participate in a prayer to a God who'd abandoned him.

That's when Rafe saw the snake slithering close beside Leopold's left knee, recognizable as a copperhead by the broad, triangular, un-patterned head, and pinkish colored body with reddish-brown cross bands, narrow on the back, and wider on the sides. Leopold finished his prayer and was about to put his hand directly on the beautiful, but deadly snake, and feeling threatened the copperhead coiled to strike. Rafe knew a bite from a copperhead could be deadly to an older man such as Leopold, but he had no pistol to shoot it with and he surely wasn't quick enough to race the ten feet to Leopold, snatch up the snake, and snap its neck before it struck. He frantically looked for a large rock to throw at the snake and then a better solution presented itself when Henry approached with his lunch. In one almost inhumanly swift motion, Rafe surged to his feet, snatched Henry's already loaded pistol from his holster, took aim, and pulled the trigger.

Three things happened simultaneously. Henry cried out in angry surprise, Leopold's eyes widened in fear assuming Rafe was trying to shoot him, and Charles drew his pistol and fired at Rafe. He felt a sharp, stinging burn in his right side and then Henry's full body weight knocked him backward. As he was falling, Rafe was able to see that his aim had been true and Leopold was safe, so he relaxed and let Henry sit on his chest, then snatch the pistol from his hand, and toss it out of reach.

"You evil demon spawn!" Henry shouted. He unsheathed his knife and shoved its tip beneath Rafe's chin, drawing blood. "Killing my brother wasn't enough to satiate your blood lust? You must take the life of your foster father as well?"

At that moment Leopold noticed the dead snake. He picked it up by its tail. "Henry, let him be. Rafe was after this copperhead not trying to kill me. He saved my life."

"Don't let that prevent you from murdering me," Rafe said taking full advantage of the opportunity to return a little of the grief Henry had given him lately. Henry reddened with embarrassment then quickly sheathed his knife and deliberately pushed on Rafe's chest as he stood up, aggravating Rafe's newly acquired bullet wound that Henry didn't notice even though Rafe grunted involuntarily in pain.

Leopold handed the snake to Charles and approached Rafe, who then scrambled guiltily, painfully to his feet to receive his inevitable punishment for harassing Henry. But Leopold surprised him. "Thank you for saving my life, Rafe, although I must confess that I thought you intended to shoot me."

Rafe wiped the droplets of blood off his chin with the back of his hand as he said, "I would need an excellent reason to shoot you, sir."

It seemed that was the exact wrong thing to say, however, for Leopold's eyes narrowed. "What good reason would justify shooting your foster father, Rafe? Would you need to be drunk or is that only necessary when killing friends?" he demanded.

Rafe was bewildered by Leopold's angry response until he realized Leopold must have taken his words as a threat. Before he could explain otherwise, Leopold added, "You're as much the son of Lucifer as Charles claims, Rafe; worse even than your father, for he was at least no murderer!"

Rafe felt the tears threatening again. *Hold your emotions in check, vile half-breed* he silently commanded himself then turned away in case he failed so that Leopold wouldn't see his weakness. Leopold's eyes widened as he finally noticed Rafe's bloodied right side. "Your side is bleeding," he pointed out concernedly. "How is that?"

"Did you not see Charles shoot me?" Rafe asked bitterly.

"What?" Leopold reached for Rafe's shirt to pull it up and examine the wound, but he quickly took a step back. "It's nothing. I'm fine," he said. But it was a lie. He was already woozy, probably from shock, for he hadn't lost that much blood yet, the bullet wound burned like a red hot fire, his head throbbed with a sudden onset headache, and his mouth was dry. The latter, however, thanks to either Leopold's earlier generosity, or perhaps a guilty conscience, he could easily remedy. The water skin was on the ground, though, so rather than leaning over to pick it up which would hurt like the dickens, Rafe sat down beside it; or rather he made a barely controlled fall, which hurt far more than if he'd just leaned down and picked up the water skin after all. Breathing rapidly from the pain of his fall, his forehead beaded with sweat, he scooped up the skin in a trembling hand then clumsily worked at popping the cork.

"Rafe, you're not fine," Leopold countered.

"I think I know my own condition better than you," Rafe said argumentatively. He finally succeeded in popping the cork on the water skin and took a long drink. The water was cool, wet and refreshing. It tasted so good that Rafe would've quickly drained the skin, except that then his body betrayed him and he lost consciousness.

Chapter Twelve

Riding beside the carriage, Charles occasionally glanced inside at Rafe lying inside, feverish, unconscious, and so ghastly pale that for the first time in his life no trace of his native blood showed in his coloring except for his coal black hair that contrasted vividly with his paleness. Leopold had done what he could for Rafe, stemming the flow of blood with tightly wrapped bandages, but neither he nor the others had the skill to remove the deeply embedded bullet that was slowly killing Rafe. Charles knew it was entirely probable Rafe would die before this day was out, and he was positive Sarah would blame him for it. He cursed Rafe under his breath. He was certain the evil half-breed had somehow manipulated events to bring about just such a situation. Rafe was always coming between him and Sarah in one way or another, such as at the trial when she'd taken Rafe's side! Charles cursed again, more loudly.

Leopold twisted around in the driver's seat. "Something wrong?"

"Rafe!" Charles spat acerbically.

"Has he worsened?" Leopold asked in alarm.

"No, he's stable. I was referring to how he's ruined my life!"

"Well from now on keep your cursing to yourself unless it's over something serious. I thought Rafe had taken a turn for the worse, and we're still nearly a day's ride from the next town," Leopold griped.

"What's the concern? Even if he does die, it will be no less than he deserves," Henry said.

"I cannot disagree with you, Henry," Leopold said. "Still, despite Rafe's disappointing decision to follow the iniquitous path of his natural father, after having spent thirteen years of my life fostering him I've developed some concern for his welfare."

Henry grunted. He could understand, but he couldn't endorse it.

A horse and rider rounded a bend in the road ahead and Charles drew his pistol and hastily loaded it. It was impossible to know if the approaching rider was friendly, a highwayman, or even someone intent on trying to rescue Rafe so he'd decided to err on the side of caution. Henry mirrored Charles's actions, as always. However, as the bearded stranger neared, it became apparent from his plain clothing that he was a peace-loving Quaker and no threat to anyone. Charles and Henry holstered their pistols and Leopold halted the carriage.

"Good afternoon, friends." The Quaker smiled affably and doffed his black hat in greeting. The late summer sun shone brightly on his golden hair, which was liberally sprinkled with gray, and his blue eyes took in the ostentatious carriage with obvious disapproval. "My name is Jacob Brody. It's a fine day for traveling. Are thou traveling far?"

"We're headed for Boston, sir," Leopold said. "But one of us has been accidentally shot. We were unable to remove the bullet, and now he lies in the carriage unconscious and in a high fever. You wouldn't happen to know of a chirurgeon nearby?" he asked hopefully.

"It seems Providence has provided, sir," said Jacob, smiling warmly. "It just so happens that I'm a chirurgeon. I will have a look at your injured friend."

Leopold brightened. "We'd appreciate it greatly." He jumped down from the driver's seat and flung open the carriage door.

Rafe, still in manacles although he was unconscious, rested on the soft, white leather cushions, looking like death had already taken him. Jacob raised an eyebrow. "Is this man thy prisoner, sir?"

"Yes." Leopold didn't elaborate further, for he was ashamed to admit to a stranger that he'd failed to wean the savage out of his foster son, who'd then become a man who murdered his friends.

"Thy prisoner is quite pale, but it's still apparent to the discerning eye that he has native blood. May this have anything to do with his injury and his status as thy prisoner?"

Charles bristled. How dare the man insinuate that he'd shot Rafe merely because he was a half-breed! "The injury was accidental, as Leopold has already said," he interposed brusquely.

Then Henry had to speak up in Charles's defense. "The Indian brutally killed my brother in a drunken rage, sir when my brother tried to prevent him from killing another."

"Namely, me," Charles said then glowered at the unconscious Rafe resentfully.

Jacob assessed Charles's healing bruises and cuts with a doctor's practiced eye and recognized that Charles had indeed endured a brutal beating that would've ended in death had it not been cut short. Noting the Quaker's silent appraisal, Charles said, "We're transporting the murderous half-breed to Boston to put him on my ship to the Caribbean, where he'll serve out his life as a slave on my plantation in penance for his crimes."

"I see," Jacob said slowly while scratching his blond, bearded chin, and regarding Rafe with a troubled frown.

Leopold knew Quakers strongly disapproved of violence and so feared that Charles and Henry had ruined any hope of gaining the Quaker's aid for Rafe. "Will you still treat him despite that he's a violent criminal, sir?" he asked anxiously.

"Indeed I will, sir, for he's a man in need of a service that I can provide. It would be a sin not to help him. My humble farmhouse is only a short ride north of here; just over that hill." Jacob pointed back in the direction he'd come. "Thy prisoner would fare far better if I operated on him there."

"Then you can save him, sir?" Leopold asked hopefully.

"I shall do my best, but his ultimate recovery lies in the hands of God," Jacob replied.

"I'm hoping my earnest prayers will have some effect on that outcome," Leopold said.

"God is the great healer, and merciful as well," Jacob allowed. "We should waste no more time. Follow me."

Jacob mounted and led the way down the road for several miles to a well-kept, good sized farm with a rambling, white farmhouse. As the carriage rolled into the yard, a blond-haired man of about Rafe's age, height, and build walked out the front door onto the porch that spanned the front of the farmhouse. He hesitated for a second as with evident envy he overlooked the ostentatious carriage and the fine horses then bounded down the steps and grabbed Jacob's horse's bridle. "I see thou not only didn't make it far on thy trip to Philadelphia, Father, but have brought home strays," he said disapprovingly.

Jacob scowled, displeased by his son's unwelcoming attitude. "I met these men on the road not far from here, Ezra. The one in the carriage is seriously hurt and needs my care. You will welcome them all as friends."

"Welcome friends," Ezra said begrudgingly to Charles, Leopold, and Henry, who all nodded acknowledgement. Then Ezra peeked into the carriage and his eyebrows shot up in surprise, but not only because of Rafe's restraints, for as a barrister he'd seen many a manacled criminal. He'd expected to see a foppish lord, overdressed in finery and ruffles, not a buckskin clad Indian prisoner. "What crime has this man committed that thou have him manacled?" he asked of Henry.

"He murdered my brother in a drunken rage and nearly killed this man," Henry explained, nodding at the bruised and scabbed Charles.

Ezra took a step back in alarm. "This man is a violent murderer?" He looked to his father questioningly. "Did thou know this, Father?"

"I did, and it makes no difference, son. The man is sorely injured and needs our help," Jacob said.

"Father—," Ezra started to object.

Jacob impatiently waved off his son's objection and addressed Leopold and Henry. "If thou will carry thy prisoner inside, Ezra will see to the care of thy horses and carriage."

Henry scowled. He'd been hoping Rafe would die on the road and justice would be served at last. That happy scenario had looked far less likely when Jacob had come along and proclaimed he could help, and now the Quaker wanted him to carry Rafe into the house so he could crush his hopes even further by operating on his brother's murderer! No! He refused to aid in this blatant injustice. "I'd rather help Ezra with the carriage and horses." He dismounted, his leather saddle creaking as if in protest of his refusal.

"I'll help Ezra and Henry," Charles said quickly, before Leopold could task him to help with Rafe.

Leopold understood Charles's and Henry's reasons for refusing to help Rafe, but it left him in a quandary, for he was in his mid-fifties. There was no way he could carry Rafe in by himself!

"I'll help you carry him," Jacob then said to his relief. The two of them gently pulled Rafe from the carriage. Then as Charles, Henry and Ezra took the carriage and the horses to the barn, they carried Rafe into the farmhouse, past a front parlor and down a short hallway to a downstairs bedroom. "This is Ezra's bedroom," Jacob explained. "I would rather use my bedroom, as the bed is more comfortable, but that would mean having to carry thy prisoner upstairs."

"That's worth considering," Leopold said, huffing and puffing under the burden of Rafe's dead weight. "But Ezra won't mind giving up his bed?"

"He's not as dutiful a Quaker as I would wish, but he knows better than to complain," Jacob said.

Leopold and Jacob positioned Rafe on the single bed covered with a colorful yellow and blue quilt. "Would thou mind if I removed his manacles?" Jacob asked. Leopold obligingly produced the key. "Thank you, sir."

Jacob removed the manacles and handed them to Leopold, who set them on a small side table beside the bed. Jacob then walked to the washstand in the far corner and poured water from the white, china pitcher decorated with dainty blue flowers. When he was finished washing up, he set to work on Rafe. As he carefully removed Rafe's bandage, the wound started bleeding again.

Leopold hovered anxiously as Jacob conducted his examination. Occasionally Rafe would moan softly and twitch as if protesting even unconscious that he was fine and to leave him alone. "How is he, doctor?" Leopold asked when Jacob finished his examination and straightened.

"His pulse is weak and he's lost a great deal of blood. I can't promise he'll survive the surgery, but without it he'll most definitely die," Jacob said.

Ezra walked in and frowned with displeasure at the sight of Rafe lying in his bed, but he voiced no complaint, as Jacob had predicted. He addressed Leopold. "Thy horses are settled, sir, and I've set out lemonade and poppy seed cakes in the parlor. Henry and Charles await thee there, if thou will follow me."

"Ezra, I need thee here to aid in the surgery. Our guest can find his own way to the parlor." Jacob looked to Leopold. "If thou don't mind?"

"Not at all, sir. I'll leave you to your work."

Ezra waited until Leopold was out of earshot then he said, "Father, Henry told me this man is a half-breed born of a wicked father, and like his father is arrogant, naturally violent, and completely lacking remorse. There are even rumors that he's killed children and then eaten their flesh!"

"He may be all of those things, son, although I find the latter hard to believe. Nevertheless, it makes no difference. I must treat him," Jacob said.

"But there's more. He was caught with his hands on Charles's wife in a dark garden, and when Charles came to her rescue this man brutally assaulted him. When Henry's brother intervened, this criminal bashed his skull in. He was sentenced to hang for the murder and the assaults, but Charles's wife, apparently taken by his charm, his numerous talents, and his extraordinary good looks, intervened with the courts and the sentence was changed to a life of slavery on Charles's plantation. It was God's justice that this man was shot, for he should rightfully die for what he did. We shouldn't interfere."

Jacob frowned disapprovingly. "God wants me to save this man, son, else why would I have been on that road at that particular time and with the necessary skills to save his life? Furthermore, it's our Christian duty to help this stranger, whoever he is, or whatever he may have done. Do thou not recall the story of the good Samaritan?"

"Yes, but this man is a wanton—,"

"Thou will aid me, or thou will go against our Father's teachings and deny help to a man in need," Jacob said sternly.

Ezra sighed in frustration. "I'll help as thou wish, but sometimes I think thou are too liberal with thy interpretation of what God wants," he complained.

"Sometimes I think thou are not conservative enough," Jacob said. "Hand me a wet washcloth so I may clean the wound before surgery."

While Ezra and Jacob had talked, Rafe had regained a hazy consciousness; enough to realize that two men argued over treating him. Then when Jacob started cleaning the wound, pain shocked him fully conscious, and he realized this stranger meant to save him! He weakly grabbed Jacob's wrist. "No," he rasped.

Jacob started in shock at this unexpected reaction, but he didn't pull free even though it would've been easy to break Rafe's weak grasp. "Thou have nothing to fear, sir. I'm a doctor. I'm trying to help thee."

"Let me die," Rafe whispered hoarsely, and then his hand dropped to the bed as he spiraled back down into unconsciousness.

"See, Father?" Ezra argued. "Even the half-breed knows that it's God's will he should die. Leave him to his deserved death."

Jacob looked at his son aghast. "How can though even suggest such a thing! That would be paramount to murder!" He leaned over Rafe. "Hear me, sir I'll not let thee die if I can help it."

Rafe didn't hear, but if he had, he would've responded with a Mohican curse word.

* * *

After what seemed an eternity to Leopold, during which he paced the room and Charles and Henry played a game of cards with a deck Henry had brought, Jacob walked into the parlor. A bloody bullet rested in his open palm along with a bloodied, tattered piece of buckskin from Rafe's shirt. "Gentleman, the surgery was a success; but see?" He pointed at the tattered buckskin. "The bullet took this piece of buckskin in with it and the wound was beginning to fester. Had I not been able to remove all of it along with the bullet, he would've most definitely died."

"Then he'll survive?" Leopold asked anxiously.

"God willing. He'll need to be watched carefully for a time, so thou are welcome to stay here until he's recovered enough for travel," Jacob said.

"How long will that be, sir?" Charles asked.

"I should think no less than a fortnight," Jacob said.

Charles exchanged a bothered look with Henry. "He can't be moved any sooner?" Charles asked.

"It wouldn't be advisable."

"As you wish," Charles surrendered disgustedly. He was unhappy at the forced delay, and from the look on his face Henry was also none too pleased.

The delay made no difference at all to Leopold, though. "Thank you for your hospitality and your help, Mr. Brody."

"Thou are most welcome." Jacob smiled warmly. "But, please, as thou will be guests in my house for several weeks, call me Jacob." He tossed the bullet and the piece of buckskin out the open window and then wiped his hands on a towel hung over his shoulder, once pure white, but now spotted with Rafe's blood. "May I ask thy prisoner's name?" he then asked.

"Why?" Charles asked suspiciously.

"I would like to pray for his soul. Judging from what I've learned, he's in great need of salvation," Jacob explained.

"Save your prayers," Charles said. "He's an abomination with no soul and even did he possess a soul, he's about as bad as they come and has no redeeming qualities."

"All the more reason to pray for him," Jacob insisted.

"He is Lord Rafael Zacharias Brookstone," Leopold answered then since neither Charles nor Henry offered. "He shuns the title though, and prefers to be called simply, Rafe."

Jacob's eyebrows shot up in surprise. "*Lord* Rafael Zacharias Brookstone?"

"His mother was of noble birth," Charles explained. "He inherited the title and a grand estate when his grandfather died with no heirs. Unfortunately his savage, rapist father's blood holds sway over the good white blood in him."

"Then I shall pray for Rafe every night; and for all of thee as well, for I sense a deep hurt in each of thee; which I and my son shall begin ministering to by fixing thee a fine meal; although not as fine as if my wife was here. Unfortunately, Mercy is visiting our daughter, her husband, and their new baby daughter in Philadelphia."

"Father would've gone with her, sirs," Ezra interposed, "only he had to stay behind for a fortnight to tend a dying patient. He was finally on his way to join Mother when he met thee on the road. Now he'll be unable to join her for at least another fortnight and they're rarely parted. It'll be hard for her."

When Leopold, Charles and Henry then abruptly looked uncomfortable, Jacob cast a scathing glance at is son. "God's plans are not always our plans," he hurriedly added. "I go where I'm needed, and gladly. It is not such an inconvenience to stay a little longer and care for Lord Brookstone as Ezra makes it sound." He grabbed Ezra's shirt sleeve and practically dragged him to the kitchen.

Charles and Henry then resumed their game, while Leopold went to check on Rafe. He touched the back of his hand to Rafe's forehead. His skin still felt hot, but not as hot as before and some color had already returned to his face. He was obviously resting easier too, his chest gently rising and falling as opposed to the ragged breathing of before. Leopold sighed in relief and returned to his companions. "How is the patient, sir?" Henry asked, hoping to hear he was at least the same if not worse.

Leopold disappointed him. "He's much improved. It was certainly fortuitous that we met Jacob and that he was a skilled chirurgeon. Otherwise, I'm certain Rafe would've died before this day was over."

"It would've been no loss if he had died," Henry said under his breath to Charles.

"Indeed." Charles agreed wholeheartedly.

Chapter Thirteen

The white, blurry—something, confused Rafe. Then his vision cleared and he realized he was looking at drawn, blue curtains on a window in an unfamiliar room. He lay on his unwounded side, his manacles had been removed, and salve had been applied to the chafed, raw, skin bracelets around his wrists. Rafe vaguely recalled the blond man who'd insisted he would save his life despite his expressed wish to the contrary. Annoyingly, it seemed the fellow had followed through. Why was it that no one ever listened to him! He rolled painfully onto his back and saw Charles sitting in a cushioned rocking chair reading a book. "Whose house is this?" Rafe asked.

Charles looked up then set the book down in his lap still open. "You're a guest of Jacob Brody, a Quaker chirurgeon and gentleman farmer we met on the road. At Leopold's request—Henry and I would've preferred to let you die—Jacob removed the bullet and bandaged you. We shall remain here for a fortnight or until you're well enough to move on."

"To a life of slavery," Rafe said resentfully, as Leopold and Henry walked in.

"You would rather we had let you die?" Leopold demanded, obviously irritated by Rafe's ingratitude.

"Yes," Rafe replied.

"No doubt so Sarah would blame me for your death and never speak to me again," Charles said accusingly, and closed his book with an angry snap as if in emphasis of his disapproval.

"Had you not shot me unjustly you would've had no worry of such a development, but indeed that prospect pleased me immensely," Rafe said, although that highly satisfying scenario had not occurred to him until Charles had suggested it.

Henry quickly came to Charles's defense. "Charles had no idea what you were up to! None of us did! Considering your recent actions you were lucky he didn't shoot to kill."

"Weren't you listening?" Rafe said. "That's what I wanted!"

"Manipulating someone into killing you is suicide, and suicide is a sin," Henry said disapprovingly.

"No worse a sin than what I'm already convicted of," Rafe countered defiantly.

Henry's eyes widened. "I don't know why Duncan befriended you. You lack even the tiniest speck of decency!"

"It would take one with decency to recognize it in another," Rafe retorted.

Charles bristled at this affront to his fellow Rafe abuser. He sprang to his feet, slammed the book on the small side table to the left of the chair that held nothing else but a single unlit beeswax candle in a holder, and the manacles, and took a menacing step toward Rafe. "You wicked, despicable—!"

Leopold hastily stepped in front of Charles. "It's a fine afternoon and we've all been cooped up in this stuffy house for far too long. Perhaps a brisk walk in the fresh air is in order," he suggested tactfully. He was surprised, however, when Charles surrendered to the suggestion.

"Even so." Charles addressed Henry. "Would you care to accompany me?"

"I'd be glad to." After a dark glare at Rafe he accompanied Charles out.

Leopold sat down in the rocker. "Why are you so intent on dying?" he asked.

"What do I gain by living?" Rafe shot back.

"You gain the rare and precious opportunity to atone for your drunken assault and murder by working on Charles's plantation," Leopold said.

Rafe snorted, which hurt his side so it was followed by a wince. "Even supposing I actually was guilty of drunken assault and murder, it would take a lifetime to atone for it in that manner. How long do you think I'll last on Charles's plantation?"

"It's beneath the gentleman I thought I had raised to continually deny your guilt, Rafe," Leopold said disapprovingly. "But as to your atonement, Charles is known for treating his slaves well, so you may be certain you'll live out your normal lifespan; which is why you should be focusing on making everything right with God. You could start immediately by repenting of your sins of drunkenness, murder and unrighteous anger, and then asking for God's forgiveness."

Rafe abruptly turned to face the wall, which hurt like someone had reached in and ripped his insides out, but effectively ended the conversation, which was what he wanted. He lay still letting the pain subside, and stared at the closed curtains on the window, brooding. It was all so useless, living. He silently cursed the day of his birth, his grandfather for having failed to properly drown him, and even John for saving him and then letting the mercenaries kill him, leaving him no option but to live life as the Lord Brookstone.

Chapter Fourteen

Charles awoke with a start, and panicked when he realized he'd fallen asleep on watch, and worse, Rafe's bed was empty! Rafe had escaped! Charles blamed Jacob for the escape more than himself, though, for if the Quaker had let them keep Rafe manacled and his ankles tied as he'd suggested that first night after dinner, Rafe would've never been able to escape. Then Charles thought of his pistol. His hand slapped his holster expecting it to be empty, but for some inexplicable reason, Rafe hadn't taken the weapon. Perhaps he'd been too afraid of waking him to try to steal it. All of these thoughts had gone through Charles's head in a split second. Now he sprang from his chair and rushed from the bedroom then hastened down the short hallway into the great room hoping against hope to see Rafe lounging in front of the fireplace in the big, comfortable chair; thus avoiding the embarrassing necessity of explaining to Henry and Leopold that he'd fallen asleep on watch. Frustratingly, though, Rafe was not in the great room. His stride growing more urgent, Charles crossed the great room and burst out into the night.

Rafe sat on the porch in one of two, white-painted, wicker rocking chairs. He wore his buckskins, which Jacob had mended and washed for him. "What are you doing out here?" Charles demanded while surreptitiously holstering his pistol.

Rafe noted the secretive movement and grinned. "Gave you a scare, did I? Serves you right for falling asleep on watch, but I'll wager the scare I gave you didn't hold a candle to the scare you gave me that time you fell off the wild horse I goaded you into trying to ride when we were boys. Remember how you lay still making me think you were dead? It still makes my heart skip a beat thinking of it even though it turned out you'd only sprained your arm." His grin widened. "Leopold caned me for that misadventure so diligently I couldn't sit down for a week!"

For a split second they were once again two boys as close as brothers. Charles even started to return Rafe's grin, which hurt his still healing mouth and cheeks and reminded him of the beating Rafe had recently given him. The budding grin was immediately overtaken by a deep scowl. "I suppose your recent attempt to beat me to death was your way of finally having your revenge against me for that well deserved punishment," he spat.

Rafe's grin vanished and he shifted position uneasily, guiltily. "No."

"So you say, but we all know you're incapable of telling the truth." Charles sat down in the other wicker rocker. Silence reigned for a moment and then Charles said, "I must admit I was surprised to find you sitting here instead of long gone. Care to enlighten me as to why you didn't escape when you had the chance?"

Rafe could've told Charles he had nowhere to go, no family, no friends, nothing to run to, except death, and that easy escape had been denied him by Jacob's ministrations. He could've told Charles that when he awoke and found his gaoler asleep, he'd considered remedying the misfortune of his continued life by snatching Charles's pistol and shooting himself. The only reason he'd chosen not to was that it was unthinkably ill-mannered to put a bullet in your head while you were a guest in someone's house, and especially when that someone had gone to a great deal of trouble to save your life. So he'd instead slipped quietly out of bed, walked outside for a breath of fresh air, and then, his legs trembling from the short walk, he'd sat down on one of the wicker rockers to rest and his thoughts had wistfully turned to better days.

Rafe could've told Charles all of this if he'd still felt close enough to Charles to open up to him. Instead he shrugged and said, "There's no use in attempting to escape. I can't ride far or fast in my current condition. You three would track me down in no time."

"Indeed we would, and I'm glad you realized that, for it has saved me a great deal of annoyance. But now that you've proven you're well enough to be out of bed I'll inform our host that we'll leave for Boston tomorrow," Charles said.

Rafe had no wish to leave. Although Ezra treated him with the same goodly measure of disrespect as Charles and Henry, and all too often Leopold too, he and Jacob had spent many hours in amiable conversation during which Jacob had never once mentioned that he was a half-breed, a child of rape, or a murderer. Jacob's unconditional acceptance, a sentiment Rafe badly missed now that Duncan was gone and God had seemingly abandoned him, was like morphine to his lonely, wounded heart, and he desperately craved more of it. "I don't suppose you'd let me rest here for merely another day, or two?" he asked hopefully.

"By no means. You've already cost me a goodly penny by making the Lady Bountiful wait in port for over a fortnight to transport a murderer to justice," Charles said.

Rafe's eyes narrowed. "If I was a murderer, you'd be dead now. Shot by your own weapon," he countered quietly.

Charles sprang to his feet and drew his pistol. "Is that a threat?"

"A fact," Rafe said, making direct and defiant eye contact.

Charles's handsome features contorted with rage. "You'd best go back inside before I'm obliged to shoot you for attempted escape."

Rafe stood up, slowly, painfully, and returned to his bed shadowed by Charles, who then retrieved the manacles, passed the chain through the bed frame, and snapped them solidly on Rafe's wrists. Even with Rafe safely manacled, though, Charles didn't holster his pistol for an hour after he was completely certain Rafe was soundly asleep.

Chapter Fifteen

It was the last night on the road before they reached Boston. Charles parked the carriage in a clearing surrounded by dense trees and bushes. A massive twelve foot boulder sat in nearly the exact center of the clearing as if planted by a giant's hand or perhaps put there by a magician's apprentice practicing his art. Charles let Rafe out of the carriage without even shoving him. Rafe walked to the boulder, which however it had been placed there would make a convenient backrest. He sat down with his back to it, stretched his long legs out in front of him and in what had become an automatic gesture pushed the hated manacles up his arms as far as they would go in a useless effort at easing the stinging pain in his chafed wrists. As usual, though, the heavy iron bracelets immediately fell back into place.

Rafe enviously watched Charles, Henry, and Leopold laughing and talking amenably as they prepared the campsite and then dinner, and then was reminded of the joyful, carefree days he'd spent in Duncan's company. A wave of profound loss and guilt washed over him. How twisted was life when it was so difficult to succeed at suicide, yet so extremely easy to kill a friend?

Leopold came over carrying two tin plates of beef stew and a biscuit, the last of the fresh rations Jacob had sent with them. Leopold sat down beside Rafe, taking advantage of the rock as a backrest like Rafe, and wordlessly offered him a plate. Rafe shook his head. Leopold sighed in exasperation. "You've barely eaten anything these last two days."

"I'm not hungry," Rafe replied.

"You must eat nevertheless," Leopold insisted. "You need to regain your strength so that upon your arrival at the plantation you'll not become a further burden to Charles, but may easily carry your load." He firmly planted the plate of stew in Rafe's lap.

"How thoughtful of you to consider Charles's needs, sir," Rafe said resentfully. "Do you also intend to personally supervise my transition from lord to slave when we arrive, and whip me if I'm deemed insubordinate? You always seemed to enjoy punishing me as a child."

Leopold bristled. During this second stage of their trip, Rafe had turned even more angry and sullen than before, and had failed to show the least bit of gratitude to any of them for saving his life. It had grown increasingly difficult for Leopold to maintain the concerned paternal attitude he'd briefly rediscovered after Rafe's near death. Now after having virtually been accused of being a slaver the anger that had been simmering near the surface for two days finally boiled over. "I'd not hesitate to whip you for insubordination if it was as well deserved as it would be now, saving that I won't be there. I must return to the estate, which is without a lord now thanks to your vile crimes."

Rafe started in shock. He'd thought Leopold would accompany him to the plantation; which meant several more weeks together not only one more day. It was far too soon. He wasn't ready for that additional loss yet. "Will—will you come to visit me from time to time, though, sir?" he asked tentatively.

"I'll be much too busy with the affairs of the estate," Leopold said coolly.

Having handled the affairs of the estate for nearly ten years, Rafe knew well that nothing would keep Leopold so busy that he couldn't occasionally travel. His beloved foster father was rejecting him as thoroughly as his Father in heaven had, and it hurt equally as much. "I miss the way things used to be between us, Leopold," he lamented, his voice breaking.

Leopold looked away for what seemed like an eternity as Rafe waited for a response, dying a little more inside each minute that Leopold continued to look in the opposite direction and didn't answer. Then Leopold said, "I too miss the way things used to be."

Rafe's spirits lifted a little. "Then do you think—might there be some expectation of—of repairing our relationship, sir?" he asked falteringly.

"Indeed, if you admit you were drunk the night you assaulted Charles and killed Duncan, and that the port was never drugged, and then promise never again to lie to me," Leopold said.

Rafe's spirits plunged to a new low. How could he admit to a lie when he'd never told one, and how could he lie about lying, while at the same time promising never to lie again? "I cannot, sir," he said sorrowfully.

Leopold turned as frosty as an ice house. "Have it your way then, Rafe. Keep to your path of iniquity, since you seem to desire it above all else!" He snatched up his plate of stew and stormed away.

Rafe snatched up his plate of stew and angrily tossed it into the nearby bushes. Then he remembered Henry's violent reaction to his food tossing on the first leg of the trip and looked warily at him. Luckily, Henry sat with his back to him, so he hadn't noticed. Rafe crossed his arms and hunched down, mourning his continued life.

Chapter Sixteen

Rafe's former estate's luxurious carriage stopped on the docks at the port of Boston directly in front of the gangplank to the Lady Bountiful. Charles jumped down from the driver's seat, opened the carriage door, and roughly dragged Rafe out. Henry remained seated on his horse, but Leopold dismounted and started to tie his horse's reins to the back of the carriage in preparation for his turn driving it. Rafe attempted to make eye contact with him, but Leopold then became studiously busy with trivial things, such as checking the carriage wheels.

"Leopold," Rafe called. Leopold flinched so Rafe knew he'd been heard, but he remained intently focused on looking over the carriage. "Leopold. Sir," Rafe called. Leopold took the driver's seat, staring straight ahead, refusing to even acknowledge Rafe's existence.

Charles impatiently grasped Rafe's arm at the elbow. "Stop making a fool of yourself! Isn't it readily apparent that Leopold no longer wishes to have anything to do with you now that you've tossed aside your honest upbringing and proven you're unworthy of his efforts?" He shoved Rafe in the direction of the gangplank.

Rafe was certain Charles had intended to cause him pain by making him stumble on his wounded ankle, but it had healed enough during his fortnight with Jacob that he only felt a slight twinge as he was forced to take a quick step forward. After one last longing glance at Leopold, who still refused to look in his direction, Rafe nimbly trod the gangplank, leaving Charles far behind and thus proving that Charles was truly the one who was unworthy of anyone's notice. He gracefully bounded from the gangplank onto the deck and presented himself with manacle chains clanking to the waiting captain with a courtly bow and a forced roguish smile. "Lord Rafael Zacharias Brookstone at your command, sir," he said with false cheerfulness.

In his black tri-cornered hat, black captain's uniform with gold fringe on the shoulders, shiny brass buttons, and crisply starched white shirt Captain Burns presented a fine figure. He was a fit man, in his mid-thirties, with dark brown hair and eyes, and a weathered face from years spent at sea. He had, of course, received a missive from Charles describing Rafe in a most unpleasant light and so the righteous, God-fearing seaman scowled at Rafe disapprovingly and refused to doff his hat as he ordinarily would to any other passenger of rank. "Murdering scum," he acknowledged coolly.

Rafe's roguish grin vanished, but the Captain missed the satisfying result of his rudeness, for Charles then boarded. Smiling respectfully, he swept off his hat and bowed low. "Welcome on board Lord Huntington, sir," he said cordially.

"Thank you Captain Burns." Charles responded. "My travel chest is lashed on top of that carriage." He pointed at the Brookstone carriage. "Please send one of your men to retrieve it."

"Yes, your lordship, sir." Captain Burns made eye contact with one of his waiting men as he donned his hat. "Mr. Craig, retrieve Lord Huntington's travel chest."

The broad-shouldered, stubble-faced sailor, dressed in tan knickers, white socks, serviceable black shoes, and beige, long-sleeved, coarsely woven shirt touched the brim of an imaginary hat with two fingers. "Aye, sir." He then summoned two other sailors similarly clad and they stepped nimbly onto the gangplank and headed for the carriage.

"Shall I have the prisoner taken to his confinement, my lord?" Captain Burns asked Charles.

"Yes. Please take the half-breed demon away," Charles said with a dismissive hand gesture. "I've had quite enough of him. I don't wish to see him again until we disembark; and mind you, don't feed or water him regularly. The animal has a violent temper, and keeping him weak will calm it."

Charles glared at Rafe, who returned the glare with interest, and then it became a contest as to who would break eye contact first. As always when Charles challenged Rafe in anything, Charles lost. Annoyed that Rafe had bested him yet again and while he was his prisoner no less Charles haughtily turned away to retreat to his private cabin. Then he remembered the key to the manacles. He pulled the metal key from a pocket in his waistcoat with his thumb and forefinger and handed it to the Captain. "The key to the animal's manacles. Be certain to entrust it to someone mentally strong or the animal may convince the man to free him, for he's a supremely gifted manipulator."

Rafe was tempted to manipulate Charles onto the deck and then manipulate his face with his fists until some fresh bruising occurred, but as he was still manacled and surrounded by men loyal to Charles besides, he judged the effort would prove unsuccessful.

Still, it would be gratifying to try… But then Charles retired to his luxuriously appointed private cabin, and settled the matter.

Captain Burns hailed two more of his men. "Davy, Thomas."

They touched their imaginary caps in salute. "Aye, Cap'n."

Captain Burns handed the small manacle key to the sailor he'd called Thomas, a red-haired, thin, wiry sailor of average height with a seemingly permanent glower. "You and Davy take the prisoner to the chain locker and secure him there. He's in your care until we land, and take heed of what Lord Huntington said about not giving him too much food or water."

"Aye, Cap'n," Thomas said with a salute. He stowed the key in his pants pocket while Davy, a barrel-chested man with beady brown eyes, stringy brown hair, a pudgy nose, and missing his top two front teeth, seized Rafe's arm. Rafe glared at Davy defiantly, but Davy was a seasoned veteran of the sea, having weathered many a violent storm, and so he remained undeterred by the puny anger of a mere man, and a half-breed bastard at that. Thomas seized Rafe's other arm, and they roughly ushered him to the chain locker. The windowless storage room smelled of long dead fish and metal chains, and was filled with a goodly amount of supplies of all sorts. The ceiling wasn't quite high enough for Rafe's six feet and he had to bend over to avoid bumping his head on the ceiling joists. Thomas removed Rafe's left manacle, passed the chain through a ring affixed to the bulkhead with a thick spike at Rafe's chest height then refastened the manacle on Rafe's chafed and bleeding wrist.

No words having been exchanged, the sailors walked out, closed the door firmly, and left Rafe alone without even a lit lantern to chase away the gloom. Rafe sat down cross-legged on the deck and rested his back against the curving bulkhead, but the manacle's chains were so short that he was forced to keep his arms raised above his head. He relaxed and let the manacles hold up his arms, although that meant enduring the pain of them digging into his sore and bleeding wrists. He glumly rested the back of his head against the bulkhead and swallowed to ease the aching lump in his throat. It wasn't so much that he was a prisoner that had him feeling wretched. Although that was definitely a major contributing factor, it was more that Leopold had completely refused to even acknowledge his existence upon his last chance of ever seeing him again, and on this most cursed of all days too, September 19th, the day of his birth. Hot tears welled up in Rafe's eyes, but he didn't blink them away this time. Isolated and in absolute darkness in the smelly, close quarters, no one but God could see him, and since he was convinced that not even God would waste His time looking down upon a rejected abomination, it was safe now to finally mourn all he'd lost.

Chapter Seventeen

Unending hours passed relentlessly the same, except for the occasional brief intervals when Rafe either Davy or Thomas brought him a scant serving of food and water, only temporarily assuaging his nearly constant hunger and thirst. He tried to relieve his boredom and discomfort with sleep, but that escape cruelly eluded him for countless days until eventually exhaustion won out.

He was deep in sleep when he was abruptly awakened by being tossed roughly aside by a sudden lurching of the ship. The searing pain of the manacles digging into his sore wrists and partly tearing off newly formed scabs as the chain abruptly reached its limits assured he wouldn't be drifting back to sleep any time soon either. At first he was annoyed that he'd been rudely awakened from the rare instance that he'd managed to actually sleep and without nightmares too. Then he realized he sat in several inches of water and that outside the chain locker the wind howled and waves thundered and pounded furiously against the bulkhead.

Rafe sprang to his feet before remembering he was in a room with a low ceiling then inhaled sharply in pain as he banged his head painfully on a cross beam. He was about to curse as well, but just then there was a deafeningly loud splintering and tearing of wood and the ship rolled hard to port. He was tossed violently aside and once again the manacles tore into his wrists, finishing tearing off the newly formed scabs that had been only half scraped off on the last jolt. Blood dribbled down Rafe's arms. He managed to set his legs under him solidly, but then the ship pitched forward making him lose his footing. He stumbled to his left and struck his forehead painfully against the bulkhead, raising a large lump and dizzying him. He righted unsteadily, but then the ship pitched violently to starboard. This time he fell to his bottom, painfully wrenching his arm sockets along with his wrists as the chain abruptly reached its limits. More water rushed in under the door and Rafe heard Captain Burns frantically barking orders and men shouting equally frantically, "Aye, sir".

Rafe's wrists soon went numb from the continual wrenching as the ship rolled, plunged and pitched to port or starboard, but he counted that as well and good, for they were now badly torn and otherwise the pain would've been intense. There came a tremendously loud crack and men screamed in fear. The ship lurched hard to port accompanied by a horrendous creaking and moaning and after that a loud thud that vibrated the deck so violently that Rafe was knocked to his knees and once again his wrists, shoulders and arms were nearly wrenched from their sockets as his chains abruptly reached their limits. He cursed in French as he struggled to his feet in calf-deep water, while on deck men shouted frantically. Although the chain locker door was too thick for Rafe to hear their words, he could surmise well enough from the hysterical tones that the ship was lost. Chained, forgotten, he would go down with the ship. Although death itself was welcome, he feared drowning. He could only guess that latent memories of his near drowning on the day of his birth were to blame for the persistent, irrational fear, for he had no fear of water itself, and he was a skilled and strong swimmer.

The chain locker door suddenly burst open and a three foot wave of seawater rushed in wetting Rafe to his waist. Thomas sloshed in behind the wave looking grimmer than usual, his shoulder-length red hair hanging in soggy, dripping, strings in his face. As the ship lurched to one side again, Rafe braced his already bruised left shoulder against the bulkhead, spread his feet wide, and shouted above the roaring of the wind, the whipping of sails, and the creaking and moaning of overstressed wood, "What's happening?"

"We're caught in a late season hurricane," Thomas shouted. He reached into his shirt pocket to and pulled out the key to Rafe's manacles. "We've lost the mainmast and the foremast, the hull is breached in three places, and water is swamping the ship. Cap'n Burns has ordered all hands to abandon ship. It's every man for himself." He unlocked the manacles then tossed the key onto the flooded floor.

Rafe's first thought wasn't for himself however, it was worry for Charles, whom he knew wasn't a good swimmer. "Lord Huntington! Where is he?"

Thomas shrugged. "Don't know. It's chaos out there. You can try to find him if you wish. No one will stop you in all the confusion. If I was you, though, I'd give up on revenge and focus on saving yourself."

"It's not revenge that drives me to find him, but concern for his welfare," Rafe explained.

Thomas looked skeptical. "No need to pretend. It's nothing to me anyway. We're probably all going to die." He slogged away through the knee-deep water.

Rafe slogged behind Thomas then climbed the stairs, gripping the handrail tightly and struggling to maintain a firm footing in the mini waterfall created by the torrents of water pouring down the stairs. When he stepped onto the main deck, he was blasted by a driving rain that stung his skin. Than a four foot wave swept across the deck and knocked him off his feet carrying him helplessly to port. He only avoided going overboard by frantically gripping the cap rail on the bulwark with both hands. It felt as if an hour passed as water washed over him, but in reality it was mere seconds.

Gasping for breath and still keeping his death grip on the cap rail, Rafe tossed his head to clear his sopping hair from his eyes and peered into the driving rain looking for Charles among the sailors busily lowering the lifeboats on the opposite side of the ship or grabbing what they thought might be of use for their continued survival. Rafe didn't see Charles among them, but he did see Davy. He struggled through the standing water on the deck to ask if he'd seen Charles. He was three quarters of the way there when another wave washed over the ship. He grabbed the stair railing on the foredeck, Davy grasped the cap rail, and that's when Rafe noticed the familiar ring on Davy's left hand. Rafe knew Charles would never surrender his signet ring under any circumstances, which meant Davy could've only gained it through foul play. A dark fury seized control of Rafe's soul. He brushed a lock of sodden hair from his eyes, leaned into the wind and the driving rain, and determinedly sloshed through the ankle-deep water to seize Davy roughly by the shoulder. "How did you come by that ring?" he shouted above the storm.

Davy pretended innocence. "What ring?"

Rafe pointed accusingly at Davy's left ring finger. "That is Lord Huntington's signet ring. He'd never surrender it to anyone. What have you done to him?"

Davy drew his knife and aimed to plunge it into Rafe's heart, but Rafe caught Davy's wrist, at the same time as another wall of water washed over them. Rafe planted his feet firmly on the deck and determinedly gripped the cap rail with his other hand while maintaining his firm grip on Davy's wrist. Then as the wave receded, he bent Davy's wrist backward until Davy cried out in pain and was forced to drop the knife. Rafe hastily swept up the weapon before it washed overboard then slipped behind Davy and held the blade to Davy's throat. "What have you done with Lord Huntington?" he demanded.

"I put him overboard when no one was looking," Davy shouted defiantly as rivulets of rain coursed down his face between the sopping locks of shoulder-length hair plastered to his forehead and cheeks. "And you should thank me for it. He was planning to make you his slave wasn't he!"

Rafe couldn't believe what he'd heard! "You tossed Lord Huntington overboard in a hurricane?" he exclaimed.

"After I coerced his fancy ring from his finger," Davy said smugly.

With the realization that his heart brother whom he still loved despite all had been drowned by this man and for something as insignificant as a ring Rafe was suddenly seized by a fury so intense that he lost all sense of right and wrong. Roaring in rage he drew the blade across Davy's throat. The sailor swayed on his feet as his life quickly bled out. Rafe hastily tore the ring from Davy's finger before his lifeless body slid to the deck then pragmatically leaned over the body as the rain pounded on his back and unbuckled Davy's knife sheath. He shoved the knife in the sheath as he straightened and then involuntarily looked into Davy's dead eyes, staring at him. Only then did the reality, the horror of what he'd done finally hit him. He'd murdered another man, and this time deliberately without a second thought; a man who was the mate of every other sailor on deck, and who would all be sure to want revenge!

Rafe started to turn around to see how many of the sailors had witnessed his crime, but just then another wall of water washed over the ship. He held Charles's signet ring tightly in his closed fist, the knife and sheath tightly in his other hand, braced his legs wide and leaned into the wave. The wall of water buffeted him so strongly that he nearly lost his footing and it did blind him and steal his breath, all while battling to force him overboard. Rafe straightened, his chest heaving with labored breathing, shoved his dripping hair off his face with his fisted hand and saw with the utmost relief that Davy's body had been washed overboard, removing all evidence of his recent crime.

Before the next wave could strike, he hastily put Charles's signet ring on his finger, where his own signet ring had once been, then buckled on the knife and sheath, and looked up to find every sailor's back to him as they stared in a sort of trance at the advancing thirty foot wave. Rafe too watched in abject terror as the titanic wave hovered over the ship for a split-second that seemed to last an hour, and then the full force of the water crashed down upon the unfortunate crew members.

Although he braced for it, Rafe was unable to resist the crushing force of this gigantic wave and he was swept helplessly overboard. Men plunged into the choppy water alongside Rafe some head first, some sideways, some feet first, along with coils of rope, bits of torn sail, shattered pieces of wood, barrels of salt pork, and all other manner of cargo. Rafe fought desperately to stop his downward plunge, but although both his leg and arm strokes were powerful, he continued to plummet until his chest ached from lack of air and water pressure. He was seriously considering ceasing his useless struggles and surrendering to his fate when his downward plunge suddenly ceased. With renewed hope he determinedly swam upward, his strong strokes fueled by adrenalin; but the surface remained elusive. Waves of blackness assaulted him. His lungs burned for air. Then at last he broke through the surface of the water.

He inhaled deeply, also taking in a mouthful of water along with the life giving air which made him cough and splutter as he was tossed about on the storm-tossed waters like another piece of flotsam. He would've liked to sink back underwater where it was at least calmer and stay under until the hurricane passed, but being no merman who could breathe underwater he had to endure as best he could as wave upon wave crashed and battered his already weakened body. He stubbornly fought the forces of nature for unending hours, treading water until his arms ached then sinking under the surface to rest until he was desperate for air, then struggling to the surface and resuming the battle all over again.

The last reserves of Rafe's strength were nearly exhausted and he was about to give up and accept drowning as his well-deserved fate when the storm suddenly broke and the seas calmed. Now that the high waves and drenching rain no longer obscured his vision, Rafe wished he was still blinded by the storm, for he was in the middle of a vast, unending expanse of ocean with no ship, no sailors, and no land in sight. His only hope for survival was to swim until he found that so desirable land, and he'd most likely tire and drown long before then. However, the fear of drowning dictated that he at least tried. He paddled around in a circle debating which direction to take—and then was amazed and relieved when he spotted a miracle.

Charles, two hundred feet distant, soaking wet, but otherwise in one piece, gripped a door-sized piece of wood, with his eyes squeezed tightly shut in apparent silent prayer. Rafe could've kissed Charles so glad was he to see that his beloved brother had miraculously survived. With renewed energy, he swam to Charles, reaching him just as he finished his prayer, surrendered to the same despair Rafe had just battled, and started to go under. Rafe grasped a handful of Charles's hair and pulled him up.

Charles blinked his eyes open in shocked surprise and then his eyes rounded in disbelief. "You! You're still alive? How can that be? I saw the ship go down and you were secured in the chain locker. I thought I was finally rid of you!"

Rafe's brotherly love for Charles fled to its place of imprisonment in the dungeon of his heart, and his joy at finding Charles alive died. "Thomas let me out, and you should be glad of it, for you would've drowned just now otherwise," he said, clipping his words in anger. He switched his grip from Charles's hair to Charles's arm.

Charles's eyes widened as he saw Rafe wearing his signet ring. "My signet ring! Davy took it from me. How did you get it?" His eyes narrowed as suspicion arose in his heart. "You and Davy were working together!"

Rafe scowled, offended, but then being offended was normal when he was around Charles. "No! I saw Davy wearing the ring and took it from him before I was swept overboard."

"That despicable man! He was always eyeing my ring. It made me nervous. Then during the storm he came to my cabin saying he'd been sent by Captain Burns to help me to the lifeboat. I went with him unaware of the harm he intended, and while the Captain and everyone else was preoccupied with the storm, Davy hit me on the forehead with a club, wrested my ring from me while I was too dizzy to fight back, and tossed me overboard. But if you're not in league with him, how did you come by the ring?"

Rafe was reluctant to say, for he was deeply ashamed of what he'd done in his anger and grief. It seemed it was far easier to kill once you'd already done it and he didn't like what that might mean the next time he was confronted violently. On the other hand, it was entirely likely he wouldn't have to worry about such a scenario, for there was a good chance he and Charles were slated for a long, lingering death by exposure. "Rafe?" Charles prompted.

"I—slit Davy's throat with his own knife then took the ring from his finger before his body was washed overboard," he confessed guiltily.

"You *murdered* him?" Charles exclaimed aghast.

"He said that he'd thrown you overboard, and—,"

"—you thought you'd seize the opportunity to take my place as Lord Huntington, and have Sarah and Laird along with it," Charles accused.

Rafe bristled. "I would never even conceive the thought of stealing another man's wife and son. Furthermore, why would I want your estate when I have my own worth five times yours!"

"You tell me, Rafe! Why is it that your wicked appetite for worldly goods is never sated?" Charles demanded.

Rafe glared darkly at Charles, who then held out his left hand while keeping a tight grip on the makeshift raft with the other. "Hand over my ring, thieving murderer!"

Rafe angrily tore the signet ring from his finger and slammed it into Charles's open palm. That's when he noticed a quarter-inch wide by two-inch long splinter of wood was imbedded deeply in his forearm. An eighth of an inch sliver on the end was exposed, so Rafe grasped it with his thumb and forefinger, yanked the splinter free, and irritably tossed the bloodied wood into the ocean pretending it was Charles; which gave him a goodly measure of satisfaction. The cut bled freely, but not enough to endanger his life, so Rafe ignored it for now and surreptitiously looked Charles over for injuries. His would be slave master seemed unhurt except for a two-inch gash on his forehead that had most likely come from Davy's clubbing, but Charles himself hadn't noticed yet. "You have a nasty gash on your forehead. Allow me to have a closer look at it," he said.

Charles uncharacteristically let Rafe examine him without making a snide comment, such as that he'd have to wash after being touched by a half-breed demon. The gash was about a quarter inch deep and was still seeping blood after all these hours, but Rafe was confident if pressure was applied, it would eventually clot. Charles would have a noticeable scar, but in Rafe's opinion that would only enhance his appearance. "You'll be fine." He couldn't risk adding a snide comment. "It's fortuitous you have such a hard head or it might've been worse."

Charles didn't rejoin with a snappy comeback, which made Rafe wonder if perhaps Charles was more severely injured than he seemed. "How are you feeling?" he asked concernedly.

"I have a terrific headache, and the vision in my left eye is blurry. What if it's permanent?" Charles said.

"Your vision will return to normal in time," Rafe reassured him, having no idea if he was telling the truth. He snagged a linen napkin from the officer's mess that happened to be floating by as if by design, wadded it into a ball, and held it out. "Hold this to the wound until it stops bleeding."

Charles rested his upper body on their makeshift raft, took the napkin, and pressed it to his head then inhaled sharply and pulled it off. "That stings!"

"It's the salt water. It'll help sanitize the wound. Put it back on," Rafe advised.

Charles reluctantly obeyed. "I thought I was the only survivor. I'm glad I'm not, although I would've preferred that the only other survivor hadn't been you."

The muscles in Rafe's jaw visibly tightened as he bit back a bitter retort. "Shall we raise you out of the water?" He helped Charles up onto the makeshift raft, but didn't try to climb up onto it judging that it wouldn't hold the weight of two grown men.

"How far do you think it is to land of any sort?" Charles asked.

"Hopefully close enough to reach it before you die of thirst," Rafe said, already burning with thirst from being denied sufficient water during the voyage, and thus doubting he'd live long enough to make it to land himself.

"We'll make it. God will provide," Charles said confidently.

"Indeed," Rafe said, although he was most thoroughly convinced that God didn't care about him; but perhaps he could benefit from God's concern for Charles?

They drifted for countless hours with the sun beating mercilessly down upon them. Charles lay on his stomach on his makeshift raft and rested his left cheek on his crossed arms. "I can't help thinking that somehow this is entirely your fault; that you somehow conjured up that abnormally fierce hurricane with your evil native mystical powers so you could escape your sentence," he mumbled sleepily through sunburnt and chapped lips.

Rafe suppressed a long-suffering sigh. "If so, it was particularly poor planning, for I wouldn't call this much of an escape."

"Perhaps you made a mistake somewhere in your conjuring," Charles reasoned and then yawned wide.

"It seems so, since you're still alive," Rafe quipped.

"I knew it," Charles mumbled as he drifted to sleep lulled by the heat, exhaustion, and the constant gentle rocking of the waves.

Chapter Eighteen

Rafe had no idea how many days they'd been drifting as he'd grown progressively weaker from the combination of dehydration, previous days of improper nourishment, and battling the forces of the storm. It was increasingly difficult to keep his grip on their makeshift raft much less stay awake and despite his best efforts, he eventually nodded off, his head slowly sinking down until his right cheek rested on the raft. His relaxed body stayed in place until the first wave hit moving him a fraction of an inch. The next wave moved him another fraction of an inch. Then another larger wave washed him completely off the raft.

Rafe breathed in water which startled him awake and he inhaled even more water. His heart pounding in fear he pushed down with his arms, kicked mightily, and seconds later burst to the surface of the water. He coughed and retched for a few moments then when that finally ceased, he saw that the raft had drifted a good fifty feet away, and Charles was still sleeping peacefully, totally unaware that his hated enemy had nearly drowned. Rafe swam to the makeshift raft, barely making it even with the aid of the short burst of strength from the adrenaline rush of nearly drowning then laboriously pulled his upper body onto the raft with trembling arms and lay motionless, calming his pounding heart, stilling his labored breathing.

One would've thought that the fear of drowning would make it easier to stay awake, but it wasn't long before he started to drift off again. As his right cheek touched the wet wood of the raft, he jerked it up in alarm then stared blearily at the unending expanse of ocean his forehead wrinkling as he forced his eyes wide trying to keep them open. Seconds later he jerked awake when his right cheek once again touched the raft.

Then he spotted it out of the corner of his eye to his left. He swiveled his head and stared. Land! Could it be real? He blinked then blinked again. The land was still there. It was no hallucination! Wide awake now he shook Charles's shoulder. "Charles! Charles!" he croaked excitedly.

"What is it? Why did you wake me? I was having the most wonderful dream about Sarah and Laird," Charles complained groggily.

Rafe pointed with a trembling hand. "Land!"

"What?" Charles cried unable to believe what he'd heard.

"Land! There's an island! A big one! Look!" Rafe pointed more insistently.

Charles could barely summon the strength to lift his head, but when he saw the island, his strength was renewed. He dipped his arms into the water on either side of the makeshift raft and paddled furiously. Rafe assisted him by pushing the raft from behind.

Three quarters of an hour later they dragged their makeshift raft onto the sandy beach and collapsed onto their backs, panting in exhaustion. "I can't believe we made it!" Charles said after he caught his breath.

"I nearly didn't," Rafe said.

"Oh please, you're better off than me. There's not a mark on you, except for that little scratch on your forearm," Charles said.

Rafe didn't bother to explain about his near drowning. As Charles lay prone on his back, panting and recovering from his recent efforts, Rafe struggled to sit up then took stock of his condition. Charles was right. Other than the cut on his arm, pervasive weakness, chapped lips, and a bright red sunburn, he was in one piece, and so surprisingly were his boots and buckskins; although they were stiff from their long soak in salt water. He also still had his recently pilfered knife and sheath, a wonderful piece of good fortune. Charles was in pretty good shape too, except for his bright red sunburn, chapped lips, and the gash on his head, and that his jacket was missing and the ruffle on his fine, white, silk shirt underneath his somewhat sturdier yellow, satin brocade waistcoat was torn and tattered.

Rafe took off each of his boots in turn and turned it upside down emptying it of water and sand, removed and wrung out his socks, then put them and the boots back on. His next action was to take stock of his surroundings. Far down shore to his right something large billowed, yellowish-white in color. He stood up unsteadily, swaying like a drunken man, and stumbled toward the yellowish-white, billowing object. Charles stayed put. He was curious, but not enough to make him stand up and walk all the way down shore.

As Rafe neared the billowing object, he saw that it was sailcloth, still attached to the mainmast. He would've whooped for joy, except that he lacked the energy, for now they had potential shelter. They could use the sailcloth and the line to build a wigwam, or perhaps even two. While Charles continued lounging down shore, making no move to come and assist Rafe although it was obvious he was struggling, Rafe drew his knife, cut the sail cloth loose, and laboriously dragged it far enough on shore to stop it from washing back into the ocean with the next high tide; a Herculean task in his current condition. Then although he was exhausted from his efforts, he returned to the mast, cut the line, coiled it and stored it with the sailcloth.

That task done, Rafe walked unsteadily back to where Charles lounged and assumed a wide stance to maintain his balance in his weakened condition, his chest heaving from his exertions. "We must conduct a search for fresh water."

"Now? But I can't even stand," Charles whined.

Rafe scowled disgustedly. "If I'm able to drag yards of heavy sailcloth onto the beach by myself, half- starved and dehydrated as I am, you most certainly can stand as well fed and rested as you are."

"That might be true if I wasn't a pure nobleman through and through and not built for hard labor," Charles said. "On the other hand, your savage blood makes you well fit for such tasks. Furthermore, the court has appointed you as my slave. You shall find the water and bring it to me."

Rafe suppressed his irritation over Charles lording it over him, but not effortlessly. "The court has no jurisdiction here, and besides we have no water skins to carry water. If you want water, you'll have to accompany me."

Charles moaned. "First you brutally assault me, then you conjure up a shipwreck, and now you threaten to let me die of thirst! You enjoy making me suffer!"

"You'll learn what true suffering is if you don't stand up and accompany me now!" Rafe threatened impatiently.

"Fine, then help me up." Charles held out his hand imperiously.

Rafe hesitated, and then he grasped Charles's hand. In his weakened state pulling Charles to his feet felt like the equivalent of pulling a cart loaded with boulders, and especially as Charles exerted no effort of his own. Straining, gritting his teeth, Rafe finally managed to drag Charles to his feet then Charles pulled his hand free unexpectedly, making him stumble back a few steps, barely avoiding a fall. He realized that a fall was Charles's intent when Charles looked disappointed that he stayed on his feet, and then was tempted to reciprocate by shoving Charles to the ground. However, he knew that then Charles would demand he pull him up again, and so he merely started walking, and Charles fell in beside him.

Within the hour they found a snaking, freshwater river, eight feet wide, and two feet deep at the point where they stood. The water ran fast, cool, and clear, and Charles dropped onto his belly and plunged his head under, drinking deeply. As thirsty and hot as he was, Rafe wanted to do the same, but he couldn't find it within himself to throw caution to the wind. Any number of unknown dangers could sneak up on him when he wasn't looking; wild animals and unfriendly natives not least among them. He knelt and keeping a wary watch, scooped water in his cupped hands until his thirst was satiated. A few moments later Charles pushed up onto his knees then leaned back on his heels, grinning, water dripping off the ends of his shoulder-length brown hair, and chin. "I never thought water could taste so good! So what's next?"

"We'll need to build shelter." Rafe pointed across the stream at a natural clearing. "There would be an ideal place to build wigwams."

"How will you build a wigwam with no axe to cut down the trees?" Charles asked.

"We don't need to cut down trees. We only need sturdy branches to strip for poles, and there's a ready supply of those," Rafe explained.

"You expect me to strip branches by hand?" Charles asked, aghast that he would have to stoop to such menial labor.

"No. I'll use my knife," Rafe said.

"You mean Davy's knife, which you stole from him after you murdered him," Charles corrected nastily.

Rafe glared darkly at Charles, who looked pleased that he'd riled him. "What will you use for the covering for the wigwams?" Charles then asked.

The sailcloth *you* failed to help me drag up onto the beach," Rafe said accusingly.

"No reasonable man would've expected me to help when I have a head wound," Charles countered defensively.

Rafe refrained from voicing the snide comment that came to mind about Charles's head wound and the possibility that his brain had leaked out of it. "It's growing late. Tonight we'll make a temporary shelter with the sailcloth and sleep on the beach. Tomorrow you'll help me carry the sailcloth up here, head wound notwithstanding, and then we'll build two wigwams; for I'll not share a shelter with you."

"Who died and made you Lord of the island?" Charles demanded haughtily.

"Everybody," Rafe said grimly, which both sobered and silenced Charles.

He stood up. "We should return to the beach now. There's much to do before sundown."

Charles stood up without complaining, for which Rafe was both surprised and grateful, and they made their way back to the beach in mutual silence, for which Rafe was also surprised and grateful. Then again surprising Rafe, Charles obligingly helped him set up their temporary shelter, and they settled down for the night.

Chapter Nineteen

Although they were only halfway to the clearing where Rafe planned to build their wigwams Charles dropped his pile of ten long, sturdy branches that he and Rafe had gathered, and Rafe had stripped of leaves. "That's it. I'm exhausted and I've done more than my fair share. I'm not carrying these branches any further, or doing anything else either. I'm done for the day." Charles sat down heavily on the sturdiest part of a nearby rotting log and fanned his face with his hand.

Rafe dropped his double burden of twenty poles and the coil of rope and took a menacing step toward Charles. He'd been silently enduring Charles's whining and complaining all morning and he'd had enough. "This wigwam is for you and you'll help build it. Stand up and pick up those poles!"

"I will not! You're the one sentenced to slavery, not me!" Charles said stubbornly.

Rafe grabbed a handful of the torn and ragged ruffle on the front of Charles's shirt and forcefully dragged him to his feet. "Pick up those poles or I'll beat you as you beat your slaves when you think they're lazy!" He shoved Charles at the small pile of poles.

Charles whirled and took a clumsy swing at Rafe, but Rafe easily dodged the blow and then cuffed Charles in the side of the head. Charles reddened with outrage. "You'll pay for that impudence, Lucifer's son!" He rubbed the new bruise on the side of his head. "It will add years to your sentence."

Rafe snorted derisively. "We're stranded on a deserted island and no one knows we're alive. I'm not too worried about paying for *impudence* by having a few paltry years added to my *life* sentence at the moment; and I've told you before to stop calling me Lucifer's son."

"Then I shall call you abomination instead, or would you prefer Satan's child?" Charles asked nastily. "Personally, I think Satan's child is the most fitting, for there's no doubt you're demon spawn."

Charles could see Rafe struggling to control his anger and his left hand strayed to the hilt of his knife. Charles was suddenly afraid he'd pushed Rafe too far. "Rafe," he said warily.

"Pick up those poles," Rafe commanded quietly, his hand resting menacingly on his knife hilt.

It was Rafe's tone more than the gesture that convinced Charles he was deadly serious. He hastily picked up the poles, but he couldn't resist grumbling, "You're heartless! You already made me help you search for the branches all morning, and yesterday you made me help you drag all that heavy sailcloth up here, and I'm still sore all over from being tossed about in the waves. You're working me to the bone on this wigwam, which was wholly your idea." Charles shifted the load of poles to free his right hand, reached across his body and tenderly fingered his ribs on his left side. "I think I might even have a broken rib, and the gash on my head is giving me a terrific headache."

"I'm hurting and exhausted too, Charles," Rafe said. He didn't bother to mention that he had a full-blown headache, vision disturbances, and nausea. "But you can't argue that you need shelter, and preferably before the sun sets. I need your help to accomplish that. So you'll help me willingly, or I'll force you to help me. Move on." He waited until Charles had started walking before he took his hand off his knife hilt.

As Charles trudged woodenly in front of Rafe, he said, "I agree that I need shelter, but as I told you this morning when we hauled that sailcloth up here, I think we should build on the beach, and we should also gather wood for a large bonfire to light when a ship passes by."

"As I told you this morning, no ship will pass by. The Lady Bountiful was blown far off course by that storm, and then you and I drifted for days. This island is not even in the shipping lanes," Rafe said.

"Even if you're correct, which I doubt, for what makes you so knowledgeable about our location and shipping lanes, I've been praying for a rescue, so God has to send someone," Charles countered.

"Because you're a high and mighty noble of pure blood who deserves an abundant life?" Rafe asked sarcastically.

"There is that," Charles said not catching the sarcasm. "However, it's mostly for the simple reason that I'm in need of rescue, and God has promised to supply all our needs."

"Well I'm not in need of rescue, nor am I praying for rescue, and since we share the same island, I'd venture to say that severely reduces your chances of ever escaping it," Rafe reasoned.

They'd reached their campsite. Charles dropped his poles on the ground. "If you were dead, then your needs couldn't interfere with mine."

Rafe dropped his burden. "If that's a threat, I should remind you that I'm quite adept at defending myself, and I also have the only weapon."

"You have to sleep sometime," Charles said pragmatically.

"Yes, but I sleep lightly."

"If you had a conscience, you wouldn't sleep at all. You'd be too upset over stranding me on this island, as well as for the lost lives of all the sailors on the Lady Bountiful," Charles accused.

Rafe snorted. "You truly do believe I conjured up that storm!"

"No, but you're responsible nevertheless, for if you hadn't murdered Duncan, we wouldn't have been on the ship in the first place, which in turn wouldn't have been caught in the hurricane and shipwrecked with all hands lost because it had to wait in port an extra fortnight for you!"

"You shot me. Unjustly. Because of that, I required surgery to save my life and then recovery time, which is what caused the delay in your ship's departure as they awaited our arrival. Thus, you are responsible for our current predicament and all those sailor's deaths, not I."

Charles bristled and placed his hands on his hips. "It was my duty to protect Leopold from assassination by an ungrateful savage!"

"Leopold's life was never in peril from me! It was the snake I was aiming at!"

Charles spat at Rafe, but it was taken by the wind and missed him. "That's a lie, even as you lied about not attempting to spirit Sarah away from me! I know you've always been jealous because she was affianced to me instead of you. You're forever trying to steal her away, baiting her with your charming smiles, your silver-tongued compliments, and your notable skills with the bow, pistol, and knife. I see the way she looks at you. I know that like all women she's enamored with you, and dreams of lying in your arms."

"No woman wants me, Charles, and Sarah least of all. She loves you, and is completely loyal to you. I only taunt you with her affection for me because you're so jealous that it's certain revenge for all the taunts you throw at me. I assure you, I've never been anything other than a good friend to Sarah, nor shall I ever be any more to her, and you do her a grave injustice by your distrust."

"You expect me to believe someone that lies practically every time he opens his mouth?" Charles said derogatorily.

"I don't lie, Charles, but even if I did, according to you I lack a soul, so I'm free to act in any way I see fit. If I should choose to lie, or kill, or steal, I may do so freely without fear of eternal consequences, for there'll be no judgment for me."

"Oh there'll most certainly be judgment for you; only it'll be in this lifetime. When we're rescued, I'll make certain of it, you—you—demon spawn!"

Rafe glared darkly at Charles. "Back to work," he threatened quietly.

Charles hesitated, but judging from his quiet tone, Rafe was barely suppressing his rage, so Charles decided it would be prudent not to provoke him any further lest he fall on him to beat him to death; and there was no one here to stop him this time. He reluctantly picked up one of the poles.

By nightfall the first small, domed wigwam was completed and as Rafe had reckoned, there was enough sailcloth and rope left over to build another. It was the first time Charles had ever built anything himself rather than directing someone else to do it. "It looks quite sturdy, doesn't it?" he remarked with pride.

"Yes, no thanks to you," Rafe replied.

"You couldn't have done it without me!" Charles huffed indignantly. "You said so yourself."

"Yes, but I had to threaten you to gain your help, so there's no room for pride. If you'd helped me willingly, then you'd have reason to be proud," Rafe shot back.

"You wouldn't have had to threaten me if you'd politely requested my help; but no, instead you insisted on acting like *Lord* Brookstone and treating me as your slave!"

Rafe was tempted to point out that was exactly how Charles had intended to treat him, for many years to come, but he didn't see the point in it. He picked up two smaller lengths of rope. "Inside the wigwam," he said, and drew his knife. Since Charles had expressed his intent to murder him, he'd have to tie Charles up. Not that he cared if he died, but only that Charles wouldn't kill him proper, but would cause him the sort of injury that would plague him for days or even weeks before he succumbed. He had no wish to grant Charles the satisfaction of watching him die slowly and in agony.

"What are you up to?" Charles warily eyed the knife and the rope.

"You've threatened to kill me so I'm tying you up for the night. You'll sleep inside the wigwam. I'll sleep out here; and let me remind you that I'm a light sleeper." He waved at the wigwam, indicating Charles should enter. Charles was initially inclined to refuse to comply, but the drawn knife and the dark threat in Rafe's eyes and tone convinced him otherwise. He meekly shoved aside the door flap and ducked inside the wigwam.

Rafe followed him in then sheathed the knife and tied Charles's wrists behind his back and his ankles together. He couldn't find it within himself to tighten the rope as securely as he knew he should, though. He didn't need the raw, red rings that still circled his wrists to remind him of how painful any sort of restraint could be and he couldn't visit that pain on someone else even if it was Charles, and even though it presented the possibility that Charles could work free of his bindings if he was persistent. It was a weakness he hoped he would not regret later.

* * *

It was mid-morning before Rafe decided it was past time to quit procrastinating and release Charles from his nighttime restraints. With a resigned sigh, he pulled back the sailcloth and ducked inside the wigwam. Even as he saw the rope he'd used to restrain Charles lying loose on the ground, Charles lunged. As Rafe had feared, Charles had managed to free himself from his bonds, and then he'd waited, anticipating a chance to attack and wrestle the knife from him. Since Rafe was on his guard, however, he easily avoided the attack by simply side-stepping, and Charles landed on the hard ground instead of on top of him. Rafe leaned over Charles grinning smugly. "I should think that by now you'd know better than to try something like that on me." He graciously helped Charles to his feet.

"I had to at least make the attempt!" Charles said, red-faced with both embarrassment and exertion. He rubbed a bruised spot on his left elbow, pulled up his right stocking which had fallen around his ankle, and straightened his dirty, tattered, once fine clothing. "I hate it here," he muttered crossly. "How long do you think we'll be trapped on this terrible island?"

"Haven't you figured it out yet? We're here for the remainder of our days," Rafe said.

"What! Oh no! You may desire it that way, but God won't allow you to escape justice that easily. You'll pay not only for murdering that poor sailor, Davy, but also for abusing me and holding me hostage! This time you won't be able to cunningly evade hanging!"

"How soon you've forgotten, Charles that the *poor sailor, Davy*, stole your signet ring and threw you overboard in a hurricane, which is attempted murder. He also attempted to plunge his knife into my heart when I confronted him. Furthermore, I've done nothing less to you than you deserve!"

Charles visibly bristled. "You really think your violence against me is justified! There's not a single iota of remorse in that black heart of yours is there!"

Rafe shoved Charles roughly, forcing him to take two steps back. Rafe advanced on him, his dark eyes sparking with anger. "Ever since I was taken from my adopted tribe, I've done everything I could to prove I was as good as any pure-blooded, white man; but you—" He poked Charles in the chest with his index finger. "You worked diligently to spread lies and rumors about me! Well now I'm in control, and I shall have my revenge!" He fluidly swept up a coil of rope and advanced on Charles. Charles backed away, arms outthrust defensively; a useless gesture since Rafe easily tackled him and shoved him face down onto the ground. He then jammed his knee in the small of Charles's back pressing him firmly to the ground, and swiftly tied Charles's hands behind his back and his ankles together; only this time he made the bindings far more secure, heedless of the pain it would bring.

Rafe stormed out of the wigwam and angrily paced in front of it while muttering under his breath in Mohican, his mood as dark as the eternal night of the depths of the universe overhead. He wouldn't be surprised if God had saved Charles of all the men on the ship merely because Charles did such a fine job of making his life sheer torture! He then began inventing hundreds of bloody scenarios that pleased his heart's desire for revenge against Charles, but none that he knew he could actually act upon, for he wasn't that far gone down the road of iniquity. Yet.

Finally, his stomach grumbled, so he abandoned his vengeful deliberations and fixed a light meal of dried fish and berries. He debated feeding Charles as well, but after some waffling decided against it. A few days without food and water wouldn't kill Charles, but it would make him far less likely to try to attack him again, with the added benefit of having his revenge on Charles for having the same done to him on the Lady Bountiful. Comfortably full, Rafe stretched out on his back on the ground outside Charles's wigwam, with his wounded ankle resting comfortably across the other, his head pillowed on his crossed arms and star-gazed contentedly until he fell asleep.

His breathing slowed to a gentle, peaceful rhythm, and he smiled in his sleep as he dreamed he was back in the green, lush forests of home. Even better, the mercenaries had never taken him away, never killed everyone he loved, and he was hunting with his heart father, John, as he would've been that night if he hadn't been ill.

Chapter Twenty

While Charles stayed pleasingly out of sight tied up in his wigwam, Rafe had been quite industrious, building another wigwam, catching fish and hanging strips to dry, harvesting berries, and crafting four wooden bowls, literal pieces of art, evenly rounded with a wood grain pleasing to the eye and insides rubbed smooth as silk. Now, his chores finished, Rafe decided he should finally feed and water Charles, who had to be suffering badly after two days with nothing. He filled one of the bowls to the top with berries, added some strips of dried fish then grabbed a second bowl and walked down to the river. He stooped, dipped the bowl in the water and filled it to the brim. With a full bowl in each hand, he approached Charles's wigwam. He stood at the door flap for a few minutes listening for any sound that would reveal Charles was up and about and waiting to spring on him like the last time, but hearing nothing, he ducked through the door flap.

Charles lay curled on the ground in a fetal position still tied securely and so still that Rafe worried he'd waited too long and killed Charles from neglect. The next moment he was relieved when Charles grunted and moved in his sleep, still alive. Silently chastising himself for overreacting, Rafe set the bowls of food and water on the ground within Charles's reach then gripped Charles's shoulder to awaken him.

Charles's eyes popped open. Upon seeing the bowls in front of him, he struggled to sit up then croaked in an angry, raspy voice, "I see you've finally condescended to provide me with food and drink, Satan's child."

"I told you to stop calling me that!" Rafe snapped irritably.

"No, you said to stop calling you Lucifer's child, and I didn't call you that," Charles countered smugly.

Rafe couldn't find fault with that argument, but he could find fault with Charles's ingratitude. "I didn't have to bring you anything. I could've let you die of hunger and thirst."

"I was beginning to believe that's what you intended. Would you untie me so I may avail myself of your bountiful generosity?" Charles asked sarcastically.

Choosing to ignore the sarcasm, Rafe knelt and swiftly untied Charles's hands and ankles then stood up and stepped out of Charles's reach in case he had another attack in mind. However, he was safe, for Charles was single-mindedly focused on the food and water. He greedily grabbed the water bowl with both hands, spilling some over the edges, and drained it in one breath. He wiped his mouth on his sleeve, grabbed a strip of dried fish and bit off half. "This isn't half bad," he said with his mouth full.

"You're welcome," Rafe replied.

"It's amazing how good everything tastes when you've been brutally starved," Charles added pointedly.

"Yes, I know. You've done it to me," Rafe responded resentfully.

"So now you're having your revenge by holding me hostage and lording it over me," Charles accused. He chewed, swallowed and then stuffed the remainder of the dried fish in his mouth.

"I do only what I must. No more, no less," Rafe said defensively.

Charles swallowed the fish. "You must keep me hostage?" He grabbed a handful of berries and stuffed them in his mouth.

"You'd stated your intent to murder me."

"It's not murder, its self-defense. We both know how much pleasure you derive from killing white men, beginning with Duncan, and then Davy," Charles accused.

More than fed up with Charles's unceasing accusations of murder, Rafe said, "I'm in dire need of pleasure. Perhaps I should kill you too."

It was his quiet tone more than his words that sent a tsunami of fear washing over Charles. "If you kill me, Sarah will have to wear black for an entire year and she doesn't look good in black," he blustered to cover his fright.

"You forget, Charles. Everyone already thinks we're dead, so Sarah is already wearing black."

"At least people are mourning my death. No one will mourn your death, including Leopold. Everyone is most likely at this minute attending a celebratory party sponsored by Leopold in what was once your grand manor house, rejoicing that the bastard, half-breed, demon-spawn, abomination is dead and all the children are finally safe from your table!" Charles spat.

Rafe's dark eyes turned flinty with anger. He shoved Charles onto his back on the ground, bound his wrists and ankles then stormed out raging in Mohican. He should've let Charles die of hunger and thirst! He punched a tree wishing it was Charles's face and bloodied his knuckles then cursed in French and cradled his bleeding and bruised left hand in his other, sullenly nursing it while wishing he truly was the murderer Charles claimed. Then he could be rid of Charles and spend the rest of his days alone on this island in exquisite tranquility, never again to be reminded by anyone, and especially Charles, of what he was, or what he was denied. He angrily kicked a round pebble directly at his feet that then soared high and landed in the river. If he'd only been allowed to stay with his adopted tribe then like in his recent dream at this moment he could be happily roaming the woods hunting, and after a successful hunt, he could've come home to a Mohican wife and children and perhaps even a faithful dog. More importantly he'd still believe God loved him. He desperately missed those halcyon days, the peace and assurance that had once been his, but was now beyond his grasp forever. If only the truth hadn't inevitably caught up to him and revealed the lie, for now he was burdened with the aching knowledge that he was missing out on something wonderful, and misery not only plagued his every waking moment, but even invaded his dreams. If not for Charles's stubborn insistence to the contrary he'd still believe himself capable of owning God's love and forgiveness. Certainly that was a lie, but the false happiness he'd once known because of that lie was far preferable to the dark misery he existed in now, which was a living death. A red hot rage boiled up in Rafe's soul. Since Charles had stolen his life, Charles should lose his life in return! A life for a life! Rafe whipped out his knife that only yesterday he'd honed to an unequaled sharpness, strode purposely to Charles's wigwam, thrust back the door flap, and burst violently inside.

Charles lay on his back looking up at the curved ceiling of his wigwam, feeling sorry for himself all trussed up like an animal; and missing Sarah and Laird. When Rafe burst in, with his knife in hand and his abnormally dark eyes stormy with hatred, Charles's eyes widened in alarm. "Rafe, what—," Rafe straddled Charles on his knees, pressed his blade into Charles's throat, and then stilled for what seemed like an eternity to Charles while struggling with what he knew was right against an overwhelming desire to slit Charles's throat. Charles swallowed audibly several times, but wisely remained silent.

In the end as much as Rafe desired to be rid of Charles, he couldn't find it within himself to break his personal honor code and kill a defenseless man, much less one he'd once loved as a brother.

He moved off of Charles, roughly rolled him over, cut his bonds, firmly sheathed his knife, and stormed out of the wigwam. Charles lay there catching his breath and calming his racing heart. The malignant hatred he'd seen in Rafe's eyes as he held the knife to his throat had convinced him that without a doubt he was a dead man this time, but then Rafe had cut his bonds and walked out. What was going on? Was Rafe perhaps waiting for him to emerge from the wigwam in pursuit so he could kill him justifiably; at least in his own eyes? Or perhaps Rafe was drunk. But how had Rafe found alcohol out here on a deserted island, unless a bottle had floated on shore from the shipwreck?

Charles didn't know what to think, but now that he'd regained his freedom he'd have answers! He stood up determinedly, straightened his tattered silk shirt and water-stained, yellow brocade waistcoat, and then pulling back the door flap to tentatively peer outside. He half expected Rafe to jump him and scalp him, although he was uncertain if Mohicans practiced scalping, but Delaware's certainly did, and Rafe had obviously inherited his father's naturally violent nature. However, Rafe was nowhere to be seen. He stepped tensely out of the wigwam determined to find and confront Rafe; although what he'd do when he finally found him, he had no idea. He had no weapon and even if he'd had one, he was no match for Rafe's quickness, agility and strength; but it made him feel better to at least be taking some sort of action. He took a few more cautious steps, and then spotted Rafe's footprints in the dirt. He followed them past the trees. Rafe stood on the riverbank with his back to him! Rejoicing in his good fortune, Charles stealthily approached. He still had no idea how he would overwhelm Rafe, but he'd find a way. No matter what it took, he must gain the upper hand and restore matters to their rightful order.

He was only three feet away from Rafe when Rafe whirled around to face him. "Charles." He gripped his knife tightly in his left hand and his eyes looked abnormally dark and menacing. Charles halted, eyeing the knife warily while silently cursing his stupidity in seeking Rafe out weaponless. "Did you truly think you could sneak up on me?" Rafe asked derisively.

Charles spread his hands and shrugged. "I was hoping…"

"Obviously your hopes exceed your abilities; but now that I've let you track me down, no easy task for you I know, why don't you take a well-deserved rest?" Rafe dipped the blade toward the ground. Charles could tell from Rafe's tone that it was more an order than a request so he sat down on the hard, uneven ground. A sharp stone pierced the underside of his thigh. He shifted position, picked up the troublesome pebble, and tossed it behind him. "I presume you didn't venture out merely seeking my friendly company," Rafe said.

Charles summoned the proper indignation for a lord offended by a lesser person. "Indeed not! I'd prefer to avoid you altogether, but I demand an explanation for what happened back there in my wigwam!"

Rafe focused his abnormally dark eyes on Charles for so long that Charles started to squirm. Then at last he spoke. "I'd decided to be rid of your annoying presence once and for all; but I let you live for Sarah and Laird's sake."

Charles took a moment to consider how to use Rafe's expressed concern for Sarah and Laird to his advantage. "Sarah and Laird would also benefit if you'd let me try to hail a passing ship," he finally said.

"If by some miracle a ship did come and I let you hail it, what would you tell them about me?" Rafe asked.

"About you?" Charles asked, stalling while he tried to concoct an answer that would please Rafe. He certainly couldn't reveal that he intended to tell them Rafe had held him hostage and murdered Davy.

"Yes, what would you tell them about me?" Rafe reiterated impatiently.

"Well, I'd…tell them you died in the shipwreck." Charles had trouble suppressing his grin of satisfaction. The lie sounded so plausible.

Rafe wasn't fooled, though. He knew Charles too well. "Truly? Because you've already threatened to tell any would-be rescuers that I killed Davy; and as you've pointed out, for this second offense I'd most surely be hung. I wish to decide when I die, not the court, so I'll not risk capture by allowing you to hail a ship should one ever pass by, which I doubt."

"Then you plan to keep me hostage until we both die of old age?" Charles cried in exasperation.

Rafe mentally recoiled from a nightmare vision of himself and Charles tottering around the island with canes and long gray beards, nearly deaf, and still arguing, but having to shout to hear each other. "I don't think spending countless years in such close proximity to you would be good for my sanity."

"What are you planning then?" Charles demanded.

Rafe sheathed his knife. "You're like a small child, Charles. What are you doing? Where are we going? I'm exhausted, in pain. When do we eat?"

"I merely wish to know what your intentions are! I have a right to know!" Charles said defensively.

"Wrong! You have no rights now that I'm in control!"

Charles scrambled to his feet. "I must return to Sarah and Laird, Rafe! They need me! I demand that you use your demonic powers, or whatever you want to call them, to summon a ship!"

"Even had I such powers, Charles, you're no longer in a position to demand anything from me," Rafe responded frostily.

Charles was desperate enough to forgo his pride and beg. He even knelt at Rafe's feet like a supplicant. "Please Rafe, you must help me! I can't live in these deplorable conditions. I'm a pure-blooded lord. I was meant for luxury and ease; and I miss Sarah and Laird so much it literally hurts."

"I can't help you," Rafe said icily.

Charles sprang to his feet embarrassed that he'd humbled himself to Rafe, and angry that Rafe had spurned his request. "Then I'm forced to resort to my original plan! I'll live on the beach and when a ship passes, I'll light a bonfire. When they come to rescue me, I'll tell them where to find you and see to it that you're hung at last!"

Rafe laughed derisively. "The enormity of your stupidity never ceases to amaze me. You'll have no shelter, no weapons, and no supplies. You don't even know how to hunt, except foxes and boars, and that from a horse with a hunting rifle. You barely even know how to set a snare, and your best skill is ballroom dancing. How long do you think you'll last?"

"I'll survive well enough!" Charles stomped off.

As easy as it would be to let Charles go off on his own and die, Rafe's sense of honor and his latent brotherly love for Charles wouldn't allow it. He grabbed Charles's shoulders from behind and pulled him roughly to the ground. "You're not going anywhere."

Charles scrambled to his feet and took a step, but Rafe hastily blocked his path. Charles hesitated, and then in desperation he attacked. They locked in a tight embrace, each struggling for mastery of the other, both determined to win. Charles fought with all his strength, but Rafe held back for fear of losing control, as with Davy and Duncan, and killing Charles. The longer they struggled the fiercer the battle became. Then Charles was lucky and gained a stranglehold on Rafe's neck and Rafe forgot he didn't wish to harm Charles. He thrust his arms between Charles's arms to break his hold on his neck. He then flipped Charles onto the ground as easily as if Charles was the small child he'd accused him of being, knelt and laced his long, strong fingers tightly around Charles's throat. Charles clawed futilely at Rafe's hands in a frantic attempt to loosen Rafe's hold, but Rafe tightened his grip and watched with detached curiosity as the color in Charles's face slowly changed from red to blue, and finding the color changes quite fascinating.

Charles's hands ceased their useless clawing and flopped onto the ground at his sides. His eyes rolled back in his head. Rafe suddenly realized he was killing Charles. He released his grip, sprang to his feet, took a step back, and stared at Charles's limp body in horror, his heart pounding in fear. What had he done? Was Charles still breathing? Had he quit too late? He knelt to check for any sign of life, but then Charles inhaled deeply, his eyes fluttered back into place and he rolled over onto his hands and knees, coughing and gasping like a man who'd nearly drowned. Rafe hastily stood up before Charles could realize he'd been concerned for his welfare. "You should thank your God that I didn't kill you," he said then turned away in case there was a residue of concern in his eyes.

Charles struggled to his feet and with the strength of desperation grabbed a handful of the back of Rafe's buckskin shirt, dragged him backward and tossed him onto his back. Rafe banged the back of his head painfully on a small, but sharp rock. Agony reignited his rage. He sprang agilely to his feet and knocked Charles to the ground with such strength that the air was forced from Charles's lungs. He looked down upon his gasping enemy with unconcealed disdain. "If you know what's good for you, you'll not attack me again," he said then walked to the within an inch of the river and stared at the swift, rushing current, guiltily thinking how extremely close he'd come to killing Charles today, not once, but twice; proving his worst fears about becoming a casual murderer, and despising himself all the more for it.

Charles struggled to his feet furious that he'd been bested by an inferior. As silently as he was able, Charles advanced on Rafe. Rafe whirled around, grabbed Charles by his arms, and flipped him head over heels. Only this time there was a swollen, rushing river in front of Charles instead of solid ground. Water splashed everywhere as Charles landed and Rafe instinctively jumped back to avoid being soaked. Then he watched in horror, as Charles, who'd never been a good swimmer was swept downstream by the swift current. Rafe hurriedly splashed in to save him. He too was caught up in the strong current, but being a far more powerful swimmer than Charles he retained control. Charles, on the other hand, was being tumbled and tossed around in the rapids and periodically going under. However, as swiftly and mightily as Rafe swam, the current was far swifter and far stronger, and Charles remained frustratingly out of reach. Every now and then Rafe caught a glimpse of Charles's pale, blood-drained face as he tumbled in the rapids. He looked terrified.

Then above the roar of the rapids could be heard a deeper, far more sinister roar, and seconds later Charles disappeared from sight over the waterfall. Rafe had no idea how many feet Charles had fallen, or even if he was still alive, but he'd soon discover the answer, for like it or not he was following Charles flight over the falls. It was the strangest, most frightening sensation Rafe had ever experienced tumbling head first with the roaring of water in his ears, while desperately trying to grasp something to stop or at least slow his fall and clutching only insubstantial fistfuls of white foam.

Rafe estimated he fell close to thirty feet before he splashed into the river. Luckily, the river was clear of large boulders at the bottom of the falls and the water was far deeper here than where they'd made their camp or he would've broken his neck. He managed to somersault before he hit bottom and then his lungs burning he followed bubbles toward the surface, finally emerging coughing and gasping. Although he had complete confidence in his abilities, he was amazed to be in one piece and not drowned. He tossed his head to clear the heavy, wet strands of hair from his eyes then spotted Charles grasping a large boulder in the middle of the raging river a few hundred feet downstream. He swam to Charles, noting that Charles's head wound was bleeding again. Rafe's overactive conscience mercilessly accused him that the bleeding was his fault for throwing Charles into the water. "Are you well? Any broken bones?" he asked guiltily.

"Nothing's broken, no thanks to you," Charles replied accusingly.

"I did warn you not to attack me again," Rafe rationalized, mostly for his conscience's benefit.

"As if that gives you the right to nearly drown me!"

"It was the river and your inferior skills that nearly drowned you," Rafe countered defensively; which was true, but didn't negate one iota of the guilt he felt. He grasped Charles's arm. "I'll help you to the bank."

Charles yanked free. "I neither need nor want your help, Lucifer's son!"

Rafe sighed silently. So it was back to the name-calling, but at least this time Charles had a good reason for it. "Then accept my advice at least. Don't fight the current. Remain calm. Allow the water to carry you and swim at an angle. Eventually you'll reach the riverbank. Do you think you can manage that?" Charles nodded while looking longingly at the opposite riverbank. "I'll be right behind you. I won't let you be swept away again," Rafe reassured him.

Charles nodded again then gathered his courage and released his death grip on the boulder, to be immediately swept downstream. At first, he struggled against the current as before, but then he tried Rafe's advice and was surprised it worked and hadn't been a deliberate misdirection meant to drown him. A hard swim later, Charles safely reached the riverbank, crawled up onto it, and lay down on his back spread-eagled his chest heaving from his exertions. Rafe soon joined him, plopping down on his back beside him. He was in far better condition than Charles, but still breathing hard and fast. He recovered far more quickly than Charles too. Then he sat up and grinned, exhilarated by the safe conclusion of their little adventure. "See how easy that was?"

"For you." Charles sat up. "Everything's easy for you," he complained enviously. He was a bit woozy, couldn't focus his eyes, and then something wet obscured his vision in his left eye. He rubbed his eye and brought his hand down bloodied. He angrily showed it to Rafe. "I'm bleeding again, and it's entirely your fault!"

Rafe irritably ripped off most of what was left of the ragged chest ruffle of Charles's shirt.

"Hey!" Charles objected.

Rafe wadded the cloth into a ball then shoved it into Charles's hand. "Press it to your head to stop the flow of blood."

Charles hesitated, unwilling at first to use his once fine shirt for such a dirty job, but then he realized it wasn't as if the ruffle could ever be sewed back on. He held the wadded cloth firmly to the gash on his forehead then winced slightly when he pushed too hard and loosened the pressure a bit. "How far do you think we are from our camp?" He craned his neck to look back in the direction they'd come.

Rafe shrugged. "The closest I can tell we're on the far west side of the island, about five miles from camp. He studied the sky, rapidly approaching black thunderclouds laced with frequent streaks of lightning off to the north. "A severe storm is coming. If we hurry, we can make it back to camp ahead of most of it." He stood up.

"I need to rest for a while longer," Charles objected.

Rafe's eyebrows shot up. "Have what little brains you once had seeped out of that wound in your head?" He asked incredulously. "We must move on immediately. Do you wish to be caught out in the open in that?" He pointed at the approaching storm.

Charles lowered his makeshift compress and gingerly probed his head wound with his first two fingers to see if it had stopped bleeding. It hadn't. He reapplied the makeshift compress. "I'm not going anywhere until I'm thoroughly rested." Even though he knew Rafe was right about the storm, he was finished with letting Rafe command him. He'd regain some semblance of control over his life, even if it killed him; which it probably would. But what did it matter since he'd most likely never see Sarah or Laird again anyway?

Rafe firmly gripped his knife hilt. "Must I use force?"

Charles snorted. "Oh please. I should think by now you'd have tired of threatening to murder me."

Rafe's strong, brown fingers tightened on his knife hilt. "It's not murder; it's self-defense. Your lack of common sense is a threat to my welfare," he said quietly.

Charles didn't like Rafe's tone. He dropped his makeshift compress, which he no longer needed anyway, and stared apprehensively into Rafe's eyes attempting to gauge how serious he was. Those dark eyes were as cold and hard as the blade of his knife. Contrarily, he recalled a time when Rafe's eyes had reflected warmth and friendship when their gazes had met; and then he wondered how they'd come to the ignominious extremity of taking turns threatening to murder each other.

Rafe's thoughts had taken a completely different tack to how not too long ago he'd been regretting how often he'd threatened Charles's life lately and here he was already doing it again. Ashamed, he released his grip on his knife and tried a less violent means of persuasion. "On further consideration the storm or the hungry wild animals will take care of you for me." He walked away, hoping he'd scared Charles enough to make him follow.

Charles glared after Rafe, wondering how he could've ever been as close as a brother to someone like him, who lacked a single redeeming quality; for anyone with decency would never desert a wounded man and leave him to the fate of an oncoming severe storm and wild animals. Then Charles started hearing strange noises all around him. He studied the surrounding forest warily, thinking he saw yellow eyes lurking behind the bushes and tree trunks and expecting a large, wild creature to rush out and attack him at any moment.

An earsplitting clap of thunder rent the air. Charles yelped and sprang to his feet quite agilely for one who claimed to be too exhausted to move. He warily studied the dark clouds closing in swiftly, with flashes of lightning zipping through them like giant fireflies in a mating dance. Then he decided Rafe had been right. It wasn't wise to stay here, not even to make a point. He hastily followed after Rafe. It was easy going at first, for the ground here was flat, but the terrain soon sloped upward in a ridiculously steep incline for a mountain goat, let alone a man. Charles had to stop twice to rest and catch his breath before he finally caught up to Rafe.

He stood as still as a statue, barely even seeming to breathe, so close to the edge of a sheer cliff that the toes of his boots overlapped into nothingness, and stared at the jagged, black rocks twenty-five feet below, and the crashing waves as they hit the rocks then expanded in fans of white foam before they broke apart and the droplets splattered on the rocks or slid back into the ocean to begin their journey anew. He didn't even seem to realize Charles was there.

"Rafe?" Charles asked tentatively.

Rafe looked over his shoulder at Charles. His eyes were no longer dark brown but as black as the deepest recesses of the Earth and they seemed to look through him as if he was transparent. Charles shivered involuntarily. Spooked. "Rafe?" he asked hesitantly.

The darkness in Rafe's eyes slid away as if a curtain had been lifted and they returned to their normal dark brown color. Then he self-consciously stepped away from the cliff. "So here you are. I thought you were too exhausted to move."

"I'm rested now." Charles stood on his toes and stretched out his neck to see over the cliff edge wondering what Rafe had found so interesting down there, but he saw nothing of interest and it gave him the willies looking down from such heights. Even though he was several feet away from the edge, he took a step back. "What were you at?" he asked.

"Sightseeing," Rafe quipped. Then he looked up at the gathering dark clouds. "We should hurry." He started downhill at such a brisk pace that Charles had to push hard to keep up with him.

They hadn't walked more than a mile when they were overtaken by the thunderstorm. Near hurricane-force winds sucked away their breath and made speaking impossible and walking a chore and the wind-driven rain stung their exposed skin like angry bumblebees. Rafe was faring far better than Charles, who was stumbling along in exhaustion. Rafe knew he'd never make it back to camp, so although he could've lasted longer, for Charles's sake he started looking for suitable shelter.

He soon discovered a shadowed, narrow expanse between two looming rocks. A three-foot overhang from one rock that extended nearly across the gap would protect them from most of the rain and blowing debris. He touched Charles's shoulder to gain his attention and then pointed to the shelter rather than speaking in the fierce winds. Charles nodded his understanding, and ran for the shelter. Rafe stayed protectively beside him, making certain he reached the shelter then Charles dropped wearily onto the relatively dry ground underneath the overhang, panting heavily. Rafe chose a spot as far from Charles as possible, sat down wearily then leaned his back against the cool rocks and closed his eyes. He was just drifting off when Charles disturbed his rest. "I'll never see Sarah and Laird again. We're trapped on this God-forsaken island forever, even as you said."

He sounded so hopelessly desolate that Rafe opened his eyes and studied Charles with a critical eye. Purple bruised ringed his neck from Rafe's aborted strangulation attempt. The cut on his head was swollen and crusted with a new scab, and a nearly black bruise had formed around the scab. His eyes were red-rimmed, skin bright red from sunburn, lips chapped, his once pure white silk stockings were gray with filth and had countless runs and holes, and what was left of the rest of his once fine clothing was mud-encrusted and ragged. All in all, Charles looked a miserable mess, and Rafe was stricken with a hefty dose of guilt for being responsible for at least some of it. He tried to assuage his conscience by comforting Charles in his own misguided way. "This place may be God-forsaken, but so am I and I've survived well enough without Him."

Charles's eyes widened. "That's blasphemy! You'll pay for your unbelief!"

Rafe didn't feel it was worthwhile to explain that he did believe, and for that he'd already paid a thousand times over in misery and despair. Charles wouldn't believe him anyway. Rather, he said, "I'm not the one who called this place God-forsaken."

Charles looked abashed. "I'm worn out and frustrated. I didn't mean it, as God well knows."

Rafe combed his thick, wet, tangled hair back from his face then sighed wearily. "We're both exhausted," he conceded. He studied the gray sky outside their shelter with a critical eye. "It doesn't look as if this storm will abate any time soon. We'll rest here for the night and then make our way back to camp in the morning."

"We don't have any food! What will we do for dinner?" Charles cried.

Rafe could've offered to catch a fish, but he was annoyed by Charles's spoiled, rich man focus on filling his belly, so instead he responded sarcastically. "Why don't you pray for manna from the heavens? Since God loves you so much, perhaps he'll come through."

"I've already been praying," Charles said failing to catch the sarcasm. "I don't think manna will fall, but perhaps a small animal will wander into our shelter to escape from the storm, and then you can snag it for us."

"Let me know when that happens," Rafe said contemptuously. He closed his eyes and tried not to dwell upon how miserable his life would be from now on, with guilt and his worst enemy as his only companions. He rested his hand on his knife hilt so Charles couldn't steal it as he slept and gain the upper hand, and soon exhaustion aided his usually long journey into sleep. However, misery and guilt insisted on accompanying him spawning a nightmare of three demons with flaming skull heads forcing him to slaughter Duncan in exchange for Charles's unworthy life. It was similar to the dream he'd had on the trip to Boston, except that this time instead of determinedly sawing off Duncan's head he slit Duncan's throat, as he'd done to Davy. As the warm blood of his dear friend flowed over Rafe's hand, he gasped awake, heart pounding, beads of sweat dampening his forehead. In the dark the misshapen rocks of their shelter looked exactly like the demons in his dream lurking in the shadows waiting to spring upon him and force him to commit a heinous murder. Rafe hastily drew his knife.

Several bolts of lightning at once lit up the sky revealing that the lurking demons were merely rocks. Rafe sheepishly sheathed his knife then glanced at Charles to see if his oppressor had witnessed his childish alarm, but Charles was still sleeping soundly. However, since he was wide-awake now, Rafe decided to take a walk. He silently, fluidly, rose to his feet, stepped gingerly over the sleeping Charles, and slipped out in to the dark and the rain. The heavily clouded sky allowed no starlight or moonlight through, but occasional flashes of lightning to the south as the storm tracked away temporarily lit up the sky. He lost track of time as he watched the storm travel further and further away, captivated by the awful power of God's creation, oblivious of the soaking rain.

"What are you doing out here?" Charles asked.

Rafe started in alarm and then silently chastised himself. This was the second time in less than twenty-four hours that he'd let Charles sneak up on him. He'd have to be more careful or he'd unwittingly grant Charles the upper hand. "Why are you sneaking up on me?" he snapped irritably.

"I thought you said I couldn't sneak up on you," Charles remarked smugly.

Rafe glowered at Charles malignantly, but it was wasted in the dark.

"You didn't answer my question," Charles said.

"I was watching the path of the storm," Rafe said while secretly wondering when the rain had stopped.

"It certainly was an angry one," Charles remarked. "Much like you."

Rafe glowered at him then retreated back inside the shelter and lay down on his back, covering his eyes with his arm. He soon drifted back to sleep, but what seemed like seconds later he was startled awake by Charles's hollering. He drew his knife as he sprang to his feet and raced outside prepared for battle.

The clouds had moved off with the storm and the moon was full allowing Rafe to clearly see the enormous black cougar perched on a boulder directly above Charles's head, yellow eyes glowing demonically. Charles hollered and waved his arms over his head attempting to scare off the creature, which would've worked on any cougar back in the colonies, but this one was unaffected. Then its leg muscles tensed and it screamed as it prepared to pounce on Charles. Rafe hastily stepped in front of him. The weight of the large cat knocked him backward and forced all the air from his lungs. He plunged his knife deeply into the cat's shoulder muscle, but when he tried to pull it out to stab the cat again it wouldn't budge.

The cougar, oblivious to the knife deeply embedded in its shoulder stood on Rafe's chest purring, obviously pleased by its easy victory. Rafe's ire rose. If there was anything he couldn't abide, it was losing, thus proving he was as inferior as everyone said. With a shout of fury he yanked his blade free from the cougar's shoulder and plunged it deep into the creature's neck. The cat howled in pain and anger and then vengefully swiped at Rafe's head with an oversized paw. Still trapped under the animal, the best he could do was to turn his head aside. The swipe missed his cheek by mere millimeters and the cat's long, sharp claws were entangled in the loose strands of his hair. Growling in frustration, the cat yanked its paw free. Rafe was so focused on the battle that he didn't even feel the pain of the significant number of hairs that were then ripped from his head. He grasped his knife hilt, determinedly pulled it from the cat's neck then plunged it into the cat's chest where he supposed its heart beat. He expected that would end the battle, but the stubborn cat didn't die. Rafe began to wonder what it would take to kill this monster.

Something dark and long flew swiftly through the air above him. Rafe couldn't see clearly enough in the blur of movement and the shadows of night to tell if it was the cat's mate or something equally deadly, but whatever it was, he was still pinned under the cat and there was nothing he could do about it anyway. He felt the breeze of the dark object's passing on his cheek, braced for a painful death. There was a loud thwack and the cougar went limp. Rafe shoved the body aside, rolled away then came to a crouch his knife held ready in his bloodied hand ready to press the attack, but no further action was needed for the left side of the cat's skull had been completely caved in. Rafe straightened and stared at the dead cougar in bewilderment. How had that happened?

"Is it dead?" Charles asked warily. He held a thick, heavy tree branch aloft with both hands like a cricket bat. It dripped with the cat's blood.

Rafe nudged the cougar's body with the toe of his boot. Nothing happened. "Yes. Most thoroughly." He smiled and approached Charles with his hand out. "Thank you for your aid."

Charles refused to shake his hand. "I was only keeping you alive so I could see you justly hung once we're rescued." He tossed aside the bloodied branch and walked back into the shelter.

Rafe sighed wearily. Then since he had no desire to subject himself to more of Charles he started searching for a suitable rock with which to scrape the cougar skin clean once he'd skinned the animal. It was difficult with only the light of the moon to see by, but he finally found the perfect flat, sharp, rock for his purpose.

The day dawned hot and muggy as he finished his work, and then it started raining again. Rafe stood up, stretched his aching back, tore a large, wet leaf from a nearby bush, cleaned the cougar blood from his knife, and used another to wipe his hands then glanced longingly at the shelter. He was muscle sore and aching all over from his exertions of the previous twenty-four hours and his eyes were gritty and burned from lack of sleep. Then too his stomach had started grumbling several hours ago and since he wasn't quite savage enough, despite what Charles thought, to eat raw Cougar meat and it would be too dangerous to wade in and scoop up a fish in the rushing, swollen river, which he'd then also have to eat raw, he'd have to hunt in the rain for berries or roots. He debated awaking Charles and making him come along, but then decided against it. The search would be far more pleasant without Charles's dour presence polluting the day.

Rafe grabbed the cougar skin, although it wasn't yet dry, and set off with the wind-driven rain at his back. His buckskins quickly became thoroughly soaked, his hair plastered to his head, the ends constantly dripping, and his boots squished in the mud. In short he was so miserable that he was almost tempted to ask God to give him a break and make it stop raining. However, he was convinced that even if God hadn't already deserted him, he didn't deserve such mercy. So he determinedly slogged.

After several seemingly unending hours of hard searching, Rafe discovered some dark green, oval-shaped, vegetable-like plants growing on vines along the ground. He plucked one, bit into it, and made a face. It was foul, similar to cucumber in both taste and texture. Rafe hated cucumbers, but hunger took precedence over taste. He managed to chew and swallow a single small plant. Then he rested for half an hour, and when he didn't sicken he loaded armloads of the distasteful vegetable into the cougar skin, fur side out, knotted the legs together and slung it over his shoulder then continued his search. The rain lessened in the early afternoon to a barely noticeable fine drizzle, and even the wind abated. With his hunger satiated, Rafe started to feel happy for the first time since he'd killed Duncan; or at least as close as he could come to happiness while laboring under the constant guilt for killing his best friend, and Davy too no matter how much Davy had deserved it. He ambled slowly along in complete freedom, with no one accusing him, or continually urging him to repent.

A roar from behind tore him from his peaceful reverie and then before he could turn around to investigate, something extraordinarily large and heavy smashed into his back. The cougar skin bundle flew from his shoulder and landed on the ground a few feet away with a dull thud. Then a paw the size of the polished tray he'd once used as a mirror before he'd become a murderer, when he was hated merely for being a half-breed, slammed on the back of his head and forced his face into the soft, muddy ground.

Rafe's nose and mouth filled with mud. He struggled mightily to throw off the monster before he suffocated, but his efforts were useless. The creature was too strong and heavy. He felt the monster's hot breath on the back of his neck and then was certain his head was about to become an appetizer, but that was a secondary concern, for he was close to passing out from lack of air and then the monster would be free to chomp him into snack-size bites at its leisure. With a Herculean effort he managed to lift his head high enough to cough and blow out the mud blocking his mouth and nose. The animal growled angrily and pressed his face back down into the mud.

Rafe desperately fumbled for his knife, but then to his surprise and relief the animal abandoned the attack and bounded swiftly away, almost as if it knew his intentions. Rafe flipped onto his back and caught a glimpse of coarse dark brown fur before the animal disappeared in the dense thicket of trees and bushes. He rose fluidly to his feet and disgustedly brushed clods of mud from his clothes, face, and hair. He was puzzled as to why the monster hadn't devoured him when it had the chance, but he was furious with it for making him feel inferior, and for that it would have to pay! He left the bundle of cucumber-like plants where it lay intending to retrieve it later, and with his knife ready in his hand tracked the muddy paw prints of a monstrously large bear. As his anger cooled, he began to doubt that his knife would do the creature any real harm and then reason argued that he should leave well enough alone and be glad he was still alive. However, an obsessive need to prove he was not inferior temporarily overruled his common sense.

At first it was easy tracking the oversized paw prints in the muddy earth and he moved quickly, but when Rafe followed the prints into a densely wooded area with a thick carpet of fallen leaves his pace slowed. The tracks led to a trickling stream and there were no tracks on the opposite side, so Rafe knew the bear had not crossed over, but either walked up or downstream. He puzzled as to which direction the wily creature had gone and then his attention was drawn to something glittering in a bit of sunlight breaking through the clouds just off to his left.

Flint! Rafe scooped up the valuable find, pocketed it then spotted a bush loaded with fat red berries only a few hundred feet distant. At the same time the drizzling rain stopped and the clouds rapidly dissipated, as if God had suddenly shoved them aside. Rafe squinted in the sudden sunlight as he sheathed his knife then started for the clump of bushes. He was halfway there when the leaves and branches rustled and an enormous brown bear emerged. It was facing away from Rafe, feasting on the berries and didn't immediately notice him. Rafe had known the creature that had attacked him was large, but this animal was monstrous, five feet in height on all four paws. Standing on its hind legs it would be twice that height. Rafe recalled the oversized cougar he and Charles had killed last night and wondered if any normal-sized animals inhabited this nightmare island and how they'd come to be here in the first place; but he wisely gave up on the idea of killing the bear armed with only a knife. Instead, he would track the monster to its lair, discover exactly how many of them inhabited the island and how far their territory extended, if it wasn't the entire island, and then avoid them altogether in the future.

The wind shifted and the bear caught Rafe's scent. It turned its head to stare directly into Rafe's rich brown eyes, its yellow-brown eyes seemingly gloating over the mud play earlier. Rafe hastily drew his knife, but instead of loping toward him to attack the bear loped away. Rafe plunged after it, but for such a large animal it moved incredibly fast. He lost sight of it quickly, being significantly slowed by having to force his way through the thick tangle of bushes here, a painful process for one lacking a protective, thick, furry hide. The smaller branches continually scratched his face and arms, and the thicker branches snagged and tore at his buckskins. This torturous progress continued for about a hundred paces, and then the tangle thickened into a nearly solid wall of branches. Rafe stubbornly persisted, hacking away at the barrier with his knife until he suddenly and unexpectedly stumbled into the open facing a narrow tunnel between two towering natural rock walls stretching as far as he could see to the right and the left.

Rafe completely forgot about the bear that was now loping away to his left, as his natural inquisitiveness took over. He had to know what curiosities he might find inside that tunnel. He sheathed his knife, sucked in his chest, and squeezed through the opening. It was a snug fit. If he'd been a heavier man, he wouldn't have made it through. As it was, a hundred feet into the tunnel it narrowed to the point that try as he might, Rafe couldn't squeeze any further forward. He resignedly tried to back up, but to his dismay discovered his efforts had wedged him tight. He was hopelessly stuck. He suffered a nightmare vision of spending the remainder of his life, which was bound to be fairly short now, wedged tightly in between these two rocks unless Charles happened to find him; which was highly unlikely, for not only was Charles lazy but he was no explorer, and he would never even think of entering the dark tunnel. Then Rafe noticed a fist-sized knob of rock barely within his reach. He stretched out his arm, wrapped his strong fingers around it and pulled. He came free with unexpected suddenness and instinctively thrust out his arms to catch himself, but there was nothing directly in front of him except open tunnel and so he ended up stumbling forward a few steps like an inebriated sailor freshly on land.

From that point on Rafe easily followed the significantly wider, twisting tunnel until he emerged into bright daylight. He blinked several times while his vision adjusted and then he stared at the sight before him in awestruck wonder. Directly to his left a wide veil of whitewater plummeted from a height of about forty feet down a moss-covered, naturally tiered, red rock wall. A rainbow arched within its spray, plunging in a roiling mass of white foam into a large pool below that disbursed into a crystal clear, meandering stream teeming with golden fish. Ferns grew thickly along the bank in lush, green grass, and trees with bright green foliage provided ample shelter from the sun's searing rays. Rafe knelt on the stream's bank to cup cold clear water in his hands until his thirst was satiated then sat back on his heels and studied the gently burbling stream.

Now that it had stopped raining, it was a stifling hot and humid day. The water looked so inviting and plainly there were no dangerous water creatures of unusual size inhabiting it. Impulsively, Rafe shed his clothing and boots and dove in. The cool water felt wonderful on his overheated skin although it initially stung his countless fresh cuts and scratches. Rafe grabbed a handful of the sparkling white sand from the pool's bottom and scrubbed the caked mud from his body. Then he retrieved his buckskins scrubbed them clean, and spread them out on the grass beside the riverbank to dry. Chores completed, Rafe swam lazily, sometimes accompanied by random schools of tiny, turquoise fish the size of his pinky, with a few larger, golden fish occasionally swimming by.

He lounged in the water until his stomach grumbled and reminded him he still hadn't eaten. He put his feet down on the river bottom then stood completely still in the waist deep water until one of the large golden fish swam by. He deftly snatched it up and held the wriggling fish in an iron grip until it quit thrashing. His dripping prize was more than large enough for two, but Charles was lazing back at the shelter, so it would be all his. With a grin of satisfaction Rafe waded from the pool with his fish. Then he gathered enough dry grass and twigs to start a fire using his newly acquired flint—far quicker and easier than the previous method of rubbing sticks. After he expertly cleaned the fish, he speared it on a branch then held it over the fire, rotating it every now and then to cook it evenly. When the fish was cooked to his satisfaction, he retreated to the shade of a nearby tree and sat down to eat.

It was the most heavenly delicious fish he'd ever eaten, by far surpassing even the fancy fish dishes he'd been served at Pierre's and Lisbeth's soirees. He devoured his meal like a starving man, which wasn't far from the truth licking every last morsel from his fingers before rinsing his hands in the pool. Then to avoid sunburn he dressed in his by now nearly dry clothing, socks and boots, buckled on his knife sheath, and returned to his shady spot beneath the tree. He lay on his back on the cushiony grass and pillowed his head on his arms and lazily watched clouds peacefully floating across the sky overhead, enjoyed the melodious bird songs drifting down from the trees. It crossed his mind that if it wasn't for having to return to watch over Charles, he could stay here forever, being the perfect home, well hidden from possible interlopers with everything he needed, even shelter, for the tunnel was more than long enough to retreat out of range of driving rain, and wide enough after the narrow pass-through for two or even three men to lie down in comfortably. He stifled a yawn. The stress he'd been under since he'd accidentally killed Duncan, his exertions of last night and this morning followed by the restful swim and then a full stomach had him feeling most lethargic. He drifted to sleep.

When he startled awake, the sun was setting. He was surprised he'd slept at all, and especially for such a long period without a single nightmare, but he cursed his stupidity. That monstrously gigantic bear or any other wild creature on this island plagued with oversized creatures could've killed him as he slept, blissfully unaware. He sprang to his feet and drew his knife in case something was lurking nearby and that was what had awakened him, but long minutes passed and no dangerous animal leapt from cover to attack. He thanked destiny for taking his side, for once, and then although he was reluctant to face Charles's hostility again, he headed out. When he came upon the narrowest part of the tunnel, he stopped and studied it for a long minute, apprehensive about making it through after his overindulgent meal when he'd barely made it through before. Then he spotted a convenient deep depression in the rock on the opposite side, barely within reach. He stretched, grasped the depression, sucked in his broad chest, and with a concerted effort, squeezed through the narrow opening. As he continued on, he made a mental note to widen the tunnel as soon as time allowed, and also to chop back the thicket of bushes to avoid a shredding each time he passed through.

He returned to where held left the cougar skin with the cucumber-like plants still wrapped in it, slung it over his shoulder, and returned to the temporary shelter. Charles waited for him, frowning; anger emanating from every fiber of his being. "Where have you been all day?" he demanded irritably.

"I was—,"

"—looking for some means of escaping and leaving me here to rot?"

Rafe understood that Charles might be upset over seemingly having been abandoned, so he suppressed his irritation. "No. There's a—,"

"—plant you can cook to make alcohol so you may drink away the reality that you're a double murderer?"

Rafe glowered darkly at Charles then untied one end of the cougar skin, and dumped the vegetables on the ground at Charles's feet as he passed him by on his way inside the shelter. He retreated to his far corner and lay down on his back using the bunched up cougar skin as a pillow then stared up at a patch of blue sky on the edge of the rock overhang while entertaining himself with countless imaginative ways to torture Charles to death.

Charles hesitantly approached him when he was in the midst of one of his most gruesome imaginings. He did his best to ignore Charles and continue his creative imaginings, but Charles wouldn't leave, so he broke off his violent inventiveness and sat up. "What?" he demanded crossly.

"I, um—," Charles shifted position self-consciously, cleared his throat, then started over. "I'm grateful for the vegetables. They taste like cucumbers. Not bad. Where did you find them?"

"If you'd come with me instead of sleeping the day away like a lazy good for nothing lord, you wouldn't have to ask," Rafe said unjustly. He lay back down and covered his eyes with his arm, hoping Charles would go away this time. Luckily, after Charles muttered something under his breath that was obviously derogatory, he stalked off.

* * *

Rafe awoke the next morning after another welcome, refreshing sleep. He stood up, stretched his stiff limbs then walked over to where Charles was still sleeping soundly. He knelt, gently grasped Charles's shoulder, and shook him awake. "Charles, wake up. It's time to return to our camp."

Charles groaned. "Now? Why can't we stay here a little longer until I'm more fully rested?"

Rafe scowled. "Don't start that again."

"But this shelter is—,"

"—far less efficient than the wigwam I had to force you to help me build. Come along or I'll leave you behind." Rafe strode briskly out of the shelter.

Charles released a long-suffering sigh then struggled to his feet and followed after Rafe. He stood there yawning and stretching and watched as Rafe piled strips of semi-dried cougar meat and the remaining vegetables into the cougar skin and tied the legs together.

Then he tossed the skin at Charles, who although he hadn't expected it, nevertheless caught the bundle far less clumsily than Rafe thought him capable of. He suppressed the urge to raise an eyebrow in surprise.

Charles scowled. "I'm not carrying this. You're the one sentenced to slavery." He tried to shove the furry bundle back at Rafe.

Rafe stepped back and refused to take it. "I was sentenced to slavery on your plantation and in case you haven't noticed we're not on your plantation. I've done all the rest of the work. It's time you did something." He walked off before Charles had a chance to object further leaving him no choice but to follow grumpily keeping a few steps behind Rafe like a humble servant. Rafe knew perfectly well that Charles's subservience was only meant to make him feel like a tyrant, but he rather enjoyed it nevertheless.

Chapter Twenty-One

Rafe pulled back the door flap of his wigwam. Rain was falling heavily. Again. He hesitated, dreading going out into the downpour when he ached all over. He also had a touch of nausea, and furthermore, it irked him that he always had to be the hunter/gatherer while Charles lay around like the lord of the island. He considered forcing Charles to come along, although he knew it was inevitable that they'd end up arguing; but an extra set of eyes and hands would be helpful, and perhaps if he was lucky the giant bear that had attacked him would attack and kill Charles. Rafe grinned wickedly. That would solve his struggle between his desire and his honor quite handily.

He sighed then resolutely ducked outside and sprinted the twenty feet to Charles's wigwam, but stopped at the door disconcerted when he heard, faintly, what sounded like a kitten mewling. Had another of those monstrous cougars killed Charles then taken over his wigwam with her kittens? He gripped his knife hilt then thrust through the door covering into the wigwam.

"Hey Rafe," Charles acknowledged, sounding almost friendly. He sat cross-legged on the grass sleeping mat that Rafe had woven for him the day after their return from the temporary shelter, cuddling a cougar kitten.

Rafe couldn't believe Charles was so thick as to harbor a cougar kitten! Didn't he know the mother would come looking for it and if the mother was anywhere near the size of the cougar that had attacked them the other night... That kitten had to die. He drew his knife. "Do you realize that's a cougar kitten, Charles?"

"Of course I do. So?" Charles asked.

"You should've never brought it into camp. Now after you've fed and pampered it, even if you release it, it'll keep returning. I'll have to kill it to prevent its mother from tracking it here and then attacking us."

"First of all I didn't bring it here. It came into my wigwam on its own. Secondly, you're not going to kill it. I'm keeping it as my pet," Charles said defiantly.

"Did you not hear what I just said? That kitten must die," Rafe insisted.

"You're only jealous that he came to me instead of you! Even a baby cougar recognizes you as a flawed, soulless creature with a single-minded devotion to killing and unworthy of life!" Charles spat.

Rafe forcefully sheathed his knife and walked out without saying another word, but he the hurt Charles had seen reflected in Rafe's eyes left no doubt that his barbs had hit home. For some reason, that made Charles feet guilty instead of gratified. It was an unwelcome emotion, so he rationalized it away by telling himself that he'd only spoken the truth about Rafe and as a bonus prevented Rafe from killing his new pet. He cuddled the purring kitten to his chest and looked into its golden eyes. "Don't worry little one I won't let the evil, half-breed, demon spawn hurt you." He stroked the little creature's body. It snuggled its head into Charles's neck, purring loudly.

Rafe walked without direction. It didn't matter where he went or that the wind-driven rain stung his skin painfully and the wind pushed and shoved him like a bully. He needed to escape as far as possible from Charles and the painful fact that he was excluded from God's love and forgiveness. Finally, however, after walking for miles in the brutal storm, Rafe's strength failed him. He dropped to his knees on the muddy ground in his now thoroughly soaked buckskins, his exposed skin raw from the unrelenting driving rain, stomach cramping, and aching where he'd never known it was possible to ache. He bowed his head, his sodden, dripping hair falling forward and hiding his face, longing to pray, to beg God to love him, to forgive him, and to grant him peace, yet fearing another painful rejection. He battled with his desire to approach God and his fear of rejection if he dared until exhaustion won out over everything else.

He struggled to his feet and stumbled back to his wigwam like a drunken man, shoved aside the door flap, and stepped inside leaving the flap open since it would take too much effort to close it. Shivering uncontrollably, he practically fell onto his woven grass mat then his stomach cramping fiercely he curled into a tight ball in a useless effort at easing the pain and stared with fever-glazed eyes at the steady stream of rain outside his door. Eventually, he drifted into an uneasy sleep haunted by horrific nightmares, but was all too soon awakened by agonizing pain in his stomach, as if he'd swallowed an entire set of sharp knives. He struggled to his feet as darkness swam in the edges of his vision, stumbled outside, leaned over, and threw up violently then straightened and tore a large, wet leaf from a nearby bush to clean his mouth. He tossed the leaf on the vomit, kicked mud over the whole mess, and started to go back inside his wigwam, but then his fevered eyes focused on Charles's wigwam, and he was reminded that he still needed to kill the cougar kitten. Despite the knives in his stomach, nausea, and that he was visibly trembling with fever and every muscle in his body ached Rafe knew he couldn't risk delaying the necessary, but sure to be distasteful task of killing the kitten until he felt better. Judging from the intensity of his symptoms, healing could be days away. By then the mother cougar would surely have tracked its kitten here. He reached for his knife, but the sheath was empty, for which there was only one explanation! Charles had stolen the knife as he'd slept the deep sleep his illness had forced upon him!

He stormed at Charles's wigwam, but a wave of severe dizziness halted him after only a few steps. He braced his left arm, palm flat, on a nearby tree and lowered his head to wait out the dizziness, but after long moments when it failed to subside, he gave up and continued his unsteady way toward Charles's wigwam.

He firmly tossed back the door flap and stepped inside. Charles lay on his back on the woven grass mat apparently asleep, with the kitten resting at his feet and the stolen knife resting on his chest. Rafe nearly snorted at how stupidly easy Charles had made it for him to recover his knife. He approached stealthily then because he was unstable on his feet knelt on one knee and reached out to snatch away the knife. Charles's eyes snapped open. He grabbed Rafe's wrist with one hand, snatched up the knife with the other, while the kitten slept on, undisturbed.

Charles pressed the point of the knife to Rafe's chest. "How does it feel to be on the receiving end of the weapon?" he snarled. "Not at all pleasant is it!" Rafe tried to pull free, but his illness had weakened him and he couldn't break Charles's seemingly iron grip. He then tried to snatch the knife with his free hand, but his reflexes had also been affected by his illness. Charles easily kept the blade out of his reach. He laughed victoriously. "Should I kill you now, Rafe, as you've tried to do to me so many times?"

Rafe was now sincerely regretting his impulsive decision not to wait until he was recovered from his illness to kill the kitten, for the only thing he'd accomplished was granting Charles the upper hand. "Try it," he challenged with bravado, although he knew he couldn't win out against Charles in his current condition.

Charles rose to the challenge. He pulled his arm back in preparation for striking Rafe in his black half-breed heart. Then a bright flash of lightening accompanied by a deafening clap of thunder startled Charles's pet awake. With an ear-piercing scream the kitten jumped straight up in the air and came back down on Charles's chest, firmly imbedding its sharp claws through his shredded shirt and into his skin. Charles howled in pain and simultaneously sat up, released his grip on Rafe's wrist, and dropped the knife so he could grab the kitten with both hands to pull it off. He carefully and painfully removed the needle-sharp claws from his chest one by one then put the kitten gently on the ground beside him—and realized he no longer had the knife. He glanced fearfully at Rafe, who'd taken advantage of Charles's distraction and scooped up the knife. He gripped it tightly in his left hand, his body trembling in what Charles interpreted as intense fury over his attempted murder. "Rafe?" he asked warily while rubbing his stinging chest.

Rafe tightened his grip on his knife, but not because he was preparing to use it, as Charles assumed. Another severe wave of dizziness and nausea had assaulted him and he feared that in his trembling and weakness he'd drop the knife and Charles would snatch it back. "This is my knife, Charles. I paid a high price for it. Don't steal it again or when I take it back again I'll sheath it in you." He firmly sheathed his knife for emphasis, swept out of the wigwam, closing the door flap behind him, and nearly fainted. He paused for a moment, supporting himself with one hand on the wigwam's framework, until the darkness at the edges of his vision receded then reeled on. Halfway to his wigwam he was assaulted by another severe wave of dizziness accompanied by nausea. He dropped onto his hands and knees and lowered his head, retching, stars shimmering in the edges of the blackness lurking at the edge of his vision.

With an effort, he managed to stop the useless retching. He slowly, unsteadily stood up and weaved his dizzy way to his wigwam, where he collapsed in a heap on his mat bordering on unconscious, but with his left hand firmly gripping the hilt of his knife, nevertheless. Charles would *not* steal it again!

Chapter Twenty-Two

Rafe battled his illness for three days, but by the fourth day he was well enough to leave his wigwam, although his head still ached and his stomach still felt like he'd swallowed knives just not as many of them. He retrieved his knife from the shallow hole near the west edge of his wigwam where he'd buried it on the second day of his illness, cleaned it, sheathed it, and walked outside into the stifling heat and humidity. Charles sat cross-legged on the ground near the river dangling a piece of shredded cloth in front of the kitten when then batted at it playfully. "Finished with your drunken binge or were you forced to quit having consumed all the alcohol?"

"I was ill," Rafe said curtly.

Charles snorted. "Of course you were." He picked up the kitten and held it in his lap. Rafe watched as it shoved its already large head under Charles's hand thinking how large and dangerous it would grow to be, and then about how large and dangerous its mother must already be. His hand strayed toward his knife hilt. "Did that kitten really wander into your wigwam or did you take it from its den?"

"Adam wandered into my wigwam during the storm even as I said. I don't lie about everything like you do," Charles said indignantly.

"Adam," Rafe said.

"That's what I've named him. God sent Adam to assuage my loneliness." He set Adam gently on the ground. It scampered up to Rafe and bounded around his feet.

Rafe hastily danced away from it. He didn't want its scent on him. "Get it away from me or I'll kill it now," he threatened, gripping his knife hilt.

Charles patted his chest. "Adam to me." The kitten obediently returned to Charles. He slid his hand under its belly and scooped it up.

Rafe released his grip on his knife and relaxed. "Is there anything to eat or did you and that animal selfishly eat it all up while I was sick?"

"Don't you mean while you were drunk?" Charles asked snidely.

"Sick," Rafe reiterated firmly.

"Lie if you must to protect your pride, Rafe, but you needn't fear for food. I'm not as selfish as you. I saved some of those cucumber-like vegetables you brought in before your drunken binge and I also found some tasty fruit yesterday. I think they're peaches, although I've never seen any without a fuzzy skin. Anyway, they otherwise look like peaches and they taste like peaches, so that's what I've decided to call them. They're in my wigwam piled in the north corner. You may help yourself to them."

Rafe looked toward Charles's wigwam some hundred feet distant. For the last three days he'd eaten nothing, and he'd had only slightly more than nothing to drink. In his weakened condition it seemed an eternally long walk to Charles's wigwam. He couldn't ask Charles to fetch the food, though, and thus reveal his continuing weakness, which Charles might then exploit. He took two steps toward the wigwam, but then was overcome by a strong wave of dizziness; only this was different than the dizziness of his illness, for it was caused by his three-day, illness-enforced fast. He sat down clumsily, and overbalanced then thrust out his left hand, fingers splayed behind him to keep from toppling backward.

"Still drunk I see," Charles said. "Vile half-breed."

Rafe chose to ignore Charles. He determinedly struggled to his feet then walked slightly more steadily than before to Charles's wigwam. The thin-skinned, smooth, yellow-red fruits about the size of a man's fist were mixed in with the foul-tasting cucumber-like plants. Since he was still slightly queasy, Rafe thrust aside the vegetables that he'd had trouble stomaching even before he was ill and picked out two of the fruits. One in each hand he sat down cross-legged on Charles's grass mat then bit into the fruit in his left hand. The skin was tart, meat sweet and juicy. It was absolutely the most delicious fruit Rafe had ever tasted. He devoured the fruit, tossed aside the pit then feeling stronger now that he'd had something to eat, he exited Charles's wigwam. As he walked, he switched the second fruit to his left hand and took a large bite. Juice ran down his chin. He wiped his chin with the back of his right hand as he approached Charles. "These are delicious. Where did you find them?"

"Adam and I took a long walk yesterday and found a tree loaded with them. It was a miracle," Charles said.

Rafe knew it couldn't be a miracle, for he was rejected by God, and since Charles was with him, that rejection of necessity must include Charles, for otherwise, God would be indirectly providing for him. Rafe hastily swallowed his half-chewed bite of fruit to argue, "It was luck."

"It was a miracle, but have it your way," Charles said.

Rafe grinned. "I always do." He leaned idly against a nearby tree and continued munching his fruit.

Charles cleared his throat. "So, uh, I've been thinking. We're the only people on this island—,"

"So we are, but how long did it take what's left of your tiny brain to figure that one out?" Rafe took another bite of his fruit, not quite smirking, but looking extraordinarily pleased with himself nevertheless.

Charles frowned, but surprisingly chose not to reply to Rafe's snide barb. "As I was saying, since we're the only two on this island, it would be wise to combine forces and work together instead of against each other."

"Indeed, but you and I are incapable of working together as long as you refuse to acknowledge me as anything but a murderer and a slave." Rafe polished off the last bite of fruit, tossed away the pit, and then feeling closer to his normal self, decided to visit the beautiful sanctuary he'd privately labeled Nirvana and have a long, lazy soak in the pool. Perhaps he'd even catch and cook a fish. "Thanks for the fruit." He walked off.

Charles sprang to his feet and accompanied him uninvited, which annoyed Rafe since now he couldn't go to Nirvana unless he wanted to reveal the sanctuary to Charles; which he didn't. "Listen Rafe, I'm weary of the constant arguing, and I'm betting you are too. It's time we set aside our differences. I'm willing if you are," Charles said.

Rafe came to a sudden standstill, taken aback by the offer, but pleased too. "It has ever been my desire to renew our friendship."

Charles's eyes widened and he took a hasty step back and raised his hands palms out, as if warding off evil. "I wasn't suggesting friendship! Certainly not! I don't even think that's possible after all the grief you've caused me. I was merely suggesting we strive to work together for the sake of survival."

Rafe was hurt as much by Charles's swift rejection of his offer to renew their friendship as embarrassed that he'd revealed his longtime desire to renew said friendship to one who'd instantly spurned him. He glowered at Charles then walked briskly away, but

Charles caught up with him once again. "You do agree we could both benefit greatly if we work together, don't you?"

"Yes," Rafe said tersely.

"Then don't you think we should sit down and discuss the division of labor?"

"We have the rest of our lives to discuss the division of labor. At the moment, I wish to be alone." Rafe quickened his pace, but he was still weak from his illness and so Charles easily kept up with him. It was quite aggravating.

"I don't think it's wise for you to go off alone, as it's readily apparent you're still weak from your—uh—illness. I shall come along to help should it become necessary," Charles insisted.

"Help yourself to my knife again, you mean," Rafe accused resentfully.

"I only took the knife so you wouldn't kill me in your drunken craze like you tried to do once before when you did kill Duncan, that's all. It was a matter of self-defense," Charles rationalized.

Adam scampered up and playfully pawed at Rafe's leg. He hastily sidestepped away from the animal. Charles snorted. "For someone so strong and skilled, you certainly are unduly afraid of a little, harmless, animal."

"That's because, Charles, as I've already told you several times, I have no wish to be tracked down by an oversized, angry mother cougar. So send your pet away or I'll kill it."

Charles hesitated while taking into consideration Rafe's current condition. Rafe was obviously weaker than normal and so he should be able to prevent Rafe from killing Adam, but then Rafe was amazingly capable like when he'd dragged those sails up onto the beach by himself after spending days adrift, and he'd been half-starved besides. Charles made his decision. "Adam, off to bed."

Much to Rafe's surprise, the kitten dashed off to Charles's wigwam. Charles beamed proudly. "Amazing isn't it? I've been training him. He's quite intelligent." Rafe refrained from commenting that Charles and the kitten probably had the same level of intelligence or lack of it; although it was difficult keeping such a fine retort to himself.

"Where are we headed?" Charles asked.

"*We* are headed nowhere."

Charles sank into a wounded sulk. He was doing his utmost to be companionable, but Rafe wasn't cooperating! He was tempted to return to camp and leave Rafe to stumble around in his drunkenness and possibly break an arm or a leg, or even to walk off that cliff he'd contemplated several months back, but then he decided to be the better man and ignore Rafe's dour attitude.

He soon discovered Rafe had been quite serious when he'd said they were headed nowhere. They wandered in circles for hours. As the sun reached its zenith, Charles could no longer contain his irritation. He knew Rafe had been headed somewhere with a purpose and had changed his mind only when he'd insisted on accompanying him. He'd hoped Rafe would eventually give in and guide him to his intended destination, but dark clouds were forming overhead. Another nasty storm was on its way. Charles had no wish to be caught out in it and was about to give up on finding out where Rafe had been headed and return to camp alone, when Rafe suddenly switched direction back toward camp having noticed the approaching storm as well.

They were still several miles away from camp when the storm caught them. It started with a few small raindrops, followed by a strong down-gust that pushed them forward a stumbling step, as if they'd been shoved by a giant hand. Then the heavens opened and drenched them with rain and the wind picked up, blowing with ferociousness akin to a hurricane and stealing their breath. The air vibrated with ear-splitting thunder as lightning bolts sizzled so close to them that their skin tingled and they could smell the ozone. Wind-driven rain stung their exposed skin, wet leaves stuck to their clothing and hair, and small branches torn from trees and bushes cut and bruised them. Charles began to fear that the trees themselves would go airborne, and indeed seconds later a tree directly in front of him ripped from the ground with a loud crack, roots and all. It crashed onto another far larger tree that then split in two with the first tree lodging between the two halves. "We must find shelter!" Charles shouted above the wind, although his sole concern was that the next tree would flatten him, not that Rafe might be harmed in any way.

Rafe's concern was for Charles as well. His dark eyes anxiously scanned the landscape, but he saw nothing large enough to shelter two grown men. He noticed that Charles was fervently praying under his breath and wanted to pray too; except that he was convinced it would be useless. Charles's prayer would have to suffice; and apparently they did, for seconds later the wind abated and the rain lightened. Rafe should've been grateful, but instead he envied Charles's ability to so easily gain God's assistance, and he was irritated too that Charles, of all people, owned what he so badly craved but could never have.

Half an hour later, Rafe and Charles ducked inside their respective wigwams.

The storm raged until nightfall when Rafe emerged from his wigwam to grab some of the tasty, yellow fruits from Charles's wigwam for his dinner. Charles sat cross-legged on his mat, holding Adam in his lap and petting him while the kitten purred loudly. When Rafe came in, however, the animal stopped purring and growled as if it knew he wanted to kill it. Charles mirrored the kitten's unwelcome attitude. "Leave my wigwam, Rafe. You are not welcome here," he spat hostilely.

"I shall accommodate your rude demand immediately after I gather some of those fruits for my dinner." Rafe started for the pile of fruit.

Charles hastily set the kitten down and stood up blocking Rafe's path. "These peaches are mine. I found them. I picked them. Go out and pick your own."

"You shared them with me this morning," Rafe argued.

"That was before you made me walk around for hours going nowhere!" Charles spat resentfully. "You'll have to find your own fruit from now on. I won't be sharing mine with you anymore."

Rafe sighed in exasperation. "Were you not the one who said we should try to cooperate?"

"Indeed I was, but I know you were headed somewhere specific today until you realized I would accompany you there. You're hiding something from me—undoubtedly something wonderful—and that breaks our truce. Leave my wigwam. I repeat, you're not welcome here."

Rafe wasn't leaving without what he'd come for. He agilely dodged around Charles and scooped up several fruits then grinned victoriously and showed them to Charles. "Looks as if I found some fruit."

Charles took a threatening step. "Put down my peaches, you thieving half-breed!"

Rafe drew his razor sharp knife and quickly and neatly sliced a four foot slit in the sailcloth wall then dived through the slit head first, rolling as he hit the ground, and deftly coming to his feet. Charles stepped through the slit in pursuit, but his trailing foot caught on the bottom edge and he fell on his face. As Charles roared with fury, Rafe sprinted away in the darkness, grinning over his successful raid.

From that point on, Charles refused to speak civilly to Rafe. He responded by retreating to Nirvana as often as possible. Once after a particularly violent argument, Rafe spent an entire week in Nirvana, sleeping out under the stars during an abnormally dry spell. He returned at the end of the week feeling more relaxed than in months, and what was even better, Charles and Adam were nowhere in sight. He slipped into Charles's wigwam to pilfer more fruits, merely to annoy Charles, for he'd found the tree soon after their argument.

Adam lounged on the mat. It stared at Rafe with its golden eyes, unblinking, seemingly gloating over his failure to kill it. Rafe drew his knife, pounced, and slit its throat. Then Charles stepped into the wigwam. He'd grown ravenously hungry for meat over the course of Rafe's weeklong absence, for none of his snares ever caught anything, and so he'd gone out searching for Rafe intent on making the half-breed treat him with the respect due a master by his slave and catch him a rabbit or two for dinner. When he saw the bloodied knife in Rafe's hand his eyes widened then they flicked to Adam's bloodied, limp body. "Adam!" He roughly shouldered Rafe aside, knelt and tenderly picked up his dead pet. He held the kitten to his chest as if it was an infant child and demanded of Rafe, "How could you! He was only a baby!"

Feeling as guilty as if the kitten had been a child instead of an animal, Rafe hid his bloodied blade behind his thigh. "I warned you more than once that it had to die. If you didn't wish for me to follow through, you should've tracked down and killed the mother."

Charles gently set Adam's limp body on the blood-stained mat then sprang to his feet. "You wicked, despicable, spawn of the devil! Epitome of evil! Curse of the world! Why didn't *you* track down the mother instead of killing the kitten? With your superior skills you could've done it far more easily than I; but you didn't because you couldn't stand it that Adam was offering me comfort! You wanted me to suffer! You blame me for the mess you've made of your life!" He advanced on Rafe menacingly, his hands clenching and unclenching at his sides as if he wished to strangle Rafe.

Rafe raised his bloodied knife defensively. "Back off, or you're next."

Charles blanched at Adam's blood on the knife then halted his offense and his sky-blue eyes filled with tears of grief and loss. "Adam was only a kitten. A baby." He knelt, picked up Adam's lifeless body and cradled it to his breast, weeping softly.

Rafe ran his right hand across his face then tried to rationalize away his growing guilt by telling himself that it hadn't been wrong to kill Adam, for it was only an animal; not like it had been wrong to kill Duncan and Charles. But then why did he feel like such a monster? When had he become the killer of defenseless baby animals instead of their protector? Why hadn't he tracked down and killed the mother instead of going after the kitten? "Charles, I'm—" he began to apologize.

"Get out!" Charles shouted hoarsely and pointed to the door. "Leave my wigwam, baby murderer!"

Rafe paled then sheathed his bloodied knife and ducked out of the wigwam. Charles's anguished cries, a grief-stricken accusation, followed him, intensifying his guilt. Rafe ran to escape from the guilt, but it no more worked than running from the reality of God's rejection. The knowledge that he'd committed a heinous crime stubbornly accompanied him every step of the way. At last realizing the futility of running, Rafe stopped. He leaned over at the waist gasping for breath. His buckskin shirt, sopping with sweat, stuck to his back. He irritably yanked the shirt over his head and tossed it on the ground at his feet. Thunder rolled in the distance. Rafe tentatively studied the gray, cloudy sky, almost expecting to see the face of God staring down on him in cold, silent, disapproval. A cold, fat raindrop splattered on his forearm, another splashed on the back of his hand, and one hit him in the eye forcing him to blink involuntarily. He cursed. He'd have to return and face Charles unless he wished to be caught out in another bad storm. He snatched up his soggy shirt, draped it over his shoulder, and headed back to camp at a brisk pace, arriving only a few minutes ahead of the storm.

Charles was just now carrying Adam's body out of his wigwam wrapped in a piece of leftover sailcloth. Rafe tentatively approached and cleared his throat intending to offer the apology Charles had spurned earlier. "Charles, I only acted in our best interests when I killed your pet, but apparently it has caused you grief. I never intended that." Even as he said it, he realized it didn't sound apologetic at all; which most likely contributed greatly to Charles purposely ignoring him. He knelt, set Adam's lifeless body on the ground, and started digging a hole in the muddy ground with his bare hands. Thinking perhaps if he helped bury Adam it might atone somewhat for killing it, Rafe tossed his shirt on the ground, knelt beside Charles and drew his still un-cleaned knife to help Charles dig.

Charles's eyes widened at the sight of the dried blood of his pet and then he went ballistic with insane fury. "Go away baby murderer!"

He shoved Rafe with such anger-fueled strength that Rafe fell backward and nearly lost his grip on his knife. He sprang agilely to his feet then forcefully sheathed his knife. "I am no baby murderer, Charles," he said vehemently then walked briskly away headed for Nirvana, forgetting to take his shirt.

The storm caught him well before he made it to Nirvana, a drenching downpour with the inevitable stiff wind and blowing debris. Rafe ducked under a close narrow rock overhang, and plastered his half-naked body against the rough rock wall behind him. The slight overhang offered only partial shelter from the flying debris, none from the wind-driven rain. As he was pummeled by flying debris, it occurred to him that God was punishing him for upsetting His favored Charles by killing Adam; and his heart filled with anger and resentment. He balled his hands into defiant fists and shouted to the sky, "Why do you love Charles and not me? I have noble, white blood too! I demand you love me as I deserve! Do you hear me, God? I demand that you love me!"

His answer came immediately in a bright flash of lightening that nearly blinded him, accompanied by deafening thunder and even heavier rain, as if God was furious that a despicable child of rape, and a half-breed besides had the audacity to demand to be loved by Him! Rafe sank to his knees, bowed his head, and wept in grief-stricken despair, oblivious to the flying debris that tore and bruised his bare skin.

* * *

Charles had just finished burying Adam when a blinding bolt of lightning seared the sky. It was followed almost immediately by an earsplitting clap of thunder then a downpour of heavy rain. Charles retreated to his wigwam, flipped over his blood-stained mat so he wouldn't have to see Adam's lifeblood on it, and sat down staring gloomily at the slit in the sailcloth where Rafe had escaped after stealing from him. He clenched both fists in anger and shook them in the direction Rafe had run. For the sake of survival he'd done his best to work alongside Rafe despite the abominable half-breed's uncooperative attitude and his drunkenness and his blatantly evil nature; but no longer. He hoped Rafe died out there in the storm!

Charles was to be disappointed, however, for Rafe survived the storm, although not without injury. He returned to camp early the next morning, scooped up his buckskin shirt and put it on, before he joined Charles sitting glumly on a downed log staring off into nowhere, and tried once again to make amends; only this time he approached it far more humbly. "Charles." He hesitated to gather his courage and then plunged on. "About the kitten—Adam—your pet. I know he meant a great deal to you, and it was unnecessary, and—and wrong to take its life. As you said, I should've tracked down the mother and killed it instead. I'm sorry I caused you pain."

It was a difficult apology, but Charles didn't even acknowledge it. Rafe was a bit peeved. He felt he deserved at least some small acknowledgement of his effort, a snort of disdain if nothing else. "Have you nothing at all to say to me, Charles?"

"I don't consort with murderers!" Charles stood up to walk away.

Rafe sprang to his feet, furious, and grabbed Charles's ragged shirt sleeve, which was so rotten that it then tore off, but stopped Charles nevertheless, to glare at Rafe for ruining his clothing. Rafe tossed the remains of the sleeve on the ground. "Stop calling me a murderer! I've never murdered anyone!"

"Duncan and Davy weren't murdered by you then?" Charles asked.

Rafe shifted position uneasily as his anger was replaced by guilt. "I've told you over and over that Duncan was an accident; and Davy tried to kill you, and me. His death was justifiable as self-defense."

"It was murder, and there's no justification for murder. I suppose I shouldn't be surprised that you claim it otherwise, however. You never could accept responsibility for your actions," Charles said.

"I always take responsibility for my actions," Rafe countered defensively. He pushed up the sleeves of his buckskin shirt, too warm in the hot and humid day.

Charles noted the fresh cuts and bruises. "You earn those in the storm last night?"

Rafe self-consciously pulled his sleeves back down. "Yes. The shelter I found was inadequate at its best."

"So you were as much as stoned. How appropriate," Charles said.

Rafe's dark eyes reflected his wounded offense. He retreated to his wigwam neglecting to lower the door covering then sat on his mat cross-legged. Rain started falling again. The tempo of the heavy drops hitting the sailcloth sounded like, mur-der-er, mur-der- er, mur-der-er. Rafe covered his ears with his hands, but although that blocked the sound of the rain, he could still hear the words echoing in his soul. It was too much to bear. Enough! He would end his life and along with it the unending guilt and the constant pain of rejection and the unceasing nightmares and the abject misery. He drew his knife with a trembling hand, closed his eyes and pressed the tip of the blade to his chest where his agonized heart beat and pushed, piercing his shirt then his skin, bloodying his knife tip.

Then it occurred to him that when he took his life he'd be abandoning Charles to a slow, lingering death, for Charles's skills were inadequate for the mean survival this island required. He tried to reason that God would take care of Charles, only to be strongly convicted that *he* was how God meant to take care of Charles. Why else had he alone of all on board the Lady Bountiful survived the shipwreck; the only one with brotherly ties to Charles as well as the skills to survive in the wilderness? It wasn't what he wanted, but his nature was such that he had no choice but to put others, including Charles, above himself and his needs. He cursed in Mohican as with the force of enraged frustration he stabbed the knife into the ground in front of him imbedding it to the hilt. Then he bowed his head, long hair cascading down on either side like a shiny, black, silky curtain, hiding his face, and sobbed in grief stricken despair.

Chapter Twenty-Three

It was a rare day without either blustery winds or pouring rain, and so it would've been pleasant, except for the ever present stifling heat and humidity. Rafe leaned casually against a tree trunk and bit into the fuzz-less peach he'd pilfered from Charles's wigwam. As he chewed, he casually studied the campsite, and then his eyes landed on Adam's grave. Guilt ruined his appetite. He tossed the half eaten fruit into a clump of bushes.

Several months had passed since he'd killed Adam, but Charles's attitude had made it seem more like several years. Charles refused to speak to him and was taking great lengths to avoid him altogether. Rafe was convinced they were destined to spend the rest of their lives on this island in mutual isolation. But there was a silver lining in that, for it spared him the guilt-inflicting accusation in Charles's eyes. He felt guilty enough already; especially since he'd realized that the reason the mother cougar had never come looking for her kitten was most likely because it had been the oversized cougar he and Charles had killed that stormy night. Left alone the kitten had eventually found its way to Charles, which meant he'd killed Adam needlessly. Why hadn't that possibility occurred to him before he'd killed the kitten? Or had his motive truly been jealousy as Charles had claimed?

Rafe was so tangled up in his guilt-inflicting thoughts that Charles's sudden, unexpected appearance made him start in surprise, but he recovered quickly. "Good Morning, Charles," he said guiltily, although he fully expected Charles to ignore him, which Charles did. He trudged straight to Adam's grave without even acknowledging Rafe's presence then stood over the tiny mound of dirt for quite some time in prayer. Afterward however, to Rafe's surprise, Charles approached him, cleared his throat, and said, "I don't know if it's even possible to forgive you for killing Adam, or for all the other grief you've caused me, but by my reckoning today's Easter. In the spirit of this Holy day, I'm willing to let bygones be bygones and resume our relations as they were before you mur—," He hastily checked himself. "…before Adam's death."

Rafe hadn't missed what Charles had nearly said, though. "You wish to resume calling me a murderer on a daily basis?" he asked resentfully.

Charles's vinegary attitude toward Rafe had become so thoroughly ingrained in his character that he automatically responded hostilely. "You are a murderer, and worse! I don't know how you're even able to sleep!"

"I don't sleep, or at least not well. Frequent nightmares don't make for peaceful rest," Rafe confessed.

Charles considered this admission with a large measure of skepticism. "If that's even true, then it's your own fault."

"Entirely," Rafe said.

Charles was left completely at a loss, for Rafe had left him no room for derogatory comments and he had nothing else to accuse him of doing. He rubbed the still semi-healed wound on his forehead that was always itching, gave up on harassing Rafe, and returned to his original subject. "So shall we celebrate Easter together?"

Rafe shook his head. "I've no desire to celebrate a holiday honoring a God who has most thoroughly rejected me."

Charles was also thoroughly convinced that Rafe was rejected by God, and that was a problem, for he couldn't argue against it, and he was desperate for companionship. "Oh. Yes. Well— hm…"

"I'd be willing to agree to a truce, however," Rafe offered tentatively, expecting rejection.

Charles brightened. "Done."

Rafe smiled, relieved. For once he hadn't been rejected.

"So how have you been occupying yourself?" Charles asked. "I think a great deal on the people and places we've left behind."

Rafe studiously avoided thinking about such things. It inevitably led to guilt and remorse, which in turn triggered hopelessness and despair, which led to a desire to self-destruct that his God-appointed task of protecting Charles wouldn't permit. It was far too frustrating. "I go exploring," he said.

"Have you discovered any places of note?" Charles asked hoping Rafe would finally reveal the secret place he was sure Rafe was keeping from him.

Rafe hesitated, but he'd unfairly kept Nirvana to himself for far too long. "There is one place in particular I like to visit when I'm in need of respite from the stress of life on this island."

"Perhaps you could show me this place someday?" Charles asked hopefully.

Now that he was at the point of surrendering his only means of escaping from Charles's harsh attitude, Rafe found he didn't wish to do it, but then if God had meant for him to look after Charles's welfare, didn't that include allowing Charles some much needed respite as well? "I'll show it to you now, if you'd like."

Charles couldn't repress his grin of victory. "I would." Rafe nodded then started off at a pace that was easy for Charles to maintain. "How far away is this place?" Charles asked.

Rafe gestured to a sharply pointed hill in the distance. "It's a mile or so over that hill." He then deliberately increased his pace so that the effort of keeping up would prevent Charles from asking any more questions. It worked well. Charles huffed and puffed maintaining Rafe's brutal pace and silence reigned. They pushed through the once thick brush Rafe had laboriously cleared with his bare hands, squeezed through the still narrow rock tunnel he'd arduously chipped wider with a sharpened rock, unwilling to risk ruining his precious knife on such a job then finally emerged from the tunnel into Nirvana.

Charles came to an awed standstill and then he grew furious that Rafe had kept this paradise secret from him all these months. "So this is where you've crept off to so often!" he accused.

"Yes, and I admit it was wrong to keep it from you. I should've told you of Nirvana as soon as I discovered it. I'm sorry," Rafe said.

"You should be sorry, you selfish demon spawn!" Charles shot back.

Rafe was determined not to be the one who broke the truce he had suggested, so he let the scathing comment pass. Charles was tempted to resume his practiced silence, but after a short but tense moment curiosity had the better of him and he sullenly gave in to it. "So why do you call this place Nirvana?"

Rafe's chosen name for his secret place sounded ridiculous when Charles said it out loud, and he felt his face grow hot with embarrassment. He looked away, as if he was merely surveying his surroundings and covered up his embarrassment with a casual shrug. "It feels like paradise compared to the rest of this cursed island."

"It's certainly as close to Paradise as you'll ever come," Charles remarked.

Rafe stiffened, but Charles didn't even notice, for he was watching a school of tiny turquoise fish about the size of his pinky fingernail swim by in the pool's clear depths. As a large golden fish swam by, Charles looked up excitedly. "Did you see that huge golden fish?"

"Yes. These waters are teeming with them," Rafe said tersely, still smarting over the paradise remark.

"Have you ever caught one?"

"Many," Rafe said.

"Then you shall catch one for our lunch today." Charles made it a command, as if he was speaking to one of his house servants or plantation slaves, but in the spirit of the truce Rafe once again ignored the affront. "Where do you keep your fishing pole?" Charles asked.

"I don't need one." Rafe kicked off his boots, rolled up his pant legs, and waded into the pool. He stood as still as a stone while Charles watched curiously from the bank. When one of the large golden fish swam by, Rafe scooped it up and brought it to Charles still wriggling.

"Would you look at the size of that fish!" Charles exclaimed. "Hurry and prepare it. I'm hungry after that long walk here. I'll gather the tinder for the fire."

Rafe nodded then squatted, laid the fish on the grass, and drew his knife to clean it, while Charles set to work collecting dry grass and wood and arranging it within a circle of rocks that had obviously been used for a fire before. Then he pulled his rubbing sticks from his pocket and set to work. Rafe set down his knife and wiped his hands on the grass then pulled the flint from his pants pocket and held it out in his open palm. "Here. Use this."

Charles's eyes narrowed. "How long have you had flint?"

Realizing his error, Rafe guiltily closed his hand over the flint that he'd never used around Charles, deliberately keeping it secret from him, and lowered his arm to his side. "You deliberately hid the flint form me, you selfish spawn of the devil!" Charles spat. "Perhaps *you* should start the fire with your prized flint, which is too good to share with your suffering companion! I'm sure you'd be much better at it than I, having had ample opportunities to practice!"

Muscles in Rafe's jaw visibly tightened as he clenched his jaw in anger. He picked up his knife. Charles's eyes widened thinking Rafe intended to use the knife on him, but Rafe only rinsed the blade in the water then wiped it dry on his shirt, walked to the circle of rocks, knelt, and struck the flint to the blade over the collected tinder.

Sparks flew, setting the tinder to flame. As Charles smoldered in his anger and the fire smoldered in the tinder, Rafe sheathed his knife and slowly added wood to the fire as each preceding piece took flame.

"I see you're as good at making flames as any demon spawn," Charles said.

Rafe angrily tossed the remaining pieces of wood on the fire and stood up, his dark eyes flashing with barely restrained fury. "I've shown you my secret place, admitted my faults, and apologized more than once. What more do you want from me, Charles!"

"I want you to show some consideration for someone other than yourself for once in your despicably self-centered life!" Charles said.

Rafe clenched his hands into tight, white-knuckled fists at his sides. It was either that, or strangling Charles. "Apparently, all the sailcloth I hauled up on the beach by myself for *your* wigwam, the mat I wove for *your* gentle repose, the bowls I carved for *your* use, the berries I picked, and the many snares I've laid are not considerate enough for you. Here then, allow me to make amends by cooking the fish *I* caught and cleaned for you here in *my* private paradise, which I sacrificed to *your* ungrateful self in the spirit of the truce that *you've* broken in less than a day!" Rafe scooped up the fish, spitefully tossed it into the flames then stomped away muttering highly uncomplimentary comments about Charles under his breath first in Mohican, then English, and then French, as Charles frantically looked for a sharp stick with which to spear the fish and rescue it from the fire.

Rafe returned to his wigwam and spent the remainder of the day working out his frustration and anger by carving three-dimensional scenes from his childhood home in the woods in randomly selected pieces of bark. Shortly after sunset Charles burst into his wigwam. "Rafe! Rafe!" he panted breathlessly.

Rafe sprang to his feet, heart pounding in alarm, knife gripped tightly, prepared to battle another large cougar or possibly the monstrous bear. "There are six canoes on the beach! Someone has come! We're rescued at last!" Charles exclaimed excitedly.

Rafe's heartbeat slowed to normal. Although there was still a danger, it wasn't immediate; but people arriving in canoes had to be local natives, and the possibility that they were friendly was remote. "Not necessarily. They may be unfriendly natives," he cautioned.

Charles's excitement dimmed and then it dawned on him why Rafe was acting so negative. "Oh, I understand. You don't wish to be rescued and then hung for killing Davy so you've already made up your mind to kill them all!"

"No! What sort of man do you think I am?" Rafe asked, offended.

"I thought we already established that you're no man. You're demon spawn," Charles said.

Rafe glowered darkly at Charles. "I'll check them out. Remain here where you'll be safe should they prove unfriendly."

"I will not remain here and allow you to go out and commit mayhem and murder!" Charles said stubbornly.

Rafe ran his hand across his face in exasperation. Why did Charles always have to make it so difficult to protect him? "Fine, come along then, but if you're hurt, don't blame me." He walked briskly away.

Charles persistently maintained Rafe's brisk pace, although the effort was obviously taxing him. As the big orange ball of the sun dipped into the sea and was extinguished, Rafe slowed. He had no wish to injure an ankle by stepping in a hole he couldn't see, as during his mad flight after he'd killed Duncan. Charles kept closer to Rafe then and because of that they kept colliding. The fifth time Charles smacked into him Rafe stopped and glared at him, a futile act in the dark. "Stop bumping into me!" he hissed softly.

"Don't snarl at me like some wild animal! It's not my fault I'm a noble of pure white blood and thus lack your unnatural demon spawn ability to skulk around in the dark," Charles snapped.

Rafe was sick to death of the derogatory label, but he resisted the temptation to pummel Charles for it, since it would only prove Charles right. "Don't keep so close and we won't run into each other! That's merely common sense! Even a noble pure-breed such as you should be able to figure that out."

Charles backed off a bit, mumbling unintelligibly.

"Quiet, before you give us away!" Rafe commanded.

Charles muttered something else and then quieted.

As they approached the beach, Rafe dropped to the ground. Charles mimicked him. They commando crawled side by side through the dense vegetation, Rafe as silently as death, Charles sounding like a stampeding herd of wild horses to Rafe. He would've chastised Charles to move more silently, except that he knew Charles was already performing at the height of his comparatively inept abilities. They eventually halted under cover of a thicket of bushes within several hundred feet of where the canoes were beached.

The moon had risen full and by its light they could clearly see the three young natives lounging on the beach, their spear shafts stuck into the sand beside them. One of the natives turned his head in Rafe's direction. Rafe recognized the distinctive war paint the boy wore. They were cannibals. Most likely come to the island and some well-hidden holy place Rafe hadn't yet discovered in his explorations to sacrifice and eat their captured enemies. Charles started to stand up. Rafe hastily grabbed Charles's forearm and yanked him back down. "No! They're unfriendly," he whispered. "We'd be wise to hide out in Nirvana until they leave."

"They're only children," Charles whispered.

"They're cannibals. These three are probably young, inexperienced warriors left behind on watch while the rest of the tribe is off dispatching and eating an unfortunate captive, or two."

"That's ridiculous! There are no cannibals in these parts! I'm not letting your prejudice against those unlike you ruin our only chance to escape from this island!" Charles said.

"It's not prejudice, Charles," Rafe hissed irritably. "If anyone has cause not to be prejudiced it's I, adopted by the Mohican, with a Delaware father, and a white mother, and I'm telling you that these natives are more likely to kill us and eat us than to help us off this island."

Charles stubbornly refused to listen. "You only don't want to be rescued and have to pay the consequences of your crimes. I'm going in!" He started to stand up again. Rafe dragged him back down, but Charles was determined. He deftly twisted free and then succeeded in taking a few steps before Rafe frantically grabbed the hem of Charles's brocade waistcoat, but like the shirt sleeve a few months before, the material was so rotten that it tore off in Rafe's hands and didn't even slow Charles down.

"Charles!" Rafe hissed quietly, desperately as Charles plunged nosily through the bushes, but it was too late. He was already seen. With angry exclamations the three young natives sprang to their feet, pulled their spears from the ground, and raced at Charles.

Charles raised his arms to his sides, palms out to show he was unarmed. "Friend!" he said, smiling. Rafe stayed in hiding, but he drew his knife, flattened his body to the ground, waited and watched, hoping that through some miracle violence wouldn't be necessary. One of the natives shoved his spear in Charles's face. Charles backed up a step, flustered by this violent reception, but his desire to escape from the island overcame his fear and his common sense as well. "I am Lord Charles Huntington. If your tribe would be so good as to convey myself and my slave to the nearest mainland then you'd be rewarded handsomely," he told the native imperiously.

Of course it was nothing but gibberish to the young native who didn't speak a word of English. He stabbed Charles in the chest with his spear cutting Charles's ragged shirt but not drawing blood, and then he spoke angry words of gibberish to Charles. Rafe started planning his attack. He could easily take down one native if Charles didn't interfere, which Rafe knew he would, and then he'd have to take down the other two swiftly before they had a chance to react. He only hoped the more experienced members of the tribe didn't return as he was dispatching their young ones, for that would surely cause some difficult complications.

"Friend," Charles reiterated in a slightly trembling voice as he began to realize his mistake. "You take us off this island?" He gestured to the canoes and then out to sea.

The first native spoke angrily to the others and then one struck Charles on his forehead with the shaft of his spear, reopening his head wound. Blood ran down Charles's face. He staggered back and looked toward Rafe's hiding spot. "Rafe! Are you still there?" he called, truly frightened now. He wiped blood from his eyes, and then rubbed his hand on his ragged shirt making a bloody smear. "Rafe? I think I might need your help now," he pleaded.

The three natives tensed and raised their spears, but when no one showed, one of the natives laughed and said something to the others in a derogatory tone then they laughed too. The first native seized Charles roughly by his shoulder, threw him on the ground on his back, and raised his spear over Charles's chest. The other two natives stepped on his arms and held him down, laughing at his vain attempts to break free.

Rafe was extremely hesitant to further sully his conscience by committing the mayhem Charles had accused him of wanting, but he knew that if he delayed any longer, the pristine white sand would soon be stained red with Charles's life blood. His conscience in turmoil he reluctantly burst onto the beach and plunged his knife up to the hilt in the back of the native who'd been threatening Charles with his spear then quickly withdrew it. The native dropped lifeless onto the sand without making a sound. Charles was as shocked by this rapid and easy kill as the remaining two natives, but for a different reason than them. When he'd cried out for help, he'd only wanted Rafe's intervention as native to native. He'd thought Rafe would have a natural rapport with them since they all had similar skin, eye, and hair coloring, and could convince them that he and Rafe were no threat. He hadn't intended for Rafe to kill anyone!

One of the cannibals threw his spear at Rafe. He dodged aside and then felt the rush of air against his face as the spear sped past, barely missing clipping his ear. As the cannibal leaned over to pick up his fallen brother's spear, the cannibal with the knife lunged and knocked Rafe onto his back in the sand. Rafe and the cannibal became locked in a fierce battle of strength, in which each fought to be the first to plunge their knife into the other's heart. It was a short battle, for the young, inexperienced cannibal lacked Rafe's strength and skill honed through years of training. Charles and the remaining cannibal, spear held tightly in his fist, watched the struggle side by side like spectators at a match, both in shock, but the cannibal had dismay added to the mix and Charles had aversion.

Rafe thrust the dead body of the cannibal aside and scrambled to his feet to face the remaining cannibal. The young warrior stared with rounded eyes of fear at Rafe then at his blade, held tightly in his left hand at his side dripping the blood of the cannibal's two brothers onto the sand. Realizing he was far outmatched, the cannibal backed warily away then dropped his recently acquired spear, turned and raced into the trees, his bare feet kicking up sand with each step. Rafe reluctantly chased after the youngster, for he couldn't let him warn the rest of the tribe of his and Charles's presence on the island.

As he followed the frightened cannibal into the trees lining the beach, he ran directly into at least a dozen natives returning to their canoes. He skidded to a sudden standstill as taken aback over stupidly running into the cannibals he'd wanted to avoid, as the cannibals were at seeing a strange, lighter-skinned native chasing one of their young warriors. The young cannibal spoke rapidly and excitedly to the group's leader while gesturing at Rafe, who raised his hands to show he had no desire to fight and began to slowly back away. Unluckily, the lifeblood of the two young cannibals staining his knife was cause enough for battle. The leader shouted a command.

A dozen cannibal voices raised the war cry and swarmed toward Rafe.

Rafe knew when a retreat was wise and this was one of those times. He whirled around and raced back to the beach. Charles's eyes widened when he saw Rafe racing out of the jungle cover with a mob of angry cannibals close in his wake. He hastily snatched up the spear of one of the dead youngsters and tossed it. It whizzed past Rafe's head, glancing off his right ear and completely missing the cannibal directly behind him. As blood oozed from Rafe's ear, Charles scooped up the other spear and tossed. This time he struck Rafe a glancing blow to his right bicep then the spear landed in the sand at the edge of the water and was carried out to sea on the next wave. Charles picked up the remaining spear and took aim.

Rafe, bicep and ear bleeding, began to wonder if his ex-friend and would-be slave master was actually trying to kill him instead of the cannibals in a bid to win their favor so they'd take him off the island. He hastily debated who was the greatest danger to him—the natives or Charles—then decided the cannibal leader close upon his heels took priority. He whirled around and plunged his knife into the unfortunate leader's chest then withdrew it. The man dropped dead at Rafe's feet having never had the chance to react to Rafe's unexpected switch in tactics. At first the other cannibals held back in stunned astonishment at how easily this strange warrior had killed their revered leader, a scarred veteran of many a battle. Then one of the braver cannibals rushed Rafe with his spear poised to plunge into Rafe's heart. Rafe snatched the weapon from his attacker with his free hand then tripped him face first into the sand and stabbed the cannibal in the back with his own spear. Yet another cannibal lunged at Rafe with his spear aimed at Rafe's heart. Rafe slashed off the tip of the spear with his blade then with is free hand pulled the spear from the back of the fallen cannibal and thrust it into the attacking cannibal's heart. Another cannibal lunged at Rafe knife blade catching moonlight. Quicker than the others, he slashed Rafe's chest, but the damage to his buckskin shirt was worse than the wound. Rafe killed the cannibal with the same quick, thrust and withdrawal that he'd used so successfully twice before then faced the remainder of the group menacingly.

Apparently, all of their bravest were now dead however, for the remaining cannibals held back warily, eyeing first Rafe and his bloodied blade and then their dead brothers piled at his feet, among them their revered leader. Then an old man with scraggly gray hair and as wrinkled as a prune shouted to the others and they fled to their canoes and paddled away from the island as fast as their wiry, muscled arms could move them. Rafe watched the retreat, the bodies of his latest victims at his feet, bloodied blade held loosely in his left hand at his side, nauseated, heartsick.

Charles had never been more revolted. In less time than it took to shave in the morning, Rafe had casually slaughtered nearly a half-dozen men and now he stood over his latest victims with his back to Charles, his knife blade dripping with blood and staining the white sand at his side, probably gloating over his slaughter with cold satisfaction. After Charles was certain the cannibals in their rapidly retreating canoes had no intention of returning, he approached Rafe. "I hope you realize that having slaughtered five of their men those natives will want revenge. As if being stranded here because of you wasn't bad enough, because you lack the self-discipline not to kill, we'll be forced to fight angry natives when they return in force for their revenge!"

Rafe was too lost in grief and remorse to pay Charles any notice, much less compose a reply. Charles interpreted it differently. "Rafe, stop gloating over your latest kills and listen to me!"

Rafe whirled around, his overly dark eyes reflecting the moonlight, looking for all the world to Charles like some demon newly arisen from the pit. "I saved your worthless life and that's all you have to say?" he demanded quietly.

There was something more than usually unsettling in Rafe's manner that made Charles shiver involuntarily and left him speechless, which was fine with Rafe. "Gather the weapons from the dead. I'll see if there are any cannibals left behind."

He hurried off, but not to search for more cannibals—he knew they'd all left the island—but because nausea had been steadily building in him from the moment the heat of battle had faded and he was determined not to display weakness by throwing up in front of Charles. He fought the urge to empty his stomach until he was certain he was well out of Charles's sight and hearing then he leaned over and allowed his stomach the relief it so urgently demanded.

Charles had angrily watched Rafe disappear into the jungle then turned away from the disgusting sight of Rafe's latest violent slaughter and started back to camp. He refused to gather the weapons as Rafe had commanded even though they were in dire need of them.

Not only had he no desire to touch the dead bodies, but he refused to meekly obey Rafe's commands, as if he was the slave and Rafe his master! If Rafe wanted the weapons, he could collect them himself!

Chapter Twenty-Four

Rafe failed to return to camp the night after the battle on the beach, which was quite fine with Charles, for he wanted nothing to do with the vile half-breed murderer. Rafe failed to return the following night as well and that too was all well and good with Charles. However, when Rafe failed to return on the third night, Charles worried. He remembered the day he'd gone to Rafe's wigwam in the rain to finish berating him for his sins. Rafe's door flap was open and so Charles had seen him sitting cross-legged on his sleeping mat, eyes closed, pressing his knife to his chest with both hands and drawing blood through his buckskin shirt. Before Charles had a chance to cry out Rafe had opened his eyes, and Charles had dodged aside so as not to be seen, but not so soon he didn't see Rafe stab the knife into the ground up to the hilt; and then he'd heard Rafe weeping! Disconcerted by this uncharacteristic display of soggy emotion from the normally stoic Rafe, Charles had silently withdrawn. Now Charles wondered if perhaps Rafe had found the courage to take his life after all, selfishly leaving him all alone on this wild, uncivilized island; a frightening prospect, for even as Rafe had said he lacked the skills to survive for long on his own.

He began his search for Rafe at the scene of the native slaughter, deeming Rafe melodramatic enough as to choose that spot to take his life. There was no sign of Rafe's body on the beach; which was only somewhat of a relief, for it only meant Rafe hadn't taken his life here. Curiously, there was also no sign of either native bodies or weapons. Only the churned up, blood-stained sand gave testament that a battle had occurred here recently. Charles couldn't understand how the bodies and weapons had disappeared, but he didn't care enough to investigate. He headed for Nirvana hoping to find Rafe there—dead or alive.

Since he'd only been to Nirvana once before and had also come at it from a different direction, he lost the path and had to backtrack twice, but four hours later he finally found the hideaway. In the dim light of waning day, Charles could barely see Rafe lying in the tall grass under a tree near the pool, apparently asleep. After having traversed nearly the entire island in search of the inconsiderate half-breed, Charles was in a foul mood. He stormed up to Rafe intent on shaking him awake and berating him for—well, for everything. As he neared his nemesis, Charles noticed new blood on Rafe's buckskins, and that his right forearm was wrapped in a bloody leaf bandage tied with a vine. Charles remembered that in the fight with the cannibals, Rafe had only been grazed in the right bicep and ear lobe and had taken a slight cut to his chest; so he had to have become involved in yet another violent altercation of some sort since then. Charles made a disgusted sound. Would the despicable half-breed never cease his sadistic killing?

The disgusted sound Charles made hadn't been loud, but Rafe startled awake anyway, and drew his knife as he sprang to his feet, not quite as fluidly as normal due to his injuries. Charles hastily stepped back, fearing Rafe would skewer him, but when Rafe realized it was only Charles who'd disturbed his rest, he sheathed his knife. "Come to finish condemning me for saving your life yet again?" he asked resentfully.

"What happened?" Charles reached for the leaf bandage on Rafe's arm to pull it back and see what sort of wound it hid.

Rafe hastily stepped out of Charles's reach. "Don't touch me!" he threatened quietly.

"I only wish to see what you're hiding under that bandage."

Rafe mumbled something obviously derogatory in Mohican, after which he said in English, "Go away and leave me alone."

"Tell me what happened to you, and I'll leave," Charles bargained.

"No you won't, but I'll tell you what happened to me anyway, because it's your fault," Rafe said resentfully.

"My fault!" Charles exclaimed.

"Yes, your fault! I was collecting the weapons you were too lazy to gather and preparing to bury the bodies when the cannibal tribe returned in force, coming from the opposite side of the island. I barely managed to escape into the jungle with my life and that only because I hid inside a hollow fallen tree until they gave up looking for me. I then hiked to the highest part of the island and watched as they collected their dead and the weapons then paddled away."

"Ah, it makes more sense now," Charles said.

"What does?" Rafe asked warily, certain he was only handing Charles another opportunity to deride him.

"When I passed the battle site and didn't see any sign of the weapons or bodies I wondered—"

"—if your stubborn refusal to do as I requested made us lose the weapons we badly needed and nearly saw me killed?" Rafe limped to a nearby seat-high boulder and sat down, wincing slightly.

"You don't seem to be hurt all that badly. You certainly reacted quickly enough when I awoke you," Charles countered.

"You startled me; and how is it that you failed to notice I'm limping, Charles?" Rafe demanded irritably.

"So you hurt your leg. That's nothing to be concerned about. As with the rest of your unnatural talents attained by your close relationship to the devil, you heal quickly," Charles said dismissively.

"Quickly enough to make all this nothing to be worried about?" Rafe pulled up his torn buckskin shirt to show Charles three stab wounds on his ribs, pushed up the sleeve on his other arm and revealed multiple cuts on his forearm and bicep, parted the thick hair on the top of his head to reveal a one-inch gash. "They nearly killed me because I had to fight two dozen of them single-handed while you were back at camp hiding in your wigwam like a spineless craven."

Charles bristled. "How was I to know what was occurring on the beach miles from camp? You should've returned with me instead of wasting your efforts burying those soulless animals, and then you wouldn't have been attacked!"

"They were men, not soulless animals," Rafe countered swiftly.

"They were natives like you, and thus also like you, soulless animals," Charles insisted.

Rafe's eyes narrowed. "You seemed to think highly enough of those soulless animals when you wanted them to rescue you from this island," he pointed out quietly.

"Animals have many uses. That doesn't mean I think highly of them," Charles said.

Rafe spat on the ground at Charles's feet. He hastily jumped back. "Hey!" he exclaimed angrily.

"I should've let those cannibals kill you!"

"It's only by the grace of God you hadn't killed me already!" Charles accused.

"Are you afraid to die, Charles?"

"What?" Charles asked, confused by the sudden turn of the conversation.

"You're continually accusing me of trying to kill you, so…"

"Well I'm not afraid of dying, for I have the assurance of eternal life. You, however, should be afraid of dying, for this life is all you have, soulless animal that you are."

"On the contrary, I look forward to the oblivion of death," Rafe confessed.

"So that's why you attacked the natives the other night before I had a chance to convince them we were friendly. You were hoping they'd kill you," Charles said, in an "aha" tone.

Rafe scowled. "I attacked them to save your life."

Charles snorted. "Considering how many times you've threatened to kill me and your tendency to lie every time you open your mouth I'm not much inclined to believe that. It's far more likely that if you weren't seeking death, you did it merely for the pleasure of killing."

"I derive no pleasure from killing," Rafe swiftly and firmly countered.

"That's a lie! I saw you looking over those dead cannibals with gory satisfaction!"

Rafe grew sick to his stomach all over again remembering that battle. His toll of lives taken by his hand was seven now—seven too many; although at least the last six had been self-defense. He swallowed bile, wondering if he'd ever be able to take a life without becoming ill, and then hoped he'd never grow so jaded. "You judge me erroneously, Charles. You always have."

"I judge you by your actions," Charles countered.

"In your prejudice," Rafe said disgustedly in Mohican. He stood up and limped to the tunnel then disappeared into it.

Charles strongly suspected Rafe had said something derogatory in his adopted language, so he decided not to offer him the chance to repeat it in English by going after him and demanding to know what he'd said. Instead, he spent the night in Nirvana joyfully free of Rafe's evil company.

Chapter Twenty-Five

Charles irritably tossed another stick on the fire as he watched Rafe clean a rabbit he'd caught for their dinner. They'd been stuck on this island for nine months; nine months of watching Rafe's snares always work, while his own snares never caught anything. He hated Rafe for making him feel inferior, but he salved his injured pride with the rationalization that Rafe had an unfair advantage over him being a natural killer. The thought of natural killers reminded Charles of the enormous bear he and Rafe had spotted yesterday in its den on the opposite side of the island. He'd urged Rafe to kill the bear arguing that it would provide meat for months and the pelt could be used to soften his bed, but Rafe had adamantly refused, saying "That bear is too large to kill with only a knife, there's plenty of other meat to be found, and you already have the Cougar pelt for your comfort." Charles was convinced Rafe was craven, and so he'd decided to kill the bear himself. That feat would surely prove his superiority at last, and then Rafe would have no choice but to defer to him and finally take his rightful place as his slave. All last night Charles had puzzled over how to steal the knife so he could kill the bear, and now he eyed Rafe and his knife covetously.

Feeling Charles's eyes on him Rafe glanced up from his work. "You're not going after that bear," he said.

"What makes you think that was what was on my mind?" Charles demanded peevishly.

"I don't think, I know. Every time you consider killing that bear you stare at my knife with that same determined expression."

"That bear is a threat, and since you're too craven to kill it I must!"

Rafe knew Charles's reason for wanting to kill the bear, and he couldn't let him do it, for the only thing Charles would end up proving was that he could die stupidly. "You're not capable of killing that bear."

"I'm capable of killing you, and that bear is less of a wild animal," Charles argued stubbornly.

Rafe sighed wearily. He was more than fed up with Charles's continuous derogatory comments, and the future only held more of the same. "You only want to kill the bear to prove you're better than me. It's wrong to kill animals merely for the sake of pride."

"I seem to remember you killing an animal for a lesser reason," Charles said bitingly.

"If you're referring to Adam—,"

"I am!"

"I was convinced it was the right thing to do, to ensure our safety. Perhaps my illness had affected my reasoning. I don't know. But I've now realized it was unnecessary to have killed the kitten, and I've apologized. Twice." Rafe held up two fingers in emphasis. "Killing that bear isn't necessary either, and to make certain you don't try, you'll sleep in my wigwam tonight where I may keep an eye on you."

Charles went sullenly silent. It was no use arguing, for Rafe always had his way anyway. He was as inferior to Rafe in having his way as at setting snares; completely under Rafe's hand, which galled him to no end, and which was why he had to kill that bear and assume his rightful place as Rafe's superior as soon as possible.

They ate dinner in stony silence and then as the moon rose, so did Rafe. He kicked dirt over the fire, drew his knife and used it as both a threat and to point at his wigwam. Charles stood up without argument, reluctantly entered Rafe's wigwam and lay compliantly on Rafe's grass mat near the east wall, pretending sleep. Rafe watched Charles with his steely gaze, but as the night wore on and Charles didn't move a muscle, he relaxed; although his hand still rested lightly on the hilt of his knife. Eventually his eyes drifted closed and his breathing deepened and slowed. It was exactly what Charles had been waiting for. He slowly, silently, sat up, watching Rafe carefully, fearing he'd open his eyes and command that he lie back down. Evidently, though, Rafe was more exhausted from his countless restless nights than even Rafe realized, for he didn't stir. Charles grinned victoriously. Now he could steal Rafe's knife and go after that bear!

He stealthily approached hoping Rafe's exhausted state would make it easier to snatch the knife, but he intended to take it from Rafe one way or another, counting on the element of surprise to go in his favor. With a great deal of trepidation, he slowly and laboriously pried Rafe's fingers from the knife hilt one by one. He had three fingers free when Rafe stirred and then grasped the hilt tightly again. Charles sighed silently in frustration. It had been far easier stealing the knife when Rafe was passed out drunk, or as Rafe insisted, sick. He set to work again and seemingly interminable heart-stopping minutes of gentle positioning and repositioning later he at last had possession of the knife. He swept back the door covering and silently slipped out, forgetting to pull back down the covering.

The moon was full in a cloudless sky, offering sufficient light for Charles to make his way to the bear's cave. When he saw the bear sleeping in front of its cave in the bright moonlight, however, its enormous head resting on its platter-sized paws, claws easily six inches long, he started second-guessing his decision to come after the creature. He looked doubtfully at the knife, the shiny, well-honed blade seeming small and useless against such a monster. Then he realized the sleeping bear was totally unaware of his presence, and his courage returned. All he had to do was to sneak up on the bear as it slept and thrust the knife through the bear's eye into its brain, instantly killing it. He'd make a necklace of those giant claws and wear it constantly, a visible reminder that he was superior to Rafe.

"Charles!" Rafe hissed from behind him. Charles nearly jumped out of his skin. He hadn't even heard Rafe approach, silent as a ghost. He whirled around to face him.

The wind blowing through the open door of the wigwam had awakened Rafe and he'd immediately noticed that Charles was gone. He'd reached for his knife and found it gone too, as expected. Cursing his latent loyalty toward Charles that had prevented him from tying Charles up like he should have, he sprang to his feet and charged from the wigwam then easily tracked him to the bear's cave. It helped that he knew that was where Charles was headed. "What do you think you're doing?" Rafe whispered, wary of waking the bear.

"You know what I'm doing," Charles whispered back. "I intend to kill the bear that you're too craven to kill yourself."

"I've told you that it's too dangerous. I won't let you throw away your life out of pride," Rafe said.

"It's not pride, and you can't prevent it. I have your knife, and if you try to interfere, you'll die," Charles threatened.

"You possess neither the guts nor the skill to kill me," Rafe said confidently.

"Try me then and learn that you're wrong." Charles assumed a fighting stance.

Rafe rolled his eyes then deftly snatched the knife from Charles's hand.

Charles stared at his suddenly empty hand in bewildered dismay. "How—how did you do that?"

"Practice and skill; the first you never do, and the latter you lack. Now give up this nonsense and return to camp," Rafe said.

Charles raced at Rafe intent on disarming him, undeterred by just having lost the knife to him, for in his pride he told himself that Rafe had only won it from him because he'd been off his guard. Besides, he was determined that no matter what it took he would prove to Rafe that he was the better man.

However, Rafe instantly proved otherwise. He slashed Charles across the belly cutting through his waistcoat, his shirt, and scratching the surface of his skin. Charles skidded to a halt and stared in shock and dismay at his now completely ruined clothing and the six-inch long scratch on his stomach. It was by far the closest Rafe had ever come to killing him. "You nearly killed me!" he exclaimed angrily, forgetting to keep his voice down.

The monstrous bear awoke and with a blood-curdling roar rose to its feet and loped toward them. Rafe wasted a second glaring at Charles for stupidly awaking the beast then assumed a defensive stance. The enormous creature advanced to within a yard of Rafe, but then stopped, studying him and the knife he held ready in his left hand with eyes seemingly too intelligent for an ordinary beast. Rafe shifted his grip on his knife and calmly awaited the attack; while Charles ducked behind Rafe, trembling in fear. Now that he was at last staring the monster directly in the eyes, Charles realized he'd been a fool to think either he or Rafe could best this enormous bear with nothing but a knife. "Rafe! Put your knife away and back off slowly, and maybe it won't see you as a threat," he advised what he thought was most wisely.

Rafe answered him without taking his eyes from the bear. "You've realized the futility in attacking this bear a bit too late, Charles. Now back off slowly while I distract it and save your worthless life."

"Now you care that I'm in harm's way; after you just tried to kill me?" Charles exclaimed indignantly.

"If I'd wanted to kill you, you'd be dead. Go. I'll keep the bear occupied until you're safe," Rafe said.

Meanwhile the bear's mate had come up silently and unnoticed from behind them, having been out hunting. With one swipe of its huge paw, she knocked Charles face down onto the ground and then slammed her huge paw on Charles's back and pressed him down as she'd once pressed Rafe into the mud, only with more force this time, for she was angry and not playful. Charles cried out in pain as a number of his ribs snapped under the bear's immense weight.

Rafe whirled around then watched in helpless horror as the bear sank its long, sharp teeth deep into Charles's skull while simultaneously tearing the skin of Charles's back with its razor sharp claws. "No!" Rafe shouted, but before he could attack the bear threatening to sully his honor and make him a failure by killing Charles its mate swiped him on the side with its platter-sized paw, knocking him off his feet. Rafe twisted as he fell so that he landed on his back, and as the bear lunged, Rafe launched into a stabbing frenzy, his sharp blade slicing deeply into the monster's flesh and muscle sometimes as deeply as to nick bone. The bear seemed oblivious to his countless strikes. Placing a single, monstrous paw on Rafe's chest it pinned him to the ground then opened its huge maw apparently intent on swallowing Rafe's head whole. Rafe abandoned his blade, currently lodged deeply in the bear's right shoulder muscle, and used both hands to shove the monstrous muzzle aside. It required all his strength and even then he barely succeeded in avoiding becoming the bear's midnight snack.

The bear roared in fury then vengefully raked Rafe's torso opening four wide, deep gashes from his neck to his groin. Rafe cried out, but not because of the intense pain. It was rage at being proven inferior. He wiped his bloodied hand on his pant leg, grabbed the knife hilt and determinedly yanked it free from the bear's shoulder then sprang to his feet and furiously stabbed the bear. Although the bear's fur soon was spotted with red from the many wounds Rafe delivered, to his dismay it remained seemingly oblivious to his strikes. He felt like a mosquito trying to pierce the hide of a rhinoceros, but he wouldn't give up until the bear was dead, or he was.

Finally, loss of blood and exhaustion drove Rafe to his knees. Expecting the bear to lunge and finish him off, he raised his knife, his arm trembling in weakness. Instead of attacking, though, the bear inexplicably retreated a few feet and sat down heavily, its sides heaving with labored breathing and obviously in great pain. Rafe tried to spring to his feet with his usual agility to take advantage of the bear's weakness and press the attack, but he instead struggled to stand. Then he studied the brown bear hostilely, swaying in exhaustion, breathing raggedly, bloodied and torn chest heaving, blade and the hand that held it slick with the bear's blood, hair, face and muscular brown arms spotted with even more of the bear's blood.

The bear glared at Rafe sullenly, waiting, watching. A stiff breeze blew a lock of sweat-soaked hair over Rafe's eyes, and a bead of sweat rolled from the end of his hair into his eye. Rafe tossed his head to clear the hair, blinked to clear his vision, but not soon enough to react to a well-aimed swipe of a platter-sized paw as the bear took advantage of his temporary inattention. Its six-inch claws tore long gashes across Rafe's right arm and he was knocked so hard onto his back that the air was forced from his lungs. As he desperately gasped for air, the bear stepped on his chest with its front feet and pinned his arms to the ground with its back feet. Rafe struggled unsuccessfully to break free as the bear roared in victory, saliva from its fangs dripping onto Rafe's forehead.

Unable to draw in a breath, Rafe knew death was imminent. Unwilling that his last sight in life be the bear's fangs he turned his head away—and saw Charles lying motionless beneath the female bear's paw. A cold fury seized control of Rafe. With nearly superhuman strength he shoved the monstrous bear off his chest then gasped in sweet, blessed air even as he rolled to his feet. The bear swiped at him, but he was somehow able to step back quickly enough to avoid the blow. Yelling out in fury he lunged and stabbed his blade into the bear's chest and right eye in quick succession. The bear roared in anger and pain and swiped at him. This time Rafe wasn't quick enough to avoid the blow. He was knocked onto his back. His legs were pinned underneath him at an awkward angle and he felt something pop in his right knee, but he had no time to acknowledge the agonizing pain, for the bear was still on the offensive. As the monstrous paw swiped at him, Rafe hastily rolled to the left saving his chest from further injury, but earning a shredded back in return. Gasping from pain and in shock, he tried to commando crawl away, but the bear pinned him in place with its enormous paw on his back then roared triumphantly.

With a cry of enraged fury, Rafe sliced off the closest of the bear's front toes. The bear howled in pain and hastily withdrew then sat down to lick its wound, its yellow-brown eyes glowing malignantly in the moonlight as it glared hatefully at Rafe. He defiantly made eye contact as he somehow managed to struggle to his feet and then assume a wavering defensive stance, his bloodied knife gripped tightly in both hands. The bear answered his unspoken challenge, roaring and rising up on its hind legs. Rafe's eyes rounded in awe. The bear was easily ten feet tall standing on its hind legs, but that didn't dissuade him from limping at it with his knife raised above his head.

The bear met him halfway, which was fine with Rafe; less territory to cover in his exhausted and weakened state. With a grunt of effort, he plunged the blade deep into the bear's chest to the hilt, savagely twisted the blade, shoved deeper, and raked downward with all of his remaining strength. The bear collapsed partially on top of him, knocking him on his back, its warm organs and the dead weight of the enormous body nearly smothering him. Desperation lent Rafe the strength to shove off the bulk, struggle to his knees then to his feet.

Limbs trembling from shock, loss of blood, and exhaustion Rafe rested one bloodied hand on the bear's furry side for support, grasped his knife hilt with his other hand, and tugged with all his remaining strength. The knife pulled free so suddenly that he stumbled backward and once more ended up lying on his back on the ground. He stayed there, catching his breath and staring in a daze at the beauty of the stars overhead as if he was merely waiting to fall asleep on a warm summer night like when he was a boy with the Mohicans. Then out of the corner of his eye he saw the other bear shoving around Charles's limp body.

Cold rage endowed Rafe with the strength to roll over, push to his feet with trembling arms, then limp at the bear, his body leadenly obeying his brain's commands. The bear turned its massive head to stare directly into Rafe's eyes and roar a warning. Rafe came to a standstill with his knife at the ready, the hilt sticky with the half-dried blood of the bear's mate. "Come to me then. I'm too tired to come to you anyway," he shouted in Mohican at the bear. It eyed the knife warily then looked at its dead mate and made no move to come after Rafe. He beckoned with his bloodied right hand. "Come! I'm easy prey. Can't you see that I'm half dead already?" he said again in Mohican.

The bear roared in triumph, as if it understood what he'd said then abandoned Charles's body and loped at Rafe. He backed up drawing it even further away from Charles. He had no idea how much strength was left in his untapped until this moment reservoir, but he was determined to continue fighting, for his honor and brotherly sentiment demanded that Charles must live at any cost to himself.

The bear roared a deafening battle cry and increased its pace. Rafe shouted a Mohican war cry in return then raced to join battle with the bear.

Monstrous animal and determined man collided with such force that the bear's broad chest knocked Rafe to the ground and he once again lost all the air in his lungs. He inhaled, refilling his lungs while thinking that he was mightily tired of that happening to him. Then he tried once more to rise, but in his weakened state, the best he could do was tightly grip his knife in both hands point up as the bear unable to stop its pell-mell pace barreled over him.

It was enough. The well-honed blade sliced the bear open from neck to rear drenching Rafe in blood and warm organs, and then the lifeless body collapsed on top of him. He cursed silently as the tremendous weight forced out the single breath he'd managed to take in and prevented him from taking another. This time he was certain he was dead. He only hoped Charles wasn't dead as well, for then all of his efforts had been a waste, and he'd die with his honor despoiled; a terrible thought for one who had nothing left but his honor. Then everything went dark.

<u>Chapter Twenty-Six</u>

Rafe slowly regained awareness, and realized he could breathe, although he was still close to smothering in fur. The bear's body had shifted in a last gasp of life and freed his lungs to take in air. Luckily, the weight of the bear had also acted like a compress and prevented him from bleeding to death while he lay unconscious beneath. His arms were now free and for a wonder he still held his knife gripped tightly in his left hand. Apparently, the stickiness of the drying blood on both his hand and his knife had worked as a sort of glue keeping the knife there. At the moment he had no need of the knife, so he shook it off. Then he gathered his strength and pushed against the dead bear. It didn't even budge slightly. He pushed again, but still nothing happened. A third push brought him no closer to freedom, but the fourth push finally succeeded in freeing him.

With a Herculean effort, Rafe struggled to his knees. Sweat, his blood, and the blood of the two bears dripped from him and his clothing as if he'd taken a swim in it. With a swipe of his forearm he brushed sweaty hair from his eyes then leaned over and pressed his right hand splay-fingered on the ground for support and muscled arm trembling clumsily retrieved his knife. Straightening up without falling backward was difficult and when he attempted to sheath the knife, his hand shook so violently that he missed. He tried again, missed again. With a roar of frustration he forcibly, but successfully sheathed his knife. Then by grabbing double handfuls of the bear's fur, he laboriously climbed up the carcass and to a stand.

Grimacing in pain, he stumbled and limped across the uneven ground to where Charles lay as still as death. He dropped to his knees beside Charles and checked for signs of life. Charles's breathing was so ragged and shallow that Rafe could barely detect it. A cursory examination revealed deep bite wounds on Charles's torso and head, shredded back, several broken ribs, and possibly a punctured lung; and like Rafe, Charles had lost an enormous amount of blood. He needed a skilled chirurgeon like Jacob and even then he might not survive. With no medical care at all Charles would suffer excruciatingly for days before he died, stubborn as he was, but he would most certainly die. Rafe couldn't let Charles suffer for days on end, and especially when it was his fault that Charles was in this mess, for he'd failed to prenent him from coming to the bear den. He would atone for his failure by easing and quickening Charles's passage into the afterlife, force feeding him a lethal dose of nightshade that he'd spotted on one of his many walks, collected, and dried, and had stored in a small covered bowl in his wigwam. Then he'd use the remaining nightshade to end his own life.

He lifted Charles, a monumental task even after his short rest that felt akin to lifting the dead weight of one of the humongous bears over his head. Out of sheer stubbornness he managed to struggle to his feet and then stagger a few steps before his injured knee gave way and he collapsed. Charles rolled out of his arms and hit the ground at Rafe's feet with a soft thud then moaned as if even in his unconsciousness blaming Rafe for his ineptitude. Rafe cursed in Mohican then struggled determinedly to his knees and gathered Charles limp, heavy body into his trembling arms; only to discover he was too weak from shock and loss of blood to rise any further. Rafe could've given up then, but he couldn't leave Charles to be eaten by predators. He himself might deserve that fate, but Charles most certainly did not. So with a colossal effort, Rafe somehow accomplished the impossible and struggled to his feet. Sweating and trembling he took one step, another, and one more. Stars swam in blackness at the edges of his vision, his limbs felt like they were made of jelly, but he stubbornly faltered on.

Eventually, despite his dogged determination, Charles's dead weight was more than Rafe could bear. He dropped to his knees and although he struggled valiantly to rise his body absolutely refused to obey his commands. Rafe resignedly laid Charles on the ground then leaned over him, supporting his weight with trembling arms, his bloody, bear-claw-shredded buckskin shirt hanging in tatters at his sides. A drop of his own blood mingled with sweat dripped from his chest and landed on Charles's cheek. Rafe clumsily brushed at it making a red streak that looked much like war paint and reminded Rafe of the nearly half dozen cannibals he'd killed to save Charles, all for naught now. "Forgive me, Pachtamawas," he whispered hoarsely to the beloved God he'd known and worshiped since childhood. He was not only begging forgiveness for the cannibal's deaths, but also for the extinction of his tribe, his best friend's death, Davy's death, and now Charles's death. If he'd ever possessed half the honor John and Leopold had tried to instill in him, he would've seen that no harm came to a single one of these whom God loved. It was further proof that as everyone said, he was an abomination, unworthy of God's love. Tears of guilt and remorse traced clean tracks in the blood and grime on Rafe's cheeks then dripped onto Charles's brow in a crude simulation of Chinese water torture. Charles moaned again. "I'm sorry, Charles," Rafe whispered.

Overwhelmed by weakness he dropped to the ground and rolled onto his back beside Charles, his bloodied and shredded chest heaving in agony and the effort of breathing. He wanted to look upon the stars as he died, but his vision blurred. Thunder rolled in the distance. Another severe storm was approaching. The inevitable blowing debris that always accompanied storms here would most definitely finish both of them, but although Rafe had no desire to be flayed to death, however appropriate Charles might find it, there was no strength left in him; which left him no other option but to pray for God's intervention. "God of all creation," he said, abandoning the more intimate Mohican word, Pachtamawas, for he was praying to Charles's God now, the One Who'd rejected him. "Forgive an abomination in your sight for seeking a favor from you, but I don't ask for myself. I've rightly earned death, so take my life if it pleases you, but you must save Charles. He doesn't deserve to die because of my crimes."

The skies opened up and rain poured down. Rafe interpreted it as yet another rejection. "Pachtamawas," he sighed sorrowfully, longingly, before he lapsed into unconsciousness and the heavy rain washed him clean.

<u>Chapter Twenty-Seven</u>

Charles awoke in a dark, windowless, damp room that smelled of illness, sweat, urine and death, and lit only by a single lantern swinging from a beam almost directly overhead, and someone had bandaged his countless wounds. As his mind fog dissipated he realized he was only one among many chained in the hold of a slaver's ship; although he was the only white captive and held aside from the others who were crowded so close together they had barely enough room to change position. Even in the dim light cast by the single lantern he could clearly see the lack of hope in those other captive's faces. He empathized, for he felt the same lack of hope within himself; but how had he come to be restrained by the wrists and ankles with rusted metal shackles, a prisoner on a slaving ship?

The last thing Charles remembered was agonizing pain as the bear clawed his back, and being surprised that his end wasn't coming by Rafe's hand. He shivered from both fever and fear, and prayed and hoped for someone to come and answer his questions; the most pressing being if Rafe was still alive, for to his surprise, he missed having the solid and reliable half-breed by his side. Charles closed his eyes and prayed for the welfare of Rafe and himself. Then he waited. There was nothing else he could do anyway; but it was taxing waiting, for he'd never been a patient man.

* * *

Rafe opened his eyes and was confused by what he saw, or rather by what he didn't see, for he lay in complete and total darkness, with no moon or stars above him. Had he died and this was oblivion? But no, by the definition of oblivion he couldn't even be aware, so apparently he was still alive. What dark place was this then and how had he come to be here? Or was it possible that he was dead after all, and in hell? Disconcerted and a little frightened Rafe reached for the comfort of his knife, but it was gone, along with the sheath. He distinctly remembered sheathing his knife after the killing the bears. Charles couldn't have taken it. Not this time. Not in the condition he'd been in. Then Rafe became aware of the smell of the sea, the creaking of ropes and snapping of sails, and the gentle rocking of the floor and realized he was on a ship. His fear dissipated and curiosity took its place. Rafe explored with his hands. He was shirtless—although there hadn't been much left of his shirt anyway—and someone had bandaged his countless wounds. Manacles again chafed his wrists, he was barefoot, and his left ankle was chained to a ring in the bulkhead. Boxes of supplies and loose chains were piled all around him. At last it all became clear to him. He was once again being held prisoner in a chain locker.

Nine months ago Rafe would've cursed in all three languages he was proficient in at finding himself a prisoner again, but now he accepted it as his due. He only hoped whoever had taken him prisoner and doctored his wounds had done the same for Charles, if Charles had even still lived. Rafe didn't hold out much hope of that though, for hadn't he asked God for a miracle before he'd lost consciousness, and wasn't he a prisoner now? That seemed more like another blatant rejection than a positive answer to his plea.

The chain locker's door swung open and light streamed in temporarily blinding him. His chains clinked as Rafe shielded his eyes with his left hand and peered blearily at the dark silhouette standing in the doorway. A second later his eyes adjusted and the silhouette metamorphosed into a beautiful woman no more than a few years older than him with an elegant figure, waist-length black hair, and soft brown, doe eyes fringed with long, thick, black lashes. Her voluminous red skirt with three wide stripes along the bottom in green, yellow and brown was topped off by a white blouse neatly tucked in. A wide belt encircled her slender waist with an oversized sheath bearing the largest knife Rafe had ever seen. In one delicate, long-fingered hand she held a tin cup and in the other a dark wooden bowl filled with a white, pasty substance so thick a spoon stood straight up in it like a firmly rooted tree. "So you are awake, pretty man. Good. Doc has instructed me to feed you and he has even prepared the meal himself," she said in a soft, velvety voice as beautiful to Rafe's ear as a love song. She dragged the spoon from the bowl hauling a large amount of the pasty substance out along with it, and held it to his mouth.

Although Rafe was starving, he turned his head away. He wanted some questions answered first. "How long have I been here and what ship is this?"

The woman laughed musically. "You amuse me, pretty man. You are a prisoner, shackled at the wrists and ankle, yet you demand answers as if matters were reversed. I admire your spirit, so I will answer your questions." She shoved the spoon into the bowl then sat cross-legged on the deck beside Rafe spreading out her skirt and resting the bowl on one shapely thigh, the cup on the other, but maintaining a firm grip on both, although Rafe didn't think it was possible to spill whatever substance was in the bowl. She smelled wonderfully fresh and clean. Rafe was almost tempted to draw her into his arms as the first woman he'd seen in quite some time and definitely the prettiest.

"You are on the Corsair. You have been here for six weeks, during which Doc has kept you drugged enough to prevent you from becoming fully aware while at the same time rendering you capable of eating and drinking. It is not surprising that you remember nothing. VonLarken is the captain of the Corsair, and my father. We deal in slaves, but that is not our primary trade. We search the waters for anything of value then sell it for a profit. People call us pirates and slavers, but those are rather derogatory terms, yes?"

"Society does have a tendency to label people offensively," Rafe agreed thinking of the many derogatory labels applied to him in his lifetime, such as the half-breed and demon spawn labels consistently used by Charles.

The woman smiled prettily. "As soon as I laid eyes upon you, I thought I would like you, and you have not disappointed me." She lightly stroked Rafe's cheek with her right index finger. Rafe hastily pulled away and she laughed, amused by his shyness. "Tell me, pretty man, how did you come to be upon the isolated island upon which we found you nearly dead?"

"We were shipwrecked."

"Shipwrecked," she repeated thoughtfully. "I do recall that a merchant ship was lost in that late season hurricane some nine months back. The Lady Bountiful, was it not?"

"Yes."

"I had also heard that this ship in addition to its usual load was transporting a murderous half-breed by the name of Lord Rafael Zacharias Brookstone. I suspect by your coloring and your educated manner of speaking that this is you?"

"Lord Brookstone is dead." It was somewhat the truth, for that part of his life was finished. "May I ask why you were on the island?"

"To gather fresh water and fruit, of course. That island has a tree which bears the tastiest, fuzz-less peaches in the world that one of our crew, a virtual genius, has carefully cultivated. You would know about that tree, for a pile of its fruit was found in one of your two wigwams. We also found several beautiful bark bowls and some wondrously fine woodcarvings. Were those your handiwork?"

"Yes."

"I thought so. You have artist's hands." She reached for Rafe's left hand, but he hastily moved it out of her reach, his chains clanking. "What do you intend to do with me now?"

"You will be sold into slavery. Such an extraordinary specimen as you, intelligent, talented, extraordinarily handsome, will bring a high price. I would say you are as close to perfection as is humanly possible." She fingered a lock of Rafe's long, soft, shiny black hair, which Rafe realized for the first time someone had washed as it wasn't stiff and matted with blood and grit. He also realized for the first time how long it had grown these past nine months, to well past his shoulder blades. "You have such beautiful, soft, shiny hair. It is too bad I cannot take it from you for myself." She playfully tugged on the lock of hair.

Rafe pulled his head to the left freeing the lock of hair. "Did you find another man alive on the island?"

"I am wondering why you should care," she said uncooperatively, miffed that her playful advance had been rebuffed.

"He's my… half-brother." Rafe lied. "We were both sailors on the Lady Bountiful."

"You do not look much like brothers, even half-brothers, or sailors either, for you wear buckskins and the remnants of the other man's clothing were obviously of fine cloth. No sailors dress like that."

"My brother is exceedingly vain and lazy. I do most of his work to keep him employed and he spends his earnings on his clothing. I prefer buckskins for their comfort and because they wear well. But enough about clothing; how fares my brother?"

"He is recovering nicely, although not as swiftly as you." The woman picked up the dark, wooden bowl of pasty substance and dragged the spoon free. "Enough questions. Eat."

It was difficult to swallow the thick, sticky, grainy substance, but Rafe managed it. Then the woman held the tin cup to his lips, but the liquid inside smelled foul. He leaned away in disgust. She frowned prettily. "You must drink. It is medicine to help you heal."

Rafe didn't fully trust the woman, but after all the effort these pirates had put into keeping him alive, it was highly unlikely they now meant to poison him. "I'd rather do it myself." He held out his hands for the cup. She gave it to him and he reluctantly downed every last drop then held out the empty cup. The woman took it back smiling, letting her fingers linger on his longer than necessary. Rafe realized then that he could take advantage of this woman's obvious attraction to him to gain his and Charles's freedom. He briefly grasped her hand, his chains clanking musically against the tin cup. "Such a strikingly beautiful woman must have an equally striking name. Won't you favor me with it?" He smiled with all the charm he could muster, which aided by his fine looks was considerable.

She rewarded him with a warm smile. "In three months we will return to New Providence. You will be sold as a slave and I shall never see your incredibly handsome face again. Since you flatter me, however, I will tell you that I am named Lauralee."

"A beautiful name for a beautiful woman," Rafe said.

Lauralee's smile revealed perfectly straight, dazzlingly white teeth. "I must go now, but I shall return." She picked up the bowl and breezed out of the chain locker.

* * *

Someone shook Charles's shoulder roughly. He opened his eyes then yelped. What was probably the ugliest, oldest man in the world leered at him toothlessly. His unshaven, grizzled, pockmarked face was abnormally long, his nose and mouth overly large, hazy gray eyes tiny and closely set. The man scowled at Charles irritably. "What is your problem?" he grumbled, scratching his bald head.

"N-nothing," Charles stuttered. "Where am I? Where's Rafe? What am I doing here? Who are you?"

"Too many questions," the ugly man grumped. "I will only tell you that you are lucky to be alive. You were badly injured, but fortunately the lovely Lauralee has convinced VonLarken he may recoup more than the cost of nursing you back to health by demanding a rich ransom for you, and selling your dark companion as a slave."

"Ransom? What are you talking about?" asked Charles, trying to shake the cobwebs from his aching head. "Who are you?"

"He is Doc," said a soft, melodious female voice. "You should thank him for saving your life."

Charles didn't see anyone other than Doc and so thought his ears were playing tricks on him, but then Doc moved aside and Charles saw Lauralee. She held a dark wooden bowl in one hand and a cup in the other, and she was beautiful. She reminded him of a statue of an angel he'd seen upon passing through Philadelphia as a boy, with the most beautiful face he'd ever seen.

"You may feed him," Doc said to Lauralee. "Although he is not as fully recovered as the other, he is also ready for more solid food." He left her to it.

Lauralee sat down on the deck beside Charles then stuffed a spoonful of a thick, grainy substance into his mouth. "Mmph!" He swallowed quickly. The grainy stuff was hot and it burned as it slid down. Lauralee shoved another spoonful at him. Charles leaned back. "Wait!" Lauralee lowered the spoon and looked at him questioningly. "Doc spoke of a dark companion. Does this mean you found another man, uniquely handsome, or so women say, darker-skinned than I and taller with long, black hair, and dark brown eyes almost the color of his hair?"

"You two are certainly concerned for each other." Lauralee fed Charles another huge mouthful.

Charles quickly swallowed. "Then you found him! How is he?"

Lauralee fed Charles another huge spoonful of the grain. "He is recovering well, and he says he is your half-brother. Is this true?"

Charles almost choked on the mouthful of grain in his rush to deny it. "Rafe is most definitely not my brother!"

"Is this so?" Lauralee's eyes narrowed. "So the extremely handsome Rafe is a liar."

"Oh he is that and much worse," Charles affirmed adamantly. "We have absolutely nothing in common, except that we were shipwrecked when my merchant ship, the Lady Bountiful, went down in a hurricane with all hands lost except us two. We were trapped on that island for nine long months before you found us, which brings me to ask, why are you holding me prisoner?"

"It is how we treat all we do not kill," Lauralee told him in a matter of fact tone. "Do not worry, though. When we reach New

Providence, if your ransom is paid, you will be freed. If not, we will kill you, but until then you are safe."

"You can't—," Charles began indignantly, but then Lauralee temporarily stopped his objections by forcing him to drink a vile liquid. As soon as he could speak again, he spluttered, "You can't hold me for ransom! I'm a lord!"

"We are quite aware of your elevated status, which is why we are asking a ransom for you," Lauralee said in a tone that indicated Charles was dull for not having realized that before. "Your fellow shipwreck victim, he is also a lord, yes?"

"Rafe was once known as Lord Brookstone, but he lost the right to claim that title when he killed his best friend and brutally assaulted me in a drunken rage, then was sentenced to life as a slave on my plantation. His vast and prosperous estate is currently held in trust by his family barrister until such time as he might prove worthy of it once more, which personally I doubt will ever occur. I'd have no objection to your holding him for ransom in my place. His barrister fostered him and despite the man's disappointment in discovering Rafe's murderous nature, I'm certain he'd be willing to pay a high price for his life, much more than you could garner for me from my much poorer estate."

Lauralee ignored the offer, since they had no intention of holding anyone in Charles's place and every intention of profiting from both Rafe and Charles. "I knew he lied about his identity," she mused aloud. She brushed a lock of hair from Charles's eyes with an almost tender, but thoroughly insincere gesture. "I presume you earned rich compensation from Lord Brookstone's estate in return for agreeing to take him on as a slave on your plantation?"

Charles bristled. "I most certainly did not! I'm an honorable nobleman as well as a Christian. I did it for the sake of justice, for the memory of our childhood friendship, which Rafe ended some seven years back by his treachery, and to preserve the last of the Brookstone family line. I'd hoped that through hard labor I could someday turn Rafe from his evil ways and back to the good ways of our Lord above, but I doubt that's possible now, for after having killed once he seems to have acquired a taste for it. He now lives only for the pleasure of taking lives."

Lauralee wasn't the least bit interested in Charles's hopes for Rafe's spiritual future. As far as she was concerned, religion was all lies and myths anyway. On the other hand she was quite intrigued by

Rafe's purported taste for killing, and she was greedily interested in his money. "How rich is this vast and prosperous estate of the extraordinarily handsome Lord Brookstone?"

Charles hesitated, unsure if it would be betraying Rafe to say, and then he realized he'd only be telling the truth, which could be discovered in any number of ways. "His estate is the richest in the territory; far richer even than mine. He's extraordinarily wealthy, for all the good it will do him as a slave."

"That is good to know." Lauralee stood up and smoothed her skirt.

"So you'll free me in exchange for Rafe?" Charles asked hopefully.

"I'm afraid not. Although what you have told me may change Rafe's fate, you must still be held for ransom." Lauralee started to leave.

"Wait!" Charles shouted desperately. "I'll pay a double ransom if you'll free me now, and I'll even broker the ransom for Rafe and then allow you to sell him into slavery. How's that for a generous offer?"

The only answer Charles had was the hatch slamming shut.

* * *

Lauralee swooped into the chain locker, skirt billowing, accompanied by a short, husky, angry man with a pock-marked face and a large, red, bulbous nose in a black waistcoat with gold trim over a white peasant shirt, black pantaloons tucked into cuffed, brown calf-high boots, and a wide, purple, satin sash wrapped around his ample waist. Rafe stood up warily wondering what was about to happen now. He didn't have to wait long to find out. The man slapped him on the left cheek, leaving behind a flaming red handprint as clear evidence of his fury. "I am VonLarken, the Captain of the Corsair, and the leader of this clan. "You have lied to us, slave!"

"I'm no one's slave," Rafe said defiantly.

VonLarken raised his hand to slap Rafe again, but Lauralee drew him aside. "Father, you will damage the merchandise. He responds well to me. Allow me to question him and I shall extract from him the truth."

VonLarken initially looked as if he would strangle Lauralee for interfering with his desires, but he kept himself under control, barely. "Do so then," he said through clenched teeth stained brown from tobacco juice, and crossed his hairy, brawny arms over his barrel chest.

"Your fellow shipwreck victim has told us all about you," Lauralee said to Rafe. "You are not brothers nor are you sailors. You are in fact Lord Brookstone, called the half-breed lord, and you were on your way to serve out your life sentence for murder as a slave on Lord Huntington's plantation."

Rafe silently cursed Charles's loose tongue.

"He also says your estate is vast and the richest in the territory," Lauralee said.

Rafe expected that next they'd say they intended to ask a ransom for him. He cared little for the family money as far as for personal gain, but he did care if it went for good or ill, and he most definitely didn't want these vipers to have any of it. "Charles lies. I have nothing to my name except these bloodstained buckskin pants. I had a buckskin shirt once too, but I seem to have lost it somewhere along the way..."

VonLarken's eyes narrowed. "In that case Charles must be severely punished. A few dozen lashes with a cat of nine tails should teach him not to tell lies." He rubbed his hands together and smiled nastily in gleeful apprehension. "I shall do it myself. Carlos is too inefficient. He always leaves some flesh intact. "Come Lauralee. We shall have some sport today." They turned to leave.

"Wait!" Rafe cried urgently. Lauralee and VonLarken stopped and looked at him expectantly. "Charles speaks true. I am wealthy," Rafe admitted.

VonLarken's eyes glinted greedily. "How wealthy?"

"The proceeds from my estate alone are worth more than you could spend in a lifetime if you spent extravagantly every day," Rafe said.

VonLarken smiled, pleased. "As I suspected. We shall ask a large ransom for your return I think."

Lauralee drew her father aside again. "I have a better plan, Father; one that has the potential to net us far more profit than we could earn from asking a ransom for this man. Would you care to hear it?"

"Proceed, my intelligent kitten," VonLarkin obliged.

"It was obvious from the evidence that Lord Brookstone single-handedly, with only a knife, killed those two enormous bears we found on the captured colonial ship then disposed of on the island several years back lacking the means to store and feed them, along with the rest of the larger wild animals from that same ship. We could use a crew member of such unique strength and skill; and he also has the education and upbringing of a nobleman. I would be willing to wager he has other knowledge and skills that would be of great value not only on the open sea, but in our dealings in port. Furthermore, his friend claims Lord Brookstone's estate is currently held in trust for his possible return and that his barrister would be willing to pay any price asked for the assurance of his safety. Why should we not have him write a letter instructing his barrister to give over half of his estate, then conscript him?"

"If he refuses to join us?" VonLarken asked.

"We shall threaten to kill his friend unless he does everything we ask," Lauralee said.

VonLarken grinned lasciviously. "I like it, but with a few changes. Listen and learn, dear daughter." He addressed Rafe. "You will write a letter instructing your barrister to transfer half of your estate to me, which I shall collect when we dock in Nassau. In the meantime, you shall be a member of our crew under Lauralee's watchful eye. If you perform to our expectations, you will save your friend's life and he will instead be sold at the slave market in Nassau. If you do not perform as required, your friend shall die and you will be the one sold into slavery."

Rafe didn't care what happened to him, but he was ready and willing to join the pirates and even to perform at the height of their expectations in exchange for Charles's life. As for Charles being sold into slavery, he'd have to find a way around that somehow; but that was in the future.

"Will you abide by this agreement, or shall we execute your friend?" VonLarkin asked.

Rafe answered without hesitation, for he truly had no choice. "I shall abide by the agreement. You have my word of honor on it, sir."

VonLarken laughed victoriously then patted Lauralee on the top of her head as if she were a small child. She scowled and ducked out from under his hand, which obviously amused her father. "As ever my dear daughter, your suggestions have proven sound. Clean up our new crew member and bring him to me in my cabin." VonLarkin hurried away.

Lauralee turned to Rafe smiling victoriously. "So?" she asked when he not only said nothing, but failed to return her smile. "Where is your thanks for the favor I have done you?"

"Favor?" Rafe saw no favor in the agreement he'd made; only the worst form of slavery, with dire consequences in the end no matter how well he performed.

"Your friend claims you live to kill. Do you not realize that you will have the opportunity to kill again when you accompany us on our raids?"

"Thank you." Rafe's tone made it sound like a question.

Lauralee's eyes narrowed. "Perhaps your friend lied when he claimed you enjoyed killing. Perhaps you both lied about your enormous fortune. Perhaps I should tell VonLarken to schedule the lashing." She turned to leave.

"No lies were told," Rafe hastily lied.

Lauralee stopped and turned around. "No?"

"I do live to kill, but was reluctant to admit it for fear you might think less of me. Truly, nothing compares to the thrill of watching my victims breathe their last, except perhaps bedding a beautiful woman." Rafe forced a charming smile then anxiously awaited Lauralee's reaction, hoping he'd judged her correctly.

She returned to his side flushed with delight. "Have no fear that I will think less of you, for I too enjoy watching people breathe their last. On our next raid you and I shall together experience the thrill and power of ending lives, and afterwards we shall celebrate privately. Yes?"

"I look forward to it." Rafe prayed his revulsion for her remained undetectable.

Apparently it did, for Lauralee laughed delightedly. "It will be a pleasure owning you."

Luckily she didn't catch the dark displeasure that temporarily altered Rafe's countenance, for she was drawing a key from a pocket hidden inside her voluminous skirt. She unlocked and removed his restraints and Rafe gratefully stood up, although feeling a bit weak in the legs. He rubbed his chafed wrists, leaned down, rubbed his ankle where the restraint had chafed, then straightened. Lauralee kissed him unexpectedly, but softly and tenderly. He'd never been kissed by any woman before, except Sarah, and that in a chaste manner on the cheek. This kiss was quite different. Desire roared through him. He willingly surrendered to it, wrapped his arms around Lauralee and returned her kiss with unbridled passion. Some minutes later when Lauralee started to draw away, Rafe resisted, not only because he was enjoying the kiss, but wishing her to believe he was thoroughly captivated by her charms. She gently but firmly pushed him away.

He assumed a disappointed air. "Was my kiss lacking in some manner?"

Lauralee smiled. "Indeed not, but there will be time enough for pursuing such captivating pleasures later. Now I will show you to your cabin where you may change your clothing and shave. Both of which you badly need."

Rafe looked down at his bloodied bandages and buckskin pants. "I agree on the bath and change of clothing, but—," he rubbed the scraggly black growth on his chin, "—don't you think a beard would make me look more formidable?"

Lauralee appraised Rafe soberly. "Hmm, well, perhaps it would. Trim the beard then after you wash up. You smell of medicine and old blood." She wrinkled her nose which was endearing to Rafe even knowing she was a demon in spirit.

"As you wish, my Lady." He made a courtly bow.

Lauralee laughed pleased both with being called a Lady and his courtly bow. She held out her dainty hand. "Come. I shall show you to your cabin."

Rafe took her hand and allowed her to lead him to his cabin, next to hers. It was tiny as it was intended for a manservant, but still a vast improvement upon the chain locker if only because he could stand completely upright and it had a porthole. Four pegs on the portside bulkhead served for hanging clothes or other items. The bed built into the bulkhead was even long enough for his six-feet and was furnished with a goose-down mattress, pillow, and a warm, gray, wool blanket. A wooden stool sat underneath the pegs on the wall opposite a washstand against the other wall with a plain white, china pitcher and bowl. A small wooden shelf built into the wall beside the washstand held a brush, scissors, razor, and a single candle in a tin holder. It was the lap of luxury compared to his living conditions of the last nine months. Lauralee poured water from the pitcher into the washstand bowl, picked up the lye from a built-in dish beside the bowl, the white washcloth hanging on a dowel below the bowl beside a matching white towel, and handed soap and washcloth to Rafe. "Clean up while I fetch clean clothing. It will not take long."

"I'll miss you," Rafe lied, with a faked winning smile.

Lauralee responded with a genuine smile then left. A dark scowl immediately erased the fake smile. Rafe was by nature a truthful man and all the lying had made him feel dirty and low. He peeled off the bandages letting them fall to the floor then scrubbed heartily, noting the countless fresh not quite yet healed scars on his stomach, chest, back, and arms, souvenirs of his battle with the enormous bears; certainly a battle worthy of bragging about, but one he wished he hadn't survived. After washing, he trimmed his beard then Lauralee walked in unannounced with folded, clean cotton underwear, fringed, blue satin sash, black pants, white shirt and socks, and black, calf-high, leather boots. Her doe eyes appraised Rafe's nakedness appreciatively, making him feel like a choice piece of meat. Face hot with embarrassment, he hastily grabbed his torn and bloodied buckskin pants and hid his nakedness as best he could. "I have brought your clothing, but I think you look better without it." Lauralee lightly ran her hand across Rafe's scarred and muscled left bicep, lesser in size after his month and a half of inactivity, but still impressive.

Rafe hastily stepped away from her. "Please leave the clothing on the cot and then allow me some privacy..." he ventured to suggest, uncertain of how Lauralee would take a dismissal no matter how polite.

Lauralee laughed. "I would have never guessed you are a shy man. How droll. I have never met a shy man so for the sake of novelty I shall indulge you, for now. Later...we shall see." She winked coyly then left the clothing where he'd asked and sassily sashayed to the door.

She winked again over her shoulder before exiting and closing the door. Rafe waited until he was certain she was gone then dropped the buckskins. Fearing Lauralee might barge in again at any moment he hastily dressed then tied the wide, fringed, blue satin sash around his waist, slipped on the boots, and then plaited his long hair into a thick, single braid that cascaded to his shoulder blades and tied it with a black velvet ribbon he'd found in the pocket of the pants. All he lacked was a weapon, for he felt naked without one, although he was fully dressed.

When he looked at his reflection in the oval polished metal on the back of the washstand, he saw a stereotypical pirate, which he was certain was wholly Lauralee's intent, and made him glad neither

Leopold nor his heart father were around to see him now, and especially not Charles. He lay on his back on his bunk to await Lauralee's return and his thoughts turned to Charles wasting away in the dank, dark, smelly underbelly of the ship, his life dependent upon how well a God-rejected, half-breed performed, while in contrast that same half-breed was relatively free and lounged in a private, if tiny, cabin. The resulting guilt was so intense that Rafe sprang to his feet and agitatedly paced the short length of his cabin, but as he was still recovering from his injuries, he all too soon wearied and lay back down. This time he drifted into a light sleep.

He startled awake when Lauralee again came in without knocking then bolted to his feet and reached for his knife in its sheath at his side that of course wasn't there. "It's considered polite to knock before you enter someone's cabin," he snapped grumpily.

"You have not yet earned that right," Lauralee said tersely, her beautiful, long lashed brown eyes glinting with displeasure.

Realizing he'd overstepped his boundaries, Rafe said, "Forgive me. I was sleeping and I was startled by your entrance, which made me unintentionally rude."

Lauralee smiled. Other than taking lives nothing pleased her more than a man apologizing to her. "You understand your place. That is well, for I will not have to waste time teaching you humility. Come, it is time to report to VonLarken."

Rafe obligingly accompanied Lauralee to an intricately carved red oak door. She knocked twice.

"Enter," said VonLarken from within.

Lauralee entered motioning for Rafe to follow. "Sir, I have brought the new crew member as requested."

VonLarken leaned over a six-by-four, rectangular, polished oak table perusing navigation charts. There was a built-in ceiling-to-deck shelf behind him on the starboard wall stocked with a goodly number of reference books, maps and charts. VonLarken rolled up the charts he was perusing and set them aside then crossed the room to a smaller writing desk and chair, grabbed several sheets of blank paper, moved a quill and half full ink bottle next to it, pulled out the chair and motioned to Rafe. "Sit."

Rafe obeyed then looked at VonLarken expectantly. "Write the letter to your barrister transferring half your estate to me. If it is to my satisfaction, you shall have earned the honor of joining me, my officers, and my family not only in our conquest of the oceans, but at table for every meal until we dock at New Providence," VonLarken said.

Rafe reluctantly dipped the quill in the ink then selected a piece of paper. Watched carefully by VonLarken, Rafe wrote in his precise, neat handwriting, instructing Leopold to liquidate half his assets and transfer them to VonLarken. Meanwhile, Lauralee crossed to the window and looked out with a bored demeanor. Rafe addressed the letter to a fictitious office address trusting that Charles hadn't blabbed that particular bit of information to his captors then gave the finished letter to VonLarken. As he slowly read it over, Rafe leaned back in the chair, stretched out his legs, crossed at the ankles and pretended to be completely relaxed. In reality he was so tense he felt he might shatter at the slightest touch, but that was proven wrong when Lauralee came over and rested her hands lightly on his shoulders and he stayed whole; although he suspected Lauralee was preparing to break his neck at a word from VonLarken should the pirate find anything suspect in the letter.

"All seems to be in order," VonLarken finally said.

Lauralee moved her hands from Rafe's shoulders proving his suspicions concerning her intentions had been correct. VonLarken carefully folded the letter then slid it into a side drawer in the writing desk and locked the draw with a small key he drew from his vest pocket. Rafe breathed a silent sigh of relief. Until they landed in New Providence and his deceit was discovered, and as long as he did everything the pirates asked of him, Charles was safe, so to speak.

"Shall we retire to dinner?" VonLarken asked cheerily.

Rafe shoved the chair back and stood up, Lauralee possessively hooked her arm in his, and they followed VonLarken to the officer's mess.

Four men and one woman were seated at a table large enough for eight. The other woman was exactly the opposite of Lauralee in coloring with waist-length blond hair, blue eyes, and light skin, but equally as beautiful. She wore a powder blue, three-quarter-sleeve dress with a white lace stomacher and lace modesty ruffle. A wide, white lace ruffle graced the end of each sleeve. She also wore a sheath holding an oversized knife with a highly decorated hilt. VonLarken took his seat at the head of the table. Lauralee sat down to his right. The other woman occupied the chair to the right of Lauralee's. Lauralee glared at her hostilely but when the woman ignored her, Lauralee shoved her viciously, nearly unseating her. "Move Delilah, I wish for Rafe to sit here."

"I will not! This is my seat! I refuse to surrender it to your current plaything! He shall have to sit somewhere else." Delilah crossed her arms stubbornly and her deep blue eyes challenged her sister.

Lauralee rose to the challenge. She sprang from her seat, whipped the wickedly large blade from the sheath, and held it to Delilah's throat. "Move or die, sister. Your choice!"

Rafe expected VonLarken to intervene, but the pirate seemed oblivious to anything but his meal. It took all of Rafe's willpower not to say or do anything as Lauralee pressed her knife to her sister's neck drawing a few drops of blood, although it helped a little that Rafe knew it would jeopardize everything he'd gained if he dared to try to stop this insanity of family members attacking each other. "Move!" Lauralee demanded of her sister.

Delilah glanced at her father obviously looking for his intervention, but he remained fully engrossed in his meal. "Fine!" she pouted. "I will move, but only because I cannot bear to endure your stink. You should consider bathing more than once a year, sister." After an indignant toss of her blond curls, Delilah moved to an empty chair at the opposite end of the table and sat down gracefully.

With a self-satisfied smirk, Lauralee sheathed her blade then motioned for Rafe to sit. Rafe reluctantly obeyed. The man directly opposite, to the left of VonLarken, and the right of Doc, looked exactly like a much younger VonLarken. He was dressed almost identically to Rafe in a white cotton shirt with billowing sleeves, a wide, blue, fringed satin sash, and brown boots instead of black. Like the other VonLarken's he also sported an oversized blade. "So you are the new plaything," the man remarked. "You are much better looking than the last one. Perhaps Lauralee will keep you longer." He shrugged. "Who knows?"

"I'm the new member of the crew," Rafe said with special emphasis on the word crew. "You are, sir?"

"Carlos," the ugly man said imperiously. "You will be under my command on raids, and you will obey me to the death or I shall kill you."

Rafe glanced at Lauralee questioningly and then at VonLarken, but they were both paying absolute attention on their meals. "Am I to answer to Carlos as well as to you, Lauralee?" he asked.

Lauralee looked up, nodded then said with her mouth full of half-chewed food, "You currently wear a blue sash which marks you as Carlos's man under me, but only on raids. Otherwise you belong completely to me." Rafe could barely suppress his irritation that not one, but two of these despicable pirates were to lord it over him. The things he endured for Charles's sake... Lauralee continued. "Only the most elite are directly under my command; those who wear the red sashes. After you have proven yourself and earned your red sash, then you will belong to me completely."

"You're Carlos's superior then?" Rafe asked.

Lauralee smirked. "In more ways than one for I am First Mate, although Carlos aspires to my place. Do you not, Carlos?" Carlos shifted position obviously ill at ease. Lauralee went on, "Unfortunately for him, the only way he will ever succeed to First Mate is if I were to unexpectedly die. That I refuse to do so makes him quite irate. He hates waiting, and although he could spare himself the wait and kill me, he is too craven. Are you not Carlos?"

"Shut up before I cut out your tongue!" Carlos hissed.

Lauralee sprang to her feet flourishing her knife, which had seemingly magically appeared in her hand. Rafe was forced to admire her quick reflexes if not her quick temper. She was nearly as fast as he, which was exceptionally rare. "I will slit your throat first little brother!"

Carlos sprang to his feet, drawing his six-inch, serrated blade then leaned across the table, his nostrils flaring like a winded horse, and flourished the blade in Lauralee's face. "We shall see whose throat is slit!"

Delilah stood up, drawing her own knife. "The pleasure of slitting her throat belongs to me!"

Doc watched the familial exchange with open amusement. The other two men at the table pretended to be intensely interested in what was on their plates. VonLarken finally reacted and banged his fist on the table, rattling the glasses and silverware. "If anyone is to slit the throats of my children, it will be me for ruining my meal!" he shouted. "All three of you unruly children sheate your knives, sit down, and shut up!"

Delilah sheathed her blade and sat down, followed closely by Carlos. Lauralee waited until her siblings were firmly seated before she resumed her seat and sheathed her knife, but not before directing a threatening slashing motion at Carlos.

With a semblance of order restored, VonLarken resumed devouring the remainder of his meal. Five minutes later he burped loudly then abruptly left. Doc and the other two men immediately arose and hastened away, leaving only VonLarken's three children and Rafe still at table. A few minutes later Lauralee set down her utensils, burped louder and longer than VonLarken had then addressed Rafe. "I have some business to discuss with one of my men. Stay here and await my return. I shall not be long." She coyly traced the line of Rafe's jaw with her index finger. Rafe trembled slightly with the desire to pull away and interpreting his reaction as a desire for her Lauralee left smiling.

Delilah wasted no time in sidling seductively up to Rafe. Carlos watched silently with a derisive smile on his wide, ugly lips. "Do you know that you are quite handsome?" she asked Rafe. "Your skin and eyes are slightly too dark for my taste, but that may be overlooked considering your other highly appealing attributes." She sat down in Lauralee's chair. "I understand you paid Father a large sum and betrayed your friend to join us." Delilah danced her delicate fingers down Rafe's shiny, thick, black braid, which currently hung over his left shoulder then rested her hand intimately on his thigh.

Rafe removed her hand. "That's not exactly true."

"No?" Delilah leaned closer to reveal her ample bosom, previously somewhat hidden behind her modesty ruffle. "Perhaps we should go to my cabin and discuss it in detail?"

Carlos snorted, but Delilah ignored him and slid her hand back on Rafe's thigh. He removed it again. "I have nothing more to say on the matter," he said coolly.

Delilah's eyes widened. None of Lauralee's previous personal playthings had ever refused her advances. However, she didn't give up. She leaned in closer and whispered in Rafe's ear. "I know a few tricks Lauralee does not. If you accompany me to my room, I shall demonstrate them to you."

Weary of saying no politely and being ignored Rafe said bluntly, "I'll not accompany you to your room or anywhere else, for any reason. Clear enough?"

Carlos snorted again. Delilah tossed him a hostile glare then turned her hostility on Rafe. "You are wrong if you think you have a better chance of surviving with mu slut of a sister! She kills her playthings faster than a lioness takes her prey!" Delilah calmed herself, with a visible effort, and then smiled sweetly. "You could have a fine future if you switch your loyalty to me."

Carlos snorted again.

Delilah shot him a withering look. "Shut up, Carlos!"

"I have not said a thing!" Carlos objected with false innocence.

Delilah maintained hostile eye contact with Carlos until he looked away then she looked back to Rafe. "What say you pretty man? Will you accept what I have to offer?"

"I've already told you no several times," Rafe said.

Carlos laughed heartily. "We have here an unusual man dear sister; one who cannot be swayed by your feminine wiles. Are you not embarrassed by your dismal failure?"

Delilah's pretty face turned several shades of red in quick succession, each a little darker than the last, then she sprang to her feet and with an indignant toss of her blond curls, stormed out of the room. A moment later Lauralee returned through a door opposite the one Delilah had exited. "Well met, Tina," Carlos said. "You just missed Lilah trying to make love to your new plaything."

"What?" she shrieked. "How dare that slut again try to steal what is mine! I will cut out her ridiculous limpid blue eyes for this!" She whipped out her knife.

"No need. Her pale looks are not to my taste," Rafe hastily intervened.

"He did refuse Lilah's advances," Carlos interposed. "Of course my presence may have had something to do with that." He shrugged. "Who can say for certain?"

Lauralee studied Rafe suspiciously for a few eternally long seconds while he did his best to look innocent. Then she sheathed her knife. "Come Rafe, let us walk."

Rafe nodded a polite farewell to Carlos, whom he truly wished to punch in the nose instead, and then stood up and accompanied Lauralee from the dining room. As soon as they were out of sight and hearing of Carlos, Lauralee grabbed a double handful of Rafe's shirt and then shoved him against the wall. "Do not entertain any notions of tasting Delilah's wares! I will not share you with her! You belong solely to me! Understand?"

A heated rage seized control of Rafe. He dropped his façade of obedient humility, gripped Lauralee's wrists and tore her hands from his shirt then held her at arm's length. "I paid your father half of my estate to avoid slavery," he said quietly.

Lauralee furiously twisted free. "You paid father half your estate to *earn* your freedom, and you have not even begun to earn it! You will start by accompanying me to my cabin and there you will do everything I ask, or your friend Charles will die!"

Rafe glowered at her darkly then recklessly walked away.

"Rafe!" Lauralee shrieked, stamping her foot. "Did I not just finish telling you—,"

Harsh laughter interrupted her tirade and then Delilah stepped from the shadows. "What is the matter dear sister? Does your new pretty boy refuse to play nice? That is a first, yes? Perhaps it is because he would prefer me."

Lauralee whipped out her blade. "Shall we fight for him then or are you afraid I will win?"

Delilah swept out her blade. "I shall be more than happy to slice you into little, tiny pieces." She held the index finger and thumb of her free hand close together with only a sliver of space in between, illustrating exactly how small she intended to slice up Lauralee.

It would've made everything far simpler in the long run to let the sisters kill each other, but Rafe's conscience was already overburdened enough. He stepped between them. "Stop! You two are family! Isn't blood worth anything to you?"

"Only when it is gushing from her slit neck!" hissed Lauralee.

"You witch! I will kill you!" Delilah tried to step around Rafe, but he blocked her. "Out of my way pretty man, before I slash your handsome face and forever ruin it!" she commanded.

"I won't allow you to harm Lauralee," Rafe said.

Lauralee laughed. "See, sister? He defends me not you. Does that not make you feel like the useless rubbish that you are?"

Delilah screamed like a banshee and rushed at Rafe, brandishing her blade, which Rafe barely had time to note had a custom hilt decorated in a complex Celtic pattern, before he deftly disarmed her and knocked her to the floor. Delilah, hair and skirt in disarray, stared up at Rafe, mouth hanging open. No one had ever succeeded in disarming her, let alone so easily and quickly! Lauralee laughed. "Well done, Rafe. I knew you and I were meant for each other. Let us retire to my cabin where you shall see how lucky you are to have chosen me."

Rafe stuffed Delilah's decorative but deadly blade between his sash and his pants. "I did not choose you," he said frostily then walked away.

Delilah laughed. "Your wiles are useless against this man, sister. How does that make *you* feel? Impotent? Ugly? Stupid?" she mocked.

"Rafe! Come back here! Now!" Lauralee stamped her foot.

Rafe ignored her which made Delilah laugh even harder, pounding the deck with glee. With an enraged scream Lauralee turned her knife on her sister. Delilah cried out in terror and thrust out her hands to shield herself. It wasn't enough to prevent her sister from slashing a wide smile across her throat.

"What have you done!" Rafe exclaimed then knelt beside Delilah, untied his sash, the knife falling with a clatter to the floor unheeded. He wrapped the sash as tightly around her neck as he dared in an attempt to stop the flow of blood while Lauralee watched, arms crossed, looking amused by his efforts. "You cannot save her," she remarked. Then Delilah proved her correct and stopped breathing.

Even though Rafe barely knew Delilah, and what little he did was distasteful, he briefly bowed his head in grief over the loss of a life. Then he stood up. "You killed your sister," he lamented.

"She was a pest; forever stealing my men. I am well rid of her. However, Father will not approve. For some inexplicable reason he harbors a soft spot in his shriveled heart for this sniveling, blue-eyed brat. I could lose my place as first mate or perhaps even my life if he ever discovers I have rid the world of her. So we must dispose of the body and be certain he never finds out. Pick her up."

Rafe balked. "Why should I involve myself in your murder?"

Lauralee's eyes narrowed. "If you do not, I will tell father you killed her! What do you think he will do to you and your friend then?"

Rafe went for his appropriated knife then saw it lying on the floor and cursed silently in French. If he reached for it in a threatening manner, Lauralee was quick enough that she could skewer him before he could retaliate. As much as it grated on him, he'd have to surrender to Lauralee's will for the time being and wait for a better opportunity to reap the justice she so richly deserved. After a dark glare filled with such malignant malice that it was surprising Lauralee didn't instantly vaporize, Rafe said, "As you wish, but I'd like to retrieve the knife first?"

Lauralee nodded. "You may do so, but make any sudden moves and you are dead."

Rafe cautiously retrieved the knife then stashed it behind his back in the waist of his pants. Lauralee remained on her guard until he'd lifted Delilah's limp, rapidly cooling, slender body, his blue, silk sash still wrapped around her neck, soaked with her life blood. Then she smiled and relaxed. "You are as wise as you are handsome."

She leaned forward to give him an amorous kiss, but he hastily stepped back, revolted by the thought of kissing her while he held her murdered sister in his arms. "How do you wish to dispose of her?" he growled.

Lauralee was miffed by Rafe's avoidance of her and his surly tone, but she had a dead sister to dispose of so she restrained her anger. "We shall dump the body overboard." She led Rafe and his gruesome burden onto the main deck.

It was a cloudy night with a new moon which made it far easier to slink around on deck without being spotted by the half alert watchman. Rafe followed Lauralee abaft acutely aware of the macabre burden he carried, ducking behind the hanging small boats when the watchman looked in their direction. He couldn't help comparing what he was doing to the day he'd killed Davy and let the body wash overboard to hide his crime. Until this moment he'd felt morally superior to these human piranhas, but now he realized he was no different and his spirits plunged to a new low. He was almost tempted to hail the watch, for then it was certain a swift and deserving death would ensue; but then Charles would lose his life as well. He had no choice but to continue to obey Lauralee; and oh how he resented Charles for that!

They reached the stern without being seen and then Lauralee waved her hand limply at the water. "Drop her into the ocean," she ordered.

Rafe obediently heaved his ghastly millstone overboard then glanced apprehensively at the watchman as the body hit the water with a loud splash that he was certain could be heard halfway across the world. However, the sailor who unknown to Rafe was half asleep and three-quarters drunk remained totally oblivious that a secret burial had occurred on his watch.

"Farewell sister," Lauralee whispered acidly then laughed softly.

Rafe, however, swallowed bile. He'd committed a number of reprehensible acts since Duncan's death, but this one definitely ranked among the worst of them.

Lauralee grabbed his hand, smiling coyly, oblivious to his distress. "Now that we are free of that annoying nuisance, let us hasten to my cabin and celebrate!"

Rafe wanted to object, but if he hadn't been rebellious with Lauralee earlier, Delilah would still be alive; and so he numbly obeyed. Lauralee paused several times along the way to her cabin to kiss Rafe seductively and it took every ounce of his self-control not to shove her away. He couldn't understand how she could feel so amorous after killing her sister. He was nauseous and racked with guilt, and his hand hadn't even taken the life. This time.

Chapter Twenty-Eight

Guilt over Delilah's murder and shame over willingly surrendering to lust and conceding his virginity to a wicked woman he loathed had kept Rafe awake all night, but at least his wakefulness had afforded him the opportunity to rethink keeping a murdered woman's blade. The possible complications should the blade be discovered in his possession weren't worth its limited usefulness. He slid noiselessly from bed without waking Lauralee, hastily dressed then stealthily made his way on deck and dropped the knife overboard. When he turned away from the railing, he spotted Carlos standing only a few yards away and looking directly at him and his heart skipped a beat in alarm. Those complications he'd feared were about to ruin him and Charles both!

He defiantly made eye contact with Carlos who smiled and nodded in return, but didn't confront him; apparently not having noticed what he'd thrown overboard. Rafe faked a genial nod then hurried to his cabin to attempt to wash away his guilt and shame with a thorough scrubbing. Despite his industrious efforts, however, the guilt and shame stayed with him, as strong as ever, for he couldn't wash away the stain from his heart and soul. Only Jesus' blood was capable of cleansing heart and soul and he was by now thoroughly convinced that he was excluded from that purification. As the ship weighed anchor near an island to collect fresh water and fruits, Rafe dressed, donning the new blue silk sash Lauralee had provided as a replacement for the one sent to a watery grave around Delilah's neck then joined the officers and family in the mess hall for breakfast.

"Where is Delilah?" VonLarken asked irritably, after waiting seven minutes for her to show."

"I have not seen her since dinner last night," Carlos said.

"Nor I." Lauralee winked at Rafe who then had to make an effort not to squirm in his seat in guilty unease.

VonLarken must've sensed his unease nevertheless. He eyed Rafe suspiciously. "How about you, Lord Brookstone, have you seen Delilah this morning?"

"I…" Rafe replied, caught without a believable lie.

Lauralee hastily intervened. "He was with me from dinner until now."

Carlos snorted.

Rafe was then powerfully tempted to surrender to his desire to curtail Carlos's snorting for a few days by applying a forceful, well aimed, punch to the nose. Unfortunately, although he suspected Lauralee would approve, he was certain it wouldn't go over quite as well with VonLarken.

"Delilah was after Rafe last night," Lauralee continued. "He would have nothing to do with her, however, preferring me. She is probably off sulking somewhere; perhaps on the island. Do not worry, Father. I am sure she will return soon."

"VonLarken slammed his fist on the table rattling the tableware and spilling some of his drink. "I will not endure such gross insubordination! Lauralee, as soon as breakfast is over, take your men and conduct a thorough search of the ship and the island. When you find Delilah, bring her to me. The spoiled child has ruined my appetite," he growled then stuffed a huge forkful of eggs in his mouth and swallowed without chewing. "For that she must pay dearly." He grabbed his tankard of ale and noisily slurped it down.

"You will accompany me and my men on the search," Lauralee commanded of Rafe.

Rafe had trouble concealing his displeasure over this command. He had no desire to waste time on a useless search. He needed to check on Charles. "Might I perhaps be excused from this search? As you know, I'm still not fully recovered from my injuries, and last night was exceedingly taxing."

Carlos snorted again. Rafe clenched his left fist under the table.

Lauralee was well pleased with Rafe so she acquiesced to his request, to some extent. "You may retire to your cabin for a short rest while we conduct a thorough search of the ship, but I wish to have you at my side when we search the island. Meet me on deck in thirty minutes."

It wasn't the full reprieve Rafe wanted, but thirty minutes was more than enough time to visit Charles. He hastily excused himself then headed for the stairs leading to the bowels of the ship. "Rafe!" Carlos hailed him. "I wish to speak with you." Rafe stopped and turned around, successfully concealing his irritability over wasting precious moments talking with a man he had absolutely no respect for and even despised. "How is it that you came into possession of Delilah's knife?"

Rafe cursed silently. So Carlos had noticed the knife after all, but why hadn't he confronted him at the time? Why wait until now? What was Carlos up to? "I don't know what you're talking about," he said, faking innocence to see what Carlos would do.

"Come now, Rafe, you know I saw you tossing Delilah's blade overboard earlier this morning," Carlos said

"You're mistaken. The blade I threw overboard was an old knife of Lauralee's that broke during knife-play last night," Rafe said.

"A lie," Carlos said. "The Celtic pattern on the hilt was unmistakable. That knife was a gift from Father to Delilah for a job well done on our last raid. She prized it above all else. I wonder…should I tell Father that you killed Delilah?"

Rafe dropped his innocent act. "If you wish to die prematurely," he threatened darkly.

Carlos had expected Rafe to beg since that's what he would've done under the same circumstance. Then he'd planned to take advantage of Rafe's fear of exposure. He raised his hands defensively. "Do not worry. I will not tell Father what I have seen." He glanced furtively around, saw that no one was looking, and then leaned closer and whispered, "If you agree to dispose of Lauralee as well."

Rafe had no objection to killing Lauralee. He wished to kill the entire wicked crew beginning with Carlos and then seize control of the ship and free Charles and the other slaves. It would take a miracle to succeed, though, and then there'd be no crew left to sail the ship, since he doubted any of the slaves had experience as deckhands. "It's as good as done," he agreed.

Carlos brightened. "Then since you have disposed of Delilah's knife, you will need a new weapon." He drew his seven-inch serrated blade from its sheath and held it out.

Rafe accepted the wicked short sword. "It may take some time for the perfect opportunity to present itself," he said as he stashed the blade in the waist of his pants behind his back and beneath his billowing shirt.

"Take all the time you need. I am a patient man. Only make sure you do her in before next hunting season. I wish to be First Mate by then." Carlos clapped Rafe on the back then sauntered away laughing softly, triumphantly.

Rafe resumed walking, but then it occurred to him that if he met with Charles, he'd have to explain his freedom. Charles would never understand. Harsh accusations would most certainly ensue. His overburdened conscience couldn't bear such a guilt-inflicting confrontation. He retreated to his cabin instead, hid the short sword between his mattress and the wall then lay down for half an hour and rested his gritty eyes before he went up on deck to meet Lauralee. They then took small boats to the island and conducted a vigorous, but of course highly unsuccessful six-hour search for Delilah.

Upon their return to the ship Rafe, exhausted, headed for his cabin, but Lauralee grabbed his arm. "Where do you think you are going? I did not dismiss you. You shall accompany me as I present my report to VonLarken." She took his arm. Rafe gritted his teeth, but obediently accompanied her.

Lauralee had been highly amused by the useless search, and so was in high spirits. She talked and laughed animatedly as they walked, blissfully unaware that Rafe silently nursed his revulsion for her and the rest of the pirates by devising highly imaginative ways of ridding the world of them, as he'd so often done on the island with Charles in mind. They entered VonLarken's quarters in the middle of one of his most gruesome imaginings. He broke it off, though, as VonLarken, standing at a table studying his navigation charts, looked up. He had no wish to jeopardize his masquerade should VonLarken see his loathing for him reflected in his eyes.

"Father, we have returned from our search." Lauralee assumed an air of distress. "We searched everywhere, but we could not find my dear sister. I do not know where she could be. It is quite worrisome."

VonLarken slammed his palm on the table and cursed, but tears glistened in his eyes, which surprised Rafe. Was it possible that the pirate's evil heart had the capacity to love? "If you did not find her, then you did not conduct a thorough search! Perhaps if you are so incompetent I should remove you as First and put Carlos in your place!"

Lauralee paled, knowing it was no idle threat. "I assure you father, we conducted a most thorough search. Rafe will confirm it."

VonLarken fastened his beady eyes on Rafe. "Answer carefully, sir, for if I ever discover you lied to me today, you and your friend will suffer horribly."

"Lauralee speaks true, sir. We conducted a most thorough search. We left no stone unturned," Rafe said.

VonLarken cursed vilely. "Then we shall leave without the ungrateful wench! Ready the ship to depart."

Lauralee had seen VonLarken quickly dispatch more than one pirate brash enough to question his orders, but she took a chance, relying on her relationship, and objected to strengthen her pretense of innocence. "You wish to depart without my beloved sister?"

VonLarken snatched an already loaded pistol from underneath a chart and aimed it at her. "You dare question my decision, disloyal daughter?" he screamed.

Lauralee edged closer to Rafe intending to use him as a shield should it become necessary. "I would never question your authority, Father. I was only reluctant to leave without my beloved sister, but as you wish, I will tell everyone to prepare for departure." She hurried out. Rafe delayed long enough to offer a polite parting bow. VonLarken nodded suspiciously in return.

Rafe caught up to Lauralee who then stopped her mad rush. Her chest heaving in anger she spat, "You see how poorly he treats me, his eldest daughter and his first mate! He bears absolutely no respect for the one who has made him so successful!"

"A father should always treat his children with respect," Rafe said.

Lauralee smiled. "I suspected all that was needed to turn you completely to my side was a night in my bed and I see now that I was not in error."

"Indeed. I'm completely yours," Rafe said, already having become skilled at lying without effort.

Lauralee laughed triumphantly. "Come. We shall retire to my cabin and revisit the pleasurable activities of last night." She winked coyly.

Rafe forced a grin in return while thinking that Charles most certainly didn't deserve the unconscionable sacrifices he was having to make for his sake, and wishing his sense of honor wasn't so strong, for then he'd leave Charles to his fate, jump overboard and swim until his strength gave out. If he reached an island, he could live out his life in peace. If he drowned instead, it would at least end his misery once and for all. Either would be better than these heart-and-mind-perverting circumstances he was trapped in.

Chapter Twenty-Nine

Rafe glumly stood among the crew, arms crossed, receiving orders from VonLarken before boarding the Pavilion, a merchant ship unfortunate enough as to cross the Corsair's path and receive the pirate welcome, which included among other things suffering downed masts. Now the pirates were preparing to board. Rafe had never approved of taking what belonged to others, and especially when the theft was driven by pure greed, so his stomach was performing nauseating flip flops in dreaded anticipation of his imminent crime. He tried to compose himself by rationalizing that he was doing this for Charles's sake, but that only made him think of how much Charles would disapprove of his crime, which in turn made him feel guilty before the fact.

"Lauralee and her men will take the first small boat," VonLarken said. "Rafe will accompany Carlos and his men in the second. Kill anyone on the merchant vessel who resists and capture the others to be sold as slaves."

"I have not been issued a weapon, sir," Rafe pointed out.

"You are trained in hand-to-hand combat are you not?" VonLarken asked.

"Yes, sir," Rafe said.

"Then no weapon is necessary. If you need cover, Carlos and his men will provide it."

Rafe cursed under his breath in Mohican. He was about to board a ship filled with desperate merchant sailors who'd kill him to stop him from stealing their cargo, which he had absolutely no interest in, and he had to depend on Carlos to keep him alive. He'd only been a part of the crew for a little over a month, but he'd already learned Carlos was addicted to coca leaves, which he smoked often, and always before raids. Carlos thought the drug lent him courage, but it actually only made him even more ineffective and useless. He was a dead man, and perhaps that was VonLarken's intent. After all, VonLarken already had his money—or so VonLarken thought—and it made sense in a pirate's mind-frame to be rid of a man he couldn't fully trust.

Rafe, Carlos, and his crew of five swarmed on board the Pavilion to be met by five merchant sailors armed with swords. As the ten men engaged in battle, Carlos hastily crouched out of sight behind the puffed up sail of the downed mast. Rafe, although no coward like Carlos, backed up against the cap rail hoping the merchant sailors had enough decency not to stab or shoot an unarmed man even if that man did look like a pirate and had boarded with them. It worked, mostly, for when the small knot of merchant sailors who'd attacked Carlos's men all lay dead, Rafe had suffered only a glancing wound to his upper left arm as he'd raised it in defense when one of the merchant sailors had come after him, before being stabbed in the back by one of the pirates. The men then enthusiastically raced off to port to join the mayhem and madness taking part on the opposite side of the ship, where Lauralee's crew was engaged in a fierce gun battle.

Rafe snatched up a saber from one of the dead sailors, slid his saber into his sash then pilfered a pistol, bullet pouch and powder horn from another dead sailor. He loaded the pistol while Lauralee joyfully immersed her soul in the slaughter of innocents. Watching her made Rafe's blood run cold. Like Satan the woman was truly a beast in a beautiful package. He'd do the world a favor if he killed her as Carlos had asked and now was definitely the time to do it, for no one would know she hadn't been killed in battle. He aimed his pistol at the back of Lauralee's head and pulled the trigger, just as a sailor so young that his mustache was little more than light fuzz on his upper lip stepped directly into his line of fire and took the shot meant for Lauralee full in his face.

Lauralee whirled around, saw the dead sailor and concluding Rafe had just saved her life smiled and blew him a kiss. Rafe forced a grin in return, but when Lauralee resumed her killing spree he leaned over the cap rail and threw up, revolted by his attempted cold-blooded murder and the tragic turn it had taken. As he started to straighten, a bullet passed so close to his head that the wind of its passage displaced a strand of hair near his temple that had worked loose from his braid. He spun around to face his attacker and was surprised to see a young boy, barely nine; and he was reloading. Rafe would've let the boy kill him, except he feared what would then happen to Charles. He hastily reloaded his pistol, finishing before the far less experienced boy, and then took aim. "For Charles," he whispered, his hand trembling slightly as he reluctantly pulled the trigger.

"Harold!" A man with graying hair dropped his pistol and hastily knelt beside the young body lying prone on the deck bleeding from a hole in the heart. "My son!" he sobbed, gathering the dead boy to his chest.

"I had no other choice," Rafe apologized softly.

The dead boy's father gently laid the boy down then glared up at Rafe, tears of grief wetting his cheeks. "I too have no other choice, filthy pirate!" He snatched up his pistol and pulled the trigger. There was a click, and nothing happened. He'd forgotten the pistol was already discharged. It then became a race between Rafe and the grief-stricken father as to who could reload and shoot the fastest.

Rafe won, for his reason to remain alive far outweighed the father's grief-stricken lust for revenge. However, it was no victory for Rafe. He held his smoking pistol loosely in his left hand at his side and stared at the bodies of father and son side by side on the deck feeling like the vilest of murderers. It was only when another bullet zoomed past his left shoulder that the need to stay alive for Charles's sake took precedence over remorse and guilt. Rafe dropped his spent pistol as he dodged another shot aimed at his head then drew his saber from his sash and killed the man with a quick lunge and thrust. After that, another sailor came at him, and realizing his best chance of staying alive was to take the offensive, he reluctantly charged into battle.

Twenty minutes later four pirates had lost their lives, but the merchant sailors, not nearly as skilled as Von Larkin's pirates in battle, had taken heavy losses. The Pavilion's Captain, knowing a lost cause when he saw one, surrendered. The abrupt silence as all fighting ceased was almost deafening. Rafe tossed his bloodied saber on the deck revolted by the innocent men he'd killed. Lauralee waltzed up to him laughing with the joy of murder, placed her bloodstained hands on either side of his head, and kissed him passionately, but he irritably broke free and shoved her away. Lauralee's beautiful doe eyes flickered with anger, but then she killed a nearby groaning, injured merchant sailor with a quick thrust of her saber into his chest and her mood improved dramatically. Thoroughly revolted, Rafe turned his back on Lauralee and headed for the Corsair and then the privacy of his cabin, where he could mourn the further stain on his character in secrecy.

"Rafe! Stay!" Lauralee commanded. Ever mindful of the cost of defiance, Rafe reluctantly stopped and turned around. "We are not finished here yet. You and I have the pleasure of slitting the throats of the wounded." She held out her bloodied blade. "You may use this. I have another."

Rafe refused to take the gore-stained blade. "VonLarken said to bring back the survivors to sell as slaves."

"Indeed, we take the survivors, but not the wounded. It cuts into our profits to doctor them."

"Charles and I were far more seriously wounded than most of these, yet you doctored us," Rafe argued.

"That was different. We suspected your value as soon as we set eyes upon you lying unconscious on the ground and covered from head to toe in your own blood and that of the bears. We gambled and won, for our suspicions that you two were the shipwrecked lords from the Lady Bountiful proved correct; and why are you not pleased at the chance to kill again since you claim to enjoy it as much as I?" Her lovely brown, long-lashed eyes narrowed. "Or was it a lie?"

"There's no sport in killing the helpless," Rafe said.

Lauralee's full, sensuous lips twisted into an ugly, displeased frown and she seized Rafe's shirt at the collar. "You will obey me or you will die as will your friend, Charles." She ran the back of the bloodied blade of her knife across Rafe's cheek to emphasize her threat leaving behind a red streak composed of the blood of her many victims, then again offered him the blade. Rafe reluctantly took it this time. Lauralee smiled. "Good boy." She patted him on the cheek, and earned a dark glare from him in return, which she graciously, at least in her opinion, chose to ignore. "Begin at the stern and we will meet in the middle. When we are finished we will aid the others in loading the cargo."

Rafe walked abaft then as Lauralee casually butchered her first victim by brutally slashing the man's throat, Rafe lightly sliced the skin of a young man probably no older than sixteen and whispered in his ear, "Play dead unless you truly wish to die." He did the same with the next wounded sailor and the next. It was the best he could do to save half of them, but it wasn't enough, for he knew he could easily stop Lauralee's killing spree if he could only find the courage to risk Charles's life. Choosing not to made him a murderer by proxy of the lowest order; and as if to confirm that conviction, as he moved methodically from victim to victim he was suddenly reminded of Matthew 12: 43-45. *When an evil spirit comes out of a man, it goes through arid places seeking rest and does not find it. When it arrives, it finds the house unoccupied, swept clean and put in order. Then it goes and takes with it seven other spirits more wicked than itself, and they go in and live there. And the final condition of that man is worse than the first.*

Rafe was then sorely tempted to take his blade to his own throat, but as with all his other actions lately heinous or otherwise he was completely ruled by the need to keep Charles alive. He finished his grisly task, grimly wiped his bloodied knife and hands on the shirt of his last *victim* and then joined Lauralee on her way to the cargo hold. Before they parted to transfer the stolen cargo Lauralee kissed him warmly, affectionately. He purposely failed to reciprocate and Lauralee was obviously miffed by his lack of ardor, but Rafe was too filled with shame and guilt to care.

The hard labor of transferring the cargo then effectively kept him from dwelling upon how completely he'd become the demon spawn Charles had so often derogatorily labeled him, but when the work was over, he once again had to deal with his conscience. The guilt was driving him to distraction, and so, desperate to escape from the soul searing emotions if only for a few hours, he deftly avoided Lauralee and headed for Carlos's cabin to ask to share some of his coca leaves.

He met VonLarken on the way there.

"I see you have returned alive and uninjured," the pirate captain observed.

"Yes and I've acquitted myself well, so next time see fit to provide me with a weapon!" Rafe brushed boldly past while fully expecting VonLarken to demand that he face punishment for his insolence, along with Charles. However, VonLarken let him go. Rafe was beyond caring or wondering why. His sole concern was to get to Carlos and the mind-numbing coca leaves.

When Carlos answered Rafe's knock on his door, it was readily apparent he was already high. "To what do I owe a visit from Lauralee's most handsome plaything ever?" he drawled his body swaying slightly like a noxious weed in a gentle breeze.

Rafe not only willingly, but eagerly chose to plunge further into iniquity. "I was wondering if you would spare some of your coca leaves for a fellow of like mind…"

Carlos grinned and chuckled. "Come in then, for I am in a generous mood. We shall celebrate our recent victory together, you and I."

Rafe stepped into the cabin, closing the door softly behind him.

For the remainder of the night, under the influence of the drug, Rafe and Carlos were the best of friends, but as Rafe returned to his cabin at dawn the next morning, the guilt and remorse he'd successfully staved off with the coca leaves returned with a vengeance with the added sting of shame over resorting to a reprehensible crutch. He desperately wanted to pray for forgiveness, but his absolute certainty that God would reject his earnest pleas presented a barrier he could not overcome. Instead, he vented his frustration and anger and guilt in a destructive rampage, tossing his chair across the room into his washstand, shattering the chair into four pieces and smashing the pitcher and bowl into unrecognizable remnants then sweeping the unlit candle and grooming items from the shelf beside his bed onto the floor. After that he turned on his bedding, dragging the blanket, pillow and mattress from his bed and shredding them with his bare hands then his knife when hands weren't strong enough and tossing the pieces about the room.

Finally, when there was nothing left upon which to vent, Rafe sank to his knees in the midst of the mess he'd made, buried his face in his hands, and sobbed in grief-stricken despair.

Chapter Thirty

By the time the Corsair docked in Nassau on New Providence two months later, Rafe had reluctantly participated in two more raids, the latest one on his twenty-fourth birthday; that cursed of all days. He'd slain many more innocent sailors without a hint of nausea and passively allowed Lauralee to slaughter the wounded while pretending to kill his fair share. To avoid dwelling on what he'd become, Rafe smoked coca leaves every night after Lauralee grew bored with him and let him go. When the drug inevitably wore off, and Rafe lay awake in the early morning hours battling guilt and shame, he was glad Charles wasn't free to witness his criminal activities. The last thing he wanted to face was Charles smugly pointing out that he'd been right all along to label him an abomination.

He stood on the deck of the Corsair numbly watching VonLarken's pirates hustle and bustle below as they unloaded the slaves and the stolen property captured on their raids while seriously considering finally ending his tortured existence by slipping into the waters and swimming out to sea until he could swim no more and drowned. After all, he'd fulfilled every demand the pirates had made and in their twisted way they were honorable even as he was. Charles would most likely be ransomed, his life purchased by countless heinous acts that Charles would thankfully remain unaware of. He gripped the cap rail tightly, his body tensed as he prepared to leap overboard, and then Lauralee came up and rested her hand possessively upon his. For a split second Rafe considered wrapping his arms around Lauralee and taking her down with him, but as much as he despised Lauralee, and even though he'd promised Carlos he would kill her, he couldn't find it within himself to add yet another murder to his already too long tally.

"We have done unusually well on our raids this season. Your considerable talents in battle have contributed greatly to our success," Lauralee said.

"Killing is what I do best," Rafe replied.

"Indeed. In that you and I are alike; and now you shall further prove your worth by selling Lord Huntington into slavery today. If you gain a fair price, you will become a full-fledged member of our crew. Does this please you?"

Rafe replied without hesitation, lies coming naturally to him now. "Exceedingly."

Lauralee smiled then leaned into Rafe and kissed him passionately. As usual he resisted the strong urge to shove her away, but this time he had a reprieve, for their kiss was almost immediately interrupted by Carlos. "When you are finished..." he remarked derisively.

Lauralee pulled away from Rafe and glowered hostilely at Carlos. "What do you want little brother?" she asked, with an emphasis on 'little'.

"Father instructed me to bring these to Rafe." Carlos shoved a shirt and pants made of coarse brown cloth into Rafe's arms while glaring defiantly at Lauralee. "These are the slave clothes for your friend," he explained to Rafe. "I have had a tub of water and some lye brought to your cabin. Make sure the slave is scrubbed clean, for clean slaves bring a much higher price." Carlos drew a loaded pistol from his sash and handed it to Rafe. "You may need this as sometimes the crowds grow unruly. Try not to kill any buyers, though."

"I can't promise that," Rafe said as he stuffed the bundle of slave clothes under his left arm and the pistol into his red, satin sash; a reward from Lauralee after the raid they'd conducted on his birthday. "Now you are mine night and day," she'd said and then she'd laughed, even as she did now at his comment to Carlos then wrapped her arms possessively around Rafe's waist. "Isn't Rafe wonderful, Carlos? You shall never be as good as he. Does this not make you insanely jealous?"

Carlos tossed Lauralee a murderous frown then turned on his heel and hastened away. Lauralee tried to resume her amorous kissing, but Rafe pulled back. "Time is short. I'd best fetch Charles."

Lauralee pouted, but she knew there were times when duty must take precedence over pleasure. "I suppose you should," she conceded reluctantly. She hooked her arm in Rafe's. "However, I shall accompany you. Since you are inexperienced in these matters, I will render help where needed."

Although it sounded like an offer, Rafe knew it was actually a command. He would've preferred some time alone with Charles to explain the situation, but over the last three months he'd become practiced at stifling useless objection. They walked arm in arm like true lovers with Lauralee chatting merrily and Rafe as dark and gloomy as a rain- soaked thundercloud, except when Lauralee looked directly at him. Then he assumed a pleasantly casual expression. The distasteful crime he was about to commit wasn't nearly as corrupt as his other criminal activities of late, but Charles's accusing glares and acidic sniping were sure to make him feel even more like the demon-spawn Charles had so often labeled him. Thus, with Lauralee attached to his arm like a beautiful leech, Rafe advanced uneasily into the bowels of the ship, feeling as if he was entering Hades with the devil at his side.

The other slaves had already been removed, leaving only Charles at the far end of the hold, sleeping, his ankles manacled, the chain passing through a nearby ring in the deck. It was readily apparent from the smell and Charles's ragged clothing that Rafe's one-time friend had endured unthinkable suffering these last three months, which made Rafe feel even guiltier for the certain amount of freedom he himself had enjoyed; although the price he'd paid for it had been far too high. He lightly gripped Charles's shoulder. "Charles," he said softly.

Charles slowly opened his eyes, but when he saw Rafe, he sat up eagerly his heavy chains clanking and rattling like a ghost haunting the cavernous hold. "Rafe! Is it really you?" He looked and sounded pleased, which exponentially increased Rafe's self-loathing and guilt. "I thought you might be dead, for after the initial news I had of you I received nothing more."

"As you can see, I'm very much alive," Rafe replied bitterly.

Catching his tone, Lauralee studied Rafe suspiciously. At times these past three months she'd sensed that her handsome playmate wasn't entirely sincere. Now she wondered if he'd been masquerading the entire time and would try to escape, taking Charles with him. Her hand drifted toward her knife. It would be a shame to have to kill Rafe, for he was by far the finest plaything she'd over owned. However, such sacrifices must be made on occasion, for the good of the clan.

"Have they freed us at last? Are we finally to go home?" Charles asked hopefully.

"Charles…" Rafe began.

Charles then noticed the pistol stuffed in Rafe's red sash, and his hopes died, even as understanding dawned. "You've joined them!"

Rafe nodded.

"I should've known when you looked so well! It's so like you to be concerned only for your own comfort while I've been suffering in this dark hold, chained like a slave and worried sick about you! Once again you've proven you're unworthy of life!" Charles spat.

Rafe wanted to argue that he'd suffered perhaps even more than Charles these last three months, although not all of it physically, but he knew Charles wouldn't care, and Lauralee would definitely be displeased, putting both their lives at risk from her quick temper. "I must admit I've enjoyed myself heartily," he lied coolly instead. "And you? How does it feel to be treated like the vermin that you are?"

Rafe's words caused two entirely different reactions. Lauralee smiled and relaxed. Charles spit in Rafe's face. Rafe wiped the spittle from his cheek without a trace of anger, for it was far less than he deserved, but Lauralee was enraged that Charles had soiled her precious plaything. She struck Charles on the cheek open-handed, knocking him onto his side. "How dare you! This man is far your better! Treat him with the respect he deserves slave, lest I allow him to kill you!"

"Rafe is incapable of killing me," Charles argued as he straightened, remembering the many times on the island Rafe had threatened his life and never followed through.

Lauralee laughed. "Will he not? I have seen him kill many men without hesitation, even to those who are wounded and defenseless."

She'd spoke with pride, like a mother bragging over her child's accomplishments, but Rafe was deeply mortified. It was bad enough that Charles thought he'd joined this viper's nest willingly and wholeheartedly, but now Charles knew the finite details of his shame as well. However, he maintained a façade of indifference as Charles looked at him aghast. "All these long months while I thought you were suffering like me and I was feeling sorry for you, even praying for you, you've been remorselessly killing and rampaging with these wicked people; and no doubt you've been cavorting with this Jezebel every night too! I never would've thought it possible that you could sink any lower, but apparently, there are no limits to your depravity."

Rafe's dark eyes flashed with fury and then he slugged Charles in the jaw with such force that it left an angry purple bruise behind. "That's some small repayment for your constant verbal abuses while we were on the island and even before that. I owe you more! Much more! But my Captain won't allow it for fear of ruining your price!"

Charles sullenly rubbed his new bruise. "Price! What price?"

"I made a deal with VonLarken. In return for half my fortune, he has allowed me to join his crew and to sell you into slavery," Rafe replied.

Charles was enraged that VonLarken had accepted Rafe's deal and not the one he'd offered himself, but he was far more enraged that Rafe was selling him into slavery when it should've been the other way around! "So not only have you taken up piracy, but you've fallen so low as to sell a friend into slavery, and a white man of noble birth besides!"

"Friend?" Rafe snarled acidly. "Since when have you been my friend, Charles?"

Charles bristled. "You know quite well that I've been your friend since we were both ten!"

"Liar!" Rafe spat. "Up until this moment you've emphatically insisted you were not my friend. Do you truly think me so dull as to believe you've suddenly changed your mind?" He turned to Lauralee and held out his hand. "The key to his restraints."

Lauralee pulled the key from one of her many hidden pockets in her voluminous skirt and handed it to Rafe. He dropped the bundle of clothing on the deck, knelt, unlocked and opened Charles's manacles, grabbed Charles's arm and dragged him violently to his feet then picked up the bundle of rough-spun, brown, slave clothes and shoved them into Charles's stomach with such force that the air was forced from Charles's lungs.

Charles grasped the bundle clumsily, and when he could speak again, asked "What's this?" as he held the rough-spun clothing away from his body with evident distaste.

"Your new clothing fit for your current station in life, slave," Rafe snarled.

Charles's eyes widened in shock and disbelief. Rafe was supposed to be the slave, not him! How could everything have turned so on its head? He looked directly into Rafe's abnormally dark eyes, searching for an iota of compassion, a pinch of sympathy, and saw nothing but an unrelenting darkness. "Oh Rafe," he lamented. "How easily you abandon what little humanity you still possessed. Do you even comprehend the matchless value of what you've so callously discarded?"

Rafe was painfully aware of the value of what he'd forfeited in exchange for Charles's life. Furthermore, since there was no forgiveness for one rejected by God, his heart would forever remain irreparably damaged by the countless heinous crimes and lustful sins he'd committed. However, maintaining his façade in front of Lauralee he boasted defiantly, "I've found something of far greater value than that which I've discarded. Acceptance."

"The acceptance of thieves and murderers! Does that mean more to you than—," Charles began.

Rafe slapped Charles's cheek open handed, cutting off his words. "Say no more, Charles! Not only do you completely lack understanding of what is of value to me, but your voice grates on my nerves."

Lauralee looked on approvingly, enough reassured to leave Rafe alone with Charles. "When you are done cleaning up the slave, bring him to my cabin," she said.

Rafe nodded acquiescence, even as he wondered what Lauralee wanted with Charles. If it was the same iniquity she'd demanded and received from him on countless seemingly endless nights, she'd be sorely disappointed, for Charles would refuse to break his marriage vows to Sarah, no matter the consequences; which could possibly be as severe as Lauralee killing Charles in anger. Then his iniquitous actions these last three months would've bought nothing except an increase of guilt on his already overburdened conscience. To avoid that guilt-inflicting scenario Rafe considered rescuing Charles now, but then decided it would be ill advised, for even his unique abilities had their limits. He could fight off VonLarken's men for only so long before they overwhelmed him, and then he and Charles would either be killed or sold into slavery. That was the way of it no matter how badly Rafe desired it otherwise.

Thus, with an aching heart and his stomach feeling as if he'd swallowed a large stone for breakfast, Rafe ushered Charles to his private cabin, which had been refurnished by an amused Lauralee after his destructive rampage a couple of months back. A copper tub sat in the middle of the room, filled with hot water, even as Carlos had said would be done. Rafe curtly instructed Charles. "Put the slave clothes on the bed, shed those rags and step into the tub; and be sure to scrub heartily. You smell like a dead skunk."

Charles meekly obeyed, while Rafe stood guard consumed by guilt and remorse but hiding it well, having become so practiced at concealing his true emotions that it no longer took the slightest effort. He watched seemingly emotionless as the clear water turned black with the three months of filth Charles washed from his body and hair. After Charles then dressed in the clean slave clothing, Rafe handed him his own comb. It took some time for Charles to detangle three months' worth of snarled hair, but he finally finished. So far he and Charles had exchanged no more words.

When Rafe reluctantly escorted Charles next door to Lauralee's cabin, Charles couldn't keep quiet any longer. "I suppose you've spent many a night in this cabin."

"Indeed. Jealous that I, a half-breed bastard, possess such a beauty?" Rafe asked smoothly, hiding his guilt and shame.

"Certainly not! That woman may be beautiful, but she's evil through and through, and so is anyone who consorts with her!"

Rafe privately agreed.

"I suppose you've been getting drunk on a regular basis as well," Charles accused disgustedly.

"On the contrary I've found something better. I regularly smoke coca leaves instead," Rafe said defiantly.

Charles gasped. "You've become a drug addict as well as a drunk?"

"As I've told you many times, Charles, I was never a drunk," Rafe said. He knocked on Lauralee's door and called out, "I've brought the slave."

Lauralee answered. "Enter, my love."

Rafe opened the door, shoved Charles inside, stepped into the cabin behind him and closed the door.

Lauralee reposed on a wooden chair in the middle of her cabin, legs crossed, impatiently drumming one dainty foot on the deck; a foot that looked as if it should be shod in a glass slipper instead of the ordinary brown leather slippers she wore. "It is about time! I was nearly ready to come looking for you." She stood up. "What took you so long?"

"It took some time to clean the countless layers of filth off of him," Rafe explained. "Unfortunately, there was nothing I could do about his soiled personality. We must hope potential buyers won't notice until it's too late."

Charles glared at Rafe, but surprisingly didn't serve him a snappy comeback, which troubled Rafe. Charles was always ready with his snide comments. If Charles wasn't throwing them at him now, then it could only mean his spirit was crushed; which added new blame to Rafe's conscience, for having failed to find some way to get them both out of this mess long before now.

"He does clean up well, my love," Lauralee remarked while studying Charles lustfully.

"He has some few redeeming features," Rafe conceded.

Charles drew himself up indignantly. "I am a lord! How dare you two talk about me as if I'm—," he began to object, but then Rafe raised his hand as if to strike him and Charles clamped his mouth shut.

"*Lord* Huntington," Lauralee said mockingly. "Please sit in this chair." She rested her hand on the back of the chair.

Charles rebelliously refused to budge so Rafe shoved Charles into the chair and then firmly gripped Charles's shoulder with his strong, tan hand, keeping him there while secretly wondering what he would do if Lauralee had something nefarious in mind. However, Lauralee only crossed to her dresser, opened a top drawer and grabbed a pair of scissors and a razor, making it clear that she only intended to give Charles a shave and a haircut. With a firm hand, Rafe continued to hold Charles still while Lauralee cut his hair, shaved him and then stepped back to admire her handiwork.

"I would never have believed it, but you are nearly as handsome as my Rafe." She patted Charles on the cheek as one would a small boy. Charles shied away from her touch. She laughed. "My, my, he is such an inhibited boy. Even as you once were. Yes, my love?"

"One of his many faults," Rafe remarked attempting to rally Charles into making a snide comment; but Charles refused to take the bait or even to look at him.

Lauralee pulled a short rope from one of her many elusive pockets and handed it to Rafe to use it to secure Charles's wrists behind his back as had been done to the other slaves. Although Rafe's conscience rebelled at restraining Charles like a common slave, he did it without outward hesitation; although he was secretly hoping Charles would finally show some spirit and berate him; which would at least make him feel better. Unluckily for Rafe's conscience, however, Charles remained stonily silent, which had a more profoundly depressing effect upon Rafe than even the worst of Charles's stinging barbs ever had.

Rafe and Lauralee ushered Charles outside, through the crowded streets of Nassau, to the slave market in front of Vendue House, a bustling, smelly place, and worse, the day was humid and hot.

After so long in the dark hold, the bright sunlight hurt Charles's eyes and gave him a headache. He shot a hate-filled glance at Rafe, who quickly looked away, but not before Charles saw a strange something in Rafe's dark eyes. He disgustedly assumed Rafe was under the influence of the coca leaves he'd earlier admitted to smoking, but Rafe was not under the influence of anything but his conscience, which was accusing him mercilessly, and which he was studiously, but unsuccessfully attempting to ignore. He guided Charles to a row of cages in the southwest corner of the marketplace then shoved him into a smaller cage at the end of the row that was barely large enough for Charles to stand upright in and far too narrow for him to sit down. Charles tossed Rafe another hate filled glance for picking this smaller cage rather than one of the larger ones, but it was wasted, for Rafe refused to make eye contact. He locked the cage with a black metal padlock the size of his palm that Lauralee had drawn from yet another hidden pocket in her skirt, and then he and Lauralee disappeared into the crowd leaving Charles on display.

He'd never felt more humiliated, as nearly everyone who passed his cage poked and prodded the rare white slave as if he were a slab of beef or a piece of ripening fruit. Every now and then someone even pinched him purely out of spite and then had the gall to laugh at his outrage! After enduring hours of this degrading treatment, Charles vowed that if he ever had the chance, he'd make Rafe pay a hundred thousand times over for his betrayal! It never even occurred to Charles that Rafe had endured this sort of ill treatment his entire life, the only difference that Rafe's suffered abuse had been more emotional than physical until he'd accidentally killed Duncan. Then the physical abuse had begun as well, made worse as it was from those he'd loved as a brother and a foster father.

Several hours later Rafe and Lauralee returned. Charles judged from the way Lauralee coyly hung on Rafe's arm that they'd been engaging in carnal immorality and although he'd vowed never to speak to Rafe again his self-righteous anger had the better of him. "It's about time you returned, Rafe! How could you leave me here in this cage to be poked and prodded like an animal while you went off to sin with that hussy? Have you no decency left in you?" he complained.

Rafe glared at Charles with such malignant hatred that Charles shivered in fear and recoiled as far as was possible within his limited confines. Then Rafe said, "We've been listing you as a slave and setting your price. They wanted to know what manner of worker you are and to ask a better price I had to lie and tell them you were an exceptionally hard worker."

"I am a hard worker! I did the largest share of the work on the island while you were off lazing in Nirvana!" Charles objected.

Rafe gripped the bars of Charles's cage with both hands so tightly that his knuckles whitened. "You spent every minute playing with Adam. I had to kill the kitten to gain any work from you, but I should've killed you instead! It would've been far better for my future peace of mind!" He shoved away from the bars then turned away his shoulders heaving with his angry breathing.

Charles was appalled by this vicious verbal attack that was not only uncalled for, but all lies! He was about to say as much, but then Lauralee pulled Rafe aside and said, "It is unseemly to allow a lowly slave to bother you. Merely sell him for a great price and have your revenge."

Rafe pulled away from Lauralee with such blatantly apparent distaste that Charles began to hope Rafe wasn't as wholly lost as he seemed. He waited until Lauralee was occupied with customers then pressed his face between the bars of his cage and addressed Rafe softly. "Rafe." Rafe looked icily at him and he found it hard not to cringe under that steely stare, but he buoyed himself with the fact that he was the lord and Rafe was his slave then said, "You haven't forgotten it's your fault I'm in this mess have you?"

Rafe didn't answer, but Charles thought he saw a trace of shame mixed with regret in Rafe's overly dark eyes, which gave him the courage to continue. "Not that I'm blaming you. I know you're hopelessly enslaved by your savage nature. Nevertheless, don't you think it's about time you took action and remedied this unfair situation?"

Rafe punched Charles in the jaw, the same place he'd hit him earlier. Charles recoiled in pain and shock, but at least he no longer had any doubt that Rafe lacked even the tiniest amount of humanity.

"Oooh." Lauralee ran her hand across Rafe's broad, well-muscled chest. "You are exceedingly desirable when you are angry my love!" she whispered and leaned closer to kiss him.

Rafe roughly shoved her away.

Lauralee whipped out her knife. "You are forgetting your place, plaything!"

"On the contrary, for the first time in months I'm remembering it!" Rafe said.

Lauralee considered where best to skewer Rafe. She wished to hurt him badly, but not mar his good looks or ruin his ability to please her in bed. Then she realized that the punishment would have to wait, for it was time to lead Charles up the thirteen steps to the auction block. She reluctantly sheathed her knife. "It is our turn on the auction block. Do not fail me in this," she warned Rafe.

Rafe nodded once, sullenly, then opened the cage and dragged the unwilling and uncooperative Charles up the stairs to the auction block. Lauralee watched from below, ready to intervene if necessary, but it turned out she had nothing to worry about, for Rafe sold Charles to a wealthy plantation owner for an unheard of high price. When Rafe descended the steps, she ran up and snatched the heavy coin pouch from his hand. "We have never made this much coin on one single slave! If we keep a bit for ourselves, Father will never know!" She pocketed a generous share of the coins then held out a handful to Rafe, who hadn't heard a word she'd said, for he was preoccupied with watching Charles's new slave master snap an iron collar around his neck and manacles on his wrists. "Rafe!" Lauralee snapped crossly. Rafe tore his eyes from Charles and looked at Lauralee with barely veiled hatred. "Here is your share of the price you earned for your friend. Do you want it or not?" she asked irritably.

"Not." Rafe resumed watching Charles as he was herded into the back of a wagon along with two other newly bought slaves, one male, one female, the latter another rare white slave like Charles.

Lauralee's eyes narrowed. "You are not suffering guilt over selling your friend are you?"

Rafe continued to ignore her as he watched the wagon drive away with Charles.

"Rafe!" Lauralee stomped her foot.

Rafe finally looked at the woman he loathed more than his cursed life.

"Did you hear what I said?" she demanded.

"Yes, and stop calling Charles my friend. He was never my friend," Rafe said.

"It hardly matters anymore, does it, since you will never see him again," Lauralee said. Then she held out the handful of coins she'd reserved for Rafe. "Here. Your share of the overage you earned in the sale of your friend. You have earned it."

Rafe roughly shoved Lauralee's hand aside almost making her drop the money. "I want none of that cursed coin!"

Lauralee was initially inclined toward anger, for it was extremely rare that she offered an unworthy playmate a share of anything. Rafe should be gushing with gratitude! Then it occurred to her that Rafe's loss was her gain. "I shall keep the coins for myself then. Do not ask me for them later, for I will not give them to you." She tucked the coins into one of the numerous hidden pockets of her skirt.

"Fine. Is the day finished? Am I free to go?" Rafe asked sullenly.

"Oh the day is far from finished, my love. Now we celebrate. Down the street there is a tavern called the Trader's Friend that serves good food and even better drink. You will accompany me there." She traipsed playfully away.

The last thing Rafe wanted to do was spend time in a bar with a bunch of drunks. It was a semblance of drunkenness that had ruined his life. Unfortunately, he had no choice, for he was not quite ready to abandon the pirates. He needed to conduct a bit of research first in Von Larkin's private library.

* * *

It took less than an hour for Rafe to discover that Lauralee's version of celebrating was drinking until she was so inebriated she couldn't see straight. As she shamelessly flirted with every handsome man in the bar and even some not so handsome, Rafe retired to a table in a dark corner and watched the room with such dark malignancy that none of the barmaids or anyone else dared approach him. Halfway through the day, Carlos tracked Rafe down.

"I have come for the pistol I lent you earlier today," he said.

Rafe pulled the pistol from his sash and slapped it into Carlos's hand. Carlos shoved the pistol into his own sash then crossed the room to Lauralee who was currently precariously seated on the lap of a drunken sailor. "VonLarken is waiting for the earnings." He had to shout it three times before in her drunken haze Lauralee understood. She searched her many pockets for the coin pouch, eventually discovered the right one then handed the coin pouch to Carlos. He poured the contents onto the table, counted the coins, scooped them back into the pouch then returned to Rafe, grinning. "Such a fine price you have earned for your friend! Father will be well pleased! Now you are truly one of us!" He slapped Rafe on the back.

Rafe's left hand fisted at his side as he was tempted to slug Carlos.

"I will see you back at the ship tonight and then we shall smoke coca leaves. Yes?" Carlos asked grinning.

"I look forward to it," Rafe lied.

"Not until after I am finished with him," Lauralee said possessively, slurring her words and hiccupping.

"Of course. He is after all yours." Carlos hastened away. He was even more afraid of Lauralee in her inebriated state than when she was sober.

Lauralee plopped onto Rafe's lap, wrapped her arm around his neck, and then he was forced to endure a sloppy, drunken kiss made only somewhat easier by the knowledge that soon he'd be free from her talons forever. Then Lauralee drunkenly sashayed off to find another handsome man to kiss. She finally passed out drunk an hour before dawn. Rafe hoisted her unceremoniously over his shoulder and carried her back to her cabin then dumped her onto her bed. She mumbled incoherently then promptly began snoring, loudly.

Rafe hastened to the Captain's cabin. VonLarken was spending the night in his favorite bordello and so he would use VonLarken's private library to access and study the street map of Nassau and of the island of New Providence. Then he'd leave this degrading life behind forever and grant his conscience a much-needed good deed as well as satisfy his honor by rescuing Charles and seeing him safely on board a ship home to the colonies. He'd polish it all off by heading out into the wilderness and doing God, his long dead adopted Mohican tribe, and society both genteel and coarse a favor by finally ending his unworthy life.

He was almost to the door to VonLarken's cabin when he was accosted by a drunken Carlos. "Rafe, well met!" he slurred happily. "Are you on your way to Lauralee's cabin?"

Rafe shook his head. "She has no more need of me tonight."

"Ah. Good." Carlos pulled a brown paper packet of dried coca leaves from his pocket and waved it in Rafe's face nearly losing his balance. "Then we two shall have a little smoke." He hiccupped.

It was an appealing offer, to forget his most recent sins in a drugged fog if only for a few hours, but the time for such immoral activities was at an end. He'd need his full wits about him from now on until the end. "Perhaps later." He brushed rudely past Carlos.

Carlos wobbled unsteadily after Rafe and grabbed his arm. "Wait! I am not finished talking to you."

Rafe irritably brushed Carlos's hand away making him lose his balance and nearly fall, but he grabbed the cap rail and sloppily righted himself. "How dare you lay hands on me!" he complained. "Have you forgotten that I am your superior? I could have you whipped for insub—in—subor—din—ation!"

Rafe was sorely tempted to demonstrate true insubordination, but Farley was on watch and Farley was well known among the crew for his conscientiousness. If Rafe harmed Carlos, Farley might well come to Carlos's aid. Rafe liked Farley. He had no wish to hurt him. He sighed in frustration. "What do you want?"

Carlos looked surreptitiously over his shoulder as if afraid he might be overheard by Farley even though they were separated by half the ship. Then he leaned forward to whisper in Rafe's ear, but he lost his balance. Rafe caught him by both arms above the elbow, not because he cared if Carlos fell on his face, but only to keep Carlos from falling on him. He shoved Carlos distastefully and roughly upright, but Carlos didn't seem to notice the ill treatment. "You sold your friend for a much higher price than Lauralee gave, yes?"

Rafe remained silent.

"No need to answer. I know you did, for Lauralee always steals a portion of the earnings. I wager she did not share any of it with you," Carlos said.

"Come to your point," Rafe snapped impatiently.

Carlos looked behind him again, saw that Farley was looking in the opposite direction, and whispered conspiratorially. "My sister cannot fight back at the moment. Now would be a good time to keep your promise to kill her."

Rafe threw reluctance to the wind and allowed himself a pleasure he'd been denying himself ever since that first night at dinner. He punched Carlos in the nose with all his might. Carlos flew backward and landed on his back on the deck with a loud thud. Rafe looked to Farley for his reaction. Farley looked at Carlos lying spread-eagled and unconscious on his back on the deck then calmly looked away. Rafe breathed a sigh of relief. Apparently, Farley's disdain for Carlos mirrored his own. Feeling easier not only because Farley hadn't raised the alarm, but because he'd finally had the opportunity to release his long pent up anger and frustration on someone deserving, Rafe waited until Farley was looking in the opposite direction then sprinted into the Captain's cabin.

He spent the next several hours researching New Providence then made his way to his cabin, skirting the washtub with its filthy water that no one had bothered to remove, the sight of which pricked his conscience, and lay down on his bunk without bothering to undress.

He'd only planned to take a short rest of an hour or two before he then left the ship, but when he awoke it was mid-afternoon. He hastily arose, shaved off his beard and mustache, re-braided his hair into a single, thick, braid, packed his few belongings in a rolled up blanket, strapped on the short sword Carlos had given him in a sheath he'd taken off a dead merchant sailor during a raid, and was ready to leave when there was a knock on his door. He cursed under his breath then hid the rolled up blanket behind the door before he opened it to find Carlos standing there. He had trouble not smiling with satisfaction at first sight of the cut across the bridge of Carlos's broken nose, and his two black eyes.

Carlos was at first rendered speechless upon seeing Rafe clean-shaven for the first time, but he quickly recovered. He stabbed Rafe in the chest with his index finger. "You punched me last night."

Having been out of his mind on coca leaves often enough, Rafe knew Carlos's recollections of last night were fuzzy at best; and especially since he'd been drunk as well. "I did nothing of the sort," he lied easily.

Carlos studied Rafe, doubt clouding his features. "Did we not talk last night?"

Rafe frowned. "Is this why you disturbed my rest? Do you think I'm any more able to remember the details of last night than you?" He started to close his door.

Carlos slapped his palm on the door and shoved it back open. "Wait! Father is on board and he sent me to fetch you."

"Now?" Rafe wondered what VonLarken could possibly want with him. Had Carlos blabbed about the money Lauralee had stolen? Had Farley told VonLarken he'd punched Carlos? Or had VonLarken somehow discovered he'd been perusing his private library? "I'm busy."

Carlos lacked the intelligence to wonder what Rafe could possibly be busy with, since his duties were suspended for a few days like everyone else's. "Nevertheless, when VonLarken calls, we answer. You should know that by now."

Rafe sighed then reluctantly accompanied Carlos to Von Larken's cabin, the door of which was propped open. He sat at his writing desk, armed with a pistol, having just finished counting the tallest of seven stacks of coins. He greeted Rafe cheerily. "Lord Brookstone! Come in. Come in."

Rafe reluctantly entered, followed by Carlos.

"I am pleased by the unusually large sum you earned selling your friend. It seems a talented killer also makes a skilled slaver," VonLarken said.

"Indeed," Rafe agreed.

VonLarken motioned to a wooden chair placed at an angle in front of his writing desk. "Sit."

Rafe took the proffered chair. Carlos headed for another chair on the starboard side of the cabin, intending to bring it over and set it next to Rafe's. "No Carlos, leave us," VonLarken commanded. "Shut the door behind you."

Carlos obviously wanted to stay, but he didn't have the courage to argue. He hastily retreated, closing the door gently behind him. VonLarken actually looked disappointed that Carlos hadn't shown some spunk and argued with him, or at least slammed the door in anger. "He's craven, that one. A thorn in my side."

Rafe agreed with the former and was delighted by the latter, but wisely refrained from commenting on either.

"Are you a father?" VonLarken asked.

"Not yet, but I hope to be someday," Rafe said.

VonLarken tilted his chair onto its back legs and stared up at the ceiling for such a long time that Rafe wondered if the pirate Captain had forgotten he was there. Without warning VonLarken slammed the chair down and slapped his palm on his writing desk knocking over the seven stacks of coins some of which then clattered to the floor. "You have no idea then what it is like to lose a child to murder!"

Rafe sat up straighter suspecting where this conversation was headed. "No sir, but as a child of ten I had to watch helplessly bound as mercenaries slaughtered my adopted tribe. I still grieve for their loss."

"Is this so? Then let the two of us who have lost loved ones commiserate." VonLarken crossed his arms and glared at Rafe so viciously that Rafe was glad he had the short sword. VonLarken leaned toward him. "Tell me what you know of Delilah's disappearance."

"Why would you think I know anything of that?" Rafe asked evasively.

VonLarken's muddy brown eyes narrowed. He drew his pistol and aimed it directly at Rafe's heart. "Come now, I am an old man, but not an old fool. Do you think I did not know Delilah was dead months ago and that you are responsible? Why do you think I sent you on that first raid without a weapon?"

Rafe's left hand strayed toward the pommel of his short sword. "Then why didn't you kill me when I returned unharmed?"

"Because you not only performed admirably on that raid and why dispose of a good man while we are on the hunt? I also admired your boldness in that you did not hesitate to speak brazenly to me, even as you have done just now. That is a good trait for a pirate, as is your willingness to kill me." VonLarken nodded at Rafe's left hand, which was almost to his sword hilt. "I would advise you not to touch your blade though, or you will die instantly."

Rafe hesitated then dropped his hand to his side.

"Wise choice. If only you were my son instead of Carlos," VonLarken lamented softly. He then shook his head as if to clear it of all hope of his son ever living up to his expectations. "So... Why did you kill my beautiful Delilah?"

"I did not kill her. It was Lauralee," Rafe said.

VonLarken surged to his feet. "You lie!" he roared keeping his pistol aimed at Rafe's heart. "I have a witness who saw you disposing of Delilah's Celtic knife the morning she disappeared!"

Rafe's ire rose. So Carlos had informed on him after all. The scum!

With lightning quick rapidity Rafe lunged and snatched VonLarken's pistol from his hand. Then he retreated out of VonLarken's reach and aimed the pistol at his evil heart.

VonLarken's eyes narrowed. "Very good, Rafe, but you shall return my pistol now and in return I shall kill you quickly instead of the flaying I had in mind."

"I would oblige you sir, for I'm most weary of life, but I have an unfinished task weighing on my conscience and thus, I cannot die yet be it quick or otherwise," Rafe said.

VonLarken studied Rafe thoughtfully for a few seconds. "You intend to rescue your friend, Charles," he then said.

"Yes," Rafe replied seeing no reason to deny it.

"It is another good trait, loyalty to a friend. It seems you are full of good traits." VonLarken sank down into his chair like a tired old man, rested his elbow on the desk, and covered his face with his hand. "She was such a lovely creature, my Delilah, like her dear departed mother, my third wife whom I had no choice but to kill when I caught her with another man when Delilah was only two. Now I have lost my little Delilah as well." VonLarken wiped away a single tear then demanded harshly, "How did you dispose of the body?"

Rafe shifted position uneasily. "Dumped overboard," he said succinctly, hoping fewer words would make the foul deed sound less horrific.

Apparently, it didn't help. VonLarken yanked open the top side drawer of his writing desk and seized another loaded pistol, but before he could pull the trigger, Rafe shot him in the center of his forehead. The pistol dropped from VonLarken's lifeless hand back into the drawer and his upper body slumped forward onto his desk. Rafe whirled around and faced the door expecting Carlos or someone else to burst in drawn by the sound of the gunfire, but an entire minute passed and no one showed, so Rafe crossed to the door, cracked it open and peered out.

No one was in sight. He closed the door, stuffed the pistol into his red sash behind his back, where it was easily accessible, but not as easily seen then pragmatically gathered the loose coins from the desk and floor, stuffing his pockets with them. He justified his theft by rationalizing that it was reasonable compensation for the heinous acts he'd been forced to commit for Charles's sake; and so for once his conscience didn't bother him.

Deciding not to waste time retrieving his small bundle of belongings from his cabin since he now had money to replace everything, he headed directly for the docks. Although it was well past noon none of the crew was about, except the lone man on watch and he was such a notorious shirker that it was easy to sneak off the ship without him noticing. As Rafe rounded the corner at the end of the dock, he made the mistake of congratulating himself on his easy escape, for then destiny perversely felt compelled to intervene. He ran headlong into Carlos.

"Where are you off to?" Carlos asked suspiciously.

Rafe rested his hand on his sword pommel as he contemplated having his revenge against Carlos for tattling to VonLarken about Delilah's knife, but one glance at the horde of people thronging the docks, every one of them a potential witness to his crime, convinced him that it would be wiser to forgo that pleasure. He hastily concocted a lie. "I'm off to buy a poison, to kill Lauralee as I promised you I would; one that will cause intense agony before death takes her."

Carlos nodded at the short sword. "Why not use that sword I gave you while she is unable to fight back, being unconscious from overindulging last night?"

"I stopped by her cabin after VonLarken dismissed me to do just that, but she's already up and asking for port to ease her hangover. You know how skilled she is. If I should attack her and lose..." Rafe shook his head. "Her death will be far more certain if I poison the port, besides that it will be highly satisfying to watch her die in agony. I'll even call you in to watch if you would like."

Carlos laughed. "I would, but then you had best hurry. You know how impatient Lauralee is and we don't want her to take another cure rather than await your return."

Rafe nodded then hurried away, exulting. He was free from Lauralee, free from Carlos, and free from the constant reminders that he was singlehandedly every bit as wicked and reprehensible as the two of them combined, plus their father.

Chapter Thirty-One

Eager to be rid of the reminder that Lauralee had once owned him completely Rafe tore off his red silk sash and tossed it to a ragged street urchin then he purchased several changes of clothes, a few other necessities such as a water skin, some beef jerky, hard cheese, and plenty of bullets and powder, a bag to carry them in with a long strap that he wore crosswise on his chest, and a thin pallet with cover and carrying strap that he wore on his opposite side. Now he only needed the name and location of the plantation Charles had been carted off to. That was easy enough if he could search the records at Vendue house, but the house was already closed for the day, and by tomorrow morning Lauralee or Carlos would surely have men on watch there. Luckily, since a white highly educated slave was a singular rarity, there was sure to be plenty of talk about the sale, so Rafe was certain if he spent a reasonable amount of time in any tavern he'd eventually have all the information he needed to track down Charles.

He first visited the Pirate's Mate, a shabby, smelly tavern in the seedy area of Nassau frequented by pirates and sailors. He took a seat in a shadowed corner and dourly watched the drunken revelers until two in the morning without hearing anything about the sale of a rare white slave. He left the tavern and rented a room in a nearby in then slept all through the day. As night fell, he headed for the Golden Unicorn in a more upscale area of Nassau.

As soon as he entered the clean, brightly lit tavern, Rafe spotted Luke, Carlos's number one man. Luke was muscular, with a broad chest, a cruel nature, and low intelligence, which made him a perfect pirate in Rafe's opinion and apparently Carlos's too. Luke had spotted Rafe at the same time as Rafe had spotted him. He sprang to his feet and barreled toward Rafe, who made a hasty exit. He then led Luke on a brisk chase through the city, until he came upon a dark alley. He slipped into the shadows, removed his powder horn, bag and bedroll and then waited like a spider in its lair for Luke to catch up to him.

A moment later, Luke stupidly blundered into the dark alley. Rafe seized him, tossed him to the ground as easily as if he was a small child then wrapped his fingers tightly around Luke's neck. Luke reached out for Rafe's neck in turn, but as Rafe's reach was longer, Luke's hands convulsed futilely in empty air several inches short of their desired grasp. Luke's realization that he was a dead man, promptly followed by stark fear, was plainly evident in his beady brown eyes, but that didn't deter Rafe from tightening his stranglehold until Luke's face turned blue. Then Rafe's conscience kicked in. He inhaled sharply and pulled his hands away as if they'd just been burned on a hot stove then scrambled to his feet and backed up a few steps. As he watched Luke intently for any sign of returning life, he remembered that he'd once done exactly this same thing to Charles, which amounted to a habit. What sort of monster had he become!

An entire minute passed without any sign of returning consciousness in Luke. Fearing he'd added yet another murder to his already shamefully long, and seemingly ever growing, tally, Rafe knelt and pressed his first two fingers on Luke's carotid artery, a trick he'd learned from observing the chirurgeon, Jacob. To his great relief he felt a pulse, weak but steadily growing stronger. Luke would suffer a lingering headache, sore muscles, and a bruised throat, but at least he'd live unlike most that'd crossed paths with him lately. He retrieved his belongings and continued on his way to the next most reputable tavern in Nassau, called the Fire Breathing Dragon.

A quarter of an hour later Rafe re-emerged onto the streets of Nassau smiling with the information he needed. Charles had been bought by the Kelley's, who owned a plantation on the opposite side of the sixty mile island near Southwest Bay. It was too far to walk when a man was in a hurry, but on the way to the tavern Rafe had passed a stable selling horses and tack.

He was almost to the stable when he spotted Lauralee coming toward him. He sighed in disgust. He'd crossed two members of the VonLarken clan within twenty-four hours. In a city the size of Nassau he should've easily been able to avoid them altogether! What further proof did he need that God hated him!

Lauralee smiled pleasantly. "Well met my handsome playmate."

"Lauralee," Rafe responded icily.

"Whatever have you been up to these last two days; other than killing Father, I mean," she asked sweetly, as if she hadn't been purposely tracking him down to kill him.

"As you well know, I've been avoiding the VonLarken clan. How did you find me?"

"I merely happened to be passing by and saw you. It was destiny, yes? We were meant to be together." She leaned forward for a kiss, but Rafe hastily stepped back. Lauralee's lovely, doe eyes narrowed. "That is no way to treat your lover!"

"Agreed, but there's never been any love between us," Rafe said.

Lauralee laughed, but Rafe could hear the undertone of rage in it. "I have missed you in my bed, and if that is not love, then what is it?"

"Lust," Rafe said.

"But is lust not as good as love or perhaps even better as it avoids the mess of entanglement?" She smiled coyly.

"Perhaps," Rafe said, and Lauralee's smile widened. "Were it any woman other than you, I might even consider pursuing such a relationship."

Lauralee's smile vanished and her hand strayed toward one of the many hidden pockets in her skirt, but the street was filling with people, many of them watching the striking couple curiously. "Let us talk in private." She nodded at an alley between two buildings.

Rafe knew Lauralee only wished to escape prying eyes so she could kill him, but his intent was no less sinister. He obligingly accompanied her into the alley then once again freed himself of his bulky items. "So, Rafe," Lauralee said, watching him warily, knowing full well he was preparing to fight. "You have been a naughty playmate, killing father and evading Carlos and me; but do not worry, I am not angry with you. On the contrary, I am grateful, for you have elevated me to Captain by your actions."

"Glad to be of service," Rafe said sarcastically.

"So then do you not think it is time you ended this nonsense and returned home?"

"I thought I'd already made it abundantly clear that nothing in this world would entice me to spend another moment with you." Rafe stepped clear of his pile of belongings.

Lauralee controlled her temper, but with noticeable difficulty. "Perhaps you do not understand the situation."

"I assure you, I understand it fully."

"Nevertheless, I shall explain to make certain there is no mistake. As I mentioned before, now that you have killed VonLarken, I am Captain, and as such I may grant your every wish. Do you wish to be First Mate? You have it. Do you wish the half of your fortune returned? You have that too and you will have me in the bargain. You will be my equal in bed and no longer a playmate. Is all that not worth returning for?"

"You made me your unwilling slave and prostitute by threatening Charles's life should I refuse to cater to your every whim. Now you offer me a different payment for my services, but even if you offered me the world on a golden platter, it still wouldn't be enough to entice me to spend another moment in your bed. Simply put, Lauralee, I despise everything about you," Rafe said.

Lauralee whipped out an already loaded pistol from one of her many hidden pockets and shoved it into Rafe's side. "Then I shall have to kill you. It is such a shame, for I did so very much appreciate your unique talents. All of them. However, I shall at least have the joy of killing."

"I'm well aware of the immense pleasure you gain from taking lives, Lauralee, but you'll forgo that bliss today." Rafe plucked the pistol from Lauralee's hand.

Lauralee stared at her empty hand in shock and disbelief, but she quickly recovered and snatched her knife from its sheath. Rafe didn't give her a chance to use it. He shot her through the heart with her own pistol. She dropped the knife, stared at the fast-spreading spot of blood on her blouse then stared at Rafe in disbelief. "You—," she cried accusingly, before she crumpled to the ground in death.

Rafe wasted a moment glaring in revulsion at the exquisitely sculpted face and body that had masked an unquestionably evil heart. Unlike the other times he'd taken a life, Rafe experienced no guilt or remorse. On the contrary he felt a certain amount of satisfaction, but he wasn't finished with her yet. He stuffed the pistol in his belt, knelt, and fluidly scooped up Lauralee's knife, grabbed a handful of her lustrous, soft black hair, stretched out her neck and slashed her beautifully shaped throat in revenge for Delilah and all the wounded innocents Lauralee had butchered in the same manner. He then grimly wiped the bloodied knife on her skirt, stuffed it back in his belt and pragmatically searched her body. He found a considerable amount of coin in the sum of her many hidden pockets and pocketed it then collected his belongings and prepared to leave.

A muffled movement to his left in the sooty blackness at the end of the alley stayed him, however. He peered into the shadows and his eyes narrowed when he spotted a small boy of mixed blood who looked to be about seven years old, with light brown eyes, brown skin, and tousled, dirty, curly blond hair. He crouched nearly invisible in the shadows against the wall. Rafe pointed at the child. "You!" he said sternly. The boy cowered, his light brown eyes wild with fright. "Come here!" Rafe pointed to a spot on the ground directly in front of him.

The child shook his head and backed further into the shadows, visibly trembling. Realizing he was scaring the child half to death, Rafe softened both his tone and his manner. "Have no fear, little one." He held his arms out to his sides, palms out. "I won't hurt you. See? I've no weapons to hand."

"I din' see nuttin," the boy cried as he cowered against the wall. "I swears not to tell no one you kilt the pritty lady."

Rafe blew out his breath in frustration. Common sense dictated he depart the scene of his crime as quickly as possible and this delay was making him uncomfortable. "Show yourself, boy," he demanded curtly.

"If I do, you'll kill me," the child whimpered. He covered his head with a tattered, gray blanket.

For the first time since he'd entered the alley Rafe took full note of his surroundings. The boy cowered among a few other shabby items of little or no note. This alley was his home. So not only did the child live in misery, but now he'd witnessed an ugly killing. *Wonderful.* "How long have you lived here?" he asked the child gently.

"I don livs heer. I was jist—uh—visitin."

The simple lie would've amused Rafe had he not been troubled by the serious problem of what to do with the boy. It was entirely possible if he merely walked away the boy would alert the authorities, if not out of fear then for the reward for his capture, which must be substantial by now, or at least it would be when the full measure of his criminal activities came to light. He considered scaring the boy into silence with a few choice threats, but the poor child had already been traumatized enough merely by having witnessed the brutality of his revenge on Lauralee. Taking the child hostage was out of the question, since that would only complicate matters with the boy constantly attempting to escape. His best option was to kill the child, but the mere thought of committing such a ghastly deed made his stomach churn.

Rafe pulled a handful of Lauralee's silver and copper coins from his pocket and tossed them at the boy, hoping it would buy some small bit of loyalty. They landed at the child's feet, but although it was a small fortune, he backed away as if was a horde of deadly poisonous spiders. "Take the money," Rafe urged. "Rent a room, and buy yourself a hot meal and some new clothes."

The boy looked longingly at the coins. He'd never seen so much money. "You ain goin to kill me wen I piks them up are you?" he asked warily.

"I don't make a practice of killing innocent children," Rafe said stiffly then walked away.

The boy hastily scooped up the coins, stuffed them inside his least tattered pants pocket then raced after Rafe, slowing as he tentatively skirted Lauralee's body while eyeing it apprehensively as if he expected it to rise up and grab him by his ankle.

Rafe cursed silently in Mohican when he heard the boys light, quick steps behind him. He glanced over his shoulder and saw the child dart behind a tree then cursed softly, in French this time, since it had the most appropriate word for the occasion. It seemed his bribe had bought a bit more loyalty than he'd intended. He considered confronting the boy, but the street was filled with people and he couldn't risk drawing attention. He considered buying a horse as he'd been about to do before he'd met Lauralee. The boy would never be able to keep up with him then; but if the boy followed him into the stables and started blabbing about the killing in front of the stable master... It would be safest to continue on foot; let the child follow him until he wearied and gave up. He was so thin and starved it wouldn't take long.

* * *

As night fell, Rafe discovered how wrong his assumption had been. He'd traveled hard and fast all day, stopping only twice; once to fill his water skin from a stream, and once to pick and eat a handful of berries from a bush beside the road. The boy followed him all day without anything to eat or drink. Rafe couldn't help but admire his tenacity and perseverance. When the moon reached its zenith, Rafe stopped at a dingy inn on the edge of a small village.

He took the stairs to his room, the boy still following him, and then waited in the shadows at the top of the stairs. When the boy came up, Rafe snatched him, placing his hand over his mouth to prevent him from crying out. The child struggled with all his puny might then realizing the futility went limp. "If you promise not to scream, I'll remove my hand from your mouth," Rafe bargained. "Do we have an agreement?"

The boy nodded.

Rafe slowly lowered his hand, but remained ready to clamp it back on at any hint of sound. However, the boy remained true to his word. "Why have you been following me all day, little one?" Rafe asked as he gently set the boy down.

The boy straightened his torn and shabby clothing then put his hands on his hips. "Stop callen me lil!" he huffed indignantly.

Rafe suppressed a smile. "Forgive me, I shall rephrase. Why have you been following me young man?"

"I hads to follow you. I din have nowheres else to go. You lef that ded woomin in my alley." The boy wrinkled his button nose. "She woulda got smelly."

Rafe raised an eyebrow. "Quite rude of me." He brushed back his braid which had fallen over his shoulder during the boy's struggles.

"It's a'right," the boy said graciously. "It was 'bout time to be movin on enyways. That place was gittin kinda shabby."

Rafe chuckled softly. "What's your name?"

"Runt," the boy said disgustedly. "Leastways that's whats ever one calls me."

"You don't like it," Rafe observed.

"I hates it." Runt stamped his tiny foot then crossed his arms. "I wanna be called Edward Teach." He drew his spindly body up to its full height of three-and-a-half feet. "Edward Teach are the meanest pirate on New Providence. Sumday I'm gonna be jus lak him." Runt tried to puff out his chest, but his scrawny, spindly body wouldn't cooperate.

The corners of Rafe's mouth quirked up in the beginnings of the first genuine smile since the tragedy at Lisbeth's and Pierre's ball. "Edward Teach is a mighty big name for such a small boy. I'll compromise and call you Ed."

Ed frowned, obviously displeased by the shortening of his chosen name, but he didn't argue.

"Now, what should I do with you, Ed?" Rafe mused out loud while rubbing an itch on his chin with the back of his left hand.

"I wanna be yer prentice. You's a big, tuff man lak Edward Teach. You slashed that pritty woomin's throat eezee as eatin apple pie. I cud learn so much frum you. Will you teech me everthin you knows, so I kin be jus lak you?"

Rafe sobered. "You don't want to be like me."

"Corse, I do. Thas why I follows you all day. I wans you to teech me how to kill eesie an qwik, lak as you did that woomin."

"I won't teach you to kill," Rafe said firmly.

"Why not?" Ed bristled. "Don you think I kin do it? Cus I kin. I lerns reel qwik. An sumone as good as you are at killin cud teech me eesy."

Rafe blanched at being called a skilled killer. "It's not that I don't think you can learn, but killing is—complicated."

"Thet may be so, but killin is the ownlee way to get ahed," Ed pronounced confidently.

"Killing is the path to ruin," Rafe swiftly and firmly countered.

Ed squinted up at Rafe. "You don seem ruint."

"I—it's—," Rafe could find no words to adequately explain the dismal state of his heart.

"Will you teech me?" Ed smiled endearingly. "So's I kin be jest lak you an Edward Teach?"

Rafe didn't know Edward Teach, but he was revolted by the mere thought of this child becoming a skilled killer, like him. Furthermore, the boy was already at a disadvantage being half African and half white. The last thing he needed was the additional disadvantage of his corrupting influence. If he turned the boy away, though, Ed might seek out some worse criminal than himself to train him, such as the aforementioned Edward Teach. At least by keeping Ed at his side he could prevent that, and then he could send Ed home along with Charles, where the boy had a good chance of adoption by a loving Christian family who would provide him with a strong moral compass. "Come." He headed for his room.

Ed grinned from ear to ear, assuming he'd been granted his request and was now Rafe's apprentice. "Yes, master."

Rafe blanched and came to a standstill. "Don't call me master. I'll be no one's master. My name is Rafe."

"Jist Rafe?"

"Just Rafe," he confirmed, having concluded, like Charles and Henry, that he was no longer worthy of either his surname or his title.

Ed grinned mischievously. "Thas an awful short name for sich a big man."

Rafe chuckled softly then affectionately tousled Ed's soft, curly blond hair. With this little companion brightening his days if only for a short while, life would almost be worth living.

Chapter Thirty-Two

Ed was hugely impressed by everything in the upscale room at the fine inn, but especially the big, soft bed. He inhaled a hearty dinner delivered to their room by the innkeeper's lovely blond, buxom daughter who flirted outrageously with Rafe. In a lighthearted mood for the first time since Duncan's death, Rafe received the flirting good naturedly, but took it no further, to the young woman's obvious disappointment, until he tipped her with a silver coin. She left smiling broadly.

After dinner Ed reveled in a hot bath until the water grew cold. Then he joined Rafe on the big bed, their backs comfortably supported by three feather pillows each, plumped up against the headboard. Rafe shared tales of his ten years with the Mohican; halcyon days of joy, love and acceptance, which Ed couldn't seem to hear enough of, but finally around midnight he fell asleep, exhausted from his long, hard day. Rafe tenderly pulled the covers over Ed's shoulders, blew out every candle but one, and retreated to the room's single high-backed, overstuffed chair.

With a sigh of contentment Rafe rested the back of his head against the chair, his arms on the armrests, wrists hanging loosely over the ends, and stretched his long legs out, crossed at the ankles. He watched Ed's scrawny chest rising and falling in peaceful slumber and wished he could live out his life with Ed at his side instead of sending him to the colonies with Charles. However, a man of his hopeless temper, willing to commit any wrong as long as it served his ultimate purpose, could never provide the proper moral and ethical upbringing required for one to become an upright man. His dark eyes filled with tears of loss. He blinked the shameful tears away then moved to the bed, pulled off his boots and lay down beside Ed for his usual nightly chasing after the peaceful sleep he'd once taken for granted, but had successfully eluded him this last year since Duncan's death.

After a restless night in which Rafe lay awake more often than he slept, he opened his eyes to the impish, smiling face of Ed, leaning over him. He couldn't help but respond with a genuine smile of his own. He sat up. "Good morning, Ed. Did you rest well?"

"Oh yes! The bed was the soffest I ever slep in. I'm hungree, whus fer brekfas?"

"Anything you'd like." Rafe picked up his boots and used a corner of the blanket to dust off the dirt of the road.

Ed's brown eyes grew big as he imagined the possibilities. "Enythin?"

"Anything," Rafe confirmed stamping his left foot into his boot. "What would you like?"

"Um…" Ed put his index finger on his lower lip and rolled his eyes to the ceiling as he mulled it over. "Two scrambled eggs, four hotcakes, three slices of bacon, a muffin, an a big peece of apple pie!"

Rafe chuckled. "You think you can eat all of that?"

"Oh yes! I'm awful hungree."

Rafe grinned as he stomped his right foot into his boot. "Then allow me a few minutes to freshen up and after that we shall go downstairs to the common room and order everything you asked for."

* * *

Ten minutes later Ed and Rafe settled in at a table for two in the inn's common room. Rafe ordered everything Ed had asked for then watched in amazement as the boy devoured every bite. "If you continue eating like that, you'll be bigger than me in no time," he commented.

"Thas whut I'm aimin for," Ed said around a mouthful of apple pie. He stood on the seat of his chair and flexed his spindly arms. "Am I gettin bigger an stronger yet?"

Rafe suppressed a grin. "I believe so. It seems you've already grown several inches and I can definitely see more muscle definition," he replied seriously.

Ed sat back down immensely pleased and resumed his feast. As usual, Rafe didn't have much appetite. He ate lightly while he surreptitiously eyed the other patrons. He'd always been uncomfortable among crowds, all too aware that his darker coloring alone made him stand out like a crow among graceful white swans. He was especially uncomfortable now that he was a fugitive as well, and his discomfort increased when he noted that several people were watching him and Ed with plainly evident distaste, but quickly averted their gazes when he looked in their direction. Rafe wondered if he'd been recognized or if it was that they disliked sharing the room with a couple of half-breeds. Then he reflected that it might be Ed's dirty, tattered clothing that was the true source of their displeasure and mentally chastised himself for not buying some decent clothing for Ed before he'd taken him out in public; a thoughtless, stupid mistake! "As soon as you're finished eating, we'll buy you some new clothes," he said to Ed.

Ed stopped his feeding frenzy so he could respond. "Why don you jus steal sum? Isn thet whut you always do?"

Rafe winced and glanced uneasily at the other patrons, even more of whom were now watching the two of them distrustfully. "Keep your voice down. This is a respectable inn, not a street tavern on the docks."

"Why don you jus steal sum?" Ed whispered.

"It's not moral to steal. Furthermore, we have plenty of money." Rafe spoke loudly enough for all those watching distrustfully to overhear.

"Whas moore-eel?" Ed asked, drawing out the word.

The innkeeper was on his way over. "Not now," Rafe said. Ed started to ask another question, but Rafe shushed him with a hand gesture. The innkeeper stopped at their table and looked down his short, stubby nose at Ed, reminding Rafe far too much of Judge McKitrick. Placing his fat, stubby-fingers on his wide, thick hips he said, "I rented you two a room last night as one man's money is as good another's, but you and this half-breed street urchin are plainly upsetting the other patrons. I'd like you to leave now."

It was the sort of prejudice Rafe had endured all of his life and he was mightily fed up with it. "Calling someone a half-breed is rude, sir. Furthermore, the boy has as much right to be here as anyone else." He fixed the man with an icy, black stare.

The innkeeper remained unfazed. He hadn't become the owner of a successful inn on an island teeming with pirates by lacking the courage to face down possibly dangerous patrons. "Pay up and leave, sir, or I'll have you forcefully removed."

"I'll pay!" Ed reached in his tattered pocket, drew out the coins Rafe had tossed at him in the alley and threw them at the innkeeper, who caught them up clumsily with both hands and then immediately started counting them.

Rafe wasn't willing to wait for the man to finish. He knew it was more than enough to pay for both their meals and their room for another night as well. "Come Ed." He grasped Ed's hand and they whisked out together. Ed couldn't resist sticking out his tongue at the staring patrons as they exited and Rafe didn't chastise him for it. "I'm sick of intolerance and prejudice! Sick to death of it!" Rafe spat as they stepped outside and assumed a brisk pace.

Ed was forced to run to keep up. "Why didn you kill them all then?" he asked breathlessly.

Rafe realized he was walking too fast for the boy and slowed his pace. "It's wrong to kill people merely because you're angry with them."

"You kilt that wooman yestiday an you was angry at her. I cud tell."

"I was," Rafe confessed. "But there was more to it than that."

"Like whut?"

Discussing his latest kill was making Rafe uncomfortable, but Ed was waiting for an answer. "It's complex, but the crux of the matter is that you don't kill people merely because they're rude, or idiots, like that innkeeper and his patrons."

"But I cud tell you wan-ned to kill the innkeeper. I cud see it in yer eyes."

Rafe came to a stunned standstill. "You could see it in my eyes?"

"Yep, an besides, you lookt reel pleesed when you finsht killin that woomin. So's I kin tell you lak to kill. Thas whys I follows you to aks you to teech me."

Rafe recalled that he'd not only felt no guilt or remorse after killing Lauralee, but quite the opposite. Was that because he'd enjoyed it as Ed believed? Charles had once accused him of living to kill. If two such different people who'd spent time with him thought he was a callous killer, then perhaps... He ran his hand across his face then he realized that if he truly lived to kill he wouldn't be distressed. It wouldn't bother him at all. "I don't know what you saw in my eyes, Ed, either in the alley or now, but it wasn't a desire to kill or satisfaction over having done it," he said with firm conviction.

"It weren't?" Ed asked sounding disappointed.

Rafe lightly gripped Ed's right shoulder. "My heart father taught me that all life is precious. One should never kill except to save a life, either your own or that of another."

Ed screwed up his face in confusion. "But yer life weren't in danger when you kilt that wooman."

"Of course it was! Didn't you see her draw first a pistol and then a knife on me?" Rafe exclaimed.

"Well sure, but she was a woomin, an you was so much stronger than her an quicker too. So she were reely no threat."

Rafe's formerly firm conviction that killing Lauralee was justified fractured dangerously, to the point where it threatened to break apart altogether. "Lauralee may not have looked like a threat, but trust me she was a threat," he argued mostly for his own benefit.

Ed shrugged un-persuaded, but not really caring. "Well ennyways, I has to kill, else hows I ever gonna be the mos bes pirate ever?"

"There are better occupations to aspire to," Rafe said fervently.

"Like whut?" Ed asked skeptically.

"You could become an upright man who helps out the less fortunate. You'll find far greater satisfaction in that sort of life."

"If'n it's so satisfyin, why ain *you* helpin peeple instead of killen em?"

Rafe winced. The child's innocent questions were as guilt-inflicting as Charles's calculated rants! "I've helped more than a few people in my lifetime and my heart profited greatly from it."

"Then why ain you still an uprite man?"

Rafe recalled Duncan's dead eyes and Davy's shock and fear when the sailor realized he was a dead man. Then there were the nearly half dozen cannibals, and the merchant and his young son on the Pavilion along with the sailor with barely a mustache he'd shot in the face while attempting to shoot Lauralee, and—the list went on and on. Guilt threatened to overwhelm him, but he hastily tossed a rationalization at it. "Sometimes life throws things at you that change your path against your will and then to survive you must do things you wouldn't do ordinarily." He resumed walking at a pace that was easy for Ed.

"There's alwis options. If you din lak killen and stealen, you wooden't do it," Ed argued.

Rafe's steps faltered. "That's—that's faulty reasoning, Ed. Sometimes there is no other choice." He steered the conversation away from this guilt-inflicting subject. "I see a general store down the street. Shall we buy you those new clothes?"

"Sure! An afer that can we git a snak?" Ed asked eagerly.

Rafe nodded absently, lost in a vortex of self-recrimination and guilt, only shaking it off as they entered the store.

He bought several complete sets of clothing, a bedroll and a bag like his for Ed and the supplies he'd need to rescue Charles, among them a spyglass. Then after a reminder from Ed that he'd promised him a snack, they bought some hot salted peanuts off a street vendor, which used up the last of the money Rafe had stolen from VonLarken and Lauralee. Tonight after Ed was asleep, he'd visit a tavern and watch a group of gamblers from the shadows then follow the winner and rob him. It wouldn't make his theft acceptable, but at least he wouldn't be taking hard-earned, honest wages. If he returned before Ed awoke, the boy would never know he'd been out hypocritically breaking the morals he'd so earnestly preached to him earlier.

As the sun dipped behind the hills, Rafe and Ed stopped in a shabby inn on the edge of a shabby village. They spent another pleasant evening chatting, until Ed fell asleep in mid-sentence. Rafe gently moved him to the bed, tenderly drew up the covers then left innocence behind to slip out into the darkness and willfully embrace iniquity.

He returned in the early morning hours with a raging headache, exacerbated by a guilty conscience, so he was relieved that Ed was still asleep and he wouldn't have to explain how he'd come into possession of the purse bulging with winnings that he'd taken at knifepoint from a young, drunken gentleman uncertainly wobbling home down a dark street after a successful night of gambling. He hid his dishonest gain in the bottom of his clothing bag then lay down next to Ed to rest.

What seemed like mere minutes later he was rudely awakened by Ed jumping up and down on the bed. "Hey sleepee hed. Les eat! I'm hungree," the boy chirped cheerfully.

Rafe's eyes felt as if someone had scoured them with sandpaper, he hadn't had nearly enough rest, and the headache was still raging. Add all that to his guilty conscience and he was in no mood for Ed's childish exuberance. He irritably grabbed Ed's ankles and yanked his feet out from under him. Ed laughed as he bounced twice on the soft bed, thinking Rafe was playing, but his laughter abruptly died when Rafe growled, "Get lost, boy! Can't you see I'm trying to rest? Don't you ever think of anyone but yourself?"

Ed's eyes widened and then he sullenly slid off the bed, retreated to the room's high-backed chair and sat down, crossing his arms and sulking. Rafe rolled over and tried to return to sleep, but Ed's sulking radiated through his senses like the crashing thunder he'd so often experienced on the island; and it didn't help that he felt guilty about yelling at the boy. He sighed in frustration and sat up, swinging his legs around the edge of the bed. "I'm sorry, Ed. I shouldn't have yelled at you. I didn't sleep well last night and it's made me irritable."

"Don you ever think of enyone but yerself?" Ed retorted.

A dark rage seized possession of Rafe's soul. He sprang from the bed and advanced on Ed menacingly. Ed cringed and raised his hands defensively. "Don murder me! I'm sorree!"

The scrawny, defenseless child recoiling in fear and begging not to be murdered by him shocked Rafe to a stunned standstill. Then he cursed the pirates and the wicked deeds he'd committed for them, which had only served to strengthen his already evil nature. "I won't hurt you Ed," he said softy.

Ed slowly straightened and even more slowly lowered his hands. "You ain goin to kill me?"

"No. I'll never harm another friend," Rafe said.

"I'm your fren?" Ed asked, brightening.

Rafe didn't hear the question, though. He was too caught up in gut wrenching recollections of Duncan's death and the speedy downward spiral into crime that had followed.

"Am I yer fren?" Ed repeated.

Rafe shook himself out of his gloomy reverie, rubbed his gritty eyes with the heels of both hands. "What?" he asked wearily.

"Am I yer fren?" Ed asked a third time.

"You are indeed my friend, Ed, although I must warn you that I'm not much good at friendships. The few I've had ended badly," Rafe said.

"Whut happent?"

"I accidentally killed Duncan and after that the others deserted me."

"But if t'wer an accident—,"

"No one believed it was an accident." Resentment crept into Rafe's tone. "They all preferred to believe I killed Duncan in a drunken rage."

"Then they was no tru frens," Ed pronounced indignantly. "Tru frens stik by you, liv or die, no matter whut."

"Then I've never had a true friend, except Duncan." *And I killed him. Some true friend I am...*

"I'll be your tru fren. Liv or die, no matter whut. If you'll hav me," Ed offered earnestly.

Rafe was deeply touched. "I'll have you gladly, Ed." He held out his hand to seal the deal, but Ed instead threw his arms around Rafe's neck and hugged him tightly. Tears blurred Rafe's vision. He returned the hug briefly then gently pried the boy's arms loose and cleared his throat. "You'd best get dressed." He patted Ed lightly on his bony bottom and gave him a gentle shove toward his neatly folded pile of new clothes on the end of the bed.

"Then will we eat?" Ed asked hopefully.

Rafe smiled. "Yes, then we shall eat."

* * *

This time no one gave them a second glance when they settled at a table in the common room, but this wasn't as fine an inn as the one they'd had trouble in. Ed ate the lion's share of the food. Then they resumed their travels. Ed was in fine spirits and chattered non-stop, keeping Rafe constantly amused by his innocent, unintended witticisms. As they left civilization well behind, Ed said, "I ain bin in the cuntreeside sins I wus borned. Wher are we goin?"

"To rescue an acquaintance."

"Whas an a-kin-tunce?" Ed screwed up his button nose with the effort of saying the word.

"An acquaintance is someone you know, but who's not a true friend," Rafe explained.

"Oh." Ed rubbed his face then swatted at a fly. "Wha you gonna reskew the a-kin-tunce frum?"

"Acquaintance," Rafe corrected. "I'm rescuing him from slavery."

"Oh. Thas bad, bein a slave. Was you ever a slave?"

Rafe recalled Charles's opinion that he was enslaved by his evil nature, which he fully agreed with now. "Yes, but not in any way you'd understand."

Ed went quiet for some time as he tried to puzzle out what Rafe had meant, but he couldn't figure it out so he gave up and moved on. "Kin I hep you rescue your ac—quaint—ance?"

"It's not a job for children."

Ed indignantly placed his hands on his hips. "I ain no chile! I'm almos eight!"

The corners of Rafe's mouth quirked up. "I concede your point, but that aside I always work alone."

"But we's tru frens, an tru frens hep each other always. An anyways, hows I gonna ever lern to be the mos bes pirate ever if you won lemme hep?" Ed argued.

"I intend for you to be an upright man, not a thief and a killer like me," Rafe said.

Ed screwed up his face as if he'd just eaten something bitter. "You meen yer not teechin me hows to kill and steel an fite like you?"

"Absolutely not," Rafe said vehemently.

"Not even a lil bit?" Ed wheedled.

"No."

Ed went quiet again. Then he brightened and said, "Isn rescuin ac—acquaint—tances a good thin?"

"Yes, but—"

"Then you has to let me hep, so's I kin lern to be a uprite man." Ed looked extremely pleased with his sound argument.

Rafe was forced to admire the boy's reasoning, but that didn't mean he was surrendering to it. "There may be killing and an upright man should not be involved in killing or even be subjected to seeing it."

"You fergit. I already saws you kill."

A tsunami of guilt slammed Rafe and he shifted position uneasily. "So you have, but I also don't wish to take the chance that you might be hurt."

"Aw, I kin take care of mysel. I'se a tuff guy," Ed insisted confidently.

"I'm sure you're quite capable." Rafe paused then decided to placate the child with a blatant falsehood. "Very well, I'll think of a job for you."

Ed hugged Rafe. "I knew we was tru frens," he said triumphantly, which only made Rafe despise himself all the more for lying to the child.

Chapter Thirty-Three

Rafe held a loaded pistol to Ed's temple forcing him to slit the throats of wounded merchant sailors as the boy wailed and begged him not to make him do it anymore, his knife dripping with the blood of innocents. "You wanted to learn to kill, boy. Well, this is what it's like, so finish them off and stop your whining," Rafe commanded harshly.

"I hate you!" Ed stabbed Rafe in the heart with his bloodied knife.

Rafe laughed. "You can't harm me boy. I'm the spawn of the devil." He pulled the knife free. Black blood gushed down the front of his shirt and then the knife wound closed up. "You messed that up boy. Let me show you how it's done." He turned the knife on Ed and the boy screamed in horror.

Rafe startled awake with a gasp, heart racing, sweat beading his forehead. Ed, still alive and sleeping soundly beside him, negated somewhat the guilt from the all too vivid nightmare, but although the boy might still be alive, the men he'd failed to save from Lauralee's lust for blood were not. Rafe wiped his sweaty brow then slid from bed and agitatedly paced the dark room. He desperately needed to escape the heinousness of his sins if only for a little while, and he knew exactly how. He only had to be certain to return before Ed awoke.

He kept to the shadows as he slinked along the mostly deserted streets to the seedy area of town where the drug dealers plied their life-stealing wares, like the coca leaves he sought. He rounded a corner and found himself in front of an opium den. He paused, considering. For the purpose of forgetting, one drug was as good as another… He stepped inside the smoky den.

A short, elderly, polite Chinese man with a waist length white beard and mustache greeted him. "Welcome, sir."

"How much?" Rafe asked.

The Chinese man stated an exorbitant price, but Rafe paid it without argument then followed him to the back of the den, his heart pounding in anticipation. However, the smoke-filled room where addicts lay on dirty, lumpy cots in a drugged stupor gave Rafe pause. Anything could happen to him while he was out of his mind. What if he was shanghaied? Then who would rescue Charles and what would become of Ed? "I—I'm sorry. I've made a mistake." He rushed out of the opium den and ran all the way back to the inn. Then he bounded up the stairs two at a time and walked briskly down the hall to his room.

Ed still deep in slumber looked so peaceful, so seemingly innocent, so young and frail, but Rafe knew this tiny child was not nearly as innocent as he seemed. At the least Ed had witnessed Lauralee's brutal death, and who knew what other horrors Ed had experienced during his short life on the streets? Rafe truly wished to preserve and cultivate what remained of Ed's innocence, but the sickly odor of opium smoke lingering on his clothing and hair was proof enough he was incapable. He tenderly fingered a lock of Ed's soft, curly, blond hair. In these last few days his lonely heart had rejoiced in the rich worldly happiness of Ed's delightful presence in his otherwise barren life; a treasure he valued above all else. He silently vowed that in their remaining few days together he would never willingly commit an act that might jeopardize Ed's happiness.

He lay down beside Ed and slept soundly until Ed awakened him asking for breakfast. He once again had a pounding headache, but this time he refrained from yelling. Instead, he sent Ed for a servant, and while Ed was gone he caught a bit more sleep.

Ed brought back a plain, dark-haired servant girl. She blushed beet red upon being addressed by the handsomest customer she'd ever seen. Rafe ordered a meal large enough for three adults, which arrived immediately after he finished cleaning up. He joined Ed at the room's small table for two and despite his lingering headache smiled in amazement as Ed inhaled his first serving then started on a second. "Enjoying your breakfast?" he asked.

Ed nodded then asked around a mouthful of food, "So, bout this reskew of yer ac—quain—tance. Whas my part gonna be?"

"It's not polite to talk with your mouth full," Rafe chastised, buying time before he had to lie to Ed again.

Ed chewed and swallowed. "So whas my part gonna be?"

Rafe reluctantly lied. "You'll be the lookout."

Ed dropped his two-pronged fork onto his pewter plate with a loud clatter. "Thas no help!"

"On the contrary, it's an extremely important job. You alone must assure that no one sneaks up on us so we may make an easy escape."

Rafe could almost see the wheels turning in Ed's head as he mulled that over. "Thas okay then, I gess." He picked up his fork to spear a large bite of sausage. "Wher we gonna live afer we reskew your fren?"

"He's not my friend, he's an acquaintance," Rafe quickly corrected. "His name is Lord Charles Huntington. You and Lord Huntington will live in New England in the American colonies."

Ed quit his feeding frenzy as he realized Rafe hadn't mentioned himself in their future plans. "Whut abut you?"

"I've made far too many enemies in New England to ever return there."

"Then I ain goin neither!" Ed defiantly placed his hands on his hips. "I'm stayin wit you."

Rafe's broken and wounded heart was warmed by Ed's desire to stay with him, but for Ed's sake, he couldn't allow it. "I appreciate your desire to stay with me, but you need a moral upbringing, and I'm incapable of providing one."

"We been doin fine so far. I ain never been so happy," Ed declared.

Rafe swallowed the aching lump that then arose in his throat. "Finish your breakfast," he said gruffly. He stood up and crossed the room to look out the blurry, wavy glass of the single, multi-paned window. Below him the street was all hustle and bustle with women hurrying to market with baskets on their arms, well-dressed children racing ahead of their nannies on their way to the park, businessmen dressed in solemn black self-importantly strolling to their offices. He envied them all their carefree, normal lives, with family to love them; a pleasure he'd never again experience now that he was a wanted man, with his crimes escalating daily. He blinked back tears then silently cursed the circumstances that had turned his life so upside down.

"I jis thot of sumthin that mite change everthin. If yur enmees in New England knows I'm yer fren, won they try to kill me?" Ed asked.

If Rafe hadn't been so depressed he would've laughed at the ridiculousness of the question. He turned away from the window. "They're not that sort. They—or rather, I…" His voice trailed off as he failed to find a way to explain the situation in New England without revealing more of his faults to Ed, who'd probably only end up admiring him all the more. "There are plenty of good people in New England who'll love you better than I ever could."

"Well even if everone is nice, I won be happy if you ain there," Ed insisted.

"You will be happy." Rafe made it a command, for he needed it to be so. Then he ended the conversation, which had become far too painful. "Pack up. We must be on the road."

Chapter Thirty-Four

"Is that wher your acquaintance is?" Ed asked pointing down at the large plantation below them.

"Yes," Rafe answered absently as he studied the plantation grounds with the spyglass he'd stolen on his crime spree the other night. The sun had set only recently and in the swiftly encroaching darkness, Rafe and Ed had climbed the hill a short distance from the plantation where Charles was enslaved.

"Thas the Kelley's place," Ed pronounced.

Rafe lowered the spyglass in astonishment. "How did you know that? I never told you."

Ed shrugged. "Is whar I wus born. One of the ladees at the orfinij whar I lived afore I runned away told me. She were reel nice, an pritty too. She even showed this place to me on a map. She's the ony one I miss from that awful place."

Rafe was glad Ed had experienced the singular kindness of at least one person in his otherwise miserable life. Leopold had been that singular kind person in his own life until the night he'd been caught alone in his parlor with Sarah, after which their relationship had become strained, although still cordial. Then Duncan had offered his unconditional friendship and Rafe had felt doubly blessed. Alas, he'd lost both Leopold and Duncan, along with God's love, and soon he'd be losing Ed too… Rafe's vision blurred with tears, but he hastily shook himself free of his melancholy. This was not the time or place for lamenting what was lost. That time would come all too soon, though. He turned his attention back to Ed. "—an she tol me that the slave master, Trent, he rape my momma, who was a slave. A few hours afer I was borned, Trent beat momma real bad for fightn back when he tooks her agin, an she died. But the Kelley's, they didn wan no baby to tak care of, so they took me to the orfinij in Nassau till I was growed enuf to sell as a slave. I runned away tho, cuz I don wanna be a slave."

Rafe almost wished he hadn't learned that both he and Ed were children of rape, for it made him feel an even closer kinship with Ed than that they were both of mixed blood, which in turn would only make it harder to give him up. "At least no one tried to drown you on your birth day," he remarked bitterly.

"Why wud anyone wanna do that when they cud sell me and make monee?"

"Yes, why?" Rafe wondered. How different his life would've been if his white grandfather had sold him into slavery instead of trying to drown him. Then he wouldn't have been adopted by the Mohicans and they wouldn't have died for sheltering him, and he never would've met Duncan, which would've been a loss for him, but fortunate for Duncan, for that good man would still be alive, along with all the others who'd died by and because of him since that tragic night. One thing would've remained the same, though. He'd still be rejected by God; still be an abomination in His sight. Would he then still have become a thief and murderer? Probably so for the penchant for crime was, after all, in his blood. *Thanks father.*

"How long ago did you run away from the orphanage?" he asked Ed.

"I dunno. A good many meals. Wen kin we eat dinner?"

Rafe smiled. "Soon." He put the spyglass back into his bag. He hadn't seen Charles, but he'd seen everything else he'd needed to see and had formed his plan. The plantation was loosely secured. Tonight after Ed was asleep he'd return and conduct a building-to-building search. If he was lucky, then he'd find Charles and rescue him. If not he'd return another night. He was in no hurry. The longer it took to rescue Charles the longer he could delay the inevitable scathing, guilt-inflicting commentary Charles was sure to punish him with; and there was another more compelling reason he was in no hurry. Once he rescued Charles, he'd have only three days left until he'd have to relinquish custody of Ed forever upon their arrival in Nassau.

"What we gonna eat tonite?" Ed asked as they descended the hill.

"If there's a rabbit in that snare I set near our campsite this morning before we left, we could make rabbit stew," Rafe said.

Ed smacked his lips in anticipation. "Souns good to me."
Rafe chuckled. "Well then let's go check that snare."

There was indeed a rabbit in the snare. After dinner Ed and Rafe had their usual pleasurable evening chat and then Rafe tucked Ed into his bedroll beneath a lean-to of leafy branches he'd built as much to hide Ed as to protect him from the driving rain that had started just before dinner. When he was certain Ed was soundly asleep, Rafe buckled on a holster with an already loaded pistol, grabbed his bag filled with everything he'd need to rescue Charles including another already loaded pistol, and hiked to the plantation.

He was grateful for the moonless night and the driving rain, both helpful if one wished to conduct a covert operation such as stealing a slave. He would've thanked God for it, except he knew it was merely coincidence. God would never favor the efforts of a man such as him. He ghosted across the plantation checking each of the slave cabins in turn, yet he didn't find Charles in any of them. Charles had been here less than a week, but what if he'd already died from abuse, or had been resold. The latter possibility held some appeal, since having to track Charles down all over again would give him more time with Ed. There was also the possibility that as a rare, white, educated slave, Charles was one of the privileged few who slept in the servant's quarters in the manor house attic. However, Rafe couldn't check there tonight, for despite the late hour the house was still brightly lit and he heard music and loud laughter. In the morning he'd observe the comings and goings of the slaves from his observation post on top of the adjacent hill and hopefully he'd spot Charles then track his movements throughout the day and discover where he bunked.

Rafe circled around to exit through the back of the plantation, merely conducting a thorough search, not expecting to find Charles. As he passed a row of storehouses, he thought he heard a soft moan. He stood still and listened, but he heard nothing except the rain splashing in puddles on the over saturated ground. He started to move on and heard another moan. He backtracked and discovered a black, metal grating of crisscrossed, black, metal bars as thick as his thumb covering a hole in the ground between two storehouses, fastened with a padlock the size of a paw of one of those oversized bears he'd fought on the island. He knelt and lit his torch then held it over the hole.

* * *

When Charles had first been sentenced to the hole for accidentally spilling a tureen of hot butternut squash soup in the lap of the obese Lord Firwood, he'd fully expected his punishment to end the following morning. No one had come to release him, though. The sun rose beating mercilessly down upon him in a cloudless sky, burning his skin and baking him like a potato in an oven. Charles could do nothing but huddle into a tighter crouch and wait. Around mid-day an unfamiliar slave brought a half-filled skin of lukewarm water. Charles thirstily guzzled it all then handed the skin back. "How long must I stay in here?" he asked. The slave shrugged and walked away. "Wait! Come back!" Charles yelled, but the slave ignored his plea. Despairing, Charles resorted to prayer. "Father in heaven, please help me. I don't know if I can take another day like this."

He fully expected someone to come and release him then, yet the day dragged on, night fell, and still no one came. Charles then latched onto the slender hope that Lydia would visit him. He'd become friendly with the pretty, green-eyed teenager since they were both rare white slaves bought on the same day. Lydia's mother had died in childbirth and her father had sold her into slavery when she was only nine to pay his gambling debts. She was what was politely termed by the other slaves as an *entertainer*, while Charles worked with the pigs. They never met during working hours, but they shared the same cabin with two other male slaves and on the first night Charles had sacrificed his single blanket and hung it on a string, dividing Lydia's bed from the men so she could have privacy. As no one had ever shown her such a thoughtful kindness before, they'd become instant friends.

Charles waited throughout the insufferable heat of the day for his only friend in this demoralizing place to visit, but at the dinner hour when Lydia still hadn't showed he realized he'd hoped in vain. Then the rains came. At first Charles thanked God for the rain, which rapidly cooled him and he could also quench his burning thirst by thrusting his head back and catching the raindrops in his mouth. But then the rain increased in intensity and the bottom of his hole started to fill with cold, muddy water and Charles was no longer thankful for it. Instead, he prayed it would stop, but it didn't, so he gathered together his aching limbs that he desperately needed to stretch and despite extreme discomfort managed to escape into sleep.

He dreamed he was home celebrating Laird's third birthday with a children's party. Hundreds of streamers in every color imaginable fluttered in the branches of the trees and from the white picket fence surrounding their yard. Mobs of small children raced screeching across the rolling lawn in front of their manse. Charles enjoyed the joyful mayhem while snuggling with Sarah in a comfortable white wicker loveseat, resting on soft, blue cushions. "I'm so pleased you were able to be here today," Sarah said. "You've been gone a long time. I've missed you."

She leaned forward to give him a passionate kiss, but then pulled back without kissing him when she saw Rafe walking fluidly across the well-manicured lawn, smiling in his charming way, so tall, and muscular, and handsome, with his long, black, shiny hair flowing free in the wind. He wore white, beaded buckskins and moccasins with his impressive, hand-made, beaded knife sheath. "Rafe!" she cried joyfully. She sprang to her feet and raced to the despised half-breed then wrapped her arms around his waist and lovingly pressed her head to his chest. Rafe grinned smugly at Charles and wrapped his muscled arms around Sarah's slender shoulders. "When I told you she was yours, I lied to salve your ego. She was never yours, Charles. She's always been mine. You will never be good enough for her," he taunted.

Charles roared in anger and tried to spring to his feet to tear Sarah from Rafe's savage arms, but his limbs refused to obey him. Rafe and Sarah laughed at his useless efforts. Charles moaned in frustration, and then he awoke. The night was pitch black, and still raining, and he wasn't home in New England, he was still in the hole. He moaned again and closed his eyes.

Then someone called his name. "Charles?" He blinked open his eyes and was nearly blinded by a bright circle of light shining directly in his them. He shielded his eyes with his right hand and then the light moved aside and Rafe knelt over the grating holding a torch in one hand which was flickering and sputtering in the heavy rain. "Rafe? Is that really you?" Charles asked in disbelief.

"Who else would come to rescue you?" Rafe asked. "Why did they put you in here?"

"I accidentally spilled a tureen of hot soup on the lap of some corpulent fop named Lord Firwood," Charles said. "So do you intend to help me out of here or did you merely come to talk me to death?"

Rafe smothered his ire. It was only natural that Charles would be grumpy considering his circumstances. He jammed his torch into the saturated ground so he could use both hands to dig through his bag, but despite his precautions the torch hissed and sputtered in the rain and then went out. Fortunately, not before he'd found his lock picks, though. Rather than try to re-light the wet torch, Rafe set to work on the lock working by feel.

"I'm surprised you quit your carousing and drug abusing long enough to rescue me from this unjust predicament you thrust me into!" Charles groused while Rafe worked on the lock.

Rafe clenched his teeth with the effort of holding back a scathing retort and continued working until the lock sprang open. He put away his lock picks, pulled the grate open and reached down with one hand, bracing his other hand splay-fingered on the sodden, muddy ground. "Take my hand and I'll pull you out." Charles weakly grasped Rafe's hand. Rafe wrapped his strong, brown fingers around Charles's wrist then easily lifted him out and set him on his feet. At first Charles's legs felt wobbly and if not for Rafe's firm, steady grip on his elbow he would've slumped to the muddy ground like a rag doll. "Are you injured?" Rafe asked concernedly.

"No, my legs are merely wobbly from long hours in that hole. Give me a second to regain my strength; and while I rest, how about using those lock picks to remove this slave collar? I can't wait to get this ghastly thing off. It chafes horribly." Charles tugged distastefully on the wide metal band around his neck.

Rafe shook his head. "No time for that now, or for resting. I'll remove the collar after we're safely away." He ducked under Charles's arm, pulled it across his shoulders then started walking.

"Wait!" Charles struggled to break free, but he was too weak so he firmly planted his heels in the muddy ground instead. Rafe dragged him another five feet before Charles's heels buried in the mud deeply enough to force Rafe to a standstill. "What are you doing?" Rafe cried impatiently. "Don't you realize we have no time to waste?"

"I'm not leaving here without Lydia."

"Lydia," Rafe echoed.

"A young lady I've befriended," Charles deigned to explain.

Rafe's dark eyes widened and then he looked disgusted. "You condemn me for my relationship with Lauralee, but at least I'm no adulterer."

Charles bristled. "Leave it to your filthy, savage mind to think that way! This is not like you and Lauralee. Lydia's barely fourteen. I promised her if I ever escaped I'd take her with me. We have to go for her."

Rafe felt sorry for the girl, but he couldn't save everyone and now that he'd found Charles he only wanted to escape before they were caught. "No, we can't take the risk." He forced Charles to take a few steps before Charles stubbornly dug in his heels again.

"I'm not leaving without Lydia!" he protested loudly.

Rafe winced and glanced around uneasily, certain Charles's outcry had roused the watch. Luckily, seconds passed and no one showed. "Keep your voice down! Do you wish to alert the entire plantation?"

"I'm not leaving without Lydia," Charles repeated, but more quietly. "I made her a promise and although you may completely lack honor, I keep my promises."

Rafe was sorely tempted to make that unjust comment about his honor true by throwing Charles back in the hole and leaving him there to rot. He resisted, however. He didn't know why. It was definitely what Charles deserved. "Rescuing the girl would mean going back into the main compound. I was lucky no one spotted me the first time through; and what if the girl is loyal to her owners and raises the alarm? We'll both be caught. We can't risk it."

Charles broke free from Rafe's grasp and sat down on the puddle-riddled, muddy, ground, crossing his arms. "I'll not take another step until you promise to take Lydia too."

Rafe tried to drag Charles to his feet, but Charles stubbornly resisted. "We have no time for this nonsense, Charles! Stand up or so help me I'll leave you here!"

"I'm not budging until you agree to take Lydia with us," Charles stubbornly persisted.

Rafe cursed in Mohican. "Then stay here and remain a slave for the rest of your life!" He stomped away, splashing in puddles and muttering darkly in first Mohican and then French, but before he'd taken more than a dozen paces he came to a standstill. No matter how much his heart desired it, his honor—that Charles said he lacked—wouldn't let him leave Charles behind. He stomped back to Charles.

Charles grinned victoriously as he shakily stood up. "I see your tiny sliver of a conscience has succeeded in breaking through your wall of selfishness and convicting you of all that you owe me," he said with evident satisfaction.

It took all of Rafe's self-control to keep from shoving Charles back inside the hole. "Where does this Lydia you're so enamored with bunk?" he asked between tightly clenched teeth.

"I'll show you."

Growing stronger and steadier with each step, Charles led Rafe through the dark, rainy night to the cabin he shared with Lydia and two others. He reached for the door knob. Rafe hastily grabbed the back of Charles's rough-spun shirt and pulled him back. "What do you think you're doing?" he hissed quietly, wary of being overheard by those inside the cabin.

"Lydia's in here," Charles whispered, pointing inside.

"Along with how many others?" Rafe asked pointedly.

Charles didn't understand why that mattered. "Two others, both male."

Rafe peered into the absolute darkness of the cabin through the single small window to the right of the door, but it was too dark to see. He rummaged in his bag until he found a candle and flint box. Cupping his hand over the wick to protect it from the rain, he handed the candle to Charles. "Shield the wick from the rain."

Charles did as he was asked without argument, for a change. Rafe drew a hunting knife, having abandoned the too cumbersome pirate blade then struck the blade to the flint over the candle wick. It lit instantly, sputtered as if it would go out, but then burned strong. Rafe sheathed his knife, put away the flint box and carefully took the candle from Charles, shielding its flame from the rain with his free hand. "On what side of the room does your *mistress* sleep?"

Charles frowned at the scurrilous label, but otherwise made no comment then pointed out Lydia's bed. Rafe held the candle up to the cabin window still shielding the flame from the rain, with the dual purpose of also preventing the candle's light from awaking the other occupants. It was easy to tell from the shapeliness beneath the single thin blanket that the occupant of the bed Charles had pointed out was a young woman. Rafe exposed the candle to the pouring rain letting it snuff out then dropped it back into his bag. He then pulled out a second already loaded pistol and held it out to Charles handle first. "If one of the others awakens, shoot them."

Charles crossed his arms and refused to take the weapon. "No. You may be able to kill without conscience, but not me."

Rafe lowered the pistol. "If you're not up to the task…" He turned away and took a step.

Charles grabbed Rafe's sleeve. "Wait! I'll do what I must."

Rafe hesitated, uneasy. Charles wasn't skilled at moving silently and he was also weak from his time in the hole. Something was bound to go wrong. He should throw Charles over his shoulder and hightail it out of here.

"Please, Rafe," Charles begged. "Please. She's so young and they're using her to satisfy the carnal desires of their guests, like that corpulent fop, Lord Firwood. We can't leave her here to be sexually abused for the remainder of her life."

Hearing it put that way, Rafe couldn't refuse. It was unthinkable that he should willingly allow anyone else to endure the same ignominy that he'd suffered under Lauralee. He held the pistol out. This time Charles took the weapon, albeit reluctantly. Rafe drew his own pistol and silently entered the cabin with Charles rustling noisily behind. The full moon momentarily peeked out from behind a cloud as if it was curious about what Rafe and Charles were up to. In its dim light Rafe could barely see the line and color of Lydia's face. He came to a stunned standstill. He hadn't expected Lydia to be white, and beautiful besides with lustrous, strawberry blond hair and the perfect features of—of the angel statue in Pierre and Lisbeth's garden! A chill raced down his spine.

Charles nervously kept his pistol aimed at the still, sleeping figures on the other two beds. "How long do you intend to stand there ogling her lustfully?" he whispered impatiently.

Rafe hadn't even realized he was staring. He stuffed his pistol in its holster and put his hand over Lydia's mouth. She startled awake and stared up at him with wide, fear-filled, emerald green eyes, but when Rafe pointed at Charles, the fear in her eyes dissipated. Rafe leaned closer to whisper in her ear. "We're taking you away from here. If I remove my hand, will you promise not to scream?"

She nodded.

Rafe slowly removed his hand from Lydia's mouth and she stayed silent as promised. Rafe gestured for Lydia to follow Charles and him out of the cabin. She nodded again, silently threw off her blanket, and slid out of bed. She quickly slipped her brown, homespun dress over her white shift and her dainty feet into her worn, black leather shoes then nodded she was ready.

They were almost to the door when Charles sneezed loudly. Rafe glared darkly at Charles as the other two slaves startled awake. Charles only shrugged helplessly. How was it his fault that he had to sneeze? Rafe was so unreasonable! The two men sat up in shocked surprise.

"Who let you out of the hole?" one asked Charles.

"Who are you?" the other asked Rafe.

Rafe's answer was to punch the first slave in the chin, snapping his head back so that he immediately lost consciousness. The other man yelped in fear, sprang from his bed, and tried to run, but before he had a chance to take more than a single step Rafe locked him in a strangle hold. Lydia squeaked with fright. Charles cried, "Stop! You're killing him!"

"Would you rather I let him sound the alarm?" Rafe asked maintaining his stranglehold.

Charles aimed his pistol at Rafe. "Let him go. I'll shoot you if I have to." Then the man went limp and it was a moot point. Rafe gently guided the body onto the bed.

"Is he—are they both dead?" Lydia asked.

"Unconscious. They'll recover with only a few sore muscles and perhaps a lingering headache," Rafe said.

Charles was skeptical, being highly familiar with Rafe's homicidal tendencies. He started to cross the room to examine the two slaves for signs of life, but Rafe grabbed the back of Charles's shirt. "We've wasted enough time," he hissed knowing exactly what Charles had been up to. He shoved Charles roughly into Lydia, who instinctively caught him in her arms. Rafe chose to deliberately misinterpret the situation. "Save your amorous hugs for later. We must go. Keep close or I'll leave you behind." He drew his pistol and slipped outside, vanishing into the dark and the rain like a shadow returning to its element.

Charles grasped Lydia's hand tightly with his free hand and literally dragged her out the door after Rafe. The three raced swiftly across the plantation in the driving rain with Rafe in the lead. The stormy night worked to their advantage by keeping everyone indoors. Charles rejoiced that soon he'd be free from this depressing place, while Lydia was troubled by the audacity of escaping, and also terrified and confused by this strange, angry man with eyes so dark that they blended completely with the black of night, and who regarded Charles with open hatred and disdain, yet was still inexplicably rescuing him. As they approached the gate, she stopped and pulled on Charles's arm, dragging him back a few paces. "No! No!" she cried, as rivulets of rain coursed down her pretty face. "Trent will come after us and whip us to death. We must return to our cabin before he discovers we've been out!"

"Child, why did you even come with us? Were you merely for taking a walk in the rain?" Rafe asked impatiently.

"Don't talk to her like that!" Charles snapped at Rafe. "She's only a frightened little girl."

With the butt of his pistol, Rafe brushed back a sodden lock of hair that had escaped from his braid and fallen over his right eye then nodded at the hulking shadow of the high hill in the distance from which he and Ed had observed the plantation earlier. "On the other side of that hill is a dense jungle. Once were in it we'll be safe. Only the most skilled trackers could find us in there in the dark and rain."

"Trent can track anyone anywhere," Lydia said. "I've heard tales of more than one slave who tried and failed to escape. Then Trent makes an example of them by whipping them to death in front of everyone. He enjoys it too."

"We need not worry about Trent as long as we have Rafe with us," Charles said.

Rafe was pleasantly surprised that Charles was actually saying something nice about him until Charles added, "This is the one I told you of, the demon spawn who sold me into slavery. He's a pirate, a skilled murderer, and a number of other things too sordid to mention in a lady's presence. He'll not hesitate to kill anyone who interferes with his plans, as you've already witnessed back at our cabin."

Lydia stared at Rafe eyes wide with fear. Rafe glared darkly at Charles then addressed Lydia. "Charles greatly exaggerates, except that I'll do whatever is necessary to remain free. If the two of you also wish to be free, then follow me. If not, stay behind. It's your choice." He again disappeared into the foggy, misty night.

Charles followed Rafe without hesitation, but after a half dozen steps realized Lydia hadn't accompanied him. He hastily backtracked. "Why are you still standing here? Come on."

"I can't go with that man." Lydia suppressed a sob. "He frightens me. He's so angry; and what you've told me about him…" She shivered. "Let's you and I go back. Please."

Charles glanced anxiously into the dense white veil of fog into which Rafe had disappeared. "I cannot go back, Lydia. I must return to my family and I won't allow you to return to slavery either, especially knowing what they're making you do. Come. In the mood Rafe's in he'll make good on his threat to leave us behind and although I'd rather not associate with him, I need his money, skills, knowledge and expertise if I'm to successfully make it to Nassau and then home."\

"But he's a murderer!" Lydia objected.

"I'll protect you. Trust me."

Charles grasped Lydia's hand and led her unwillingly into the veil of fog. They'd delayed long enough that they had to push hard to catch up to Rafe, although he'd purposely slowed. Still suffering the effects of his time in the hole, Charles was soon huffing and puffing, which changed to gasps for air as they rapidly ascended the hill. Concerned, Rafe said, "Here, Charles, put your arm across my shoulder and I'll support you."

"I don't need *your* support," Charles panted then defiantly placed his arm across Lydia's shoulders instead. She looked at Rafe apprehensively as if she feared he'd punish her for aiding Charles.

Offended by both of them, Rafe deliberately increased his pace, forcing them to work harder to keep up. Then Lydia slipped on the wet grass almost taking Charles down with her. Rafe hastily reached out to catch her, but she fearfully shied away. He self-consciously dropped his hand then redoubled his pace, vowing silently that even if Lydia and Charles slipped six hundred times in their efforts to keep up, he'd never again grant them the pleasure of spurning his aid.

At the top of the hill he turned around to check on Lydia and Charles's progress. They were still several hundred yards downhill and Lydia was struggling under Charles's weight. Rafe wanted to go down and help them despite their earlier rejection, but he stuck to his vow and instead waited in assumed impatience with an impatient frown and crossed arms.

"Took you long enough," he grumped to hide his concern when they finally caught up.

"Forgo the rude behavior, Rafe and remove these slave collars as you said you would," Charles commanded breathlessly.

Lydia grabbed Charles's wrist. "We can't remove the collars! I heard that they ordered Trent to beat a slave to death for taking off his collar merely because it was chafing his neck." She wrung her hands. "Oh, this was a mistake. We still have time to return before anyone misses us." She pulled on Charles's arm but he refused to budge.

"It seems your mistress prefers slavery to freedom," Rafe remarked disgustedly having no respect for one who'd choose life as a slave rather than taste freedom no matter the cost.

"I told you she's not my mistress!" Charles shot back heatedly. "Stop calling her that! Her name is Lydia."

Rafe was pleased he'd succeeded in returning a bit of the grief Charles had thrust upon him these last eight years. He goaded him again, working on evening the score. "Have no fear, I'll not tell Sarah about you and Lydia."

"Sarah?" Lydia asked.

Rafe didn't need to pretend shock. "Charles didn't tell you he was married and has a son?" He looked at Charles askance.

"It was too painful talking of them when I thought I'd never see them again because of you, who, by the way, have no room to judge. You used Lauralee merely for sport with absolutely no intention of ever marrying her. How many innocent, naive women have you coerced into your bed with your charming smile and good looks, I wonder?"

Rafe's countenance darkened. "None," he said tersely. He could've added that he'd sacrificed his virginity to Lauralee for Charles's sake, but Charles wouldn't believe it anyway, and it was too personal to talk about in front of Lydia.

"Oh, of course. What was I thinking? You don't bed innocents, only whores like Lauralee. Their kind are the only ones willing to bed an abomination," Charles said.

Rafe glared at Charles, his eyes as black with anger as the inky, starless depths of the sky above. "Perhaps I should return your mistress to the plantation and you to the hole I found you in and allow you both to continue to live the life you so richly deserve," he threatened quietly.

"It's you who deserve a life of slavery being already sentenced to it, but you, with your usual lack of honor sentenced me to it instead. That you rescued me only partially negates the crime. Now remove this wretched collar, as you said you would." Charles tugged on his slave collar.

Rafe sullenly pulled out his lock picks and set to work on Charles's collar. A few seconds later Charles heard a barely discernible click and then Rafe removed the collar and tossed it aside. Charles was so relieved to be free of the despicable ornament that he felt like jumping up and down for joy like when he was a small child on Christmas morning. Then he was convicted that he'd intended to make Rafe wear one of those collars. Like the Kelley's, his slaves wore collars constantly as a reminder that they were not free and thus subject to severe punishment at his command should they become surly, lazy, or attempt to escape. Now that he knew how degrading slavery was and how uncomfortable the collars were Charles couldn't follow that practice any more. He even privately vowed to improve his slave's living conditions; all except for Rafe, of course. The abomination would still have to suffer endlessly for all of his crimes—if he could even make Rafe serve out his sentence now…

Lydia watched Rafe remove Charles's collar with trepidation mixed with dread. The fear of punishment was so ingrained in her that she fully expected Trent to magically appear and whip the dark and angry stranger to death for his audacious act. When nothing happened, however, she realized freedom without punishment was actually possible. She tentatively approached Rafe. "Will—will you remove my collar as well?"

Rafe respected courage and high-spiritedness. Ed possessed such qualities, which was partly why he'd taken Ed in. Lydia, though, was of a completely different nature being meek and compliant. Besides, she made him uncomfortable, reminding him too much of that angel statue pointing accusingly at him on the night of Duncan's death. He crossed his arms. "It's unwise as well as dangerous for a wanted man to keep company with those who lack the courage and conviction to do whatever is necessary to remain free. It would be best if you returned to the compound as you yourself have suggested several times tonight."

Lydia turned away, sobbing. Charles aimed his pistol at Rafe. "You wicked child of Satan stop harassing her and remove her collar or so help me I'll shoot you in your cruel, black heart!"

Rafe rolled his eyes then plucked the pistol from Charles's hand. Lydia was so surprised that she stopped sobbing. Charles could barely restrain his rage. Rafe had stolen the knife from him on the island with that same ease. He'd been bested and shamed twice now in the same manner, and worse this time in front of Lydia. "Return my pistol!" he commanded imperially and held out his hand.

"It's not your pistol, Charles. I merely loaned it to you, but try and take it from me if you think you're capable," Rafe said.

Charles advanced on Rafe menacingly. Rafe assumed a defensive stance. Lydia hastily stepped between the two of them facing Charles. "No, Charles."

Charles stared at Lydia in disbelief. "You're taking Rafe's side?"

"You said you needed him to lead us safely to Nassau. If you harm him, you'll lose his aid."

Rafe snorted disdainfully. "Charles is incapable of harming me. I'm too quick and skilled, and he knows it, which is why he resorts to continually flinging barbed comments at me instead."

"Those so called barbed comments are merely the truth," Charles asserted firmly.

"Truth as you erroneously comprehend it," Rafe shot back.

"Enough of this! Will you remove Lydia's collar or not?" Charles demanded.

"Not," Rafe said and crossed his arms.

Charles's face reddened and his chest puffed up in anger, making him look as if he was about to explode like an overfilled, old water skin. Lydia put her hand lightly on Rafe's forearm. "Please, sir, I was frightened before when I spoke of returning to the plantation. I didn't mean what I said. I truly do wish to be free like Charles. You may bed me as often as you wish and even share me with your friends if you'll remove my collar and allow me to accompany you."

"Rafe, don't you dare accept that offer!" Charles commanded. Rafe ignored him and beckoned to Lydia to come closer. "Rafe," Charles warned.

"Charles," Rafe threatened quietly.

Charles desperately turned to Lydia. "You're a free woman now. There's no need to offer your body to Rafe or any other man."

Lydia closed her eyes and lifted her chin to Rafe, waiting for him to taste her lips and grope her body to see if she was worthy of the taking, as so many other men in her young life had already.

Rafe pulled out his lock picks and set to work on her collar.

Lydia's eyes popped open in surprise and a moment later her collar joined Charles's on the ground. Her hand flew to her bare neck as if she couldn't believe she no longer wore a collar. "Oh, thank you, sir!" she gushed.

Rafe nodded curt acknowledgement as he put away his lock picks.

"Do you want my services now, or later?"

"Rafe, if you dare take advantage of her—," Charles began.

"Shut up, Charles!" Rafe snapped irritably. Then he addressed Lydia. "Your body is yours to be freely given only to the one you will someday marry."

Charles's mouth fell open in surprise. Lydia's mouth fell open in shock. For the first time since she was ten years old a man had given her control of her body! She was stunned speechless by the magnanimity of the gift that this dark, scary stranger had given her.

Rafe noted both reactions and was offended twice over that they hadn't thought better of him. He turned and walked off without another word. Charles caught up to him, but Lydia walked a bit behind still in stunned wonder. "You of course have a wagon or horses or some such stashed nearby for our transport to Nassau," Charles said.

"No," Rafe said.

"What? Then how do you expect us to get to Nassau!"

"On your feet," Rafe said curtly. He increased his pace.

Charles dropped behind to walk beside Lydia, and complain loudly about Rafe's lack of concern for the welfare of his betters. Rafe ignored him. Actually, he was busily congratulating himself on how easily the rescue had been pulled off despite Charles's complicating it by insisting they take Lydia along. Then the sharp crack of a whip cut the air. Rafe sighed in disgust. After all his previous experiences with his bad luck, he should've known better than to congratulate himself before the task was completed. He stopped and turned around to face this new complication.

Trent had been making his nightly rounds armed with his treasured whip and a pistol when he'd seen Charles, Lydia, and a dark stranger crossing the plantation. He'd followed them covertly, curious as to what they were up to. When he realized they intended to escape, he considered going for help, but then it occurred to him that it would be far better to capture them singlehandedly and thus not have to share the reward. He would hide the dark stranger in his private cabin and enjoy slowly torturing him to death for the audacity of trying to steal his slaves and make him look bad. Charles would go back in the hole for a few more days. Lydia he'd request as part of his reward; that she be his alone for one full night as with that other slave woman a little over eight years back.

He'd watched hidden in the tall grasses on the hill when the stranger stopped to tinker with Charles's slave collar, curious as to what he was up to. A few seconds later the collar opened and the stranger threw it aside. Then the stranger easily removed Lydia's collar. Trent had snapped his mouth shut, which he only then realized was hanging open, and decided that instead of torturing the dark stranger to death he'd torture him into submission. He could imagine countless uses for a man who could open locks as quickly and easily as this man. All of the potential uses were illegal, of course, but he would use the dark stranger's talents to become rich beyond his wildest dreams using Charles's and Lydia's continued life as incentive for the stranger to obey his every command. Then he'd let the man be captured and executed for his crimes.

Trent had been so preoccupied with imagining the riches he would amass that he almost waited too long. The slaves and their would-be rescuer were heading for the jungle, and it would be difficult if not impossible to track them in there in the dark and the pouring rain. He sprang to his feet and cracked his whip. All three whirled around simultaneously. Charles gasped and Lydia's eyes widened in fear, although to her credit in Rafe's eyes she didn't cry out or try to run. Rafe merely looked annoyed. "You sir!" Trent said pointing at Rafe with the his whip handle. "Where do you think you're taking my slaves?"

Lydia snuggled close to Charles, trembling and he wrapped his arms protectively around her thin shoulders while watching Trent with obvious trepidation. Trent's ego was stroked by the slaves' reactions, but the dark stranger ruined his triumph by focusing his unusually dark eyes on him unyielding. "These two are no longer your slaves. Return to your plantation and I'll spare your life."

Trent bristled. The audacity of the man! "Who do you think you are to threaten me?" he demanded imperially.

"I believe I'm your superior in every way," Rafe said then smiled smugly.

Trent's face reddened and his eyes nearly popped out of his head as he went ballistic with insane fury. How dare this dark-skinned, dark-eyed, Indian claim superiority over a pure-blooded, blue-eyed white man! The impudent animal would have to learn some proper manners the hard way! "I'll show you who's superior!" he roared. He lashed out with his whip.

Rafe casually lifted his left hand caught the whip and snatched it away as easily as if he was taking it from a small child then seemingly oblivious to his cut and bleeding palm disdainfully tossed the whip on the ground a few yards away. "You'll have to do far better than that," he said deprecatingly.

Trent stared at Rafe in stunned astonishment. Here was someone who didn't recognize his authority, and who had skills beyond belief! He'd never had to face someone quite like this before. For the first time in his adult life, Trent knew fear. He drew his pistol and shakily aimed it at Rafe. "You shall return my slaves and I'll show mercy and not kill you," he blustered.

Rafe was thoroughly disgusted by this egomaniacal man who was only brave because no one had ever dared to question his authority. Then he realized that this was the man who'd raped and killed Ed's mother. A cold fury seized control of his soul. "Return to your plantation if you value your life." He was hoping Trent would refuse so he could take vengeance upon him for Ed.

"Rafe! Don't you dare kill him!" Charles commanded.

"He won't have the chance," Trent said. "I shall kill him first for the audacity of not only trying to steal my slaves, but for threatening me." He started to pull the trigger on his pistol.

With lightning-like rapidity Rafe drew his knife and threw it. The wicked slave master didn't even have the chance to be surprised that someone had summoned the impudence to kill him before he took his last foul breath.

"Is—is he dead?" Lydia asked tentatively.

"Most certainly. Murder is what Rafe does best," Charles said.

Rafe angrily rounded on Charles. "Would you rather I'd let him take you back and beat you to death as an example to the other slaves?" he demanded.

"You could've hurt him enough that he couldn't follow us, without killing him! However, as usual you couldn't forgo the pleasure of killing," Charles accused.

Rafe firmly sheathed his knife, the handle bloodied from his cut hand, and pointed to the trees. "Move on or I shall not forgo the pleasure of killing you," he said quietly.

Charles snorted disdainfully. "Spare me your empty words, Rafe. I stopped believing you'd kill me somewhere around the tenth time you made the threat and didn't follow through; and by the way, it's quite ungrateful of you to threaten me after I saved your life three times."

"You only saved my life once," Rafe swiftly countered.

"Three times." Charles counted off on his fingers. "The first was when you were sentenced to be hung for Duncan's murder and I managed to divert it to slavery on my plantation. The second was when you were attacked by that large cougar and I smashed its head in. The third was when the cannibals attacked and I scared them off by throwing spears at them. Considering all the murders you've committed since you slaughtered Duncan, though, not to mention joining with pirates and selling me into slavery, I wish I'd let you hang!"

Rafe could've argued that it was Sarah who'd rescued him from hanging and that instead of saving him from the cannibals Charles had injured him with those thrown spears—twice. Rafe also could've revealed his reasons for joining the pirates and selling Charles into slavery. It would be a waste of time, though, for Charles would undoubtedly find something unethical, immoral, or both in whatever he said. Rafe merely walked away without a word, and Lydia and Charles dutifully followed him.

Half an hour later as the day dawned they neared the camp where Ed slept. Rafe had no wish for Charles to hear him lying to Ed about why he'd rescued his acquaintance without Ed's help, so he said, "Wait here," and pointed to a fallen, mossy tree log with his cut and bloodied left hand.

"Why?" Charles asked suspiciously.

"My camp is near and I have a friend waiting there to whom I must explain your presence." Rafe obviously chafed at having to explain this to Charles.

"The slut, Lauralee, I presume?" Charles asked snidely.

"She was never my friend." Rafe walked swiftly away. During the seemingly interminable walk from the plantation he'd been tempted more than once to pummel Charles into oblivion. He feared that if Charles continued harassing him, he'd surrender to his desire before he saw Charles safely off the island. Then everything he'd done—the killing, the stealing, the unending nights in Lauralee's bed—would all have been for nothing.

He silently entered the camp where Ed still slept peacefully under the leafy lean-to. After he cleaned and bandaged his left hand, he knelt and gently grasped the boy's shoulder. "Ed, wake up. It's time to move on."

Ed stirred but didn't open his eyes. "Not yet," he mumbled sleepily. "I wanna sleep sum more."

Enduring Charles's acerbic comments, severe sleep deficiency, and over a year of stress and loss, combined to deny Rafe the patience to deal with disobedient children. He grabbed Ed by his scruff and irritably yanked Ed to his feet. "You'll rise now!"

Ed rubbed his eyes and yawned still half asleep, not registering the rough treatment. Stretching, he asked, "We gonna save yer acquaintance now?"

"It's already done." It wasn't exactly the way Rafe had intended to break the news, but in his irritation and exhaustion, intent went the way of the wind.

Ed was wide-awake now. "You alreddy did it? Wifout me? But you sed I cud help!" his lower lip quivered. "You lide! You were never takin me wit you!"

"It was the only way to make you stop bothering me. Take it like a man. I'm sure you've been lied to before and survived," Rafe snapped.

"I never been lide to by a tru fren afore," Ed accused sullenly.

Guilt roared up in Rafe. He countered it with a rationalization. "I warned you I don't do well with friendships. Now break camp and don't dawdle. I'm in a hurry. The others are waiting."

Ed crossed his arms and refused to budge. Rafe grabbed Ed roughly by the back of his brand new, white, silk shirt, lifted him off the ground and planted him firmly in front of his bag. "Pick it up!" he commanded; but Ed remained stubbornly defiant. Rafe snatched up the bag and shoved it into Ed's stomach with such force that the child doubled over in pain and air whooshed from his lungs. Rafe winced. He hadn't meant to hurt the boy.

"Yer mean and you lie! I don wanna be your tru fen enymore and I don wanna be like you either! I'm ne'er even goin to tok to you agin!" Ed sat down on the ground cross-legged with his bag resting in the hollow of his legs and crossed his arms.

Rafe ran his left hand across his face. His relationship with Ed was mirroring his relationships with Charles and Leopold. It wouldn't be long before he'd lost the child's regard forever, if he hadn't lost it already. Apparently, he was as incapable of cultivating a friendship that didn't end in either anger or bloodshed as he was of owning God's love. He kicked dirt on the remains of the fire under the lean-to and then picked up Ed's bedroll, took Ed's bag from his lap, picked up his own bag and bedroll, and walked away expecting Ed to follow.

Ed delayed for a moment, but since Rafe was walking away with all of his new things, he finally sprang to his feet and followed him at a distance. Despite a sense of urgency, Rafe didn't hurry. He had nothing to look forward to, except Charles's hostile attitude, Ed's sulking, and Lydia's overt fear of him, a triple combination of misery certain to make him feel wretched. Rafe suddenly wished he could simply abandon them all and end his life now, but his sense of honor coupled with the certainty that none of the three were capable of making it safely off the island stood in the way. He attempted to console himself with the knowledge that in three days they'd reach Nassau. Then Charles could buy berths on a departing ship for himself, Lydia and Ed, and Rafe would no longer be responsible for all of them and could end his life. Three more days to the end of his misery. He could do anything for three days…

Rafe rejoined Lydia and Charles far sooner than he wished. Ed came up a moment later and eyed Charles and Lydia curiously. Forgetting he'd determined never to speak to Rafe again, Ed pointed at Charles with his thumb. "Is him yer fren?"

"He's Charles, the ungrateful wretch I rescued tonight."

Charles scowled at Rafe and he returned it in kind.

"The ac—quaintance?" Ed asked.

Rafe nodded once in acknowledgement. Ed pointed at Lydia. "Who's she? She's reel pritty."

"Ask her," Rafe said in no mood for polite introductions.

Ed happily approached Lydia holding out his hand. "Well met. I'm Ed."

Lydia smiled and shook Ed's hand. "I'm pleased to meet you, Ed. My name is Lydia."

"What are you doing with Rafe, young man?" Charles asked suspiciously. "Is he holding you for ransom? We'll make him return you to your home immediately."

Rafe laughed derisively. "Yes, Charles, gallantly force me to return Ed to his loving and wealthy parents."

"I will!" Charles said indignantly. "You'll return this child to his parents this day or I'll report you to the authorities no matter the consequences to myself!"

"Or Lydia?" Rafe asked pointedly.

Charles hadn't thought of Lydia. Here was a dilemma.

"Don't worry for me, Charles," Lydia said. "Returning this child to his parents is far more important than anything else."

Charles gloated openly. "Take note, Rafe. You have before you two people who are willing to sacrifice themselves to aid another. You could benefit from our example were you even capable of such nobility."

Only Lydia noticed the answering hurt in Rafe's eyes, which confused her. From what she'd already seen and everything Charles had said, Rafe was thoroughly evil and completely lacked a conscience. He shouldn't even be capable of caring about lacking altruism.

Sensing that Lydia was looking at him, Rafe's dark eyes flicked in her direction. She quickly averted her eyes.

"I demand that you return this child to his parents," Charles commanded imperiously.

"But I ain got no parens," Ed objected.

Charles's eyebrows shot up. "Then what is Rafe doing with you?" He looked at Rafe askance. "Exactly what nefarious use are you making of this child?"

Ed hastily came to Rafe's defense. "He's my tru fren, and he's gonna teech me hows to kill reel qwik an eezee, lak as he did the woamin in my allee."

Ed's declaration earned three different reactions. Rafe winced, Lydia stifled a gasp, and Charles looked stunned. "What woman?" Charles asked, his eyes narrowing.

"Ed..." Rafe warned. He most definitely did not want Charles to know he'd killed Lauralee. It would only grant his ceaseless tormentor another opportunity to claim he was irredeemable, and he didn't need to be reminded of what he was already certain of.

"The woamin in the alley wheres I use ta live. Rafe kilt her, real eezee. Shot her in the hart an then slit her throwt, lak this." Ed grabbed the hair on the top of his head with one hand and grimacing, made a slashing motion across his neck with the index finger of his other hand. "She ne'er had a chance," he added proudly.

Charles looked to Rafe, aghast. "You brutally murdered an innocent woman in a dark alley and this child witnessed it?"

"I ain no child!" Ed heartily objected.

Charles ignored Ed. "Rafe?"

"She was far from innocent," Rafe said.

"How do you know she was far from innocent? Are you God that you can see into people's souls?"

"It was Lauralee," Rafe said.

Charles's eyes widened. "You killed your lover?"

Lydia gasped again and sidled further away from Rafe.

"There was no love between Lauralee and me."

"Yes, well, we've already established that you're incapable of caring about anyone but yourself," Charles said. "But even so, how could you kill a woman you'd known intimately?"

"I'm a natural born killer," Rafe said defiantly, knowing Charles would never believe his claim of self-defense. Ed didn't even believe it and he'd seen Lauralee threaten him.

Lydia stifled a whimper of fear. Ed patted her forearm reassuringly. "Don worry, Lydia, Rafe won hurt you. Yer too pretty an too nice."

"He'd best not harm her," Charles said, "or he'll discover what I'm truly capable of."

"Perhaps you'd like to discover what *I'm* truly capable of, Charles," Rafe threatened quietly. His tone, if not the threat itself, silenced everyone not just Charles. Then having enough of all three of them, Rafe walked away. The others followed him hesitantly, silently.

Finally, Ed couldn't keep quiet anymore. "Wher are we goin?"

"Nassau," Rafe said tersely.

"Why are we goin there?" Ed ventured to ask when Rafe didn't rip his head off for asking the first question.

"So you may all catch a ship to New England," Rafe said.

"New Providence has always been my home," Lydia risked objecting. "I have no wish to live anywhere else."

"If she's stayin, I wanna stay too," Ed said.

Rafe was exhausted, his cut hand throbbed, he ached all over from his long day, and all the arguing, incriminations and ungratefulness grated on his soul like sandpaper on a fresh burn, but he gritted his teeth and held his temper in check. Barely.

"You two are wasting your time," Charles told them. "Rafe doesn't care what you want. He only wishes to be rid of us as expeditiously as possible so he may continue thieving and killing innocents without hindrances."

That did it. Rafe lost his tenuous hold on his temper. He whirled around, drawing his knife. "Enough!" he roared. "I will cut out the tongue of the next one who says a word!"

Ed sullenly crossed his arms. Tears welled up in Lydia's eyes. Charles bristled indignantly. "Vile threats may have been acceptable among the pirates, Rafe, but not in front of children and I'll not stand for such abuse either!"

Rafe tightened his grip on his knife. "Apparently, you wish to lose your tongue, Charles."

Lydia gasped. "Oh please sir, don't cut out Charles's tongue." She wrung her hands in distress. "I assure you, it's not his intent to show disrespect. He merely hasn't yet learned to stoop to his superiors."

Charles snorted. "Rafe is most definitely not my superior!"

"I shall grant your wish, Lydia," Rafe said. "I won't cut out Charles's tongue."

"Oh thank you, sir," she said.

"I shall slit his throat." Rafe took a menacing step toward Charles. "We'll see who's superior as your life blood drains from your neck!"

Charles's eyes widened and he took a frightened step back. Rafe lunged forward, intending to scare some respect into Charles by slicing his shirt open as he'd done at the bear den on the island.

"No!" Ed rushed in between them.

Rafe inhaled sharply and hastily lowered his knife as he skidded to a halt, the toes of his boots kicking up pebbles. Then he forcefully sheathed his knife, grabbed a handful of Ed's shirt at the chest and lifted him up onto his toes. Breathing heavily from the adrenalin rush of fear over nearly slaughtering Ed by accident, like Duncan, he said "Never do something as foolish as that again, boy! I could've killed you!" He roughly released Ed, shoving the boy back a step.

"I coodin hep it. I din wan you to hurt Charles," Ed said as he straightened his clothing. "I lak him! He's nice, lak Lydia, an not alwis mad, lak as you are."

Rafe's dark eyes plainly reflected the pain of the betrayal he felt. "I see. Then I'll leave you with your nice new friends who are not always mad." With astonishing speed he disappeared into the surrounding jungle growth.

Lydia was immensely relieved that Rafe was gone, but Ed was stunned speechless, and Charles couldn't believe Rafe had deserted them and in the middle of a jungle too! It didn't make sense after Rafe had gone through all that trouble and risk to rescue them; but then Rafe's choices never made any sense. Ed started to race after Rafe, but Charles grabbed his scrawny arm. "No, Ed."

Ed struggled. "Lemme alone! I has to go afer him! He's my tru fren an I hurt him. I culd see it in his eyes. I has to say I'm sorree."

"I can't let you go after him, Ed. I know Rafe quite well and when he's as angry as he is now, he wouldn't hesitate to hurt even a true friend like you."

"I has to go afer him," Ed insisted, tears filling his eyes. "I need him."

"We all need him," Charles conceded. "But I'll be the one to go after him. You must stay here where it's safe." He made eye contact with Lydia. "Watch after him." She nodded acquiescence and then Charles raced after Rafe.

After a few anxious moments Charles finally caught sight of Rafe. "Rafe!" he called, but the evil half-breed ignored him and continued walking briskly away. Charles suppressed his anger at being ignored by an inferior, but only because he needed to pacify Rafe and anger, no matter how justified, wouldn't accomplish that. He finally caught up to Rafe and grabbed his sleeve to make him stop. "You can't walk off and leave us," he said breathlessly.

Rafe angrily yanked free. "I'm through with you! With all of you! You're on your own now!"

Charles humbled himself to the lowly half-breed criminal. It wasn't easy, but necessity demanded it. A woman and a child depended upon him to convince Rafe to return. "We need you."

"You only need someone to continually disparage so you can feel better about yourself and I won't be that for you anymore," Rafe said resentfully.

Charles thought it was quite gracious of him to ignore the completely untrue jibe. "On the contrary, we need your guidance and superior skills."

"My guidance and skills," Rafe repeated scornfully.

"Yes. We don't know the lay of the land and as you're aware, I'm not as skilled a hunter as you. Also, we have no money."

Rafe opened his coin pouch and grabbed a handful of coins, all of them either silver or gold crowns. He tossed the small fortune at Charles's chest. Charles clumsily caught the coins, dropping several which then rolled on their edges on a curving, wobbly path, eventually stopping some face up and some face down underneath several ferns. "You have money now. As for the rest, you'll either learn or die," Rafe said. "I don't care which." He walked away.

Charles hastily pocketed the coins he'd caught then chased down the errant coins and stuffed them into his pants pocket along with the others. By this time Rafe was so far away he could barely be glimpsed among the trees. Charles raced after him once more. He was so worn out by the time he reached Rafe that he had difficulty maintaining Rafe's brisk pace. "Rafe—,"

"Stop following me!" Rafe demanded.

"I can't. We still need you. The money's only any good when we find a town. I don't even know where one is and I don't have a map. We could wander lost for days, weeks."

"Then you'll have plenty of exercise," Rafe said unmoved. He knew the island wasn't that big. Eventually, Charles and the others would wander into civilization.

"What about Ed? I thought you cared about the boy. How can you leave him out here to wander lost until we starve to death?" Charles was panting hard from his exertions.

Rafe deliberately increased his pace so that Charles was forced to jog to keep up with his much longer stride. "Head east to Harold Pond and then turn north. Even a halfwit like you should be able to manage that."

It wasn't as easy for Charles to ignore being called a halfwit by Rafe as it had been to ignore the earlier jibe, but desperation helped considerably. "Rafe." He paused catching his breath as well as searching for some way to tell his adversary he feared going on without him without having to actually admit to it.

"Well?" Rafe prompted impatiently.

Charles couldn't maintain the pace any longer. "Could you please stop?" he exclaimed, nearly winded. "I can't keep up with you and talk at the same time."

Rafe obligingly came to a standstill then looked at Charles expectantly. Charles suddenly discovered he was completely out of arguments. "I, um, uh..."

"If you have nothing else to say, I'm moving on," Rafe threatened.

Charles hastily blurted out the first words that came to mind. "I can't tell direction out here in the jungle."

Rafe raised an eyebrow. "The sun rises in the east and sets in the west even in the jungle, Charles." He resumed his brisk pace.

Out of excuses and out of energy Charles sank down onto a nearby fallen log, his chest heaving and stared after Rafe at a loss. Then Ed raced past him, caught up to Rafe and latched tightly onto his bandaged left hand forcing him to a pained standstill. "Don go! Don leeve me! I'm sorry for makin you mad at me agin!" he sobbed. "Pleese, Pleese don leeve me. I'll be good. I promise."

Rafe's vision blurred with tears. He knelt to be at eye level with this child whom he'd come to love so dearly in such a short time. "Ed," he said softly, lovingly. "I'm not mad at you. It's time for us to part, is all. I told you we'd have to part eventually, remember?"

"Yes, but I was hopin it wuld be afer I was all growed up," Ed said tearfully.

Rafe couldn't help but smile. "I'd love to see you grow into a man, Ed, but I'm not fit—" His voice broke. He wiped his right hand across his face, reined in his emotions, then started over. "I want you to be an upright man and you can't learn to be an upright man if you stay with me; not with the sort of life I'm forced to lead now. You must stay with Charles. It's what's best for you." He gently pushed Ed toward Charles.

"No, no!" Ed protested. "I wanna stay wit you." Tears streamed down his cheeks as he tried to grab Rafe's hand again, but Rafe pulled away. Ed sank to the ground sobbing wretchedly.

It was too painful to look upon Ed in such misery when he could do nothing to ease it. Rafe turned away. Charles misinterpreted it as heartlessness and decided they were better off without Rafe after all. He scooped Ed into his arms. "Forget Rafe, Ed. We'll be fine without him. You'll see. You and Lydia and I are a good team. We don't need him."

Ed squirmed free, raced back to Rafe and grabbed Rafe's forearm with both hands. "Pleese, Rafe! Don let Charles take me away frum you! Pleese," he sobbed.

Rafe determinedly pried Ed's hands loose and shoved him at Charles. "Take him," he commanded hoarsely.

Charles gathered Ed into his arms. The distraught child buried his face in Charles's shoulder, wailing loudly. "How can you be so heartless?" Charles rubbed Ed's back in a futile attempt at calming him. "Can't you see the child is quite enamored of you for some strange, incomprehensible reason?"

"I see it," Rafe said softly.

"Then why are you treating him so poorly?"

Rafe wasn't about to waste his time explaining to someone as prejudiced against him as Charles. "Just take him and go." He had difficulty keeping his voice from trembling.

Lydia had raced after Ed when he'd run after Rafe, but then she'd become a bit lost in the jungle. She'd followed the voices and arrived on the scene in time to see Rafe turn away from Ed. She deduced that Rafe had refused Ed's and Charles's requests to stay. "Sir, although I'm grateful to you for freeing me, I think we'd all be better off without you and your angry, violent ways. However, I like Ed and I can see he cares for you deeply. So for his sake I beg you to stay with us at least until we reach Nassau."

The wording of Lydia's plea was more than a little insulting, but since her opinion of him had been influenced by Charles, Rafe granted leniency and didn't become angry. He looked at Ed's tear-stained, pleading face then looked at Charles who surprisingly also looked anxious for him to stay. It would be a terrible emotional strain to stay, but still it wasn't that hard to make his decision, for he truly had no wish to leave Ed yet. "I'll stay until we're a few miles out from Nassau, but only if each of you and especially you Charles, promise to refrain from whining and complaining and accusations. Do you think you can all do that?"

They each nodded solemnly.

"Return my money, Charles." Rafe held out his hand. Charles reached into his pocket, grabbed the coins and handed them back. Rafe stuffed the small fortune back into his coin pouch then possessively snatched Ed away from Charles.

Ed wrapped his arms tightly around Rafe's neck and sobbed into his chest, "I'm glad yer stayin. Even if it is ony fer jus a lil wile."

"Me too, little one," Rafe whispered, his voice hoarse with emotion. He buried his face in Ed's soft, thick curly hair as tears stung his eyes. "Me too."

<h1 style="text-align:center">Chapter Thirty-Five</h1>

Rafe walked into the parish alone in the dead of night. He'd loaned his pallet to Lydia and left Charles to sleep on the ground then waited until he was certain everyone was soundly asleep before he'd left on his private errand to the fine manor house they'd passed a few miles back. The master and lady were riding out the gate in their open carriage and they'd looked about the same size as Charles and Lydia, which had given Rafe an idea.

As silently as a leaf on the wind Rafe walked around the red brick manse checking the windows. Finding the dining room window unlocked he slid it open and slipped inside then closed the window, ghosted up the stairs, and down the hallway until he came upon the master's bedroom. As the master and lady slept blissfully unaware of the uninvited guest in their room, Rafe brazenly searched through their wardrobe. He picked out two complete suits and undergarments for Charles and two dresses and undergarments for Lydia, took a brush and a comb off a side table, and a blue wool blanket off the end of the bed to carry all of his stolen goods. He left the majority of his small fortune on the dressing table as a guilt offering then left the house through the front door.

Charles happened to awaken from another bad dream about Rafe and Sarah just as Rafe returned to camp. "Where have you been? No doubt, up to no good!" he groused.

Rafe wordlessly tossed the bundle at Charles. Clothing spilled out, burying Charles's head underneath the dress and petticoats. Charles hastily pulled the clothing off. "Where did these come from?" Charles demanded. "You stole them, didn't you! Did you kill their owners?"

Rafe ignored him and lay down on the ground beside Ed for a few hours of rest. Charles knew Rafe well enough to realize that further questioning would be useless, so he sighed in exasperation then pragmatically lay down and went back to sleep.

* * *

The next morning after breakfast Charles and Lydia changed into the clothing Rafe had stolen then buried their slave clothing under a bush. The spare sets of clothing were once again wrapped up in the blanket which Charles carried under his arm when they resumed their travels.

Rafe remained silent all day, but Lydia, Charles, and Ed talked amiably. At sundown they stopped at the single inn in a small village and rented a room for the men and another for Lydia. Lydia joined them in their room for dinner, which Rafe had a servant bring up, then stayed to visit with Charles and Ed. Rafe retreated to the shadows on the opposite side of the room and laid out his pallet for a little rest and recuperation.

When Lydia retired to her room for the night, Charles took the only bed, and Ed placed his pallet beside Rafe, who pretended sleep. As soon as Rafe was convinced Charles and Ed were sleeping soundly, he silently arose then stole out into the night to replenish their coin by continuing his recently adopted practice of robbing drunken gamblers at knifepoint. Charles opened his eyes as the door creaked shut behind Rafe, for he'd only been lightly sleeping, too tense and wound up by recent events to fall into the deep sleep he normally found without effort. Having no desire to chase Rafe into the dark of night and most likely to a drug den or a bordello, he decided to instead confront Rafe upon his return. He moved the room's single stuffed armchair to face the door and sat down, dozing off and on as he waited.

When he slept, Charles dreamed of home and of Sarah, and Laird. Thankfully, Rafe was absent from his dreams this time. When Charles was awake, he mulled over the events of the last twenty-four hours, and his conscience accused him that he'd treated Rafe shoddily. At the least he'd been ungrateful, for Rafe could've left him to rot in slavery, but for some motive known only to Rafe the half breed had saved him, and Lydia too, although reluctantly. Inexplicably, he was then reminded of the cross-stitch done by his mother that had hung on his wall in his nursery for as far back as he could remember. *Make sure that nobody pays back wrong for wrong, but always try to be kind to each other and to everyone else. 1 Thessalonians 5:15.*Charles knew it was past time he should begin applying that verse to Rafe, but he still found it hard to forgive Rafe for brutally assaulting him at the ball and for selling him into slavery; and he still blamed Rafe for the shipwreck too. Sneaking off tonight to commit crimes, drink until he was in a stupor, and/or smoke coca leaves risking not only his own capture, but the safety of the three innocent people totally dependent upon him didn't go far toward promoting any good feelings toward Rafe either. As the night wore on and Rafe failed to return, Charles's anger increased exponentially; an anger he intended to unleash upon Rafe with a vengeance when Rafe finally crawled back in high or drunk like the despicable insect he was!

* * *

It was the small hours of the morning when Rafe finally returned, exhausted, but with a full pouch of stolen coins tied to his belt and the means of permanently ending his misery safely tucked away in his left pants pocket. Being the second night in a row he'd had little to no sleep, his weary body was begging for rest, so when he saw Charles not only awake, but lying in wait, he cursed under his breath in Mohican. "It's about time you returned!" Charles ranted. "What were you doing? Drinking? Abusing drugs? Stealing? Murdering innocent women in dark alleys?"

Rafe released a longsuffering sigh. "Even if it was all those things it's no business of yours. You're not my master, nor will you ever be, much as you wish otherwise."

"I am indeed your master, by decree of the court, and even if that were not so, what you do is my business if only because your actions affect all of us. Not only do you put us in danger with your criminal activities, but you're an exceedingly poor example for Ed. I'd be willing to wager my life that before you rescued Lydia and me you've been leaving the poor child alone in inns every night while you drank yourself into a stupor or smoked coca leaves; and I wouldn't be at all surprised if a tumble with some prostitute wasn't included as well."

Rafe laughed mirthlessly. "You'd lose that wager."

"I don't think so," Charles countered.

Rafe scowled. "Why must you always assume the worst where I'm concerned? I may be a bastard half-breed, lack a soul, and certainly have faults, but all things considered I deserve better from you!"

"On the contrary it's I who deserves better from you! I'd wager my life you haven't paused once to consider the countless unbearable and unjust hardships I've suffered ever since you assaulted me at Pierre and Lisbeth's ball, you selfish demon-spawn!" Charles spat.

Rafe's hands fisted at his sides, his eyes narrowed, and he tensed. "That's the second time tonight you've wagered your life and been wrong, Charles. If you're not careful, I might collect," he said quietly.

Charles ignored the obvious warning signs of an imminent violent flare-up and opened his mouth to point out that Rafe's threat only proved his point.

Rafe drew his pistol. "Don't," he warned quietly.

Charles didn't know if the pistol was loaded, but he snapped his mouth shut. Rafe kept the pistol out for a moment longer before he holstered it.

"Surely you're aware that you're only proving your irredeemable nature by continually making threats on my life," Charles then couldn't help pointing out.

"How could I not be aware of it when you do such a fine job of continually pointing it out, Charles?" Rafe said resentfully. "I suppose I should thank you though, for as a result of your unceasing efforts I no longer fool myself that there's hope for one such as me."

"A remorseless criminal?" Charles said snidely.

"I am not a remorseless criminal, Charles! Every criminal act I've committed since the shipwreck, no matter how despicable, was thrust upon me by circumstances beyond my control!"

Charles snorted derisively. "You honestly can't expect one who knows you as well as I do to believe you don't choose to sin," he scoffed.

"I'd be a fool to expect that," Rafe agreed bitterly.

"Indeed, you willingly plunge deeper into iniquity with every passing moment."

Rafe muttered under his breath in Mohican then brushed past Charles and lay down on his back on his bedroll, covering his burning eyes with his arm. Within moments he was asleep, but all too soon he gasped awake from a horrific nightmare. He stared at the whitewashed walls of their room, which looked more gray than white in the half-light of early morning when no decent person was awake. How he envied Ed and Charles their peaceful slumber. He'd had nightmares nearly every night since he'd killed Duncan, except when he was exhausted beyond dreaming, or he resorted to smoking coca leaves; which reminded him… He silently, fluidly rose from his pallet, pulled the expensive corked, four-ounce, dark purple, glass bottle of enough laudanum to assure his death several times over from his pocket, and buried it in the bottom of his clothing bag. Then he returned to his pallet and waited for sleep if it came, and a return to his turbulent dreams.

What seemed like a second later, Rafe was snatched from another virulent nightmare by Ed shaking his shoulder violently and crying out, "Wake up! Wake up!" Rafe bolted to his feet while drawing his knife, his heart pounding, scanning the room for the threat. When he saw only Ed, Charles, and Lydia in the room and realized there was no threat, however, he irritably sheathed his knife. "Ed, don't ever wake me like that again!" he chastised sternly. "I thought it was an emergency."

"It is a mergency. I'm reel hungree," Ed said.

Rafe rubbed his face and sighed wearily. Judging from the sun's position in the sky out their room's single window he'd only snatched about two hours of sleep, but as Lydia had joined them, returning to sleep was out of the question. She stood beside Charles, who lounged in one of the two chairs in the room and was pointing out something to her in a single-page newspaper. They discussed the article in muted tones, but deducing from the uneasy glances Lydia tossed at him from time to time Rafe guessed it was probably about him and his criminal activities – Charles's favorite subject.

"When we gonna eat?" Ed asked impatiently, drawing Rafe's attention away from Charles and Lydia.

"Soon. Pack up," Rafe said absently.

As Ed set to work rolling up his and Rafe's bedrolls, Rafe walked across the room to Charles to see which of his recent crimes he and Lydia were discussing so intently. Lydia stepped hastily away as he neared. It hurt that she continued to fear him; especially after he'd told her he had no intention of ever harming her, but he saw no way of changing her opinion as long as Charles continued to feed her apprehensions.

Charles shoved the newspaper at Rafe. "Read this and then deny you were sneaking out on killing and thieving raids every night!"

Rafe took the paper and hastily perused it. Several articles mentioned his criminal nocturnal activities, among them Trent's death. They were calling him the half-breed savage; not terribly imaginative. Surely they could've come up with a better tag such as moonlight marauder, or ghost bandit. Then he became aware that Ed was watching him intently. He crumpled up the paper. "There's no proof this is me. Plenty of people on this island meet this description."

"It's you!" Charles spat. "They say you've taken at least eight lives since we were taken from the island. Is this true or do you even keep count of how many murders you've committed?"

Rafe did keep count. He knew the exact number. It was twenty-one if he counted the half-dozen cannibals and the merchant sailors he'd killed by his own hand on the three pirate raids, thirty-six if he added the wounded he'd failed to save from Lauralee's butchering hand, one-hundred-six if he added his slaughtered adopted tribe to the tally. He wasn't about to tell Charles that though, and especially not with Ed listening. "The papers exaggerate. You know that."

"In your case, I don't believe the facts are exaggerated. That aside, let me point out that if we're captured in your company, we'll all be considered accomplices to your crimes," Charles said.

"Have no fear. Under no circumstances will I allow any of us to be captured," Rafe reassured him.

"How will you make certain?" Charles demanded. "Will you slit the throat of everyone who looks at us in a manner that annoys you and then claim it as self-defense?"

Rafe angrily threw the crumpled up newspaper at Charles's chest then retreated to the window on the opposite side of the room and stared blindly outside, seriously considering walking out altogether and taking Ed with him; except that would be tantamount to throwing away Ed's future. He told himself he only had to endure Charles and his dour attitude until tomorrow night, when they'd reach Nassau. He'd suffered worse for longer. He could do this; but then he'd lose Ed... Rafe wondered which local family would adopt Ed and how long it would be before Ed gave his heart to God. That was certainly what he wanted for Ed, except that then Ed would hate him for his crimes instead of admiring him. Although by then he would be dead, Rafe cared a great deal about how Ed would remember him. He tentatively approached Charles, who had begun packing. "Charles?" he asked softly so that Ed who had finished packing and was playing hand games with Lydia across the room wouldn't overhear.

"What!" Charles demanded.

Rafe nervously cleared his throat. "Would you possibly do me a favor?"

"You have the unmitigated gall to ask me for a favor after all the harm and grief you've caused?" Charles demanded heatedly.

Lydia and Ed momentarily stopped their play, but as Rafe's knife remained sheathed, they quickly resumed their game, knowing it was merely another heated argument; normal between Rafe and Charles.

"I admit I don't deserve any favors, Charles, and especially not from you, but once you return home Ed will find God and then—"

"He'll despise you for your many crimes," Charles said with a hint of smug satisfaction.

Rafe glanced wistfully in Ed's direction then looked back at Charles. "I'd like you to explain to him when that time comes that I only broke the law out of necessity and not for any other reason, such as greed or malice."

"I won't justify a single one of the heinous crimes you've committed. On the contrary, I will make certain Ed despises you for every last one of them as he should," Charles said.

Rafe nodded resignedly. So in death even as in life he'd be thoroughly reviled and hated. He deserved no less, but it still hurt that not a single person would remember him fondly. "Is there nothing that would persuade you to change your mind?" he asked, without any real hope of an affirmative reply.

"No. Nothing," Charles replied firmly.

Rafe nodded again. Then unable to remain in the same room with Charles, Lydia, and Ed, who all played havoc with his emotions in one way or another, he snatched up his bag and bedroll and crossed the room in three long strides.

Ed hastily abandoned the game with Lydia and raced to Rafe. "Wher are you goin? Yer not leevin me are you?"

"Not yet. I only need some fresh air," Rafe said.

"I'm goin with you." Ed raced to his bag and bedroll, scooped them up then raced back to Rafe and grasped his right hand possessively.

Rafe's arid heart blossomed with joy that this small child whom he'd come to love so completely in such a short time had chosen his company over that of both Charles and Lydia. At the same time, his heart ached with the knowledge that soon Ed would despise him as much as everyone else. He wrapped his strong tan fingers possessively around Ed's tiny brown hand and they walked outside together.

They sat down under the shade of an old, twisted, oak tree across the street from the inn to wait for Lydia and Charles. Five minutes passed. Charles and Lydia didn't show. Rafe picked up a long, thick stick, broke it in two and drummed a rhythm on the hard ground while absently listening to Ed's non-stop prattle. Eight minutes passed. Lydia and Charles still failed to show. Rafe fumed. What was taking those two so long?

Twelve minutes later Lydia and Charles finally came out of the inn. Rafe tossed aside his sticks and stood up. Ed scrambled to his feet and grabbed Lydia's hand. "Finally!" Rafe said. "What were you two doing alone together in the room for so long? Is it something Sarah shouldn't know about?"

Charles reddened and was about to utter a spiteful retort, but Lydia squeezed his forearm and shook her head while glancing fearfully at Rafe. For her sake Charles bit back the retort, which left him with nothing to say but the actual reason for the delay. "Lydia and I were discussing whether it was more circumspect to remain with you despite your murderous nature or to go off on our own. We've chosen to remain with you."

"I'm gratified by your faith in me," Rafe said sarcastically. Then he walked away.

Charles, Lydia, and Ed followed Rafe instead of walking beside him, which was fine with him. He was struggling with his emotions on this last day of having Ed in his life and he wanted to keep his turmoil private. Charles took the opportunity to witness to the youngsters. He thought it wouldn't hurt Rafe to hear it too, but he was mistaken. It was heart-wrenchingly painful to hear of the love, peace, joy, and forgiveness through Christ's death and resurrection that Rafe now firmly believed was unavailable to all those like him. Any other time, Rafe would've hidden his anguish under a façade of indifference, but since he was as much as walking alone, he uncharacteristically allowed himself to grieve openly.

However, Charles was familiar enough with Rafe that he could tell Rafe was distressed merely by the way he walked, with his head hanging, shoulders slumped, and without his usual energetic, confident step. His distress added truth to Rafe's avowal last night that he suffered guilt and remorse, which left Charles no option, but to conclude that he'd badly misjudged Rafe. But then how was that possible when he'd based his opinion of Rafe on Rafe's iniquitous lifestyle? In his pride, Charles desperately needed to prove he'd judged Rafe correctly, but the only way to prove that was to have a serious talk with Rafe and he knew Rafe's moods. Rafe would refuse to talk to him now; but before he and Rafe parted forever he would have to find time for that talk and confirm the truth if only for his own peace of mind.

<u>Chapter Thirty-Six</u>

Rafe and his charges stopped at a well-kept inn on the southern edge of Nassau for the night. Rafe paid for two rooms, and after a bland, but filling mutton stew for which Lydia once again joined the men in their room, Rafe loaded his pistol in case trouble found him as it was prone to do these days, made sure his knife was loose in its sheath, then as it had started to rain, slipped on his coat, and headed for the door.

Ed hurried to Rafe's side. "Wher you goin? I wanna cum too."

Rafe found it hard to deny Ed, but he needed time alone to mourn the boy's imminent loss. "Not this time, but I promise I'll return before bedtime." He quickly stepped out and closed the door before Ed could object or Charles could make a snide comment about committing crimes, drinking, or abusing drugs.

He was halfway to the stairs at the end of the hall when Charles caught up to him. "Where are you off to at this time of night?"

"What business is it of yours?" Rafe asked frostily.

"I thought I'd come with you."

"To make certain I don't kill, steal, smoke coca leaves, or drink myself into a stupor?" Rafe demanded resentfully.

Charles almost automatically answered in the affirmative with an accusatory retort added on for good measure, except he knew that then Rafe would never let him come along and time was running out for him to discover if he was truly wrong about Rafe. "I thought we might have a pleasant chat."

Rafe snorted. "You and I could never have a pleasant chat, Charles; and I also wish to be alone." He increased his pace.

Charles tried to keep up, but Rafe's longer legs gave him the advantage. He slipped downstairs and reached the busy common room well ahead of Charles who determinedly bounded downstairs two at a time. As he breathlessly entered the common room, he spotted Rafe already at the door. "Rafe!" he called out.

Rafe winced and glanced uneasily at the full crowd of diners and drinkers. Luckily no one seemed to be paying him any particular heed. However, he didn't want Charles yelling out and drawing attention to him again, so he impatiently waited for him. Then he grabbed Charles's forearm and drew him outside. "Don't ever call out my name in public again! It could see me caught!" he hissed.

"You were leaving without me and I had to stop you somehow," Charles rationalized.

"I was leaving without you, Charles, because as I've already told you, I wish to be alone," Rafe said tersely.

"You'll have plenty of time to be alone after we're on a ship home, and I must talk with you," Charles said.

"Talk with me or accuse me and call me names again?" Rafe asked resentfully.

"I promise there won't be any accusations. You have my word on it," Charles said.

Rafe knew Charles would break that promise. After seven years of constantly deriding him, the behavior was thoroughly ingrained in Charles. But then it was their last night together, and after selling Charles into slavery Rafe felt he owed Charles at least one more opportunity to thoroughly dress him down before they never saw each other again. "As you wish, but when you break your word as you inevitably will, at least make an effort to confine the biting comments to my most recent crimes. I'm weary of hearing about the others."

"I'll do my best to be civil if you will," Charles bargained.

"I'm not the one who always initiates the offensive comments," Rafe returned heatedly then resumed walking.

Charles bit back the retort that if his comments were offensive, Rafe should stop doing the things requiring them. Such a comment, however true, would only serve to further anger Rafe, and then he might refuse to talk with him altogether. He caught up to Rafe and fell in beside him then made casual conversation to put Rafe off guard before broaching the most important topic. "The stars are extraordinary tonight don't you think?"

Rafe shrugged and didn't even look up.

"I'm reminded of a story my mother used to tell me when I was a child of a little angel whose job it was to polish each star until they sparkled and gleamed and then place them in the night sky as beacons of hope to a lost and dying world. Isn't that a great story?"

"Hope is overrated," Rafe remarked miserably then kicked at a round pebble in his path that soared off into the darkness. "Furthermore, you've made it abundantly clear that it's not for such as me."

Rafe's unmistakable despondency went far toward proving Charles's suspicions that he might have been wrong about him. "In light of our conversation the other night, I've been reconsidering. It seems you're not as wicked as I once thought," he said.

Rafe laughed bitterly. "Certainly I'll sleep easier knowing I'm not as evil as the great *Lord* Huntington once thought," he said sarcastically.

This was the second time in two days that Rafe had used his title in a derogatory manner! Charles huffed indignantly, "I'm doing my best to show compassion and you respond with sarcasm and disdain! I don't know why I even try!"

Rafe was all too familiar with how Charles felt. He'd felt that way himself many times because of Charles's negative reactions to everything he did for him. "Forgive me, Charles. I spoke in bitterness over the unpleasant turn my life has taken. It was unfair to you, for it's not your fault. In truth, I'm gratified by your change in attitude toward me, but you should focus instead on someone you may actually help, such as Ed. As you've noted he idolizes me, but under your firm guidance he could become an upright man instead of—someone like me. He already likes you and even though he's a half-breed and child of rape like me, you were able to overlook those blatant faults in me until the incident with Sarah. Might you once again find it in your heart to show kindness to one with a cursed origin and take Ed on as your ward?"

Charles's eyes widened. "You're asking me, the man you singularly hate, to foster Ed?"

"I've never hated you, Charles, although I've been mightily angry with you now and again. I suppose I've already made that clear enough by my actions, though."

"You most certainly have," Charles agreed resentfully.

Rafe nodded guiltily. "As you've so often said, there's no decency in me, but about Ed… Will you foster him?"

"I will do more than foster him, I shall adopt him. He's a wonderful boy with many fine traits. I know Sarah will love him too, and he'll make a fine big brother for Laird."

"Then Ed is yours to cherish from this moment on. See to it that you don't fail him." Rafe looked and sounded as if he'd given away his only friend in the world, which in truth he had.

"I won't fail him," Charles promised earnestly.

Rafe couldn't speak past the egg-sized lump in his throat so he merely nodded acknowledgement. They walked in silence then as Rafe mourned his loss and Charles thought on Sarah and Laird and home. Shortly, they came upon a scribe's office which despite the late hour was still open. Charles stopped, looked longingly into the shop window at the scribes inside then heaved a heavy sigh.

"Would you like to write Sarah a letter to let her know you're still alive?" Rafe offered.

Charles looked at Rafe hopefully. "You'd allow that?"

Rafe nodded. "We're nearly at the end of our journey. It's safe enough now."

Charles brightened then started to enter the scribe's office, but stopped upon remembering he had no coin. "I'll need money to pay for the paper and ink and the cost of sending the letter."

Rafe obligingly pulled a piece of silver from his coin pouch and held it out. "This should be more than enough."

Charles didn't take the coin. "I noticed your money pouch was nearly empty the other day, but after last night it was full again. Where did you come by all the coin?"

"You already know the answer," Rafe said evasively.

"Indeed I do, and I'll not use your stolen money to contact Sarah," Charles declared.

Rafe sighed in exasperation. "You've had no objection before now to using my stolen money."

"I was as much as your hostage and had no other choice," Charles rationalized.

Rafe chose not to waste time pointing out that Charles had never been his hostage, had even begged him to stay with them back in the jungle, and had chosen to willingly stay with him after that.

"Now that I do have a choice," Charles continued, "I won't use stolen money."

"Not even to pay for a letter to your beloved Sarah so she'll know you're still alive and vigorously harassing me every second of every day?" Rafe asked irritably.

Charles bristled. "I merely point out your sins. If you didn't commit so many of them, then you'd have no complaint against me!"

Rafe repressed an angry retort. "Do you wish to write the letter to Sarah, or not?" he asked impatiently.

"Not if I must use your dishonest gain. I'll visit a local barrister in the morning and arrange with him to write the letter to Sarah, on account," Charles said.

Rafe angrily stuffed the silver piece back into the coin pouch. "Your choice, but since you won't use my money, be certain to instruct Sarah to send you enough funds to pay for everyone's passage home and any debts you'll incur in the meantime."

"Or I could turn you in and collect the reward," Charles said.

Rafe's eyes narrowed and he gripped his knife hilt. "Try it and you'll regret it," he said quietly.

Charles raised his hands defensively, palms out. "There's no need to turn dark and menacing, Rafe. I was only joking." Rafe took his hand from his knife and Charles dropped his hands. "I'll do as you suggested and ask Sarah to send money. The only problem is that with no money until then where shall we stay?"

"I paid a week in advance for the rooms we currently occupy."

"With stolen money," Charles pointed out disapprovingly.

"Yes and if that knowledge grates on your pristine conscience, then camp out in the jungle. It's no concern of mine. I'll be leaving in the morning," Rafe snapped irritably.

"You mean you don't intend to stay with us the entire week?"

"No."

"But where are you off to in such a hurry?"

"A place where I'll be free at last," Rafe grimly replied.

"You mean Nirvana?" Charles said, referring to their hideout on the island.

Inasmuch as ceasing to exist would be Nirvana, Rafe nodded.

"Well I certainly have no wish to ever return to that island, but you always seemed content there; and you are a wanted man, so I suppose Nirvana is the best choice for you. Certainly you won't be looking over your shoulder anymore."

"No," Rafe agreed. There was no looking over one's shoulder in oblivion.

"Well then, it's growing quite late and you did as much as promise Ed that you'd tuck him in. Shouldn't we return to the room?"

Rafe shook his head. "That responsibility is no longer mine. He's your son now."

Rafe sounded so despondent that Charles actually found it in his heart to pity him. "You don't have to give Ed up, Rafe. If you returned to New England with us, something might be worked out with the law."

"I'd still have to serve out my original sentence and I'm certain you'd waste no time tattling to the courts about what you insist upon calling my murders. Then there are my pirating activities, armed robberies, and thefts. All of which merit hanging," Rafe said.

"Well, you did—,"

"Stop right there, Charles!" Rafe interrupted irritably. "I know full well I'm an abomination, a bastard half-breed, an unnatural, soulless being, and that no one can expect anything good from the likes of me! There's no need to keep drilling it into me!"

"That's not what I intended to say!" Charles huffed.

"Then you intended to say that I'm a child murderer and worse and deserve everything the courts would mete out. I've heard enough of that as well," Rafe said.

"I wasn't going to say that either! I was about to point out that you did save my life several times. That might count for something with the courts."

Rafe took a moment before he spoke. "Forgive me. I thought you were—that is, I'm so accustomed to your constant—," He sighed heavily, ran his hand across his face. "Never mind. As I said earlier, it's growing late. You should return to Ed now." He walked briskly away.

Instead of returning to the inn, however, Charles determinedly fell in beside Rafe. "I'm not leaving you alone. In the mood you're in..."

Rafe didn't hear another word, for he was distracted by the sight of four mercenaries following them. He cursed in Mohican then reached for his pistol, but he didn't draw it yet. Charles, however, thought Rafe was preparing to threaten him. Again. He bristled. "You would threaten my life yet again? When will you—,"

"Charles—," Rafe interrupted.

"—stop this constant—,"

"Charles!" Rafe used the name as a rebuke.

"What!" Charles responded in the same tone.

"We're being followed," Rafe explained, "by a group of four mercenaries."

Charles's heartbeat quickened in fear. He'd heard of New Providence mercenaries from the other slaves. To put it succinctly if one wanted to live to a ripe old age, any confrontation with them should be avoided at all costs. He looked over his shoulder at the four large, muscular men following them at a not so discreet distance, all armed to the teeth with pistols and knives.

"Don't look at them!" Rafe hissed. "It's to our advantage if they don't know we're aware of them."

Charles swiftly changed the direction of his gaze hoping to make it seem as if he was merely taking in the scenery. "How do you know these men are mercenaries or even that they're after us? Perhaps they're only four men out for a walk."

"They're mercenaries and they're after us," Rafe said with firm conviction.

Charles didn't want to believe Rafe was correct, but then they crossed the street and so did the four men, turned a corner and so did the four men, and he couldn't deny it any longer. The next street they turned onto was pitch-black lacking even the dim reflected light of a single candle in a window. Charles was certain Rafe had chosen this street deliberately, but how had he known about it and that it would be so dark and isolated? "Now what?" he asked.

"We kill them before they kill us," Rafe said resignedly.

Charles looked at Rafe aghast. "You talk as if killing men is no different than swatting mosquitoes! We're not killing anyone. Absolutely not!" he exclaimed breathlessly, already tiring from matching Rafe's brisk pace and wondering how long they'd have to keep this up.

"Would you rather we let them kill us?" Rafe asked irritably.

"Of course not, but there has to be another way."

"Let me know when you discover it. Better make it soon, though." Even as Rafe spoke, five mercenaries seemingly materialized out of the darkness in front of them. Rafe and Charles came to a standstill. "Never mind," Rafe said dryly.

Charles glanced over his shoulder. The original four mercenaries were closing in. Soon they'd be surrounded. Rafe cursed softly under his breath in Mohican, while Charles uttered a quick, silent prayer for delivery. One of the five mercenaries in front of them approached. He wore a skull earring in his left ear. Charles wondered if it had hurt to have the ear pierced and then wondered why he was wondering about such an inconsequential matter when he was about to be brutally murdered by nine scary men for no apparent reason.

The skull mercenary addressed Rafe. "You and your companion will accompany us," he said; a fully confident statement, for no ordinary man would think to challenge nine skilled, highly trained mercenaries. Rafe, however, was no ordinary man. He drew his pistol, shot the skull mercenary, smoothly holstered his spent pistol, drew his knife then sliced the throats of two others, all before anyone had a chance to react. Charles watched in shock and awe. He'd seen Rafe fight the cannibals, but the mercenaries had skills the cannibals lacked and still Rafe was prevailing against them singlehandedly. Then Rafe shouted at him, breaking him from his stunned trance. "Run, you fool! Do you wish to die?" He dodged a pistol shot from one of the men, who then drew a second already loaded pistol and aimed at Charles. Rafe shoved Charles out of the line of fire nearly knocking him down. The bullet whizzed between them so close to Rafe's head that the wind of its passage displaced one of those bothersome shorter strands of hair that were always coming loose from his braid. "Go! Get out of here!" he shouted, as the strand of hair slowly drifted back into place.

Charles hesitated, feeling guilty about leaving Rafe to fight all these men alone, but then he saw another mercenary take aim at him. Panicking, he leapt over the bodies of the dead mercenaries and raced away. He didn't look back even when he heard Rafe cry out amid the blasts of multiple pistols discharging. He didn't slow down even when he felt a sharp, cutting pain in his lower right rib. He ran until his legs refused to obey him then after glancing behind to make sure he wasn't pursued, he collapsed onto the ground, drenched in sweat, chest heaving.

After he'd caught his breath, Charles unbuttoned his waistcoat, pulled up his bloodied shirt, and gently probed the bleeding wound he'd earned in his flight with his left index finger. He was fortunate in that the bullet had glanced off bone, but the wound was deep and hemorrhaging freely and would need bandaging. He had to return to the inn as soon as possible. Charles wiped his bloodied finger on his pant leg then stood up shakily and took a few wobbly steps in the direction of the inn. His conscience convicted him of cowardice. How could he leave Rafe to fight off all those mercenaries on his own? He should return to help him. He changed direction, and then reason stopped in his tracks. With no weapon and injured besides he couldn't possibly be of any use. It would be better to summon the authorities. Charles looked up and down the street wondering where to find a constable. Then he realized that although notifying the authorities would ordinarily be the best option, at the moment he and Rafe were on the wrong side of the law for such countermeasures.

A heated rage seized possession of Charles's soul. All because of Rafe's instinctive aggressiveness he was caught in a web of violence with no means of escaping, except to leave Rafe to his fate; and a well-deserved one it was at that! Ignoring his conscience, Charles turned back toward the inn. A few blocks later, however, to Charles's ultimate amazement, he saw Rafe, looking bedraggled and weary, approaching from a side street. He stopped and waited for Rafe to catch up to him. "You're still alive!" he then exclaimed.

"Yes, and you're not the only one who's disappointed," Rafe said.

"I'm not disappointed, I'm simply amazed! Even though I know well enough you're a highly skilled fighter, I never would've imagined in my wildest dreams that you could singlehandedly kill nine skilled mercenaries!"

Rafe raised an eyebrow and looked at Charles as if he was someone he'd never met. "You're not going to harass me for killing again?"

"Those nine mercenaries would've killed us if you hadn't killed them," Charles said.

Rafe raised his other eyebrow. Charles never justified killing, for any reason. This latest brush with danger must've finally knocked some sense into him! "Well, we're still in danger, for I only killed six mercenaries. The other three ran away, and they'll want revenge. We must hasten back to the inn. The children could be in danger."

"You think they know where we're staying?" Charles asked.

"I think it most likely, so it would be wise to move on without delay." Rafe then noticed that Charles had his hand pressed to his side. He frowned. "Are you injured?"

"Yes, but it's not serious. How about you? Are you injured?" Charles asked.

"Not that you'd notice." Rafe resumed walking at a pace that was easy for Charles to maintain.

When they passed the well-lit window of a tavern, however, Charles saw that Rafe was bleeding from knife wounds in his right shoulder, left arm, and right thigh. Alarmed, he gripped Rafe's right forearm, stopping him. "You said you weren't injured!"

"I said not that you'd notice," Rafe clarified.

"How could I notice? It's dark and I don't have your sharp eyes!" Charles objected.

"No you don't," Rafe said.

Charles was uncertain if Rafe was accepting his excuse or affirming that he was inferior, but decided now was not the time to pursue an explanation. "Do you need a doctor?"

Rafe shook his head. "I've been hurt far worse than this and survived, like when you shot me."

"I had no idea you only intended to shoot a snake! We all thought you were aiming for Leopold!" Charles said defensively.

"You could've trusted me," Rafe shot back resentfully.

"Trust must be earned."

"And you made certain no one would trust me by speaking ill of me at every turn and even stooping so low as to spread rumors that I killed and ate small children," Rafe said, sounding hurt.

"You have no proof it was I who spread those rumors," Charles said.

"Deny it then," Rafe challenged, but Charles remained guiltily silent and even looked down at his feet. "As said," Rafe confirmed bitterly.

Rafe resumed walking with a limp that Charles hadn't noticed before. He reflected that Rafe had also been injured saving him from the cannibals and he'd never once thanked him for his efforts. His conscience convicted him that he should thank him now. "This is the second time you were injured protecting me," he said; not quite a thank you, but it was the most his pride would allow, and it did at least salve his conscience.

Rafe grunted, thinking of how he'd intended to poison Charles after the fight with the bears to shorten Charles's misery as he passed from life into death. Thankfully God had prevented what would have been a tragic mistake by rendering him unconscious before he could take action. "Yes, but don't begin thinking of me as your savior. If God hadn't intervened, you'd be long dead," he said.

Charles bristled. "So but for God's intervention you've would've let me die; and since you couldn't be rid of me any other way, you sold me into slavery!"

Now it was Rafe's turn to bristle. "I rescued you didn't I?" he countered testily.

"As if that makes up for the original crime," Charles griped and then went sullenly silent.

To avoid being seen entering the inn in their bloodied and rumpled condition, they went around to the back and Rafe broke the lock on the kitchen door, which he knew would be empty at this late hour. They cautiously tread the squeaky floorboards then the creaking stairs and once had to hastily duck into an empty room to avoid being seen by an exhausted-looking, bedraggled, gray-haired servant woman delivering a nightcap to a guest at the opposite end of the hall. Upon reaching their room, Charles raised an arm that felt like it weighed ten times normal to open the door, but then to his ultimate surprise Rafe snatched Charles's wrist and dragged him halfway down the hall. "Unhand me, half-breed!" Charles objected loudly while struggling to break free from Rafe's iron grip. "What is wrong with you!"

Rafe released Charles. "Forgive me, but I sensed that something's not right in there."

"You *sensed* something's not right," Charles said skeptically. "Rafe, have you been drinking or smoking coca leaves?"

Rafe scowled. "When would I have had the time, Charles?" he snapped irritably.

"Well, we were separated for a few—,"

"Charles!" Rafe hissed.

"What?" Charles asked innocently.

Rafe ran his left hand across his face in exasperation. "Ever since I witnessed the slaughter of my village I've been able to sense if something's not right in a room even before I enter it. It's a sort of uneasy feeling, and it's never failed me."

"That must come in quite handy when you're out thieving and murdering," Charles quipped.

Rafe's answering dark glare dimmed the entire corridor. "This is no time for your malicious comments," he said. "If I'm right, Lydia and Ed are in danger."

That sobered Charles like nothing else would have. "Do you think it might possibly be the remaining three mercenaries?"

"I can't say for certain. Stay here and I'll discover soon enough," Rafe said.

"Nothing doing, I'll accompany you," Charles insisted.

Rafe looked at Charles askance. "Do you truly think you wouldn't be in the way?"

Charles drew himself up indignantly. "I've received the same martial training as you, from the same masters."

"Yes, but I took my training seriously, while you were far more interested in catching Sarah's eye. Furthermore, I also possess the unique fighting skills my heart father taught me, which you have no knowledge of. Thus, you shall remain here out of danger, *Lord* Huntington."

Charles irately placed his hands on his hips. "Stop abusing my title to insinuate that I'm incompetent!" he objected loudly.

Rafe winced then glanced apprehensively at the door to their room expecting someone to burst out shooting, but luckily, no one did. "Keep your voice down! Do you want them to hear us?"

Charles glanced fearfully at the door to their room then obligingly lowered his voice. "I couldn't help it! Your intimation that I'm useless was so absurd! Need I remind you that I've survived countless threats against my life since we left New England, most of them by you, I might point out? Yet you still haven't succeeded in killing me."

Rafe didn't bother pointing out once again that if he'd really wanted Charles dead, he'd be dead. He figured he'd said it enough times. "Nevertheless, you'll wait here and when it's safe, I'll—,"

"I'll not wait here," Charles countered with stubborn determination.

Rafe was exhausted, in a great deal of pain, and wanted to have the impending fight with whoever was lurking in their room over and done with, so he gave in for expedience's sake. "As you wish, but I'll enter the room first. Stay out of sight until I summon you." He started reloading his pistol.

"Wouldn't it be better if I—,"

"No," Rafe interrupted curtly, with a dark glower that dared Charles to argue and suffer the consequences. For once Charles submitted to wisdom and refrained.

Rafe pulled a pilfered mercenary pistol from his left coat pocket, hastily loaded it then held it out. Charles balked at taking it.

"Surely you know better by now than to expect me to murder anyone."

"I'm not asking you to *murder* anyone. I merely expect you to defend my life, even as I will defend yours," Rafe said impatiently.

"Well then that's different." Charles took the weapon.

Rafe ghosted silently to the door followed by a much noisier Charles. He motioned for Charles to take position against the wall to the left of the door then burst into the room.

Ed and Lydia snuggled on the divan, cowering from Carlos who held a loaded pistol in each hand, one aimed at Lydia, the other at Ed. The young pirate looked not at all surprised by Rafe's abrupt entrance, and Rafe concluded Charles's loud protestations were to blame, ruining his chance at catching Carlos unaware. It didn't really matter though, for even injured as he was he was confident he was more than a match for Carlos.

"Here you are at last!" Carlos said. "The mercenaries I hired to capture and torture you to death told me you had escaped; at least those you left alive told me. I hurried here to kill you myself, but I've been here for ages. What took you so long?"

Rafe could tell from Carlos's manner and bloodshot eyes that he'd smoked coca leaves recently. He wasn't surprised. Carlos was too craven to attempt something brazen without a crutch. He aimed his pistol at Carlos's heart. "Provide one good reason why I shouldn't kill you first."

"I shall provide you with two; this child and this young woman. Drop your pistol or they both die!" Carlos threatened.

Rafe made brief concerned eye contact with Ed, who looked frightened half out of his wits, and then he leaned down and set his pistol on the floor near his feet. Straightening, arms held out to his sides to prove he was no threat, at the moment anyway, he said, "I'm curious. How did you find me?"

Carlos grinned with pride. "It was not easy. I had completely lost track of you until Lauralee's body was discovered in that dark alley shot through the heart and with her lovely throat brutally slashed. I immediately knew it was you who was responsible, for you are the only other besides me who hated Lauralee enough to kill her twice. Yes?" Rafe made no answer so Carlos continued. "Thank you for finally keeping your promise to kill her, but it was foolish. You should have left the island on the first ship instead. I never would have found you then."

"You still haven't told me how you did," Rafe said.

"Ah, but I am not as dimwitted as you think. I knew you would free your friend next and then return to Nassau to buy passage to the colonies. I deduced your general whereabouts from your dubious nocturnal activities faithfully reported in all the papers then hired the mercenaries, who tracked you here."

"It seems I grossly underestimated you," Rafe begrudgingly admitted.

Carlos smiled smugly. "Thank you, but despite your flattery you still must die, for regrettably you killed my father and as his sole surviving heir it is my duty to present your head on a silver platter to the clan, else no one will respect me enough to accept my leadership. Nothing personal, you understand."

Ed jumped up and faced Carlos with balled fists, his fear forgotten now that he thought Rafe was in danger. "I won let you kill Rafe! I'll kill you firstest!"

"Ed!" Lydia grabbed him around the waist and dragged him back onto the divan fearing for his life.

He struggled to break free. "Lemme go! I has to protek Rafe!"

Rafe shot Ed a warning glance and the boy stilled, but he crossed his arms indignantly and pouted. Seeing this, Carlos's mouth twisted into an evil grimace. "The small one adores you and I see in your eyes and your manner that you return his affections. The girl, you love her also? Is this why you killed Lauralee, to make a place for this new, younger lover?"

"Lauralee was evil incarnate and lived to kill. You, on the other hand, don't have the guts to kill anyone. You're so craven you had to hire mercenaries to kill me and when that failed, you had to smoke coca leaves to give you a semblance of courage so you could face me," Rafe said.

Carlos purpled with rage and aimed the pistol he held in his right hand at Rafe. "I shall prove you wrong by killing you. The boy will die next, but I think I will keep the girl for myself. She's a pretty young thing. Yes?"

Rafe was preparing to snatch the pistol from Carlos's hand when Charles unexpectedly stepped into the room and shot Carlos. The pirate fell lifelessly to the rough and worn wood floor, a steady stream of blood leaking from his shriveled, black heart and down his left side to pool around him. Charles lowered his still smoking pistol. "Is—is he dead?"

"Yes, most assuredly," Rafe said.

"I—I had to do it. He said he would shoot Ed and take Lydia as his personal slave. I couldn't let him do that," Charles reasoned.

Rafe couldn't help but note that Charles had neglected to mention Carlos's intent to murder him, but he added his hurt over this most recent slight to the collection of other hurts he kept tenuously imprisoned in the dark, cobwebbed recesses of his soul and moved on. "No you couldn't let him do that, and indeed, I would've killed him if you hadn't." He scooped up and holstered his pistol.

"Now I'm a murderer like you," Charles lamented in a trembling voice.

Rafe was all too familiar with the heavy burden of guilt and remorse Charles was obviously laboring under. He offered the same rationalization he used to ease his own pain and guilt, although it had never worked. "There's no sin in killing evil men, Charles." *Or evil women,* he silently added.

Charles responded in a completely unexpected manner. "How dare you try to draw me into your wicked mindset with that immoral rationalization, you demon spawn!" he raged then threw his pistol at Rafe's head.

Even though he was thoroughly taken by surprise Rafe successfully dodged the missile then glared at Charles malignly. In return for attempting to ease Charles's pain he earned a near bruise on the head! He was sorely tempted to punch Charles in the nose in turn, but then he noticed Ed staring at the dead body in wide-eyed fear. He had to do something about that. "Ed."

He hadn't raised his voice above normal, but Ed started as if he'd been yelled at then stared at Rafe in obvious shock. "Wait out in the hall," Rafe instructed gently.

"Why? I seen ded boddies afore. I ain afraid," Ed said. But the trembling of his chin betrayed his lie.

Rafe pointed at the door. Ed slowly slid off the divan then warily skirted Carlos's body and exited the room, but he left the door open a crack and peeked in. "Shut the door," Rafe said sternly.

As soon as Rafe heard the door latch, he retrieved Charles's pistol, stuffed it into his belt then limped to Carlos. He painfully knelt and leaned over the body, his long, shiny braid sliding over his left shoulder, the softly bristled end dangling less than a quarter inch above Carlos's bloodied chest. He flipped his braid over his shoulder then pried the two pistols from Carlos's still warm hands and struggled painfully to his feet. He stored Carlos's pistols and Charles's pistol in the bottom of his bag displacing several rolls of bandages that he'd stolen on one of his forays in case of injury. He pulled out the bandages and held a roll out for Charles, who made no move to take it. "Here Charles, bandage the bullet wound in your side. Then we must move on in case the remaining mercenaries show," he prompted.

Like Charles, Lydia had also been staring in shock at the dead body littering their floor, but upon hearing that Charles was hurt she came to her senses. "Charles has been shot?" She hurried to Charles to examine his wound then glared at Rafe. "Did you do this to him?"

Rafe was as much offended by Lydia's swift assumption that he'd hurt Charles as by her obvious lack of concern for his multiple injuries. He tossed the rolled bandage at her. "Bandage his wounds since he won't do it himself." Lydia deftly caught the roll then gently led Charles to the divan compassionately tended his injuries.

Rafe limped across the room to a table for two, sat down on one of the hard, wooden chairs then drew his knife to dig a bullet out of his right calf. After a few moments of teeth-gritting pain, he tossed the bloodied bullet on the floor. It rolled into a shadowed corner unnoticed, for Rafe was surreptitiously watching Lydia. He desperately longed to be treated with the same gentle caring as she was giving Charles, but although he continually sacrificed body and soul for the benefit of others he never earned anything in return but abuse, and anger, and ungratefulness. Even God didn't appreciate his desire to serve Him. A lump formed in Rafe's throat and his vision blurred with tears. He swallowed hard, blinked away the tears, and then in an effort at forgetting the unfairness of life hyper-concentrated on bandaging his leg.

Lydia finished bandaging Charles before Rafe finished his self-ministrations. Having spent her formative years as a slave, instead of taking the initiative she waited for Rafe to notice she was done and tell her what to do next. When after a reasonable period of time he didn't look up from bandaging his arm, she finally found the courage to ask. "I'm done, sir. Is there something else you wish me to do?"

Rafe suspended his bandaging and looked up. "Go to your room and pack then return and pack Charles's things for him."

"Yes, sir," Lydia said meekly and headed for the door.

Ed tried to peer into the room when Lydia exited, but she effectively blocked his view with her body then hurriedly closed the door. Rafe was grateful to her for that. He resumed bandaging his arm, which had only been grazed by a bullet then moved on to the knife cut on his right shoulder, thankfully not deep enough to require stitches. He looked up when he was finished to find Charles hatefully glaring at him. "What, Charles?" he asked wearily.

"You made me a murderer! If you hadn't forced that weapon on me, I wouldn't have—," Charles suppressed a sob.

"Carlos would've killed us all. It wasn't murder," Rafe said.

"Yeah, yer a hero!" Ed said, peeking in through the slightly open door which apparently hadn't latched when Lydia exited.

"Ed!" Rafe chastised sternly. Ed quickly shut the door and Rafe heard it latch securely this time.

Charles continued as if they hadn't been interrupted. "You may use self-defense as an excuse to justify murdering someone every time you turn around, Rafe, but that doesn't make it true or right."

"I don't—,"

The door opened again. Rafe was about to chastise Ed for his disobedience, except it was Lydia carrying the rolled up blanket with her spare dress wrapped up inside along with her brush. She closed the door softly behind her, once again blocking Ed's view of the room.

Rafe resumed his defense. "I don't use self-defense to justify murder, Charles."

"You most certainly do! You used that excuse to murder Carlos's entire family. You're evil to the core! It's you I should've killed, not poor Carlos, who was only seeking justice against you for slaughtering his father and sisters!"

Rafe inhaled sharply and to his dismay tears stung his eyes. He took out his hurt on Lydia, who looked as if she wished she wasn't there. "What are you staring at?" he demanded harshly.

"N—nothing, sir," Lydia stammered. She turned away, set her bundle down on the floor, and studiously rolled out the blanket to add Charles's spare suit and his comb.

"How do you live with all the killing, Rafe?" Charles asked.

Rafe was ready to reply he didn't live with it at all well, but before he could Charles said, "Oh, never mind. I forgot for a minute that you're demon spawn and lack a conscience."

Rafe gritted his teeth. If he hadn't known Charles was in shock, he would've congratulated his one-time friend on successfully breaking the record for malicious comments directed at him in less than half an hour, but even so he'd endured enough. "Ed and I will wait for you and Lydia outside." He grabbed his and Ed's bags, both bedrolls, slung the four straps over his shoulder, strode stiffly to the door and opened it.

Ed, who'd been leaning against the door peering through the keyhole started to topple inside the room. Rafe's left hand shot out and grasped Ed's scrawny arm, preventing a fall. Ed wobbled upright and then grinned up at Rafe sheepishly. He looked so endearing that Rafe couldn't help but grin. More, he yearned to snatch Ed up in his arms and hug him tightly for long minutes, but he couldn't demonstrate such unrestrained want in front of Charles and Lydia, who would undoubtedly find something unclean in it. Instead, he firmly grasped Ed's tiny hand and they walked outside together.

Chapter Thirty-Seven

Rafe and his self-imposed charges stopped at a clearing in the trees five miles outside of town and well off the road and settled down for the night. Exhausted from their recent emotional ordeal and the long day Ed and Lydia lay down and quickly fell asleep. Charles took a seat on the only firm spot on a decaying log directly across from Rafe who sat on the ground with his back resting against a wide tree trunk, left leg bent, injured right leg stretched out in front of him, eyes drooping as he unsuccessfully fought to stay awake and keep watch in case they'd been followed by what remained of Carlos's hired mercenaries.

"You and I are exactly alike now," Charles commented.

Rafe startled fully awake. "What?"

"I said, you and I are exactly alike now," Charles repeated.

"We're not at all alike, the most significant difference being that you're not a half-breed, and thus you own everyone's respect, while I am—was—lucky to own a single friend. Furthermore, you possess the reassurance of God's love and forgiveness, which I—cannot." Rafe scooped up a handful of dried leaves from the ground beside his left thigh and slowly crumbled them directing his anger at the unfairness of life onto the leaves.

Charles watched those strong thin fingers working and was jealously reminded of Sarah once remarking that Rafe had beautiful, artist's hands. Charles supposed that was true if one considered killing an art. His own hands were large and strong, his fingers fat and ugly compared to Rafe's slender digits. Apparently though his comparatively fat, ugly hands were every bit as good at killing as Rafe's—something else they now had in common. "No matter what you say, the fact remains that I'm a murderer now, which nullifies everything else and makes me exactly like you," Charles argued.

Rafe angrily tossed the handful of crumbled leaves into the wind. "Stop calling me a murderer, Charles!"

"The truth is the truth, Rafe, whether you continue to deny it or not," Charles said stubbornly. "I must admit, though, I do now regret treating you so harshly. As a fellow murderer, I now understand how forgiveness might do your heart good, and I'm afraid I haven't been very forthcoming in that area."

If Rafe had ever harbored any doubt that Charles was in shock, that statement would've confirmed it. Charles would never say such things otherwise. His anger melted away replaced by concern for Charles's sanity. "I'll keep watch. You'd best catch some sleep."

"And have nightmares like you? That would be worse than staying awake!" Charles sighed and rubbed his burning eyes with the heels of both hands.

"You need only pray for forgiveness and you'll receive it. Then your heart will be eased and you'll sleep like an innocent," Rafe said.

There was envy in Rafe's tone, but Charles was too self-absorbed to recognize it. "How do I find the courage to approach God with my sin, though, when the uncertainty of His willingness to forgive my heinous crime stands in the way?" he asked despairingly.

Rafe understood Charles's dilemma all too well, for he as much as owned the rights to it, but Charles possessed the solution he himself lacked. "You are God's own child, Charles. He'll love you and forgive you no matter what you've done. You may be certain of it."

"I suppose you're right, but how do I ever forgive myself?" Charles asked.

"That is the hardest part," Rafe conceded, having never been able to accomplish it himself. "I suspect, however, that with the support and unconditional love of your family and friends, self-forgiveness will come in time."

"But how shall I live with what I've done in the meantime?" Charles bemoaned. "Oh, if only I could kill without conscience as you do."

Rafe slammed his fist on the ground unsettling the remaining dry leaves. "I may be a half-breed bastard, a child of rape, and an abomination in God's sight, Charles, but I'm not the heartless animal you think I am! Like you I have desires and needs, suffer regrets and remorse. I'm capable of love and I crave the love and acceptance of others. When everyone who'd claimed to be my friend suddenly withdrew their support after Duncan's death, it so devastated me that I wanted to die. But I don't expect you to believe that. You would never believe anything good about me, not even in the face of incontrovertible evidence!" He struggled painfully to his feet, limped to the edge of the clearing and then stood with his back to Charles, staring gloomily out into the darkness and regretting that in a moment of weakness he'd revealed one of his deepest hurts. Any time now, Charles would come over and say something derogatory, such as that he deserved to die and should've been hung over a year ago. Both were true, but it would still hurt to hear it and he was so weary of hurting. His only consolation was that soon now he could end it all.

Even as Rafe had said, Charles was initially inclined to dismiss Rafe's avowals as his usual manipulative melodrama, but then he recalled that after he'd shot Rafe on the trip to Boston, Rafe had said he'd wanted to die from his wound; and there was the aborted suicide attempt on the island to be considered too. But if Rafe truly wanted to die, then why had he aborted that latest attempt, and why hadn't he tried to take his life since? Charles hated uncertainties. He couldn't spend the rest of his life wondering which was true, his beliefs about Rafe, or Rafe's assertions to the contrary. He joined Rafe at the edge of the clearing.

Rafe glowered at him unwelcomingly, but that didn't deter Charles since it was Rafe's usual reaction to him. "Rafe, on the island when you were contemplating stabbing yourself in the heart—,"

"How do you know about that?" Rafe interrupted harshly.

"I followed you to your wigwam. You didn't seem to realize how badly you'd hurt me when you killed Adam and I wanted to make it quite clear. I saw you sitting cross-legged with your eyes closed and your knife at your chest drawing blood. At first, briefly, I thought you were performing some savage magic ritual, but then I realized your actual intent. I was about to cry out, but then you opened your eyes and stabbed your knife into the ground and I ducked away so you wouldn't see me and come after me next."

"Undoubtedly you were as sorry as I am that I failed to end my life that day," Rafe said.

"Yes and no. I didn't like you much at the time, but I was relieved that I wasn't robbed of your considerable skills. Then too your barely tolerable companionship was better than absolutely none at all," Charles said.

"Companions do make an otherwise unbearable existence worthwhile," Rafe agreed. "Ed has done that for me, and before I accidentally killed Duncan…" His voice trailed off in pain and guilt.

"God can fill that gap even better than flawed, mortal man," Charles dared to venture and then intently watched Rafe for his reaction hoping to gain the answer to the questions about Rafe that had been bothering him for days.

Rafe nodded. "For you and others that is true. As for me, I once thought I knew the great comfort of Pachtamawas—your God. I believed he was my steadfast loving companion who accepted me unconditionally when almost all despised me for my mixed blood, the color of my skin, and my ignoble origin." He paused briefly then continued softly. "After I killed Duncan, I realized it was all a lie. Your God has never loved me, nor will he ever love me. Salvation and forgiveness are impossible for a soulless, abominable, half-breed like me no matter how badly I wish otherwise." He swallowed audibly. "Death is the only way to end my pain."

"If you believe that, then why did you abort your suicide on the island, and why haven't you tried again since?" Charles asked.

Rafe stared into the night for a long moment then he said, "My sense of honor demands that I fulfill certain—obligations first."

Charles now had far more answers than he'd ever wanted and with them the awful conviction that he was substantially to blame for Rafe's current state of mind, having done Satan's work for him and diligently worked to remove all hope of God's love and forgiveness from Rafe's heart. "Rafe, while I have up until now been quite vocal in insisting you could never be loved by God and that you lack a soul, I realize now that I was in terrible error. If you lacked a soul, you'd be incapable of lamenting the loss of God in your life, for it's the soul that cries out to God and desires to worship Him."

The irony was that Rafe would've given up his soul had he felt he possessed one for that to be true. He was thoroughly convinced, though, that if he ever again had the audacity to believe he was more than the abomination in God's sight that he was, then God in his righteousness would be forced to prove the lie in a most painful and guilt-inflicting manner as He'd done first with Duncan's death and then with the many misfortunes that had befallen him since. Rafe couldn't endure yet another round of heart breaking confirmation that he was worthless and unlovable. "As I said before, you should take this opportunity to sleep, Charles. I'll take the watch," he said.

Charles recognized a slammed door when he saw it so he reluctantly let the matter drop for now. "You've only had a few short hours of rest over the last seventy-two hours. Why don't you let me take the watch while you sleep?"

"So you may tie me up as soon as I'm asleep then turn me over to the authorities for the reward? I think not," Rafe said.

"I give you my word I'll not do that," Charles said.

Rafe was uncertain if he could trust Charles, but he was certain he was exhausted since he'd been shamefully falling asleep on watch when Charles had started this conversation. "I suppose I have no choice but to trust you."

Charles smiled, pleased. "You won't regret it."

Rafe had his doubts about that, but he didn't say so. He placed his bedroll beside Ed's, lay down on his back and in a matter of minutes was soundly asleep.

<h1 style="text-align:center"><u>Chapter Thirty-Eight</u></h1>

The sun shining directly into his eyes awoke Rafe. He sat up groggily and to his dismay discovered he was alone. His first thought was that everyone had abandoned him while he slept, and while such a thing was to be expected of Charles, and even Lydia, he was deeply hurt that Ed hadn't even bothered to say goodbye. Then he saw that everyone's belongings were still in the camp, and immediately after that he spotted all three of them returning from the direction of Nassau. Charles held a wrapper of sausages, Lydia, a loaf of freshly baked brown bread and brick cheese, while Ed's scrawny arms were loaded with honeydew melons.

Upon seeing Rafe awake, Ed dropped his melons to run to him. A few of the melons split open, but Ed merely jumped over them unconcerned. He skidded to a halt in front of Rafe breathless from his short run and smiling broadly. "Mornin Rafe. We wokt into Nassau and bot some break-fast!" he said the last word slowly and deliberately. "Did I say it right? Break-fast? Lydia taught me."

Rafe smiled. "Perfectly."

Charles hurried up. "Ed! Didn't I tell you not to awaken Rafe? He needs his rest."

"It's fine. I was already awake." Rafe stood up stiffly. "How did you pay for these purchases when you have no money?"

Charles looked uneasy. "I, um, uh—I stole a handful of coins from you while you were sleeping," he admitted shamefacedly.

Rafe's eyebrows shot up in surprise.

"It was only because everyone was hungry and you were finally sleeping peacefully and so soundly that I couldn't bear to awaken you," Charles explained.

"You were in need. Necessity trumps everything else," Rafe said dismissively.

Charles drew himself up self-righteously. "Stealing is always immoral no matter the circumstances and it's exactly that sort of criminal thinking that turned you into a wanton, remorseless murderer and thief!" When Rafe then stiffened, Charles realized he'd habitually reverted to his previous judgmental manner. "Rafe, I'm sorry. I didn't mean—,"

"I think you did," Rafe interrupted coolly.

"I'm starving. Wen can we eat?" Ed asked.

"How about right now?" Lydia said grateful for the opportunity to distract Rafe and Charles from their most recent disagreement. She portioned out the meat, bread, and cheese.

Rafe's appetite, however, was ruined by the specter of Ed's imminent permanent departure from his life. He sat on the ground cross-legged holding the bread and cheese in one hand the sausage in the other then forced a bite of the sausage, but had some difficulty swallowing. Unable to force down another bite he set the bread and cheese on his pallet and the sausage on top of that.

The others, including Charles, ate heartily while they laughed and conversed animatedly. Rafe attributed the complete turn-around in Charles's attitude to seeking and receiving God's forgiveness, and he envied him. Why couldn't God love him too?

Ed, sitting to Rafe's left, nodded at Rafe's untouched bread, cheese, and sausage. "You goin to finish yer breakfast?"

Rafe shook his head. "You may have it."

Ed pounced on the food and devoured it as if he hadn't already eaten a full serving. Rafe watched in wistful amusement, knowing it was the last time he'd ever see the undernourished child eat enough for two grown men. Then he gathered up his pallet and bags making ready to leave. Ed sprang to his feet and started to gather his things as well. "No, Ed. It's time for us to part."

Ed froze in the middle of rolling up his pallet looking stricken.

"What?" Charles sprang to his feet. "Now?"

"You can't go yet!" Ed slipped his slim, brown arms around Rafe's waist in a gentle but possessive hug.

Rafe hardened his heart and gently pried Ed's arms loose. "It's time, Ed. I warned you it was coming. Take it like a man."

Ed nodded, valiantly suppressing tears. Rafe was proud of the boy's self-control, which perversely made leaving him all the more difficult, but he refused to let his own desperate need to be loved sway him from what he knew was best for Ed.

"I've sent off a letter to Sarah this morning. Can't you at least stay with us until I hear back from her?" Charles pleaded.

Rafe shook his head. "It's too risky. You know my description is in all the papers."

"Yes, but you yourself pointed out that many people fit that description and furthermore, what if those mercenaries find us again? I don't have the skills to prevail against them," Charles argued.

"All the more reason why we should part, for it's me the mercenaries want. They have a debt of vengeance to satisfy and if you're with me, they'll include you in that debt," Rafe said.

"Won't you risk staying anyway, for Ed's sake?" Lydia pleaded.

Rafe looked at Ed who was still valiantly suppressing tears, but no matter how fervently he wished it otherwise the child would be far better off without his wicked influence. Furthermore, he knew that despite their pleas, Lydia would truly prefer him gone, and so too Charles. "I cannot stay any longer," he said firmly.

Charles drew a loaded pistol from beneath his shirt behind his back. Rafe recognized it as one of the mercenary pistols which apparently Charles had also stolen from him as he slept. First Charles was killing and now he was stealing; the same iniquitous path he himself had taken. He was obviously a corrupting influence on Charles as well as Ed; another reason for parting immediately.

"I can't let you leave." Charles stayed well out of Rafe's reach so he couldn't snatch the pistol from him. He'd learned that lesson well.

After their talk last night, Rafe had thought he and Charles had made solid inroads toward renewing their friendship. Now he silently labeled himself an idiot. "So despite your talk of how wrong you were about me, you intend to turn me over to the authorities after all."

"I'm not turning you over to the authorities, Rafe. I only want you to stay with us a little longer. I—I owe you so much and I still must make amends," Charles said.

"Aiming a loaded pistol at someone is a strange way of making amends," Rafe commented dryly.

The pistol wavered in Charles's trembling hand and then he self-consciously lowered it to his side. "I didn't know how else to stop you from leaving. I wouldn't have hurt you."

"I wouldn't have let you hurt me," Rafe corrected.

Charles nodded then flipped the pistol and offered it to Rafe handle first. Rafe shook his head. "Keep it. You most likely won't need it, but I'll feel better knowing you're armed."

Charles nodded and stuffed the pistol into his belt.

Rafe turned to leave.

"Rafe!" Charles called. Rafe turned back around. "I've something important to say. Will you at least linger long enough to hear me out?"

Rafe had no wish to hear any more apologies or painful talk of God's love, but he felt he owed it to Charles. He nodded once.

"Come, Ed, let's take a walk," Lydia said.

"I don wanna. Rafe mite leeve wiles I'm gone," Ed objected.

Rafe remembered all too well the bitterly intense pain of Leopold's refusal to say fare well when he boarded the ship in Boston. He wouldn't do that to Ed. He wasn't so cruel. "I won't go without saying fare well, Ed. You have my word of honor on it. Go with Lydia."

Ed reluctantly let Lydia pull him away and Rafe wistfully watched them go. Then Charles drew his attention away from them. "I've been wrong about you, Rafe."

"Yes, you have; but you've admitted that already, so if you have nothing new to confess, I'll say my fare well to Ed and be on my way." Rafe took a step. Charles grabbed Rafe's left wrist. Rafe glared at him darkly and Charles hastily released his grip.

"I have more to say, much more. Please hear me out?" Charles begged.

Rafe surrendered to the entreaty in Charles's eyes and nodded. "Have your say."

"I watched you sleeping last night. You were obviously struggling with horrific nightmares until dawn when you finally settled into a peaceful sleep. It's proof enough you suffer guilt and remorse even as you've been insisting all along. Combine this with your desire to be loved by God and that's solid proof you have a soul."

"Animals have nightmares, but they don't have souls," Rafe argued.

"You're not an animal, Rafe. You're as human as I."

"Yet you claim I kill instinctively, like an animal," Rafe said.

"If you're referring to Duncan, although it was a horrible mistake and then you compounded it by killing Davy and joining up with the pi—," Charles caught himself before he launched into a full-blown diatribe against Rafe. "What I mean to say, is that Christians aren't perfect. If you have any doubts, I'm ample evidence of that.

Furthermore, my sin is far worse than any of yours. So much worse that it borders on unpardonable."

"Killing Carlos—," Rafe began.

"I'm not referring to killing Carlos, although that was bad enough. The sin I'm speaking of is insisting you were irredeemable to the point of firmly convincing you it was true," Charles said.

Rafe frowned darkly. "I know you don't truly believe I'm redeemable, Charles. Are you perhaps trying to delay me until the Constables you contacted this morning in Nassau arrive to arrest me?"

"I didn't contact any Constables!" Charles shouted vehemently.

Rafe raised an eyebrow.

Charles sighed and raked his fingers through his hair. "It's been a long, slow, painfully humbling process, but I've finally been convicted of the truth and now I'm attempting to set things right."

Rafe was skeptical. His one-time brother turned enemy was up to no good, if not by turning him over to the authorities, then by making him believe a lie so he'd return with them to New England, where Charles could then have the satisfaction of seeing him hung for his crimes. Rafe's proof lay in that no one changed their opinion of him so completely and rapidly, and especially not Charles. "We both know it's not possible to set things right between us, Charles, and now I'd like to say fare well to Ed." He started to walk away again.

This time Charles knew better than to grab Rafe. Instead, he blocked his path. "I can't let you leave when you're still trapped in your unbelief and it's my fault! I must remedy the situation before we part forever, for both our sakes."

Charles looked and sounded desperate and Rafe pitied him; a unique experience for one accustomed to finding him insufferable. "I do believe, Charles, but it's impossible for a blade of straw to flower and therein is the problem to which there is no solution."

"What? What are you talking about?" Charles exclaimed exasperatedly. "What does gardening have to do with humanity and souls?"

Rafe shook his head then sidestepped around Charles. He was finished with this futile conversation and with Charles.

Charles wasn't finished with Rafe, though. He raced in front of him and blocked his path again. "Please Rafe, return to New England with us. With my testimony that you rescued me from slavery and the help of my barrister and Leopold, I'm certain all charges against you will be dropped."

Rafe shook his head. "I don't believe in fairy tales Charles, and after all you've been through neither should you." He gently moved Charles aside and continued walking to where the youngsters relaxed beneath the shade of a large tree.

Ed scrambled to his feet and raced to Rafe, while Lydia followed more sedately then stopped at a discreet distance. "Is yer leavin me forever now?" Ed asked, unshed tears in his eyes.

"Yes little one. It's time," Rafe said.

Ed's chin quivered, but he reined in his emotions and held out his hand. "I'll miss you." Despite his best efforts his voice was uneven, which made it difficult for Rafe to remain stoic.

He knelt and gathered Ed into his arms never wanting to let him go. Finally he gently gripped Ed's skinny, tan arms above the elbow and held him at arm's length, gazing lovingly into the boy's warm brown eyes. "I know you want to be like me, but if you follow my path, you'll reap only misery and despair. I wish for you to be happy and the only road to happiness is that of an upright man. I'd like to be the one to guide you on that road, but I'm hopelessly lost. Under my influence you could never become an upright man. Charles will be a good and faithful guide, and that's the reason I'm sending you with him; not because I wish to be rid of you. Do you believe that?"

Ed nodded solemnly.

"Charles has promised to make you his son. Promise me that in turn you'll make him proud to be your father," Rafe said.

"I promise." Ed smiled bravely while tears rolled freely down his cheeks.

Rafe smiled sadly then taking Ed's right hand he offered an Apache blessing he'd learned at the Stockbridge missionary school from a visiting orphaned Apache girl who'd been adopted by a fur trader. "May the sun bring you new energy by day, may the moon softly restore you by night, may the rain wash away your worries, the breeze blow new strength into your being, and may you walk gently through the world and know its beauty all the days of your life." He pulled Ed into another, quick, hug, which Ed fervently returned and then in a voice trembling with emotion said, "I'll always love you, Ed. Make me proud and walk with God." He lost his composure, hastily stood up and turned away to hide his tears.

Ed wrapped his scrawny, brown arms around Rafe's waist from behind in a quick hug and then he raced to Charles and buried his face in Charles's stomach, stifling sobs. Charles put his arm protectively around the boy's shoulders.

Lydia shyly approached Rafe, who hastily dragged his emotions into check, ran his sleeve across his tear-filled eyes. "Sir, I'm grateful for everything you've done for me," she said. "I should've thanked you long before now, but I thought you were most thoroughly evil and so I was afraid of you."

Rafe nodded. "That's the prevailing attitude toward me and especially those influenced by Charles." He glanced resentfully at Charles.

"I'm not afraid of you now, though," Lydia said. "I've seen how dearly you love Ed and anyone who could love a child so completely couldn't possibly be evil."

Rafe didn't know how to answer that. After an awkward silence, he cleared his throat then said, "I know you care as deeply for Ed as I. Will you watch over him for me? Don't let the others tease him about his size, or his skin color, or call him a bastard half-breed, or an abomination. Help him through the rough times. Stand by him as a true friend. He'll need that more than anything else."

Lydia sensed that Rafe spoke from personal experience, and her heart went out to this man who'd suffered so much scorn and derision from others, Charles included, yet still found it in his heart to aid anyone who needed it. "I'll be the truest friend Ed could ever have," she promised earnestly.

Rafe forced a smile. "Thank you, Lydia."

Lydia silently reflected that when he smiled, Rafe was the most handsome, yet somehow, still the saddest man she'd ever met. She blushed and nodded acknowledgement then joined Charles who handed Ed over to her care and approached Rafe.

"Would you allow me to pray with you before we part?" Charles asked.

Rafe shook his head. "It would be a waste of time. God has nothing to do with me."

"God loves you," Charles countered. "The evidence is clear if you only look for it."

Rafe looked up at the sky, longing, hoping, as he'd done so often before, to catch a glimpse of God smiling lovingly down upon him. He saw only the dark clouds of an impending storm. He sighed, his heart hurting anew as with each time he was rejected. "Take good care of Ed," he commanded, and then he turned and walked away.

He'd taken no more than a few steps when an abject pang of loss stopped him in his tracks. He turned back around. "Charles—," He paused, consumed by a firestorm of conflicting emotions—forgiveness and anger, guilt and defiance, love and hate.

"Yes?" Charles prompted hopefully.

Rafe struggled for the words to express all he felt and then he found them. He grinned. "Try to avoid hurricanes from now on."

Charles chuckled. "Good advice, which I'll certainly do my best to follow." Then he sobered. "And you stop neglecting your sleep."

Rafe thought of the laudanum buried deep in the bottom of his bag and the permanent sleep it would provide. "I will," he promised carefully keeping the grimness from his tone.

Charles stepped up and held out his hand. Rafe hesitated then he gripped Charles's hand warmly. When their eyes met, each saw a friendship renewed, but it was far too late for Rafe. Nothing could sway him from his intended self-destruction now. Rafe broke the clasp, adjusted the straps of his bag and bedroll, nodded once at Charles in acknowledgement and farewell then quickly disappeared into the dense green jungle.

Lydia and Ed sobbed so heartrendingly that Charles was almost tempted to chase after Rafe and force him to return, but against all human reasoning Charles somehow knew that letting Rafe go was the right thing to do.

Chapter Thirty-Nine

Rafe had parted from Ed, Lydia, and Charles six days ago, but he'd never strayed far from them, for his sense of honor demanded he keep watch over them until they were all safely aboard a ship home. He'd surreptitiously followed them to Nassau and then to an inn. At night he retired to a shabby room above a tavern in the seedy area of Nassau where criminals like him belonged. Early each morning he returned to the fine, respectable inn Charles had chosen for himself and the others and when they came out, watched them from the shadows as they took walks in the park or shopped at the market. One day he even risked talking to one of the indentured servants at their inn and discovered that the barrister Charles had engaged to contact Sarah was a cousin to Charles's neighboring plantation owner in the Caribbean and had been more than willing to loan Charles enough funds to pay for their every need while they awaited the arrival of the merchant ship, Lady Essex, on which they'd bought passage home.

Ed, Lydia, and Charles were obviously well content in each other's company, which both pleased Rafe and caused him pain in that Ed so easily forgot him. On more than one occasion jealousy encouraged him to emerge from hiding and demand that Charles turn Ed back over to his custody, but certainty that he was the wrong mentor for Ed always restrained him. On the day the Lady Essex arrived in port Rafe walked down to the docks. He needed to see the ship that would carry Ed away from him forever. He watched despondently as sailors unloaded the ship's cargo of cotton and picked up a new cargo of sugar cane, mahogany, and tobacco. At sunset, weary from standing for hours, Rafe ambled slowly back to his shabby room. On the way, he had to pass the Silver Chalice tavern. Although his sort generally weren't welcome in the more upscale taverns such as the Silver Chalice, he impulsively decided to enter.

Like all taverns the place smelled of stale tobacco smoke and countless years of ale spills that had soaked into the wooden floor, but it was well lit and clean. Rafe chose a seat at a table for two in a shadowed corner where it would be less apparent that he was part Indian, and leaned back in his chair, further evading the light. He brooded in the shadows for a full quarter hour before the barmaid finally noticed him and approached with a friendly smile and one hand on her ample hip. "What would you like, sir?" she asked as she brushed a stray curl from her eyes.

"A bit of love or a handful of caring would be more than welcome," Rafe said wistfully.

The barmaid's friendly smile vanished. "Sir, this is not that sort of establishment. We only serve food and drink here. If you wish for more than that, Lady Crawley's establishment is not far. I could give you directions if you'd like."

Rafe was glad for the shadows that hid the bright red blush that crept across his handsome face. *Why had he said that out loud!* "No. Thank you. I'd like a mug of water, please."

"Now look here, we don't normally serve your type here, but I figure one man's money is as good as another's, and as long as you stay in the corner unnoticed..." She shrugged. "However, if your intent is merely to occupy a table that would otherwise be occupied by a paying customer—,"

Rafe's embarrassment metamorphosed into full blown irritability. "Bring me some bread and mutton then," he snapped.

"As you would, sir," the barmaid said huffily and turned to go.

"Also…" Rafe said, causing her to turn back around. "Bring me a mug of water," He added perversely. The barmaid rolled her eyes and shook her head then hustled off to fill the order.

Rafe leaned back into the shadows, rested his feet in their dusty boots on the table ankles crossed, and sighed heavily. He was sick to death of this miserable existence that others called living, but at least it wouldn't be long now before he could end it all… He listlessly looked around the room and then he saw someone that made him sit up straight in shock and amazement his boots thumping loudly to the floor and shedding the dust of the road. Upon seeing that he was recognized, Leopold gathered up his black hat and gloves from the table then crossed the room.

"Well met, Rafe. I traveled to New Providence to hire mercenaries to try to find you and indeed I met with them not an hour hence in this same tavern, but I never thought to find you myself on my first night in Nassau, and frequenting a fine tavern too. I've been watching you since you came in, but until we made eye contact I wasn't completely certain it was you. You're leaner, with a certain hardness to your eyes, and you've let your hair grow too long." Leopold nodded distastefully at Rafe's nearly waist length braid, which was currently draped over his left shoulder. "You know I hate it when you let your hair grow past your shoulders. Combined with your darker coloring it makes you look like a savage."

Rafe self-consciously flipped the offending braid behind his back. "I am a savage, sir. Have you not read the papers? But will you join me nevertheless?" He nodded at the chair opposite his.

"Thank you." Leopold pulled out the chair and sat down, setting his hat and gloves on the table to his right.

Rafe shifted position uneasily as he was flooded with bitter memories of the suffering he'd endured from Leopold and the others after Duncan's death. "I presume you arrived on the Lady Essex, sir?" he asked.

"I did, along with Sarah. She was most anxious to see Charles again; especially after giving him up for dead. According to the letter Charles wrote, you two have had quite the adventure, shipwreck, pirates and all."

"Not as much an adventure sir, as life-ruining events I'd prefer to never repeat," Rafe said. "Why have you come searching for me? Do you intend to make me serve out my sentence? If so, I must warn you that I'll not—"

"You sentence has been annulled," Leopold interrupted.

"What?" Rafe exclaimed loudly, drawing the attention of several well-dressed gentlemen at a nearby table behind Leopold, who frowned with overt displeasure at the sight of an Indian in *their* tavern. Rafe self-consciously leaned back into the shadows. "How is that possible, sir?" he asked in a more normal tone.

"It's a long story, but the short of it is that upon my return from Boston I discovered Cabel had laid claim to the estate. He'd even moved all of my possessions into the local inn. Of course, I immediately called the Constables, but when we arrived to arrest Cabel, he produced a birth certificate proving his father was Lord Brookstone's wayward, disinherited only son, Rafael Theodore Brookstone, your namesake, who was knifed to death in a drunken street brawl a few years before you were born. Cabel's mother was a prostitute and so to avoid scandal your grandfather secretly paid her the tidy sum of twenty thousand pounds in exchange for giving up her son's rights to the estate forever, unless there was no other heir. Since for all we knew you were at the bottom of the sea, there was nothing we could do but surrender the estate to him.

"Cabel then acted the prodigal and wasted the estate's money in the taverns, on prostitutes, on gambling, and drinking. It made me long for better days when you were lord of the estate. At Lisbeth's and Pierre's annual anniversary ball, however Cabel brought about his own downfall when he drunkenly bragged to all who'd listen that he'd drugged your port at the previous anniversary ball then paid a servant to make sure you drank it. The draught had been meant to kill you, but owing to your distaste for alcohol, which Cabel was unaware of, you only drank two sips which instead only made you act out of character, beat Charles and kill Duncan. But it was good enough, for then you were sent away for murder and assault and Cabel still had the estate."

"I didn't act so out of character that night after all, as it turns out, sir," Rafe remarked.

"Whatever do you mean?" Leopold asked.

Rafe's eyebrows shot up. "You don't know? I thought surely Charles would've told you all the sordid details straightaway. Perhaps his changed attitude toward me was more than temporary after all…"

"Tell me what!" Leopold exclaimed impatiently.

Rafe glanced uneasily around the crowded common room. The gentlemen that had glanced disapprovingly at him before were doing it again. "Not here. But about Cabel; if he wants the estate so badly then transfer it to him."

"You'd give Cabel everything after what he did to you?" Leopold exclaimed.

Rafe nodded. "You know I've never cared for the money or the title, only the people I could help by them. I only wish Cabel had told me of his claim earlier rather than resorting to attempted murder. It would've prevented a great deal of harm. I would ask, though, that you assure he treats the estate's workers and their families with respect and dignity."

"Well, Rafe I must admit it's quite noble of you to surrender your estate, but it's too late. Cabel was hung early last week, two days before Sarah received the letter from Charles informing us that you had both survived the shipwreck and were here in New Providence."

Rafe paled. "Hung! But Cabel's crime was less than mine!"

The disapproving gentlemen at the nearby table showed their displeasure again. Rafe glared menacingly at them and his hand strayed toward his knife hilt. Leopold had started to answer, "Cabel—

," but then he turned around to see what the trouble was, just as the three gentlemen hastily stood up and walked out. He turned back around. "What was that about?"

"Nothing," Rafe said. "You were saying?"

Leopold hesitated. Something had occurred between Rafe and those gentlemen that could've resulted in violence, but as it had apparently been solved without violence, he decided not to pursue the matter and resumed the conversation. "Cabel tried to kill you and stole your inheritance, which is at least as bad in the eyes of the court as your crimes. Furthermore, he had no title, no beautiful woman or influential men taking his side."

Rafe bristled. "You accuse me of manipulating the courts, sir?"

"No, Rafe. I merely state the facts. I know Sarah and Charles acted on their own accord. At any rate, it's a moot point, for all charges against you in Duncan's death have been dropped. You're free to return home."

The barmaid returned with a pewter plate laden with bread and mutton and a tin mug of water. Rafe waved her away. "Take it away. I don't want it anymore." He drew a gold crown from his coin pouch and handed it to her. "For the meal and the rest for your trouble."

The barmaid brightened. "Thank you, kindly sir!" She walked off smiling broadly.

Leopold frowned. "You've always been generous with your money, but how is it that you have gold crowns to spare on serving women when you've never contacted me for funds?"

Rafe shifted position guiltily. "Suffice it to say that gambling was involved, sir."

"You've taken up the vice of gambling?" Leopold exclaimed disapprovingly.

"In a manner of speaking," Rafe hedged.

"Surely you are aware that gambling is unwise! The odds are always against you!"

"The odds have been against me, sir, from the moment of my unpropitious conception," Rafe said. Abruptly the stale smells of the tavern were too much to bear. He needed fresh air. Now. "Shall we finish this conversation outside?" He shoved back his chair and stood up.

Leopold quickly gathered up his hat and gloves and accompanied Rafe outside into the dark, unlit street. Then they walked east. "Where are you staying?" Leopold asked.

"I have a room above a tavern," Rafe said evasively.

"A tavern! That's no place for the Lord Brookstone! You must take rooms more befitting of your station!"

"No, sir," Rafe said.

"But surely you don't intend to remain at the tavern until we leave," Leopold said disapprovingly.

"I'm not leaving, sir, or at least not with you and the others."

"While I understand that you might wish to return on the next ship to avoid the discomfort of traveling with those you've harmed—"

"I don't intend to return at all, sir," Rafe said.

Leopold looked aghast. "But Rafe, now that you've been acquitted of all charges in Duncan's death and Charles's assault, you must resume your rightful place as Lord Brookstone! The estate needs you."

"The courts put the estate in your care. You need only keep my changes in place and it will prosper in your care even as it has prospered in mine," Rafe said, making it a command.

"You would shirk your duties? Did not I and your heart father teach you better?" Leopold objected.

Rafe winced guiltily. "Indeed you did, sir, but I've committed countless crimes since the shipwreck, many for which I deserve to hang; and if I should ever return, no doubt I would hang soon thereafter. Discounting that, I refuse to return to where even those who once called me friend were all too eager and willing to label me *liar*."

"You can hardly blame them, Rafe. Even I could find no evidence to support your claim," Leopold reasoned.

Rafe came to a standstill as a tsunami of unpleasant memories washed over him. "Yes, I remember it quite clearly, sir. I also remember that you labeled me a drunk as well as a liar, accused me of lacking remorse, and even went so far as to purposely ignore what we all believed was my final fare well. Tell me sir, was that, as Charles claimed, because you wished I'd never been born?" He added, "As I then wished," his voice breaking, then looked away and swallowed hard.

Leopold took a moment to answer. Then he said, "I must admit to my shame that I did indeed wish you'd never been born. I was convinced you'd inherited the wicked nature of your drunken, rapist father. Curse the man! I never could stand him and especially after he ruined my life!"

It took a minute to register through the fog of Rafe's misery. "You knew my father?"

"I wish with all my heart I could say no, but yes I knew him," Leopold spat.

Anger superseded Rafe's angst. "You never told me! All those years! Why?"

"After what he did to your mother, it was difficult to talk about him," Leopold replied defensively.

"Talk about him now," Rafe commanded reverting to his long unused lordly manner. "Begin with his name."

Leopold considered for a moment then sighed heavily. "I suppose you do have a right to know... His name was Buckonegahelas and he was a scout like your heart father. That was the only thing they two had in common, though. Buckonegahelas was cruel and arrogant and self-centered. If he wanted something and it wasn't given to him freely, he'd take it claiming it should've been his in the first place; and then of course it goes without saying that he drank too much. He wanted your mother like he'd wanted nothing before, but Ophelia wanted nothing to do with him, not only because of his wicked nature, but because, well, you see, I was the sick person she was tending the night your father waylaid her then raped her. We were engaged."

Rafe's eyes widened. "You and my mother? Engaged to be married?"

Leopold nodded. "When Ophelia discovered she was with child, she broke off the engagement unwilling to saddle me with Buckonegahelas's son. Desperate not to lose her I offered to bring you up as my own son, but she knew I was lying; that I hated you even before you were born because you were *his* son!"

"Were you by her side when she died then?"

Leopold nodded.

"Then you were also there when my grandfather took me away to drown me," Rafe accused.

Leopold nodded again.

"Did you even try to stop him?" Rafe demanded.

"To my everlasting shame, no I did not. However, in all fairness I had no idea he intended to drown you. I thought he was taking you off to an orphanage. I only discovered the truth of the matter when he hired the mercenaries to bring you back from the Mohican—,"

"Steal me from the Mohican," Rafe interrupted harshly. "And you didn't try to stop that either!"

Leopold nodded guiltily. "So as you can imagine, I was glad of the chance to negate some of my shame and do my duty to your mother by fostering you."

"Now at least I understand how you so easily adopted the bitter attitude toward me that Henry and Charles shared," Rafe said resentfully. "I was never more to you than a duty, and a disagreeable one at that!"

"I tried to love you, Rafe, but you so closely resemble your father. Then too, I couldn't help blaming you for causing Ophelia to break off our engagement. It was difficult enough to continually overlook those two things and then when I saw you turning into Buckonegahelas in other ways, such as in the incident with Sarah and when you killed Duncan…"

Rafe nodded somehow making it seem bitter and resentful.

"It should be understood that I battled hard against the hatred. I tried to stay on your side. You must remember how I fought for you at your trial. In the end, though, I couldn't help despising you even as I despised your father," Leopold said defensively.

Rafe disgustedly labeled himself a fool for naïvely believing Leopold had ever cared for him simply because he'd rarely treated him like the half-breed bastard that he was. "I understand," he said softly.

"No, I don't think you do understand. I knew then and I know now that it was extraordinarily selfish and wrong for me to blame you for your father's sins, and although I may never be able to say I love you as a father should, when I thought you were lost in the shipwreck, I realized that I am at least fond of you. I know it's not the love you crave, but it's the best I can manage. So for the anguish I've caused you by my petty selfishness, I humbly beg your forgiveness."

Tears blurred Rafe's vision. "It's I who should beg your forgiveness, sir, for you were right about me. Like my natural father I made all the wrong choices. I've lost my friends, my honor, and—," he almost said God's love, but he had no wish to move Leopold to argue that God loved him, as Charles had. This conversation was painful enough already without having arguing about even more of what he wanted so badly, but knew he could never own. "My white grandfather was right to try to drown me, for the world would've been a far better place without me in it." A tear escaped and rolled down his cheek. Rafe hastily swept it away with the back of his hand.

"Rafe." Leopold reached out to him.

Rafe hastily stepped back fearing Leopold's touch would open the floodgates and he'd shame himself further by bawling like a baby in front of a man who'd always despised him.

Leopold awkwardly dropped his hand to his side. "You're no abomination, Rafe. You're a good man with many fine qualities; chief among them that although in general people have treated you poorly, you nevertheless always put the welfare of others above your own."

Rafe laughed mirthlessly. "I'm afraid Charles would heartily disagree with you on that point, sir."

"No I don't think he would. Return with me to the inn and I'll prove it to you, and also that it's indeed possible for you to resume your life as the Lord Brookstone."

Rafe shook his head. "Lord Brookstone is dead, sir. He died the same night as Duncan."

"But Rafe, whatever will you do if not resume your old life?" Leopold exclaimed in exasperation.

"I will end the nightmare," Rafe said grimly. He made eye contact with Leopold and his eyes were as black and void of light as the deepest reaches of the universe, but it was more his tone that sent a shiver down Leopold's spine.

"What do you mean, Rafe?" Leopold demanded.

Rafe shook his head.

"What are you planning to do?" Leopold persisted.

Rafe took a step back preparing to leave. "You showed me tenderness and caring when no one else did. Because of that I have loved you like a father and still do despite the knowledge that you have no feeling for me beyond a slight fondness—more the fool I. Fare well, foster father. I wish you all the best."

Before Leopold could cry out in protest Rafe quickly vanished into the gloom and the shadows of the darkest night New Providence had ever known.

Chapter Forty

Rafe trudged despondently into his room above the dingy tavern and shut the door softly behind him. Although the room was pitch-black, he didn't bother to light a candle. He didn't need to see and no earthly illumination could chase away his dark depression. He pulled the straps of his bag and bedroll over his head and wearily dropped them on the floor then lay down on his back on his bed without bothering to undress or even to remove his dusty, muddy boots or his loaded pistol or knife. Despite the drunken uproar from the tavern below he slept—and dreamed.

He was home, wandering his dark and shadowed manse at night with no candle to light his way. Upon descending the stairs, he came face to face with a shining, golden haired man dressed all in white. The man's presence lit up the entry like the sun at mid-day, except where Rafe stood. He was still wrapped in inky black shadows. The man spoke with a voice like the loudest thunder Rafe had ever experienced. "In the time of my favor I heard you, and in the day of salvation, I helped you. I tell you, now is the day of salvation."

"I don't believe you! Salvation is not for such as me," Rafe argued stubbornly.

"So be it!" the shining man boomed, and then the floor beneath Rafe's feet misted away revealing a fiery chasm. Rafe jumped back, away from the hole, but it widened behind him and he fell, screaming…

He startled awake with a gasp, brow beaded with sweat, trembling from head to toe. The darkness in the room clutched at him, smothering him. He sprang from the bed and fled out of the room and down the stairs seeking fresh night air and the comforting light of the moon and stars. The common room was deserted at this late hour, except for the tavern keeper who was cleaning tables with a wet rag that had once been white, but was now permanently stained gray with overuse and shoddy and infrequent laundering. As Rafe hurdled down the last stair into the room, the tavern keeper abandoned his work, leaving the dirty, gray rag lying in a wad on the table he'd been *cleaning.* Wiping his damp hands on his dingy apron, he asked, "Is there something wrong, sir? Anything I may do for you?"

"There's nothing anyone may do for me," Rafe said. He barreled past then shoved through the inn's front door, made of a single piece of wood. The innkeeper stared after him in dismay then shrugged and resumed his work.

Despite the late hour and the deserted street Rafe felt the presence of pursuers. He drew his knife and whirled around expecting to have to confront a group of angry mercenaries, but there was no one there. Rafe turned around and ran anyway, his knife in his hand, his long, thick braid lightly pounding his back. He raced around a corner, passed a two-story boarding house then skidded to a standstill in front of a plain, white stone building with a twenty-foot high wood cross topping a steeple and stared at the church in bewilderment, his chest heaving from his exertions, his knife forgotten in his hand at his side. Rafe was absolutely certain that when he'd passed this way after his conversation with Leopold there'd been no church here. Was he still dreaming? He brushed a loose lock of hair from his sweaty brow with his trembling knife hand then reached out with his other hand, also trembling, and tentatively touched the smooth, cool stone first with only his fingertips then flattening his palm against it.

The building didn't mist away like the floor in his dream. It was definitely real. A strong inner voice urged him to go inside, and so despite intense misgivings he sheathed his knife then climbed the flight of seven stairs. He paused uncertainly at the double cedar doors decorated with smaller inlaid wood versions of the cross on the steeple as he gathered his courage then with a large measure of trepidation grasped the looped, antique brass door handle and pulled. Rafe hoped the door would be locked, so he could leave in good conscience having tried his best, but the door opened easily. He resolutely stepped inside, onto the highly polished wood floors of the sanctuary. A small part of him felt comforted, as if he'd finally returned home after a long, taxing journey, but that emotion was almost instantly overwhelmed by a much stronger conviction that he was trespassing. An abomination in God's sight had no right to contaminate this holy place with his presence.

Thus, instead of continuing confidently, Rafe proceeded with the footsteps of a now practiced thief. Silently, stealthily, frequently looking over his shoulder he walked down the central aisle of the empty sanctuary lit only by the silvery moonlight streaming in through the twelve arched windows, six on either side. Upon reaching the podium he turned around and looked out upon row upon row of empty pews, and waited. He was unsure what he was waiting for, although deep down inside he hoped God would speak to him, and say something like, *Welcome home, son*. But after long minutes of waiting and nothing happening, Rafe grew irritable. "Well God, why did you lead me here? What do you want?" he demanded.

One word echoed back at him. "Want–want—want."

Rafe laughed softly, embarrassed by his foolishness. The laughter bounced off the stone walls, seemingly mocking him for seeking a God Who'd already thoroughly rejected him. Rafe could almost hear the words in the echoes. "Fool, half-breed, abomination." Unshed tears blurred Rafe's vision. Rejected again, and this time in God's house; but this time instead of merely accepting God's rejection as he'd always done before, he railed at the injustice of it! How was it his fault that he'd been conceived in rape, or that his mother and father had been of different races, or that his mother had died giving birth to him? Why did that make him less valuable or lovable than anyone else? Had he not since he was a young boy until the night of Duncan's death faithfully worshiped God and followed His teachings? Why then did the Father/Creator/Spirit continually turn his face from him? Why was he not good enough to be loved? Why? Why?

Rafe fell to his knees, sobbing, his heart aching so acutely that he felt it would burst at any moment, but no instant death came and relieved his misery. Then he remembered the bottle of laudanum and at the same time realized he no longer had to wait to end his life until he was certain Ed, Charles, and Lydia were safely homebound, for Leopold was there to watch over them. He could end his misery now, and in so doing taint God's house by committing the sin of suicide on this holy ground; revenge and solace in one package, a perfect and highly satisfying solution.

Stilling his sobs, Rafe stood up, reached into his pants pocket and drew out the full bottle of laudanum. His hand trembling in eager anticipation, he popped the cork stopper and carelessly let it fall on the floor, tilted his head back, and without hesitation poured the entire contents of the bottle into his mouth. He choked and gagged as he struggled to swallow the foul-tasting liquid, but grim determination aided him. The bottle empty, he tossed it aside. It hit the floor with a clang that didn't even register in his consciousness. With a sigh of relief that his troubled and miserable life would soon be over, he lay on his back on the last pew and smiled serenely up at the beamed ceiling above him as the laudanum slowly infused his system bringing a welcome numbness to body and mind.

Chapter Forty-One

Rafe resisted the encroaching awareness and snuggled deeper under the covers on the soft, comfortable bed. Perversely, however, sleep insisted on leaving him. He reluctantly opened his eyes and drowsily marveled at the shining magnificence of the dust motes in a beam of sunlight streaming through the opening of the partially closed blue and white checked curtains on the window to his left. What a glorious world God had created, where even the smallest, most insignificant things in life were beautiful.

Wait! Life?

Rafe sat up quickly. He'd swallowed enough laudanum to kill four adults! How was he alive? Whose house was this? How was he here? He couldn't have come here himself, for he'd taken such a large dose that walking would've been impossible. Someone must have found him, brought him to their home, and doctored him back to health.

In Mohican Rafe roundly cursed whoever that person was, in English he cursed destiny for ruining his perfectly staged death, and in French he cursed himself for not realizing that God would protect His sanctuary from being soiled by the suicide of an abomination. He should've realized it was impossible to win when playing against the all-powerful Father, but how maddeningly frustrating! Now he'd have to steal more coin, buy more laudanum, and drink the foul stuff all over again! This time he'd be wiser and forget about seeking vengeance against God, though, and instead retreat deep into the jungle as he'd originally planned, where nothing and no one could intervene and prevent his passage from misery.

Rafe looked around the room and spotted his clothing, cleaned and neatly folded resting on a nearby white chair to his right. His black boots, polished to a high sheen, sat side by side on the floor to the left of his bed. His knife, in its sheath, rested on a night table to the right of the bed. Rafe threw back the covers, quickly dressed then vaulted over the bed, snatched up the knife and sheath and buckled it on. He didn't know why his captor hadn't taken the knife, but all that really mattered was that he still had it. He drew the knife and held it ready as he crossed the room, opened the door—and came face to face with a large, wide-shouldered, barrel-chested Bahamian man in his sixth decade, his black hair liberally salted with gray.

Rafe stepped back and raised his knife, but the man only smiled, his warm brown eyes twinkling merrily. "Good afternoon, young sir," he said in a deep kindly voice. "My name is Zebulon, but you may call me Zeb as do all my friends. I'm the caretaker of the church you overdosed in a few nights back and you are a guest in my house. You may put your weapon away. I would never harm a guest."

"You have it backwards, sir. It's I who won't harm you if you step aside and allow me to pass," Rafe threatened.

Zeb deftly snatched the knife from Rafe's hand. Rafe was definitely not pleased at being on the opposite end of such a trick and he was even a little frightened. He realized his victims must have felt the same as he did now, and hated himself all the more for it. "You're mistaken if you think that makes me less dangerous," he blustered. "I don't need a weapon to kill you. Bare hands will suffice."

Zeb deftly slipped the knife into the waist of his pants behind his belt. "I have no doubt that is true, sir, but killing me would be a mean way of thanking me for saving your life. Don't you agree?"

"I wanted to die! I thought my misery was ended and now you've—you've—," Rafe had to stop or he'd break down and cry, and he had to blink away tears, nevertheless.

"Oh you'll die in your time, but the number of your days has not yet reached their fulfillment. Now is your appointed time to live and if you wish to live in peace, you must turn your heart to God," Zeb said.

Rafe's throat tightened as he recalled his most recent rejection by God in the sanctuary of the church. "Death is the only solution to my problems and you've callously denied me that escape by your unwelcome ministrations."

"I'm sure your friends at home would disagree," Zeb said.

"I have no friends and there is no home for such as me. I'm half of one world and half of another. In the white world I'm an outcast and an abomination, and in the other I'm the catalyst for the destruction of all those I care about." Annoyingly, tears threatened to make their appearance again, but Rafe determinedly held them back.

"Then allow me to offer you the hospitality of my home, sir. You may stay as long as you wish and while you're here we'll work on the confirmation you so badly need. Then you'll no longer have the desire to run away from your problems."

Rafe bristled. "I wasn't running away, sir! I'm not craven! I sought death merely because it's the only way to—," He cut off his words before he revealed his innermost despair to a complete stranger. It was bad enough he'd revealed it to Charles and had come close to revealing it to Leopold; and why was it that lately he couldn't keep the emotional turmoil of God's rejection to himself when he'd done it easily enough for over a year before?

As if Zeb could read Rafe's mind, he said, "God would never reject someone who earnestly seeks him."

"Unless that person is an abomination, like me," Rafe said.

"You are not an abomination in God's eyes," Zeb assured him.

When Charles had insisted much the same thing, it had been easy not to believe, for Rafe had sensed Charles desperate need to right a wrong, first and foremost for his own conscience's sake. With Zeb, however, it was quite clear there was no selfish agenda. The thick barrier of doubt Rafe had erected in his heart started to crumble, and he shifted position uneasily. "You don't know all that I am, all that I've done, sir. Even if what you say is true, I'm unworthy of God's love."

Zeb chuckled. "I know much more about you than you think, and I assure you that no one is any more worthy of God's love than you."

Rafe decided he'd endured enough of this extremely upsetting talk. It was time to move on, buy more laudanum and end his life, properly this time. He tried to push past Zeb, but the man was like a stone wall, solid and immovable. "Step aside and let me pass, sir," he commanded with all his lordly aplomb.

"As you wish, but first allow me to point out that you're headed in the wrong direction. I would be glad to direct you to the right path," Zeb said.

Rafe cursed under his breath in Mohican. He didn't want direction he only wanted his miserable life to end! He'd try one more time to walk out and if Zeb continued to stand in his way, he'd fight Zeb until Zeb killed him or he killed Zeb. "If you won't allow me to leave, I'll be forced to harm you, sir," he threatened quietly.

Zeb showed no fear. He only looked disappointed. "I won't keep you here against your will, but please take this one small bit of advice. You'll find God's love only when you stop justifying your crimes and your attempted suicides with the excuse that you're a soulless half-breed, rejected by God."

Rafe's dark eyes widened. How had Zeb known he felt that way? "What makes you think I've ever—,"

"Haven't you?" Zeb asked.

Rafe felt Zeb's warm brown eyes delving into the deepest dungeon of his soul where the truth was chained, waiting to be freed. He shifted position uneasily, looked to his left, his right, down at his feet, anywhere but into the eyes of this strange man who seemed able to read his mind. "It's only because my origin *is* the source of all my problems," he rationalized.

"Is it? Or is it your lack of faith that is to blame?"

"My faith is as firm as anyone's, sir," Rafe insisted stubbornly.

"Don't fear the truth. It will free you," Zeb said.

Rafe made inadvertent eye contact with Zeb and was suddenly firmly convicted that love, acceptance and forgiveness awaited him. *No!* Zeb was attempting to make him believe a lie; a lie he desperately wanted to believe, which made it all the harder to battle it. He broke eye contact, but with an effort akin to fighting off those seven mercenaries all on his own. Sweat beaded his brow and his chest heaved with exertion. "What are you?" he demanded harshly.

Zeb smiled warmly. "I already told you. I'm your friend."

"I don't want your sort of friendship!" Rafe spat vehemently.

"Are you certain?" Zeb asked still smiling.

"Yes! More certain than I've ever been of anything in my life."

Zeb's smile vanished. "Then allow me to show you to the door, sir," he said frostily.

For some inexplicable reason it bothered Rafe that he'd lost Zeb's good regard. Almost, he impulsively offered to stay for a few more hours, perhaps even a few days, but a small, harsh voice deep inside him warned that staying here would be a grave mistake. He'd lose all of his self here. He should escape as soon as possible.

He followed Zeb down a flight of thirteen stairs to a small entryway at the front door. Zeb then stepped aside allowing Rafe to open the door himself. Frigid air smacked him in the face, raised goose bumps on his arms. It was a vast change from the cozy warmth of the house, and absolutely wrong too, for New Providence was never this cold. Rafe hesitated to step out into that frigid weather, but the harsh voice urged him on and Rafe found himself crossing the front porch, buffeted by a strong, glacial wind.

"Have a safe journey, young Lord Rafael Zacharias Brookstone. If you change your mind, I'll be here waiting." Zeb started to close the door.

Rafe whirled around and slammed his palm against the door preventing it from closing. "How is it that you know my full name and title when I never told it to you?" he demanded.

Zeb smiled. "I have ways of discerning things."

Rafe accepted that explanation, but only because he was certain it was all he'd ever have from Zeb. It brought up another question, though. "There must be a substantial reward for my capture…"

"And you're wondering why I haven't collected on it."

Rafe nodded.

"God sent you to me for guidance, Rafe. Turning you over to the authorities would not accomplish His purpose."

A chill raced down Rafe's spine as he recalled the shining man in his dream and his subsequent flight. "God didn't send me, sir. I stumbled upon your church purely by accident."

Zeb smiled knowingly. It was infuriating. Rafe decided to wipe that irritating smile from Zeb's face. He took a menacing step forward. "It's more likely I was sent by Satan to kill you, as I've killed countless other innocents this last year."

Zeb's smile remained intact, warm and genuine, without a trace of fear. "You'll not hurt me." Rafe's knife suddenly appeared in Zeb's hand with the blade pointed at Rafe. He hadn't even seen Zeb reach for the weapon and he wasn't at all pleased by the threat. "You'd kill me with my own knife? Somehow that doesn't seem fair," he complained.

"Have you not done the same to others?"

Rafe was guiltily reminded of Lauralee, VonLarken, and a few others. "Indeed I have, sir," he confessed. "Proceed then. In this case it's justice, and as you know, I'm more than ready to die."

Zeb deftly flipped the knife so that the hilt was facing Rafe then held it out. Rafe didn't try to take it, for he was certain Zeb was playing a twisted game and would snatch it back and then laugh at his failure, which would be humiliating, if not irritating. "Please take it. It is, after all, yours," Zeb urged.

Rafe gathered his courage and snatched the knife then was surprised he'd succeeded. Flushed with triumph he decided to ram the knife into the wall of the house directly to the left of Zeb's head, if only to prove he was the one in control here, but although he struggled mightily his hand wouldn't move from his side. His eyes went wide in shock and dismay.

"You can't hurt me unless you truly wish to do so," Zeb explained. Scowling, Rafe firmly sheathed the knife, and then much to his dismay he shamed himself by bursting into tears! Zeb lightly rested his large, strong hand on Rafe's shoulder. "Tell me all about it. I'll help you find the answers," he offered.

Inexplicably, Rafe wanted to reveal everything to Zeb, even the many merchants he'd failed to save from massacre when masquerading as a pirate. It frightened him that he was willing to divulge such a horrific secret to this disquieting man whom he didn't even know. He wondered if Zeb was some kind of shaman who'd placed a truth spell on him or something equally sinister. "Release me," he wept.

"Nothing is keeping you here but your own desire. You may leave whenever you wish," Zeb assured him.

Rafe pulled his emotions into check, swiped his sleeve across his eyes then tentatively stepped onto the first of the four porch steps while warily watching Zeb. Zeb made no move to stop him. Rafe took the next step and the next. Only one step was left, but Rafe hesitated. He had a single burning question that he needed the answer to and he was certain Zeb was the one to give it. He turned around.

"You have a soul," Zeb said.

Rafe's mouth dropped open. He realized it and snapped it shut. "How did you know I intended to ask you that? Have you been talking to Charles?"

Zeb smiled warmly. "I have never met your friend, Charles, but please come inside and I'll give you all the answers you need to renew your peace."

Rafe sensed if anyone could help him find peace again, it was this bewildering man, but the harsh voice told him if he stayed, he'd only ruin this man's life too as he'd ruined the lives of everyone else he'd ever known. Did he truly want to add yet another ruined life to his already overburdened conscience? "I thank you for your concern, sir, but I destroy the lives of everyone I meet and you seem to be a good fellow. It would be best if you avoided me."

Zeb smiled. "There's no need to be concerned for my welfare, Rafe. God is on my side and if God is for me, who can be against me?"

"Trust me, I can. It's what I do best; ruin people's lives." Tears threatened to shame him once again. Rafe hastily blinked them away while silently cursing his new and exasperating inability to control his emotions.

"Let's talk about a solution then," Zeb offered. "We may sit out here on the porch if you don't wish to go back inside. It's a beautiful day." And just like that the frigid air and glacial wind were replaced by warm sunshine and a gentle breeze.

Rafe shivered, nevertheless. It was abnormal.

"Have a seat." Zeb nodded at one of several wicker chairs.

As had been the case ever since Rafe had first met Zeb, something in his tone made Rafe obey; although to maintain a semblance of control he perversely chose to sit on the top porch step instead of in the chair. The white stone church sat directly in front of him, a mere several hundred yards away, which reminded him that he'd chosen to end his life in the sanctuary instead of out in the jungle solely to defile the place. It was a childishly defiant act, and shame washed over him.

Zeb sat down beside him. "You sought revenge based on what you believed, but if one's belief system is flawed, it naturally follows that any solution you design is flawed as well."

Rafe was no longer surprised Zeb knew what was on his mind. "I suppose that's true," he conceded.

"That was not your first attempt to take your life," Zeb stated.

"No, but apparently I haven't made the effort often enough to succeed," Rafe said bitterly. "It's the single portion of my life in which God feels compelled to intervene. I think He derives pleasure from watching me try and fail."

"God derives no pleasure from your pain, Rafe. On the contrary, it saddens Him deeply, for He loves you," Zeb assured him.

"So you've said, sir, and so others have said as well, but it's not possible."

"What makes you so certain?"

Rafe shook his head. "You don't wish to hear about my sordid life. It gives me nightmares and I've grown accustomed to violence and bloodshed."

"I've seen and heard far worse than anything you could imagine. You need have no fear of revealing all. It will neither shock nor frighten me, nor will I judge you for it," Zeb avowed.

Rafe didn't even want to think about his crimes much less reinforce his guilt and remorse by talking about them. He dredged up another excuse. "A number of good people have tried to help me, sir. They all failed. What makes you think you can succeed where they did not?"

"You have nothing to lose and everything to gain by letting me aid you; but take a moment to think it over. I wish for you to be sure," Zeb said.

Rafe considered his past, his possible future, then concluded Zeb was correct. He had nothing to lose, for he'd already lost it all. The harsh voice deep within Rafe urged him to run before he'd told all his secrets to this stranger and opened himself up to derision and rejection, but overpowering need drowned it out. Rafe started talking even though the harsh voice warned him that Zeb would reject him or in the least revile him.

Zeb listened to every horrendous detail with quiet sympathy and showed no sign of rejecting him. "You've suffered immensely, but that is about to end, for now is the day of salvation."

Rafe's eyes widened. "I heard those exact words in a dream the night I stumbled upon your church!"

Zeb nodded. "God used that dream to bring you here to me, where you could be renewed in His love."

Conviction seized Rafe. He desperately fought it off. "No! That can't be! I came upon your church during my walk. It was pure happenstance. That dream was only a byproduct of my guilty conscience! God had nothing to do with any of it!"

"Are you so certain of that, even now?" Zeb asked gently.

Rafe shifted position still uncomfortably convicted of the truth and still unwilling to surrender to it. "I'm not only a half-breed, but a child of rape. My birth killed my mother, my presence killed my tribe, and my friendship killed the only man who ever accepted me unconditionally. You've heard of the other lives I've ruined. I'm rightly called abomination. It's too much to expect God to accept a cursed one such as myself into His household, much less to ask Him to forgive me for all I've done. It's useless to even try."

"A spirit-wise pastor in my youth once told me that God saves because of who He is, not because of who you are. Furthermore, the Bible says, "*I, even I, am he who blots out your transgressions, for my own sake, and remembers your sins no more.* It's faith that saves, not actions and not who you are, or are not. I know you believe in God and His Son so don't you think it's time you stopped rationalizing and started repenting?" Zeb urged.

Rather than admit that the rationalization he'd used to justify his actions this last year was wrong, Rafe angrily blamed Zeb. "You've put some kind of spell on me so I can't think clearly and will believe your lies, but I know the truth and I'm finished with this conversation!" He stood up to leave.

Zeb stood up too. "Or perhaps you wish to continue to believe you're soulless and thus avoid accountability for your actions."

The blood drained from Rafe's face. "That's—that's ridiculous!" he denied. "I wouldn't willingly choose darkness over light! Pachtamawas—your God— abandoned me not the other way around! I'm not responsible! I was merely struggling to survive without Him in the best way I knew how, and even then I only did what was necessary when I could've done far worse."

When he'd finished his tirade, Rafe strained to hear the harsh voice reassuring him that he was right, but it had been silenced by the truth. He then remembered Duncan's words at Pierre and Lisbeth's anniversary ball. "*Charles was correct where choices are concerned, but Rafe, God is the God of all. If you believe, then you're His. Promise me you won't ever let anyone, or any untoward circumstance, convince you otherwise.*" Rafe had promised he'd keep the words in mind, if not keep the promise itself, but he'd forgotten them almost immediately and instead plunged fully into iniquity. He broke into a cold sweat, and a wave of nausea and dizziness passed over him. He gripped the stair railing so tightly that his knuckles whitened and then he dropped heavily onto the top step. "I've been so wrong. All this wasted time, the unnecessary pain…"

Zeb rested his hand lightly on Rafe's left shoulder. "Would you like to ask God back into your life?"

Rafe nodded, for his voice wouldn't come. Zeb sat down beside him. Led by Zeb, Rafe admitted his sins, asked forgiveness, and re-committed his life to God.

Afterward, Rafe sighed long and heavy like a man who'd completed a daunting task against all odds. "You probably somehow already know this, Zeb, for you seem to know everything else. Deep down, I always felt as if God was merely letting me tag along since the Bible didn't exclude me specifically. He was stuck with me as if He'd signed a bad contract. Perhaps that's why it was so easy to let myself believe God couldn't possibly love me and why I was blinded to the fact that the unconditional love I've so fruitlessly chased all my life up to now was only one prayer away. Thank you, sir, for opening my eyes to the truth."

Zeb smiled warmly. "You must never forget that unlike temporary, worldly love that fades, God's love is eternal. He will never leave you nor forsake you. In the future when circumstances go awry, hold on to that assurance and remember you're justified through faith in the shed blood of Jesus Christ. Your actions neither save you nor condemn you, but are only a mirror of your faith."

"I'll remember, sir. I've spent too much of my lifetime mired in misery and darkness. I don't want to return there. Ever." He stood up and then so did Zeb. "I should like to stay with you a little longer and perhaps find some way to pay you back for saving my life, both physically and spiritually, but I am still a wanted man, so I think it best I leave."

"You may pay me back by leading a Godly life from now on and never returning to your old ways," Zeb said.

"I will," Rafe promised then held out his hand.

Zeb clasped it warmly. "Fare well, Rafe. If ever you pass this way again, be sure to pay me a visit. I'll be waiting right here, a true friend you may always count on."

Rafe smiled gratefully, and then he gently pulled free from Zeb's grasp and still smiling, walked away into a new life filled with hope and the light of God's love.

Epilogue

The letter Charles held in his trembling hand had no return address, but Charles recognized Rafe's neat, precise handwriting on the envelope. Six long months had elapsed since that dark night when Leopold had returned to their inn in New Providence and told them he'd met Rafe by accident in a nearby tavern. Charles blamed himself for Rafe's refusal to return with Leopold. He was convinced that if he'd treated Rafe as the true friend he'd always been instead of an enemy, matters would've gone differently. He was almost afraid the letter from Rafe blamed him as well and so he slowly, apprehensively opened it.

"My dear friend, forgive my lack of details, but time is short. I've finally accepted that God loves me, have repented, and I'm once more walking in His will."

Charles was so thrilled by this news that he whooped loudly. Sarah hurried into the room looking concerned. "What is it? Is something wrong?" she asked anxiously.

"No, something is quite right. Quite right!" Charles showed Sarah the letter. "Rafe's written that he's returned to the Lord."

"How wonderful! You must write and tell him Ed and Lydia have become Christians too. He'll be so pleased."

Charles's joy dissipated somewhat. "I would love to let him know, but I can't write him; or at least not yet. See here?" He pointed to the next paragraph then read it out loud. *"The Governor of New Providence is industriously ridding the island of all pirates. I have no wish to be caught and hanged among them, so I've hired out on a departing merchant ship leaving within the hour. When I find a place to settle down, I'll write again."*

He'd signed the letter simply, *Rafe*. No title. No surname.

"He didn't even give the destination of the ship he's hired out on!" Sarah complained.

"I don't think he wanted us to know." Charles stared absently out the six-foot tall leaded glass window to his left at a beautiful sunset, but he didn't see it. He was wondering where in the vast world Rafe was now and worrying about him, for although Rafe may have found his way back to God, he was still a wanted man. Would Rafe's re-discovered faith carry him through the difficult trials he'd certainly face as a fugitive? If he had no choice but to kill again to remain free, would Rafe make that choice, and would that decision then thrust him back onto the winding path to Perdition? Charles put his palm on the window as if reaching out to touch Rafe, his friend wandering out there somewhere, alone, newly returned to God, in a world fraught with temptation and danger. "Hold fast to the Lord, Rafe. I'll be praying for you, my brother, my friend."

www.ingramcontent.com/pod-product-compliance
Lightning Source LLC
Chambersburg PA
CBHW060934120726
47910CB00002B/329